# EIGHTEENTH-CENTURY NOVELS BY WOMEN

Isobel Grundy, Editor

Advisory Board

# THE HISTORY
## OF
# SIR GEORGE ELLISON

Sarah Scott

~

BETTY RIZZO, EDITOR

THE UNIVERSITY PRESS OF KENTUCKY

Copyright © 1996 by The University Press of Kentucky

Scholarly publisher for the Commonwealth, serving Bellarmine College, Berea College, Centre College of Kentucky, Eastern Kentucky University, The Filson Club, Georgetown College, Kentucky Historical Society, Kentucky State University, Morehead State University, Murray State University, Northern Kentucky University, Transylvania University, University of Kentucky, University of Louisville, and Western Kentucky University.

*Editorial and Sales Offices:* The University Press of Kentucky
663 South Limestone Street, Lexington, Kentucky 40508-4008

Library of Congress Cataloging-in-Publication Data

Scott, Sarah, 1723–1795
    The history of Sir George Ellison / Sarah Scott ; Betty Rizzo, editor.
        p.    cm. — (Eighteenth-century novels by women)
    Includes bibliographical references (p.    ).
    ISBN 0–8131–1938–3 (alk. paper). — ISBN 0–8131–0849–7 (pbk. : alk. paper)
    1. England—Social conditions—18th century—Fiction.  2. Social reformers—England—Fiction.  3. Feminism—Fiction.  4. Utopias—Fiction.  I. Rizzo, Betty.  II. Title.  III. Series.
PR3671.S33H577    1995
823'.6—dc20                                                      95-30288

# CONTENTS

~

# ACKNOWLEDGMENTS

~

Isobel Grundy, the general editor of the series of which this edition is a part, and Jan Fergus, a member of the edition's board, carefully reviewed this manuscript and made a number of valuable corrections and suggestions. Despite the increasing helpfulness of such databases as the Eighteenth-Century Short Title Catalogue and the Readex Microprint Edition of Early American Imprints, to which I am much indebted, a number of archivists and libraries contributed to such projects as this. I particularly thank Mary L. Robertson of the Huntington Library, San Marino, and her library assistant, Ms Hoang-My Dunkle, for their substantial and timely assistance, Marie E. Lamoureux of the American Antiquarian Society, Worcester, and also the archivists of the Rare Books and Special Collections in the Firestone Library of Princeton University, the special collections of New York University's Fales Library and Union Theological Seminary, the Sterling Library of Yale University, and the W.S. Lewis Walpole Library in Farmington, Connecticut. Sarah Wimbush of the Courtauld Institute and Mrs. Evelyn Newby of the Paul Mellon Centre for Studies in British Art tried in vain to track down a portrait of Sarah Scott done by William Hoare in 1749. Thanks to Linda Bree, Diane Chardin of Trinity College Library, Cambridge, Barbara Dunlap, Peter Sabor, Beverly Schneller, Barbara Schnorrenberg, Keith Williams, and Carolyn Woodward for valuable information; and to Linda Merians, who, as always, provided sterling advice and assistance when appealed to. Professor Merians also advertised a recalcitrant quotation on e-mail, for which Jack Kolb and Greg Clingham provided an identification.

# INTRODUCTION

~

## THE LIFE AND WORKS

Sarah Robinson Scott was born to many advantages of education and up-bringing that made her a writer, but if she had not needed the money, she would scarcely have turned out the nine books (at least) that made her a professional author.

In 1712 her father, Matthew Robinson (1694-1778), of Edgeley and West Layton Hall in Yorkshire and of a younger branch of a respectable Yorkshire family, married Elizabeth Drake (*c.* 1693-1746), a Kentish heiress, daughter of Councillor Robert Drake of Cambridge. Together they produced twelve children of whom seven sons and two daughters survived. In Yorkshire were baptized Matthew (1713), Thomas (1714), probably Morris (c. 1715), Robert (1717), Elizabeth (1718), and Sarah (1721); at Cambridge were baptized William (1727), John (1729), and Charles (1731).[1] It was a family of clever, loyal, close-knit siblings, most of whom remained intimately connected throughout their lives.

Elizabeth Drake Robinson's mother, Sarah Morris Drake, had married as her second husband, Dr. Conyers Middleton, the noted Cambridge scholar. The Robinson family spent some part of each year in Cambridge, and Middleton took considerable care with the education of all the children including the two clever girls. There were so many children that the family could not afford to live in London, Matthew Robinson's place of preference. Their circumstances became an additional advantage to the children, however, since, in order to make do in the country, their father turned the family into a club in which witty debate and contention for superiority in argument were the chief diversion. Elizabeth Drake Robinson became known, for her moderation, as "The Speaker."

The capacities of the elder children flourished under these unusually propitious influences. Matthew, Thomas, Elizabeth, Sarah, and William all are noticed in the *Dictionary of National Biography* (Morris, John, and Charles are briefly noted under their brother Matthew's entry), and all appear to have capitalized on impressive rhetorical and writing abilities. Matthew, who inherited his mother's Kentish estate of Mount Morris, or Monk's Horton, entered Parliament and was an author of political pamphlets; Thomas wrote a classic legal text before his early death at thirty-three; Morris studied law and became a solicitor; Robert was a sea captain for the East India Company and died in China in 1756; Elizabeth Robinson Montagu became a famous bluestocking, business magnate, and author; William, a clergyman, was a lover of literature and close friend of Thomas Gray; John by 1749 was mentally ill and seems never to have recovered; Charles went briefly to sea with Robert, then entered the Middle Temple and after being called to the bar became recorder of Canterbury in 1763, a bankruptcy commissioner, and M.P. for Canterbury from 1780 to 1790.

By the 1730s the family had removed entirely to Mount Morris. Elizabeth and Sarah, the only two girls, were each other's intimate companions. "Remember the days," Elizabeth wrote in 1749, when the sisters were no longer of one mind, "when as Hermia says, we set on one stool, work'd one sampler, &c. and you will then imagine how much the happiness of your sister depends on you."[2] The girls were precocious, but not as precocious as has been imagined: their baptismal records show that Elizabeth was two years and Sarah three years older than had been previously recorded. In those early days their good looks and vivacity were so similar that Sarah was known as "Pea," for "peas in a pod," or as Bridget, as a complement to Elizabeth's nickname "Fidget." Yet Sarah's two nicknames, both contingent on comparison to Elizabeth as model, also suggest that she was the copy and Elizabeth the original. The distinction between them grew clearer when Elizabeth struck up a friendship with Lady Margaret Harley, daughter of the Earl of Oxford, and, after Lady Margaret's marriage in 1734 to the Duke of Portland, enjoyed London society as companion to her friend. Sarah, left alone in the country, wrote loving, sometimes longing letters, but Elizabeth, intent on establishing herself in another life, could no longer reciprocate whole-heartedly. Sarah's cry of pain at her desertion in October 1741 helps to explain a lifelong motivation for her writing: "The love of writing you see, enters into me as soon as you go out of the house; while you are with me I have all I desire, content is then my companion: but when you are gone I can't help writing in hopes you will send me some return for the affection and spirits that are gone with you, all of me that is portable you carry with you."[3] Elizabeth, however, happy in her liberation, was at the same time writing to her cousin and mentor, Dean William Freind, "Her Grace has a friendship for me I can never find in any one else; nor indeed would it give me the same pleasure from any other person; because then I must be ungrateful, as it would be impossible for me to love any one as I do her. The duty and love I owe at home will make me leave her next spring, but (which is a secret) I do not propose to do it before."[4] Elizabeth would subsequently regret and revise this priority of affection, but Sarah would never recover from its effects or entirely forgive.

By this time Sarah could no longer have hoped to follow her brilliant sister into society. The distancing of the triumphantly successful Elizabeth, celebrated in court circles for her liveliness and her wit, had been definitively emphasized when in April 1741 Sarah contracted the severe case of smallpox that ruined her complexion and her beauty. During her illness, for fear of infection Elizabeth was removed to the home of a neighboring farmer, from which she was not prevented by anxiety from writing the most amusing letters about a local conquest; the sisters were belatedly reunited in the open air, symbolically at a four-foot distance, without touching, and with Sarah's face veiled.

One of the most compelling preoccupations of Sarah Robinson Scott throughout her life was the relationship with her sister. Perhaps even without the catastrophe of the smallpox she had felt inadequate to the social challenge of equalling Elizabeth's triumphs. She may have been comparing the two in *The History of Sir George Ellison,* for she was never reluctant to denigrate Elizabeth's brilliant éclat: "Those who have specious manners, a good address, an easy assurance, and what we call the savoir vivre . . . have all the qualifications requisite to render them acceptable in the gay world; but such as are deficient in these particulars, however replete with unadorned good sense, integrity, strict honour, and general benevolence, will make but an indifferent figure there; and are much more judicious, when they fix in a less crouded scene" (*GE,* 191).[5] Sarah was never comfortable at her sister's brilliant parties. After her smallpox it seems probable that she tried to adjust to the ruin of her beauty as Louisa Tunstall does in *The History of Sir George Ellison.* Louisa's vivacity had been so unbounded as to incline her mother "to think that the ravages a very severe small-pox had made in her face was no small blessing. . . . but, fortunately . . . the extreme plainness of her face . . . made her much disregarded, and in some measure damped the redundancy of spirits which, if animated by vanity, might have proved dangerous" (*GE,* 199). Louisa accepts this view of the matter and becomes a serious student, acquiring French, Italian, Latin, Greek, geography, astronomy, geometry, history, and philosophy, and there is reason to suppose that Sarah Robinson occupied herself in the same way, thanking God for having saved her from frivolity with smallpox, as did Harriot Trentham in *Millenium Hall*:

> In a very short time she became perfectly contented with the alteration this cruel distemper had made in her. Her love for reading returned, and she regained the quiet happiness of which flutter and dissipation had deprived her without substituting anything so valuable in its place. She has often said she looks on this accident as a reward for the good she had done . . . and that few benevolent actions receive so immediate a recompense.[6]

In making these radical adjustments, Sarah differentiated herself yet further from her sister, who studied in order to display her knowledge and intellect and read all the fashionable new performances in order to display her brilliance, whose spirits *were* in fact (as her friends were later to admit) animated by a vanity that grew inordinate.[7]

Elizabeth, however, in 1741 had a genuine use for all her assets. The family had developed a problem, perhaps to do with the growing incapacity of Mrs. Robinson, who was to die five years later, probably of cancer; and Elizabeth sought the opportunity to escape, and if possible to be useful to her siblings, by marrying. In August 1742, at twenty-three, she married the rich fifty-year-old Edward Montagu, grandson of the first Earl of Sandwich and a coal magnate. Almost at once she brought her three youngest brothers, aged about fourteen, thirteen, and eleven, from their Yorkshire school to the Montagu home at Allerthorpe for their holidays: though probably visited by their parents, they had not been home—perhaps because of the distance—for five years and were virtually unknown to their sisters.[8]

As a result of Edward Montagu's intercession, William and Jack were sent forthwith, in January, to Westminister School, and Charles was sent to sea with Robert (LEM, 2:226). Elizabeth Montagu also conscientiously sought to make a home for Sarah, who had been with her since her marriage and was present to welcome the boys, but who increasingly resisted living with the Montagus, though after 1746 their home appears to have been her base and the repository for her clothing. The two sisters would never cease to love each other—as time passed Elizabeth seems particularly to have yearned after Sarah—but their increasingly divergent courses were now irrevocably set.

That Sarah did not do the usual thing after her mother's death and find a home with her father, who moved to lodgings in London and then to a house, or with her unmarried eldest brother, who was now the master of her old home, Mount Morris, or with her sister, is indicative of her obstinate and self-sufficient integrity. Her father, a rather bawdy roué as well as a wit, may already have begun that liaison with his housekeeper that was to set the tone for his last years, and her brother, a brilliant but eccentric recluse on whom Sir William Ellison is apparently modeled, could accommodate neither her company *nor* her housekeeping, which he managed on his own plan. Elizabeth Montagu usually insisted on her prerogative as elder sister to direct Sarah's choices, which may have rendered her constant company oppressive, and Sarah could not but have observed that her own abilities did not shine in the fashionable world.

Sarah Robinson nursed her mother till her death but afterward was a wanderer, sometimes staying with the Montagus, sometimes visiting such Kentish friends as Caroline Scott Best or her cousin Lydia Lumley Botham, and once visiting Tunbridge with her father. In December 1747 she went to Bath with the Montagus. Her headaches, a lifelong affliction, were somewhat alleviated there, and when in May 1748 the Montagus went home, Sarah stayed on. She had met and struck up a sympathy with Lady Barbara Montagu, an invalid with heart problems, younger even than herself, and the daughter of the first Earl of Halifax.

Of Lady Barbara, her cousin George Montagu was to write after her death, "She was the one I always loved and passed all my youth with in daily gaiety and joy, for she had all the wit and humours of the family, generous, and beneficent; her constitution so delicate that her life has been a sufferance for many years."[9] Sarah Robinson had a slender provision from her father, Lady Barbara only a meager fortune of £5,000,[10] and each needed a companion with whom to pool resources. More important, Lady Barbara had eschewed the fashionable life of her own sisters, and the two young women, both serious Christians, were of one mind as to how to live. In August 1748 Sarah Robinson moved into her friend's house in Trim Street and, with minor interruptions, the two remained together, part of an important Bath community of women, till Lady Barbara's death in 1765. They were almost indeed like "two lovely berries molded on one stem." The novelist's longing for an inseparable and equally devoted sister was thus, for years, to be satisfied.

In these early days, however, she was not yet committed to the idea of a celibate life in a community of women, for she was in love with the brother of her friend Callie Scott Best. George Lewis Scott was a great burly man of multiple talents twelve years her senior who, though a member of the bar, had as yet no prospect of supporting a wife. The Scott family of Canterbury had been friends of the Robinsons, and Sarah had known George Scott well for many years. She may have been recollecting his courtship of her in the courtship of Louisa Tunstall by Mr. Blackburn that took his object so by surprise: "The uncommon qualifications of Miss Louisa, the excellence of her temper, heart, and understanding, had entirely captivated his affections, and given him such a prejudice in favour of her person, that although he perceived she had no beauty to boast, yet he thought it perfectly agreeable" (*GE,* 220).

The couple awaited only a subsistence in order to marry, although Sarah had no intention of deserting Lady Barbara, who was to live with them, as was indeed appropriate at the time. In these circumstances Sarah Robinson showed her resourcefulness. Her sister vehemently opposed the match, and perhaps not entirely on grounds of the impecuniosity of the pair, for her husband knew George Scott well. But Sarah Robinson was able to rouse her cousin Anne Knight Cresset to enlist her husband, James Cresset, secretary to the Princess of Wales, in her fiancé's aid, and with the help of others as well, he was in 1750 named sub-preceptor to the Prince of Wales. In the meantime Sarah had determined to do what she could herself, and wrote her first novel, *The History of Cornelia,* which was published by Andrew Millar on April 19, 1750, according to an advertisement in the *Daily Advertiser.*

In *The History of Cornelia,* the rich and beautiful heiress Cornelia is the object of the passion of her guardian uncle, who attempts to abduct her. In order to elude his pursuit she must leave home alone and incognito and remain so. A wanderer in the world without an identity (as female identity depended upon relationships with males), no longer afforded the protection of the patriarchal roof, she undergoes many trials and adventures including imprisonment, attempted rape, disguise as a university student and tutor, and romance with the worthy Bernardo, whom eventually she marries. For Sarah Scott marriage is no success unless the community benefits; and this couple makes the whole neighborhood happy by perfecting their own hearts, educating their offspring, loving one another without abatement, and distributing their money to all in need.

Scott in this novel poses the same question that other women writers like Charlotte Smith, Frances Burney, and Mary Brunton were later to pose: if absolutely free of all patriarchal supervision/oppression, absolutely on her own, how might a woman fare? Cornelia fares well, and for subsequent writers Scott's novel is an important influence. Moreover, as has been noted, although the book precedes Walpole's *Castle of Otranto* (1764), it is almost Gothic.[11] That is, it expresses the oppression of the abusive and tyrannical patriarch, whose relentless will motivates the plot, and the failure under his aegis of the family unit. In order to disguise the indictment of the English social hierarchy, it utilizes symbolic (distancing) scenes and situations such as a continental setting, immurement in castles, abductions, and attempted rape. An element Radcliffe may have found here and used in *The Mysteries of Udolpho* is the calumniation of the hero as a libertine, so that having found him, Cornelia must demonstrate her moral strength and rational control over passion by rejecting him and continuing on her lone adventures again. The Gothic element missing, however, is the terror of the heroine resulting from imaginative powers which she must learn to subordinate to her reason; Cornelia instead is consistently fortitudinous, resourceful, and rational. The book in some ways expresses Scott's sense of her own situation, forced from home by failures of her family into the world where as a woman much on her own she must certainly have encountered perils, and opposed in her wish to marry by a sister who calumniated her lover. It expresses as well her determination to cope and survive.

The novel was no great success and probably did not earn enough to hurry Scott back to her desk, though she may already have been working on the tales that comprised her next book. At any rate, employment was found for George Scott at the end of 1750. The couple married on June 15, 1751, at St. Michael Bassishaw in London, and moved into a house in Leicester Square close to Leicester House, the residence of the Prince of Wales.

The remarkable thing about this disastrous marriage is that instead of dragging miserably on for thirty years and draining all of Scott's energies, which would have been the usual event of a mismatch, it ended dramatically nine months later with her removal from under her husband's roof by her father and brothers—an extreme and almost a unique response to marital incompatibility, and a response in which she must have been fully complicit, even instrumental. A wife's fleeing from her husband would have been of no legal significance whatsoever, but the involvement of the Robinson males, of whom Matthew Robinson Sr. and Morris were trained at the bar, made the separation—there would be no divorce—decisive. George Scott and the two Robinsons settled the finances: George Scott returned half of his wife's fortune to her father and undertook to provide her with £100 a year. Considering Elizabeth Montagu's later claim of responsibility for this extraordinary event (see below) it is indeed possible that in it she finally had her way—something she was always willing to labor hard to achieve—about the marriage.

The explanation for this debacle, however, was never publicly provided. As George Scott's employment was so very sensitive, his reputation had to be protected, and the stipend he paid his wife guaranteed her family's discretion. A silence fell into which Montagu whispered that "she and the rest of her friends had rescued her [sister] out of the hands of a very bad man, but for reasons of interest they should conceal his misbehaviour as much as possible," but that her sister was "very innocent."[12] George Scott's "explanation" to the Princess of Wales, retailed to Montagu by Scott as a ridiculous fiction, was that because of her brother Jack's madness she had broken their engagement, whereupon he had instead agreed to a celibate marriage, a condition he had found difficult to keep. The implication was that she had been removed because he was importunate, though the princess, very much the husband's advocate, was also making remarks about Sarah Scott's untoward extravagance in "setting out."[13] Perhaps Montagu touches most closely on the truth in a subsequent letter to Scott of autumn 1767 when Scott hesitated about signing a lease for Hitcham because she was a "femme couvert": "As to being femme couvert, helas vous ne l'etiez jamais," wrote her sister, and suggested she could sign as "you are posses'd of property yr nominal Husband cannot touch (I dont here mean a double entendre)." Montagu's implication that Scott's was indeed a *mariage blanc* because of George Scott's incapacity is evident, but that in itself seems not reason enough for the violence with which they were separated, and probably he was detected in some more heinous practice.

Both Scott and Lady Barbara, who had been with her throughout the marriage, went back to Bath; and Scott, now neither maid, wife, nor widow, might have been marginalized as one of those dim, unclaimed, peripheral ladies of no interest to patriarchal genealogies and conscious of her insignificance. Instead, she determined, now that she had shed the final male overseer, to make her life significant.

To the efforts she and Lady Barbara subsequently made, Sarah Fielding was an important contributor. Fielding, ten years Scott's senior, had thought out many of the problems women like herself faced and had dealt with them in her writing. There was a great advantage to being unmarried, these women knew, because only unmarried women were free to work toward their own ends. And in regard to work they refused to be hampered by delusions of their own gentility. It became an important tenet of Scott and her circle that any honest labor became a lady or gentleman who needed a subsistence, and that no work was demeaning that was useful. In *The History of Sir George Ellison* the importance for both genders and all classes and ages of devoting one's life and most of one's time to meaningful work is consistently emphasized. Scott therefore out of financial necessity—her husband's stipend and her father's allowances (varying bits of money) would not go far—determined on a useful life of both writing and social experiment to remedy insofar as she could the injustices to which the events of her own life and the lives of the members of her circle had made her sensitive.

Her conclusions were shared by a small but powerful community of immense importance to her. Sarah Fielding, still writing herself, was a crucial member. Lady Barbara functioned almost as an alter ego, helping Scott build an excellent library, reading, discussing, and writing. Elizabeth Cutts, herself an occasional author, was an important member; so were the less well-defined (though only to us) Miss Arnold, a young, rather gay and fashionable woman who later wrote history, and Mrs. Adams. At Batheaston just outside of Bath, with her friend Margaret Mary Ravaud, lived Margaret Riggs, the hearty daughter of Captain Southwell Piggott, who had flirted with Scott at Bath.[14] She was mother of the future Lady Miller of Batheaston vase fame.[15] Riggs and Ravaud were soon to draw Scott and Lady Barbara to Batheaston. These women shared an important idea of community, based on writings by Mary Astell and Sarah Fielding among others, which inspired them to work together, to incorporate many colleagues and clients temporarily or permanently, and to annex many influential friends.[16] The crucial point was that only women personally disconnected from the control of men could study, talk, think, work, and write as they themselves determined. It was for this reason that Astell had originally suggested a college, rather like a convent, for women. But Scott and her circle detested the very idea of a convent; they believed women should work as much in the world as possible and did so themselves to a greater extent than did the fictitious women of Millenium Hall.[17]

Perhaps it was also among these women that Scott became a committed politician, studying the political events of the time and taking a great interest in the minutest alterations in government, as letters abroad to her brother William and his wife in the early 1760s demonstrate. Her trespasses on this male domain would be tactfully presented in her histories, but she was by no means confined in her interests to feminine benefactions.

Scott's biographer, Walter Crittenden, has identified what he considers a neurotic tendency in her to change her habitation. Although a certain restiveness may have been involved, in fact most of her moves can be attributed to one of two relentless conditions, ill health and poverty. She and Lady Barbara were constantly in search of cheaper satisfactory housing that would not exacerbate their ailments. When after trying a variety of houses and lodgings in Bath they moved into a farmhouse in Batheaston in 1754, they were, for the time being, entirely happy. Batheaston was a delightful spot, and Lady Barbara, who had secured the lease, erected a tent at the bottom of the garden overlooking the Avon; Bath was a two-mile walk along the river. Scott was always in best health in the country, and the tiny Batheaston neighborhood afforded the pair a well-defined arena for their social experiments.

Life even before Batheaston was busy, every moment filled. Social theories had to be put into practice, people in trouble befriended or taken in, servants helped through pregnancies, and babies boarded. The clients were of course endless. As early as 1752 Scott had been experimenting in employing the unemployable—two women servants, one totally deaf, the other mentally deficient. She and Lady Bab were already assuming responsibility for the unfortunate wherever they were met with. In addition, as she herself confessed, Scott loved ornaments and was a gifted painter and needlewoman, specializing in crewel. Both she and Lady Barbara painted and embroidered flowers, decorated various objects like the "toilette" she did for Montagu (which was sent to the Duchess of Portland for inspection), collected acorns, cones, and shells to make decorative swags for borders and walls; and probably marketed the results of their labors when they could. Each time they moved they took great pains with the arrangement of their home.

In Batheaston Scott and Lady Barbara put their schemes into a regular system so that when Montagu visited them in 1755 she thought (knowing the history of the idea) that the household, because of its regularity, resembled a convent—an idea Scott would have repudiated. After an early rising and household prayers, Scott cut out the sewing work for the twelve poor girls whom she and Lady Barbara were schooling; the girls made childbed linen and clothes for the neighborhood poor. She taught them writing and arithmetic. A school for twelve boys was also provided, and on Sundays Scott held Sunday school for all the children before church. The poor women in the neighborhood knitted simple items that Scott and Montagu sold to their acquaintance (LEM, 4:17).

Somehow Scott found time for writing with the intent both of earning money for their projects and of disseminating her—or the community's—

ideas, particularly about the forming of girls' values. In early 1754 two of her books appeared. One was a translation, published by R. and J. Dodsley on January 24, 1754, of a French novel by Pierre de la Place, *La Laideur Aimable.* As Scott and Lady Barbara read all the new publications, both English and French, Scott's interest in translating this particular novel was motivated by her desire to demonstrate to young women that worthy plainness in a woman is superior to charming beauty; but the book must also have been a gloss on her relationship with her sister. One of two stepsisters is beautiful and charming, the other plain and good. The pretty sister is chosen to go out into the world as companion to Mademoiselle de Beaumont, but because of her flirting is disgraced and dismissed. When the second sister is given her chance, she develops her good parts and is valued for them. She follows her father's orders and marries a man other than the one she loves, but eventually her husband dies and she is enabled to marry the man of her choice—and to bring happiness to an entire community. Her sister, however, corrupted by her own charms, is disgraced and has to retire to a convent.

The other book, *A Journey Through Every Stage of Life,* is supposed to have been "Drawn from Real Characters. By a Person of Quality" and in fact Scott demonstrably often did draw upon real characters. The book is a series of separate tales. The first and longest is the story of beautiful Leonora, who runs away when her stepmother tries to make her marry a fifty-year-old miser, taking with her a cruelly-treated dependent cousin and a servant, and seems to be a fantasy of what might have happened if Miss Melvyn of Millenium Hall had refused to marry the odious Mr. Morgan and had had female allies. Leonora, disguised as a clergyman, proves irresistible to women, preaches a sermon so well that a lady offers her marriage and a living, slips off to London as tutor to a young gentleman, in London becomes a beau and a successful painter, next a successful schoolmaster, and, in short, liberated from petticoats, successfully employs all the talents Scott possessed before she resumes her sex and wins the man she has come to love. It is a fantasy of liberation which can also be read as a reproach to a society that did not allow women to enter the professions.

Those few critics who have addressed themselves to Scott's fictions have noted her failure to utilize the humor and satiric wit so prevalent in her letters.[18] Scott the novelist adopted a high moral tone that was very like that of Sarah Fielding. For one thing, Scott had adopted the Johnsonian tenet, best expressed in *Rambler* 4, that "it is . . . not a sufficient vindication of a character, that it is drawn as it appears, for many characters ought never to be drawn"; that when good and bad qualities are mingled in a writer's principal personages, readers begin to lose abhorrence of their faults; that, as Johnson added, "in narratives, where historical veracity has no place, I cannot discover why there should not be exhibited the most perfect idea of virtue." Novelists like Richardson, Sarah Fielding, and Johnson himself who take this line do not ordinarily indulge in levity.

And then, as a woman writer who needed to publish and earn, Sarah Fielding had not been able very often to indulge the irony, jests, and facetious tone her brother used to such good effect; women with wit were under suspicion of moral failure; even Elizabeth Montagu, that celebrated wit, had written, "I am sorry to say the generality of women who have excelled in wit have failed in chastity" (LEM, 3:97). She spoke in a climate in which the sexual freedoms and the wit associated with them enjoyed by such writers as Aphra Behn, Delariviere Manley, and Eliza Haywood had to be lived down and repudiated by a new, more respectable generation. The tone of Scott's novels, even more than of Sarah Fielding's, is therefore determinedly and deliberately earnest and worthy in a manner in which she, evidently, was often not, and the humor, irony, and fun so remarkable in her letters are far less obvious in her published works. Scott's biographer Crittenden gives one comic passage from Scott's second novel worthy of inclusion in any contemporary comedy, in which Mrs. Colraine learns that her new maid's name is Wilhelmina, disdains the whole as pretentious, and successively rejects each part: "*Will,* no, no, that is too like a Fellow, that will not do; let me die if I should not be scandalized; Will, bring me my Shift; Will, put me to Bed; Will, pull off my stockings; Oh! frightful! who would not think it a He creature?"[19] and in her last novel Scott relaxes so far as to exhibit a comic Welsh family, but these broadly humorous passages are rare. Scott had ample talent to anticipate Burney's *Evelina* in satiric fun (and popularity), but women writers could not have risked that in the 1750s, when even Eliza Haywood was trying to live down the Haywood stigma.

Nevertheless Scott does consistently exhibit a sly wit in her novels, a wit that if it is not anticipated may be overlooked. Indeed, the witty first sentence of The Preface to *Sir George Ellison* is not without malice. Her wit often sparks the novel: in the observation that fools may always call a little fresh folly to their aid (26); in the satire on London citizens' taste (145-46); in the simile of children dressed with the assistance of pins and more full of wounds than the anatomical figure in an almanac (197 and note); in sentences like "Mrs. Grantham had little taste for the dignity of abstaining from the enjoyment of splendor" (187) and passages like that on the bill of mortality of beauty (201)—bill of mortality parodies were a familiar form of humor at the time.

Her letters, moreover, by way of proof of her abilities, are lively, amusing, at times malicious or even bawdy. She could cheerfully call her neighbor fool and coolly assess the advantage to him of the death of his wife: encountering Mr. Le Marchant at Tunbridge in 1747, she wrote her sister, "I enquired after Mrs. LeMarchant, which produced a countenance more dismal than any of Mr. Sable's Chief Mourners, with many other signs denoting affliction, from whence I gatherd that he had cause to rejoice, & try'd to hide I did so for him by lengthening my chin as much as so short-a-faced woman coud contrive. I have had a visit from him this morning & as I touchd on none of the benefits he had lately receiv'd from Providence he was very chearful & agreable."[20] On her maid's little girl Nanny whom she was looking after,

> I don't think little Nanny has a heart that can be soften'd, in short I am afraid she has nothing that people mean by a heart when they talk of it in any other light than a Surgeon wou'd do, but I see she will soon have sense enough to be a good Hypocrite. I don't think it safe to try the way you mention to soften her, for she has long had a Doll, & the only proof of affection she gives it is taking it to bed with her, & since tendering of her temper takes this turn, two sober virgins can't encourage it, indeed her Doll is of the feminine gender, but if she learns to shew her love in that way one don't know how far she may extend it in time. [9 Feb. (1749)]

In a letter in 1762 to her brother William, Scott is malicious about their cousin Richard Robinson, newly made Bishop of Kildare, who was to rise to be Prelate of Ireland, and whom all the Robinsons, Elizabeth Montagu in particular, spoke of publicly with the highest respect. She adds acid remarks about the bishop's younger brother Septimus, formerly preceptor to the king's younger brothers, now knighted and named gentleman usher of the black rod:

> I hear our Cousin Robinson does not much like his Promotion to Kildare; I suppose he does not entirely relish rising step by step; all travelling is expensive, & I believe none more than the passing thro' the various stages of Bishopricks; but I think he may be contented to rise a petit pas; nature went but a slow pace when she made him, & did not jump into one perfection, so that his rising at all seems to proceed only from a want of any thing to stop him, according to the philosophical

axiom that put a thing in Motion & it will move for ever if it meets with nothing to obstruct its course. Sr Septimus is tolerably contented with his fate in a World so regardless of real merit, & therefore so little likely to reward his superlative deserts. I hear that a Week before he had this blackrod given him (a proper reward for a Preceptor) he declared that whoever wou'd eat Goose at Court must swallow the Feathers; but now they have been so well stroked down at least, he finds they go down easily enough.[21]

To the same brother she wrote an account of the effects of a fashion edict:

A Court Dress is going to take place at St. James's, the same as in France, which greatly distresses the old Ladies, who are quite clamorous upon the occasion, at a loss how to cover so much Neck as the stiffened Bodied Gowns are made to shew, & which they are sensible is not very appettisante after a certain Age, and likewise how to supply the deficiency which churlish time has made in their once flowing Tresses. Some Younger Ladies to whom Nature has been rather a step dame than a kind Mother join in their lamentations, & London is in an uproar, the exultation of those who conscious of their charms rejoice in laying aside as much covering as possible being as little silent as the distress of the others; they look on this allowed display as a sort of Jail delivery to their long imprisoned Attractions, & as Beauty is Nature, insist that it should be shewn at Courts, at Feasts & high solemnities, where most may wonder at the Workmanship, & that fashion has been hitherto unjust in concealing part of the superiority Nature has bestowed upon them. The consumption of Pearl Powder will certainly be much encreased, for when there is such a resource even fourscore will exhibit a snowy breast, & the Corpulent Dowagers will unite the Lillies of the Spring with all the copious abundance of a later Season.[22]

Scott's tone in these passages is remarkably like the tone of the witty Elizabeth Montagu in her own letters; apparently the suppressed Pea could still on occasion privately emerge, and perhaps what she had most to fight in her sister was her own likeness—for her only route to equality, even superiority, was through the high moral ground she was ever increasingly to take.

In general Scott seems to have written consistently but to have readied her work for publication only when she needed a sum of money for a particular purpose. For eight years, until 1762, she published no known books, but Lady Barbara and Scott as well were involved with Samuel Richardson in 1758-59 in a Lockeian project to publish a set of cards to teach children geography, chronology, and history "with greater Ease" as "an Amusement, rather than a Labour"; the cards, printed by subscription, included maps, accounts of the soil, climate, government, and manners, the chronology of England, France, Germany, and Turkey from the eleventh century, and short histories of these kingdoms.[23] The scheme was to benefit a poor aged gentlewoman of Bath, but the price, a guinea, necessitated by the great expense of printing, prohibited their sale save to the charitable subscribers.

Publishing, in fact, was a means the Bath group used to raise money for others. In 1759 Lady Barbara also paid for the publication by Richardson of a novel by an anonymous woman, *The Histories of Some of the Penitents in the Magdalen House*;[24] and in 1775 Elizabeth Cutts published her verses *Almeria; or, Parental Advice* to benefit two indigent persons. But a need for additional money of Scott's own was gradually emerging; Lady Barbara was in best health at Bath, where she could drink the waters, and her health was worsening. The two women went into lodgings at Bath at periods, particularly in the winter, but it was becoming apparent that the invalid needed to move permanently to Bath. Scott, suffering from painful arthritis that sometimes prevented her even turning in bed, in addition to her headaches, was in best health in the country. For a period in 1760 and 1761 Scott probably hoped to raise enough money to support two establishments. She could work swiftly, and soon after the death of George II on October 25, 1760, she had completed her *History of Gustavus Ericson, King of Sweden, with an Introductory History of Sweden from the Middle of the 12th Century*, "by Henry Augustus Raymond, Esq.," a book very positively received. Scott took the then conventional view of history that it ought to provide exemplary and cautionary models. She had always been a great reader, and her knowledge of and interest in her subject, an exemplary monarch of the sixteenth century, may also have derived from her work on the pedagogical cards. At the moment when the popular young George III had just succeeded, she pointedly presented the portrait of a model king who "left his kingdom furnished with every encouragement of industry, ample regards for knowledge, relief for the poor, and consolation for the sick and diseased, in the magazines, the schools, and the hospitals which he established." The work was timely and well reviewed— and Scott had her own (if oblique) opportunity to attempt the education of the monarch to whom her husband had been sub-preceptor.

It was probably in 1761 that she arranged with John Newbery to publish a series of works, most likely for a fixed sum that would have met her need.[25] The first of these works, *The History of Mecklenburgh*, was another timely work that provided the background of Charlotte, the chosen queen of the newly-ascended George III, and defended her forebears the Vandals as hospitable, benevolent, just, temperate, wholesome lawgivers. This work may also have derived from the historical and geographical work on the cards; it was published in March 1762 and dedicated (over Newbery's signature) to the new queen. It received excellent reviews. *A Description of Millenium Hall,* published by Newbery in November 1762, was also part of the larger, uncompleted scheme, and for it, as only a minor part, Scott had contracted for no more than £30. As the rest of the scheme was not realized, probably because her health or other commitments interfered, she failed to earn the money to save Batheaston. In the autumn of 1762 the friends gave up their home and moved to a new house on a high, airy Bath street.

*A Description of Millenium Hall* was, however, in spite of the derision of the *Critical Review* (which referred to the author's costive brain), Scott's most successful work. It is of course the novel of which *The History of Sir George Ellison* is the sequel. It is a Utopian work, descriptive of an ideal community, as the title suggests, and is a telling critique of the economics, inhumane values, and hypocritical Christianity of Scott's contemporary society. The community is centered in the Cornish home of the founders, a group of women who succeeded to significant fortunes which they pool to finance their various schemes, but it comprises enough variety of habitations and inhabitants to make a sizable village, which is conventual only in the sense that the organizers themselves must remain celibate to be effectual. They have organized a home for indigent gentlewomen, schools of various kinds, a retreat for exceptional persons who do gardening; cottages for the old, who are employed in gardening, nursing, and knitting; a carpet industry; extensive landscaping; a policy of decency to animals; and a sensible, ecologically balanced domestic economy. The women travel freely and visit abroad, foster marriages, nurture and educate the young. Into their environment wander two travelers, the returned Jamaican planter George Ellison and his thoughtless young companion, Lamont, and to them the community is gradually revealed and explained. The past histories of the women organizers provide the stories, which demonstrate the injustices and cruelties to women encountered in the world.

Scott lacked a strong inventiveness, and her acquaintance are often recognizably adapted for presentation in her novels—one can detect Mary Delany's experience in Miss Melvyn, for instance—but never is this so blatant as in the portrait of Elizabeth Montagu as Lady Brumpton in *Millenium Hall.*

Lady Brumpton is an excessively vain patroness of parties at which wit is every-one's object and solid information considerably less obtainable. Moreover her name derives from Steele's play *The Funeral*, in which Lady Brumpton schemes to be heir to all her husband's possessions and guardian of his de-pendents—exactly what Elizabeth Montagu attained at her husband's death in 1775.[26] That Montagu forgave her sister, perhaps as the best way of repudi-ating the resemblance, cannot mean that Scott's graceless action—another ef-fort to establish the moral differences between the two sisters—was not deeply felt by her. But the effect was to lead Montagu, who could bear no moral inferiority on her own part, for some years to try to win Scott's approval on Scott's own high-minded terms.

*Millenium Hall* may have been written in a month, but its well-considered content had been the work of the whole community of women for years. Lady Barbara is sometimes credited with co-authorship;[27] but her con-tribution was to the content, not to the writing, something Scott claimed for herself when she said she had written it in thirty days. The book firmly estab-lished Scott's reputation, and there were four editions within the next sixteen years. What Scott had not been able to do in this book, however, was to dem-onstrate how an ordinary family might apply her benevolent systems. The idea of presenting George Ellison, the visitor to the Hall, as a convert and follower of its philosophies may have struck Scott at once, but, typically, she did not publish her sequel until she was once more in need of funds for a special project.

In early 1763 Scott was treating with Millar for an unfinished geogra-phy that was to come out in the summer.[28] Perhaps the book was laid aside because in 1763 Lady Barbara was awarded a £300 pension on the Irish estab-lishment—too late to save Batheaston but enough to ensure the comfort of the pair. But Lady Barbara's health had been steadily failing, and by the sum-mer of 1765 she was dying; she was dead in August. Elizabeth Cutts was with Scott throughout the devastating ordeal and remained a faithful friend and support, but Scott had again lost in Lady Barbara the sister she had lost when Montagu deserted her twenty-five years earlier.

Scott, encouraged to the last by Lady Barbara, may have known already what she would do next: undertake a new community like Batheaston and, perhaps to raise money for the project, write the sequel to *Millenium Hall.* By October she had given up the cold, drafty, and expensive new house in which it was impossible to keep warm and moved into rooms in the house where Elizabeth Cutts lodged. She worked with care on *The History of Sir George*

*Ellison,* exposing him to every common cross-purpose and eventuality to show how a Christian might really live. When the novel was published by Millar in April 1766, it was well received by the reviewers and the public, though with a general incredulity that such a character could be. (The *Critical Review* was complimentary but suggested that Ellison was an inferior derivative of Sir Charles Grandison.) Montagu's own close friend, the scholar Elizabeth Carter, who after one lavish encomium had rarely mentioned Scott to her again, noted that she had called on Scott and Miss Arnold in London in May, and from Kent in June declared, "Sir G. Ellison is in high reputation among our reading people here."[29]

Throughout the latter part of 1767 Scott worked on the arrangements of the new community, abetted by her sister, who was eagerly determined to make as much a part of the scheme as possible, particularly as her husband seemed to be rapidly declining. Her letters of the period express a great warmth and longing for her sister, and a need to impress her with her millennial activities. From Denton in Northumberland she writes of having engaged a schoolmaster to teach reading and writing to her coal miners' boys and her plans to begin a school for girls as well (7 Oct. 1767). "I know," she adds,"my brother Coal owners will hate me & abuse me for this, because it may in time oblige them to the like, but every one must be guided by the dictates of his own conscience." And she makes a point of her having incorporated the entire family of her steward, the poet James Woodhouse and his wife, her housekeeper, into her establishment, noisy children and all.

Only the practical arrangements for the community are noted in the sisters' correspondence and none of the plans for life and work, but Montagu referred twice to the community as Millenium Hall and once as "our Bower of bliss." Clearly Hitcham's inhabitants were to practice first the domestic economy, then the charitable activities of the Hall. The garden and the animal stock were to render the community as independent as possible; there was to be a democratic society run by rules and implemented by good will; and there would be a school, a Sunday school, and various schemes for employing the local poor. The house pitched upon was Hitcham House in Hitcham, Bucks, where Scott had once taken Lady Barbara for her health. It was only about two miles across the Thames from Maidenhead and about thirty miles from the neighborhood of the Montagus' Berkshire estate, Sandleford, just outside Newbury. Both Hitcham and Sandleford were near the Bath road, Hitcham about twenty-eight miles from London, Sandleford fifty-six, so that Montagu could take in Hitcham on her way to and from Hill

Street. Anticipating using the house as a country retreat from her great establishments, and incidentally being identified as a prominent member of the community, Montagu was enthusiastically helpful. She would be one of the four major shareholders in the venture—with Scott, Cutts, and her newly widowed cousin Grace Freind—paying her £50 share but willing also to assume many other expenses. (She had in her husband's growing incapacity assumed full responsibility for his coal mines and other ventures, and had, as she liked to crow, much increased the profits.) If Sarah Fielding, now dying in Scott's lodgings in Miles Court at Bath, was well enough to join them, Montagu would pay her share. She would send her butler, Joseph Woodhouse (brother to her steward Woodhouse) over to inspect and oversee the preparation of the garden. She was at pains to find a proper gardener who could also protect "the virgins." She stocked the poultry yard from Sandleford and sent other livestock. As she loved eatable ice, she begged that the ice house be furnished with care. After twenty-five years of marriage, she was excited at the prospect of living once again with her sister even though—or perhaps, now, especially—on her sister's terms.

From the beginning there were formidable problems, many of them financial. Grace Freind, widowed in November 1766, was insufficiently provided with money, so that the Hitcham scheme seemed ideal for her. Hitcham House and forty acres were available for £13 a year—probably a reduced rate—from her son, its owner, but were sublet to a tenant; both had to approve the lease. But Freind's younger son William (and perhaps her elder son Robert as well) was at odds with his mother and was delaying the lease to bring her to heel. His feckless sister Grace, whose father had bequeathed her £4,000 to be paid only at the death of her mother, had recently eloped with a conscienceless fortune hunter, Duncan Campbell, a lieutenant of marines, who now demanded a handsome maintenance in order to keep her and was probably jockeying for the payment of the entire fortune; in fact he extorted considerable sums, which his mother-in-law could not afford. William Freind —"a fool by nature, & a knave by habit" said Montagu—was his partisan. Another problem was that the Hitcham scheme, though simple, proved more expensive than Scott had reckoned, as a great deal of repair, putting in order, and bringing in of supplies was necessary before the desired domestic economy could be instituted. Then Edward Montagu, rather inconveniently, did *not* die as he had seemed about to do, but instead remained in precarious health, demanding his wife's attendance. Finally, Scott's own health was poor; she had been ill with headaches for months, had left Bath earlier that year for

Bristol to seek help, and was still much impaired, in no condition to undertake the major work of organizing the community.

Hitcham was an L-shaped early seventeenth-century house with two stories, an attic, and a good garden.[30] Montagu consulted mightily with Scott about the furniture and contributed to the store. When the lease was at last settled, Scott had to delay moving in during the final illness of Sarah Fielding, who it had been hoped might be included in the scheme. Fielding died on April 9, 1768, and Scott, further worn down by nursing her friend, was in Hitcham shortly afterward. She was joined not only by Elizabeth Cutts and Grace Freind but also by Miss Arnold. A little testimony remains of how the spring was passed at Hitcham, where Montagu made a visit at the end of April and then sent her respects to "the happy spirits of Millenium Hall," thanking Scott for "ye pleasing hours you gave me in yr millenium, as it resembles yr millenium in quality I wish it did so in quantity. "In spite of the difficulties, it seems a good start had been made.

Scott's health, however, worsened under the strain, and in August she was in Chelsea at the establishment of Dr. Dominiceti, who offered a regimen of medicated baths and fumigations for almost every ailment.[31] She was accompanied to London by Cutts and Arnold, which left Grace Freind alone too long at Hitcham. In October Scott was still in Chelsea but planning to let some of the land at Hitcham and buy in some cattle; at the end of November, back in Hitcham, she announced the end of the experiment: "I woud cherish any chance of continuing at this place coud it be done, but even coud the expence be brought within proper bounds, I see not how it coud be." If she could keep it on without Grace Freind, Freind, now impoverished, would wish to stay on as a boarder, and Scott would not have her now "on any account" (Nov. 30, 1768). Freind had brought her daughter into the house, perhaps at the occupants' expense, for Montagu responded by noting her disillusionment in Freind (whom she had loved and respected from childhood), her sorrow that Freind and her family had drawn Scott into such expense, and her rage at Freind's behavior to Cutts. In fact, Grace Freind, in a desperate attempt to provide for her foolish daughter, had rendered the Hitcham experiment no longer feasible. A new tenant had been found to assume the lease, and Montagu was already eagerly looking for a new location for their scheme. But though many houses were investigated with vigor, none was ever taken.

In the end, perhaps, it was Scott's ill health that most critically injured the project; her absence for almost four months had left their weak link,

Grace Freind, the only member with double loyalties, alone and at the mercy of her children, who wished to use Hitcham as a convenient home for the Campbells and perhaps considered that their due. Scott was now forty-seven and would probably never again have the energy or the consistent good health for an undertaking of which she was the driving force and inspiration. Had she been able to be present, she, Arnold, and Cutts could have controlled Grace Freind. In those circumstances, shortness of funds might have prolonged the time necessary to establish the household economy but would not have destroyed the scheme. But the scheme was not renewed elsewhere, and henceforward Scott seems to have confined herself to proselytizing by writing.

She had never ceased to write. While at Dominiceti's she noted to Montagu that Cadell had refused a translation she had made, and at the end of December Montagu retrieved two manuscripts for her and sent one of them, a novel, to Cadell. No more is known of these works (though some may have appeared unrecognized as hers), and there may have been many others over which she labored, working on exemplary fiction, exemplary history, and geography. She was very ill in November 1771 but had at least three projects in train. One of these, the geographical work Carter mentioned, apparently came to nothing.[32] Of the others, she published for herself her last novel, *A Test of Filial Duty*, issued by Carnan, in January 1772, and Edward and Charles Dilly published *The Life of Theodore Agrippa d'Aubigné* in May. *A Test of Filial Duty*, told in the letters of two young women, was written, Scott notes in a preface, to emphasize "one of the greatest duties of social life," "filial obedience . . . in the important article of matrimony"—a theme common to many of her works.[33] She was thinking of Grace Campbell when she wrote, "If I am so fortunate as by the following sheets, to be the means of saving one family from the complicated affliction which is usually the consequence of such [clandestine] marriages, I shall think myself greatly rewarded for my time and trouble." Two of her young women, though frustrated in their predilections, are patient, refuse to elope, and eventually marry as they wish, but a third elopes with unfortunate consequences.

Her last work, the life of Theodore Agrippa d'Aubigné, is both history and the biography of an exemplary Huguenot life, that of a Sir George Ellison with a political and religious cause. Like her other histories, it was highly praised.

After 1772 Scott is not known to have published again—though it is very likely that some of her works have escaped bibliographers—and seems to have lived quietly among her friends, visiting Bath, London, Tunbridge, and Sandleford, Montagu's Berkshire home. On Edward Montagu's death in 1775, Elizabeth Montagu settled an annuity of £200 on her sister, and on her father's death in 1778 Scott acquired the income for life of a Yorkshire estate and an additional annuity of £50.

In the winter of 1784-85 Scott spent three months with a Mr. and Mrs. Freeman in Norwich and found herself free of headache. Despite Montagu's objections at her removing so far from her friends, she then settled in Catton, just outside Norwich, in May 1785 and, though she continued to travel, made her home there for the remainder of her life.[34] She died there on November 3, 1795, at age seventy-five. After her death, her executor, at her direction, burned her private papers.

The reputation of Scott's writing in her own time was inextricable from her own reputation for piety and good works, as she intended; she lived the life that validated the work and pruned the work to validate the piety. Even before her marriage hers was a remarkably self-directed, uncompromising life. Scott demonstrated both what a woman could achieve in her time and the cost of the achievement. Her influence on her successors is to be tracked in their works; in the Wanderer figure utilized by Burney, Charlotte Smith, and Mary Brunton; in the Gothic plots of Ann Radcliffe, in the character of Louisa Tunstall in *Sir George Ellison,* adapted by Burney as Eugenia in *Camilla;* and in the phrase "sense and sensibility," which she may have been the first to use (*GE,* 220). Though her followers outdid her own novels, she was for them an important model.

## THE HISTORY OF SIR GEORGE ELLISON

The Sir George Ellison of this novel is not precisely the Ellison of *Millenium Hall,* a forty-year-old retired West Indian planter who revealed no particularly benevolent past. This new Ellison is thirty-five on his return and already remarkably attuned to the society he encounters. But his utility to Scott is clear: it is as if she thought, "Suppose we had the money and were of the sex who might carry out our plans within an ordinary family and neighborhood. Suppose we had the power to alter society rather than being crushed by it." If Sarah Fielding demonstrated that the community of *The Adventures of David Simple* was unable to protect itself, Scott intended that Ellison's would be stronger.

*The History of Sir George Ellison* (1766) contrasted English society in all its corruption to the society Ellison, a disciple of Millenium Hall principles, constructs in and around his home. Ellison, who has been absent from England for fifteen years—the course of his adult life—has returned a widower with one son and a fortune to discover his native society afresh in the traditional manner of the outside observer used by Montesquieu in the *Persian Letters* and Goldsmith in the *Citizen of the World*. In the course of the book he anatomizes and does what he can to amend the West Indian systems of slavery and education and the English systems of marriage, child rearing, the education and the status of women, charity, justice, imprisonment for debt, Parliament, the church's clergymen, and the treatment of the mentally alienated.

In the course of the book Ellison contrives to reform the condition of his slaves, establish a family with an ideal domestic economy, relieve and employ the poor of his neighborhood, educate all the young and assist them to appropriate marriage, reconcile neighboring families, instruct a farmer elevated to a dukedom in decorum and restraint, raise the status of educators and the clergy, and make annual tours of nearby prisons to relieve the worthy among the debtors.

Scott contrived to endorse a gradualist and meliorist approach to reform and to apply instrumental arguments, an approach which appealed to, reassured, and enlarged her audience; but her uncompromising revelation of the corruption of her society is clear-sighted, arresting, and hard-hitting. Ellison's own tolerance—"I am no leveller," he says—is contrived to procure Scott a hearing, but his analysis of such institutions as Parliament made the reviewers gasp.

Yet feminist critics of Scott's two Utopian works, particularly of the first, have reluctantly concluded that she was politically and socially conservative, endorsing the class and even the gender structure of her time.[35] A close study of *Sir George Ellison* suggests an alternative theory. When Scott's own model, Sarah Fielding, was publishing *The Governess,* a collection of tales exemplifying how to moderate character flaws in children, her printer, Samuel Richardson, knowing her opinion, argued that she should speak out against corporal punishment of children. Her friend Margaret Collier responded for her that though the book contained many sly hints, still "There is no occasion that she should teach the children so punished that their punishment is wrong."[36] Nor was there any occasion for angering potential readers and thus preventing their adopting other important views, such as that morality was as necessary to be taught to children as was learning.

Altogether Scott seems carefully to have calculated those reforms she could safely advocate (and still hope to be influential) and those she could not. She could and invariably does present Ellison as a genuine Christian, thus reminding her readers of what they too as Christians might be expected to perform. There are arguments she apparently cannot safely make, and she takes the safe side on the question of miscegenation, perhaps because of sensitivity to her audience and what it would bear (139). Any other agenda, such as an argument for gender, class, or racial equality, Scott relegates to "sly hints"—which, however, are not undetectable. That gender, class, and racial equality are her ideals is undeniable because they are the conditions she attributes to heaven. "When you and I are laid in the grave," Ellison tells his wife, "our lowest black slave will be as great as we are; in the next world perhaps even greater; the present difference is merely adventitious, not natural" (13). And what is natural, Scott tells us again and again, takes moral precedence over what is merely socially constructed. Ellison makes the distinction when he says he has no natural right to enslave, only a political one (16); he makes it again when he notes that the Blackburn children have both a natural and a legal right of inheritance of their grandfather's estate (128). In this context Ellison's note that "nature's Agrarian law has been abolished by political institutions" (41) is telling; by nature land is distributed more equally, and natural right is morally superior to political. And Scott notes that tyrants in marriage as well as in slavery have no natural right: but "Human nature always abuses a power which it has no right to exert" (16). The very abuses of marital partners and slave owners are the effect of their not being naturally empowered.

These are sly hints enough to suggest that Ellison's (and Scott's) meliorist positions are an accommodation and that underlying Scott's accommodation is a sense of outrage controlled by an intellectual perception of what she could and could not propose. She could, for example, banish corporal punishment from Ellison's plantation. She could not abolish the institution of slavery; she could only insist on its injustice.

In terms of class divisions, her acceptance at first seems more unquestioning. She seems to uphold the class divisions, based on money and privilege, of her society, envisioning in the conventional way a three-part social division into the landed and idle rich, the profitably employed merchants, tradesmen, and shopkeepers, and the laboring poor. All benefits bestowed including education were bestowed with the condition of the recipient in mind. And yet Ellison gives another sly hint when he reminds Lamont that rank and fortune are indispensable steps to honor, poverty an impenetrable cloud concealing merit, whereas a great estate or high birth frequently exalts those who are unfit (41). Ellison attributes the corruption of the country to "the necessitous state of too many of the individuals" (188), a hint at the inequity of distribution. A telling argument against class is Scott's belief that honest labor is honorable for anyone, that one should forget one's condition and do the work that makes one independent and useful, even though it be the labor ordinarily assigned to lower stations (34). Ellison protests he is no leveller (79), but labor, that great leveler, Scott requires of everyone: of the protégés of Millenium Hall, of Ellison's enfranchised slaves, of the poor children and the elderly of his neighborhood, of the poor gentry, of the privileged upper classes in behalf of the less privileged, and even of Ellison's schoolchildren in vacation lest they esteem idleness a pleasure. Moreover, to some extent it is suggested that appropriate labor be apportioned to the individual according to circumstance and talent rather than station.

Education is also of prime concern to Scott, and better education, we learn in this novel, more closely approximates both slaves and women to free men. If everyone were to labor and if labor were not class-determined, if all were to be educated, even if only according to class, if money were to be more equitably distributed, as Scott gently suggests, what then would become of class distinction?

Ellison dissociates himself from the Levellers and would apparently also have endorsed the anti-democratic 1654 manifesto of the Baptists requiring the saints to await the last judgment before the "Rule and Government of the World should be put into their hands, meanwhile patiently to suffer from the world."[37] But such a direction gives a new significance to the name Millenium Hall, that place where the saints do indeed rule and govern their world.[38]

Scott appears also to attack the class pretensions (and distinctions) of the professionals, those educated but dependent upon their earnings and without the resources to ensure their children's gentility. She believes not only that genteel but unprovisioned dependents ought to abandon class pretensions and take positions as teachers, personal attendants, or servants, but also that the test of their worthiness is their willingness to do so. Both slaves and women are seen to improve with proper education, which for Scott is the key to a better society. Children are born with particular natures, and educators must carefully adapt their instruction to each. Ellison's son is the primary example: he is born with his mother's "natural violence and imperiousness of temper" (138), but we see his father devise a successful education that considers the training of his passions to be as important as the training of his mind. His poorly educated mother, on the other hand, is imperious and manipulative.

The control of the passions, "the deceitful varnish of passion," "the intoxication of passion" (183, 184), is a great object of education for Scott. She is suspicious of the passion of love, which can be avoided by attending to one's work, but which, if it is incurred, must be controlled. That is the point of Ellison's courtship, disappointment, long patience, and final success with Miss Allin: passion might assail him, but in each crisis, including his brush with death just before he marries her, his behavior is exemplary, as it remains after marriage when the temptation to forget his duties to others and slip into domestic bliss must be fought. That he is human is amply proven by his joy on hearing of the fatal illness of her first husband, his friend; but that he is thoroughly controlled is proven by every response he makes.

A proper moral education, such as that Ellison provides for his slaves and all his other charges, is essential for moral behavior. Ellison's efforts with his own children, the Granthams, and the Blackburns are so successful that whereas by nature so many would not have proved deserving (205), all eventually do. Scott notes again and again that the teachers of the young deserve generous wages for the important work they undertake and she labors hard to raise the prestige of the profession. On this point and on other educational issues Scott, like Richardson and Sarah Fielding, follows Locke in his *Thoughts on Education* (1693); the line of influence is clear. Pamela deliberates at length over Locke's advice in *Pamela II,* Sarah Fielding echoes it in *The Governess* (1749), and Scott in this volume follows Pamela's (or Richardson's) ruminations on Locke in the conclusions that the tutor must be very carefully chosen and treated with respect, that a tutor at home with a group of five to eight pupils is the best plan of education, that leaving children in the care of the lesser servants, who are often, in Locke's words, unbred and debauched, is pernicious. Scott works consistently to raise esteem for the educators of children, and to emphasize the importance of their work, which was to establish both intellectual and moral foundations and which had also to be reinforced by parents. And as a particular duty of the mother, educating the daughters and the younger sons implied a necessity for her own careful education.

Scott labors in other subtle ways to raise the position of women. When Ellison leaves Jamaica, it is his sister-in-law and Miss Reynolds who are made monitors of his steward's treatment of the slaves, and not his own brother. And whereas Henry Fielding never introduced a learned woman in his novels without ridiculing her pretensions or impugning her chastity, Scott equates

learning in women with virtue and right thinking: the best women in her
novels tend to be learned. Mrs. Tunstall and her daughters, particularly
Louisa, are joined by young Ellison's beloved Miss Blanchard, who has begun
her studies under his direction.

Scott also impugns the inequity of concentrating family inheritances in
the eldest son. Whereas Ellison's father was comparatively impoverished as a
younger son, Ellison himself insists on a more equal division with his brother
and sister. The story of Mrs. Alton, left entirely dependent upon her brother
and treated like a servant by his wife (101-9), is a blow against such a custom;
and Ellison himself makes a point of saving fortunes for the younger Blackburn and Grantham children and intends to provide additional stipends for
his unmarried daughters. The evils of entrusting the family fortunes entirely
to the husband are twice glanced at, in the Tunstalls and the Blackburns,
cases in which Ellison has to convey money secretly to the wife, who is far
more competent to handle it.

Marriage as an institution also comes under Scott's scrutiny. An unen-
lightened marriage is dreadful, as Scott suggests by moving directly from an
examination of slavery to that of Ellison's first marriage. "Perhaps few have
more severely lamented their being themselves enslaved by marriage," writes
Scott, than Ellison does at becoming the owner of slaves (10). Ellison is enslaved by the passions of his first wife, as Mrs. Reynolds is by those of her
husband; the proper form of marriage is that of Ellison and his second wife.
Finally, the monkey imagery in the novel actually suggests the superiority of
women. For young Lamont women are playthings for men, "a race somewhat
superior to monkeys; formed to amuse the other sex during the continuance
of youth and beauty, and after the bloom was past, to be useful drudges for
their convenience."[39] For Ellison, however, the spectacle of a rich man accessi-
ble only at the end of a suite of elegant rooms is like that of a monkey in a
temple (80). And Ellison also notes that a wife's submission to a capricious
husband "is such as might be expected from a man enslaved by a race of monkeys . . . ; he would be passive from a sense of their power, but despise them
for the capricious manner wherein they exercised it" (28). The callow young
man sees women as very like monkeys, but the reliable Ellison assigns that
likeness to prideful or tyrannical men, and in the last analogy, assigns the
superior position to women.

Scott would probably not have chosen to distract attention from her
task of examining almost every social institution by introducing an exciting
plot even if she could have done so. Ellison examines and, if he can, reforms

the institutions of slavery, marriage, education, law, local justice, imprisonment for debt, and parish charity. He devises his own systems for employing
the local poor, managing his estate, settling his expenses, and handling the
lunacy of a near relation. He refuses to stand for Parliament and gives a full
indictment of its corruption and its system of elections. He insists on interfering in every neighborhood contretemps as one of his primary duties. Aware
that he works hand in hand with Providence, he interests himself in the distresses of everyone he encounters.

The book fits, therefore, into several categories. It is primarily a Utopia
—Ellison is indeed "fit for Utopia" (133)—and Scott knew the genre.[40] Its
first part is a West Indian tale that might be profitably coupled with Aphra
Behn's *Oroonoko*. It is a Christian exegesis and exemplum that demonstrates
how a genuine Christian lives and dies and suggests that Providence cooper-
ates with the just, testing but ultimately rewarding. Its structure is thematic,
about rising to proper and falling to improper behavior, a structure reinforced
by the rise and control of the passions, the success or failure of right reason,
the alternate endorsement and suggested collapse of the striations of class,
gender, and race. A constant reference to implicitly understood vertical distinctions derives from a belief in two levels of reality, earthly and heavenly.
Rising to successfully correct behavior or falling to incorrect behavior, the
characters are each barometrically analyzed. The frequent contrast on this vertical scale of such characters as Reynolds's two wives, Sir William and Sir
George when thwarted in love, Mr. and Mrs. Blackburn and Dr. and Mrs.
Tunstall as parents and domestic economists also produces a consistent vertical ranking the recognition of which, in fact, is what Scott most requires of
her readers.

## THE MAN OF REAL SENSIBILITY

In 1774 *The History of Sir George Ellison* assumed new life under the title
*The Man of Real Sensibility* in a condensation made for a special purpose.
All of the books of this title, published by different publishers, repeat the
same text, prepared apparently for James Humphreys, Jun., in Philadelphia in 1774. American piracy of English publications was then a common-
place, and Humphreys was an industrious pirate;[41] Scott almost certainly had
nothing to do with the project, which attracted publishers because the question and the problems of slavery had become important considerations, particularly in America.

The condensation therefore prints all of the opening of Scott's novel to the point where Ellison leaves Jamaica. It then condenses the remaining plot to focus on Ellison's courtship and marriage. The effect is to provide the plot with a consistent theme of slavery: Ellison ameliorates the conditions of his slaves and then is himself liberated from the slavery of his first marriage into the partnership of his second.[42]

The climate into which Humphreys's novel was released, that of Philadelphia in 1774, was contentious on the subject of slavery. Many Pennsylvania slave-holding Quakers had fought the movement by abolition-minded Quakers to prohibit slavery for members of their meeting. In 1772 the slaveholders had attended the annual meeting and defeated the movement. In 1774 the meeting first moved to ban slaveholding.[43] Humphreys, a prominent printer, may have been commissioned by an abolitionist Quaker to publish the condensation of Scott's work, for Scott emphasizes the equal humanity, spiritual and intellectual potential, and (to use an anachronistic term) the human rights of Ellison's slaves. However, her meliorist position, her failure to insist on abolition of slavery, might also conceivably have provided the slave-holders with an attractive justification and program.[44] The title of the condensation may have been a reflection on James MacKenzie's popular *The Man of Feeling* (1771), about a protagonist with extreme sensibility of no use either to himself or to others.

Subsequent editions pirated from the first (see bibliography, 233-34) were probably undertaken by publishers who foresaw a good market: three more in Philadelphia, two in Edinburgh, one in Delaware, one in Massachusetts. If Scott did know of this publication and its uses, she was undoubtedly happy and proud about it. Though it assumed only a meliorist position, like its original it questioned man's natural right to enslave, revealed that slavery of any kind is oppressive and unnatural, and both explicitly and implicitly denied the inferiority of blacks and women. Probably in the event it was Scott's most influential work.

# NOTES

1. Information from the International Genealogical Index of the Church of Latter-Day Saints adjusts and corrects the birthdates. Elizabeth Robinson was christened at Holy Trinity, Goodramgate, York, on October 13, 1718; Sarah Robinson was

christened there on March 5, 1721. At least the three youngest children were born in Cambridge at the home of their maternal grandmother, wife of Conyers Middleton (see n. 8). John entered Trinity Hall in 1747, but took no degrees at Cambridge, though he is reported, surely erroneously, to have been a fellow of that college (1750-1805). As the correspondence of his sisters and his father's will show, he actually lived in custodial care from about 1749 until his death in 1800.

2. From a letter of Elizabeth Montagu at Tunbridge to Sarah Robinson at Bath dated 29 August 1749, now in the Lewis Walpole Library at Farmington, Connecticut, quoted by permission. For the allusion, see *Midsummer Night's Dream,* where Helena (not Hermia) paints a picture of the two girls as the Robinson girls might have been, creating "both one flower, / Both on one sampler, sitting on one cushion, / Both warbling of one song, both in one key. / . . . Two lovely berries molded on one stem" (III.ii. 204-11).

3. From a letter in the Montagu Collection at the Huntington Library, and quoted by permission. Subsequent quotations from letters in this collection, quoted by permission, are identified in the text by date.

4. *The Letters of Mrs. Elizabeth Montagu*, ed. Matthew Montagu, 4 vols. (London: T. Cadell and W. Davies, 1809-13), 2:8. Subsequent references to this work are by volume and page number in the text with the abbreviation LEM.

5. *The History of Sir George Ellison* (London: A. Millar, 1766). Citations in the text are to this edition, using the abbreviation *GE.*

6. Sarah Scott, *A Description of Millenium Hall,* ed. Jane Spencer (New York: Viking Penguin, 1986), p. 199.

7. On this subject see, for instance, *Lady Louisa Stuart, Selections from her Manuscripts,* ed. James A. Home (Edinburgh: David Douglas, 1899), pp. 157-58; Hester Chapone, *The Works of Mrs. Chapone,* 2 vols. (New York: Evert Duyckinck, 1818), 1:124; Betty Rizzo, *Companions without Vows: Relationships among Eighteenth-Century British Women* (Athens: Univ. of Georgia Press, 1994), pp. 127-28.

8. Elizabeth Montagu, *Elizabeth Montagu, the Queen of the Blue-Stockings,* ed. Emily J. Climenson, 2 vols. (London: John Murray, 1906), 1:121. A letter from Dr. Conyers Middleton to Montagu on the occasion of her marriage, dated 4 Oct. 1742, notes that he is pleased with her account of her brothers "who after being exposed as it were on the mountains of Yorkshire, were discovered at last, like Enfans trouvé, by a sister unknown to them." He also notes that the three boys were all born under his (Cambridgeshire) roof (Montagu Correspondence, Folder 9, Princeton Univ. Library), printed in LEM, 2:201.

9. Horace Walpole, *The Yale Edition of Horace Walpole's Correspondence,* ed. W.S. Lewis, 48 vols. (New Haven: Yale Univ. Press, 1937-83), 10:169. George Montagu perhaps uses the word *sufferance* in three senses: as something to be endured, to be suffered, to be barely tolerated (*OED*).

10. The usual dowry of a duke's daughter was £10,000 and that was considered small for the grandeur of the marriage she was expected to make, except that her connections were also conceived of as contributing to her fortune. Lady Barbara's money, invested in the safe government bonds that yielded only 3 to 5 percent, could

have given her an income of £250 *at most*; a London establishment with servants and a carriage required an annual income of at least £1000.

11. Walter Marion Crittenden, *The Life and Writings of Sarah Scott—Novelist (1723-1795)* (Philadelphia: Univ. of Pennsylvania, 1932), p. 67.

12. Mary Delany, *The Autobiography and Correspondence of Mary Granville, Mrs. Delany*, ed. Lady Llanover, 6 vols. (London: Richard Bentley, 1861-62), 3:115. For more on this subject, see Rizzo, *Companions without Vows*, pp. 303-5.

13. For the text of Sarah Scott's letter see Rizzo, *Companions without Vows*, p. 305.

14. For these women see ibid., pp. 383-84, nn. 28-30.

15. Anna Riggs (1741-81) in 1765 bestowed her large fortune on John Miller, an Irish baronet in 1778. By 1775 Lady Miller had set up an antique Italian vase in their Batheaston villa as the recipient for verses with which their guests competed for wreaths of myrtle. Attendance for this fashionable amusement was select and four volumes of the poems were published: see R.A. Hesselgrove, *Lady Miller and the Batheaston Literary Circle* (New Haven: Yale Univ. Press, 1927).

16. Vincent Carretta has pointed out the important contributions of both Richardson and Johnson (and, a bit parenthetically, of Charlotte Lennox, who was first among these) to the development and endorsement of the idea of a women's community of scholars and/or unmarried women (see his "Utopia Limited: Sarah Scott's *Millenium Hall* and *The History of Sir George Ellison*," *Age of Johnson* 5 [1992]: 303-25); but he has failed to note the debt of all three to Mary Astell, who in 1694 in *A Serious Proposal to the Ladies* suggested an all-female college or Protestant nunnery where women could live the life of the mind (see Ruth Perry, *The Celebrated Mary Astell* [Chicago: Univ. of Chicago Press, 1986], pp. 98-119; Perry also notes precedents for Astell's idea, pp. 118-19). Carretta emphasizes the ratification of the idea by Richardson and Johnson, but that had little practical effect and generated little subsequent endorsement. As he notes, the vision of a Protestant nunnery for women appears in Lennox's *The Female Quixote* (1752), Richardson's *Sir Charles Grandison* (1753-54), in which the hero proposes the establishment in every county of Protestant nunneries "in which single women of small or no fortunes might live," and Johnson's *Rasselas* (1759), in which the Princess Nekayah dreams of a college of learned women over which she might preside. Astell's view of the sequestered nature of the place is emphasized in all these schemes: a convent, a nunnery, or at the least a college. Sarah Fielding, too, in *The Countess of Dellwyn* (1759) proposes a scheme for a community of gentlewomen, and as she was an intimate friend of Richardson's may well have convinced him herself in conversation of the worthiness of the scheme, whereas Johnson may have been most influenced by his friend Charlotte Lennox. Scott of course knew the work of all these writers: as Bridget Hill notes, she probably took a hint from Astell when she named Millenium Hall; see Carretta, p. 306, and Bridget Hill, "A Refuge from Men: The Idea of a Protestant Nunnery," *Past & Present* 117 (Nov. 1987): 107-30, but see also n. 38 below. Scott took various points from Astell's works and was in intimate communication with Sarah Fielding. But she much disliked the concept of confinement in a convent: see next note.

17. The fuller title *A Description of Millenium Hall and the Country Adjacent* . . .

suggests Scott's dislike of confinement. She expresses her distaste for conventual life in *The History of Cornelia*; see also her letter to her brother of 26 May 1762 (Huntington, quoted by permission) on shutting oneself up in a cloister: "No one can be very free, but it is strange that any shou'd endeavour to render themselves absolute Slaves, without a possibility of Manumission; & as strange that people shou'd think an useless life, a life of religion."

18. See, for example, Crittenden, *Life and Writings,* pp. 73-74; L.M. Grow, "Sarah Scott: A reconsideration," in *Coranto* 9, no. 1 (1973): 9-15.

19. Crittenden, *Life and Writings,* pp. 73-74.

20. Undated letter of Sarah Scott to Elizabeth Montagu (Winter 1748-49) in the Huntington Library, San Marino, California, quoted by permission. Mr. Sable is the lugubrious undertaker in Steele's comedy *The Funeral; or, Grief a la Mode* (1701), from which Scott would also take the name "Lady Brumpton" for Montagu (see below).

21. Letter of Sarah Scott to William Robinson dated 26 May 1762 in the Huntington Library, quoted by permission.

22. Letter of Sarah Scott to William Robinson dated 10 April 1762 in the Huntington Library, quoted by permission. Portions of some of Scott's letters to William Robinson and his wife, formerly in the possession of Sir Egerton Brydges, were published (see bibliography), but such passages as these were not.

23. T.C. Duncan Eaves and Ben D. Kimpel, *Samuel Richardson: A Biography* (Oxford: Clarendon Press, 1971), pp. 462-63, also note that Lady Barbara paid Richardson £56 to produce the cards; see also the *Daily Advertiser,* 30 April 1759, where they are fully described.

24. Eaves and Kimpel, *Samuel Richardson,* pp. 463-64. Montagu wrote to Elizabeth Carter, "There is a novel published which I believe to be chiefly written by your friend Mrs. Fielding" (LEM, 4:216). Entirely fictitious, it was a pious attempt to warn women, but if Fielding wrote it she did not wish to have her authorship known.

25. See *A Description of Millenium Hall*, ed. Walter M. Crittenden (New York: Bookman, 1955), p. 15.

26. Ibid., pp. 145-48; Rizzo, *Companions without Vows,* pp. 127, 296-97.

27. The claim of co-authorship derives solely from Horace Walpole's notation in his copy of the work that it "is the work of Lady Barbara Montagu and Mrs. Sarah Scott." Walpole's information would have come from his friend George Montagu, Lady Barbara's cousin, who may have been confused by a knowledge of Lady Barbara's participation in planning the work into assuming she had also participated in writing it.

28. Crittenden, *Millenium Hall*, p. 15. The book may be what Elizabeth Carter was referring to in July 1772 when she wrote to Montagu that she had seen a geographical work on a very large plan advertised which she was afraid would interfere with Scott's (Elizabeth Carter, *Letters from Mrs. Elizabeth Carter, to Mrs. Montagu, Between the Years 1755 and 1800,* 3 vols. [London: F.C. & J. Rivington, 1817], 2:146).

29. Carter, *Letters,* letters dated 24 May and 29 June 1766, 1:296, 305.

30. Royal Commission on Historical Monuments, *An Inventory of the Historical*

*Monuments in Buckinghamshire*, 2 vols. (London: His Majesty's Stationery Office, 1912), 1:205.

31. Bartholomew Dominiceti, in 1762 a druggist and apothecary bankrupt in Bristol (*Daily Advertiser*, 24 May 1762; *A Short and Calm Apology in regard to the many injuries and repeated affronts . . . met with . . . in Bristol* [Bristol, S. Farlew, 1769]), author of medical works, including *A Plan for Extending the Use of Artificial Water-baths* (1771), in August 1767 petitioned for a patent for his method of making "arbitrarily heated and medicated baths, pumps, and stoves, both moist and dry, and a variety of fumigations from herbs, seeds, &c., and an infinite variety of machines for applying the above to the human body" (*Calendar of Home Office Papers of the Reign of George III, 1766-1769*, ed. Joseph Redington [London: Longman, 1879], p. 268). Dominiceti at least prevented some deaths by dehydration. His establishment was in Cheyne Walk, Chelsea. (See also Reginald Blunt, "Aesculapius Fumigans, Dominiceti of the Baths," *In Cheyne Walk and Thereabouts* [London: Mills & Boon, 1914], pp. 137-55.)

32. Carter, *Letters,* letters dated 24 May and 29 June 1766, 1:296, 305.

33. On this subject see Caroline Gonda, "Sarah Scott and 'the Sweet Excess of Paternal Love,'" *Studies in English Literature, 1500-1900* 32, no. 3 (Summer 1992): 511-35.

34. Letters between Montagu and Scott of 1785-86 from the Huntington Library, quoted by permission. I am indebted to Barbara Schnorrenberg for lending me her copies of these letters and to Mary L. Robertson, curator of manuscripts at the Huntington, for additional information about Scott's movements at this time.

35. Moira Ferguson, for instance, includes an interesting discussion of *Sir George Ellison* in *Subject to Others: British Women Writers and Colonial Slavery, 1670-1834* (New York and London: Routledge, 1992), 100-105; she detects a very faint anti-patriarchal whisper, but in general concludes of Scott's meliorist and gradualist approach that, as with any charity, "The unstated subtextual monster is profit, cornerstone of the rising and predacious capitalist-colonialist economy" (p. 104). I would add that Scott, rather than playing along with the prevailing profit motive, was urging the moral position to the utmost extent she thought productive.

36. *The Correspondence of Samuel Richardson*, ed. Anna Letitia Barbauld, 6 vols. (London: Richard Phillips, 1804-6), 2:62.

37. Quoted by E.P. Thompson, *The Making of the Working Class* (London: Victor Gollancz, 1980), p. 32.

38. See note 16.

39. P. 40. Lamont is eventually, at the end of the novel, reformed under Ellison's influence but is appropriately paired with the worthy Mrs. Blackburn, who also has no great sensibility. However, as a measure of Lamont's improvement, Scott allows him to be captivated by an experienced woman whose bloom is specifically stated to be past.

40. Scott had evidently read Thomas More's *Utopia*: competition among gardeners is permitted at *Millenium Hall* as it was the only form of competition permitted in More's Utopia.

41. The *Eighteenth-Century Short Title Catalogue* lists 122 entries for Humphreys

between 1774 and 1810, including almanacs, grammars, sermons, political treatises, law cases, charitable prospectuses, plays, histories, novels and tales, and, during the British occupation, army proclamations. Among his other 1774 piratical publications were Hannah More's pastoral drama *The Search After Happiness* and Sterne's works in six volumes.

42. Moira Ferguson, pp. 110-11, 114, discusses *The Man of Real Sensibility* as an anti-slavery document and notes the thematic connection to the subject of marriage, but assumes that the pagination is the same in all editions and that Scott was herself responsible for its preparation. She may here follow Crittenden, *Life and Writings,* who knew only of the Chapman Whitcomb edition and assumed wrongly that it was published in England in about 1770 (p. 43). Of course no English edition has been found.

43. Jean R. Soderlund, *Quakers and Slavery: A Divided Spirit* (Princeton: Princeton Univ. Press, 1985), p. 172.

44. Matthew ("Monk") Lewis (1775-1818), novelist and West Indian planter, for instance, was a great meliorist but no abolitionist; see his posthumously published *Journal of a West Indian Proprietor* (1833). Lewis, like Ellison, abolished harsh punishments, lessened labors, increased comforts and holidays, and arranged a system whereby in his absence his slaves could not be mistreated; he was idolized by the slaves throughout Jamaica. Scott may well have been an important influence on him.

# CHRONOLOGY OF EVENTS

## IN

## SARAH ROBINSON SCOTT'S LIFE

~

| | |
|---|---|
| 1718, 2 Oct. | Elizabeth Robinson, sister of Sarah (later Scott) is born. |
| 1720, 21 Sept. | Sarah Robinson (later Scott) is born. |
| 1721, 5 March | Sarah is christened at Holy Trinity, Goodramgate, York. |
| 1730s | Robinson family removes to Mrs. Robinson's estate at Mount Morris, Kent. |
| 1741, April | Sarah contracts a severe case of smallpox that destroys her beauty. |
| 1742 | Sarah visits Bath as the companion of Williamina-Dorothy Cotes. |
| 5 Aug. | Elizabeth Robinson marries Edward Montagu in London. |
| 1743, Sept.-Oct. | Sarah again visits Bath with Mrs. Cotes. |
| 1746 | Elizabeth Drake Robinson (mother) dies. |
| 1747, Dec. | Sarah visits Bath with the Montagus and remains. |
| 29 Dec. | Thomas Robinson (brother) dies. |
| 1748, Aug. | Sarah moves into the house of Lady Barbara Montagu, "Lady Bab," in Bath. |
| 1750, 19 April | Millar publishes Scott's first novel, *The History of Cornelia*; an Irish edition is published by John Smith; reviewed in *Monthly Review*, May 1750, p. 59. |
| 1751, 15 June | Sarah Robinson marries George Lewis Scott at St. Michael Bassishaw, London. |

| | |
|---|---|
| 1752, April | Scott's father and brothers remove her from her husband's home. |
| 1754, 24 Jan. | R. and J. Dodsley publish Scott's *Agreeable Ugliness*, a translation of *La Laideur Aimable* by Pierre de la Place; reviewed in *Monthly Review*, Feb. 1754, p. 144. |
| 26 March | Millar publishes Scott's *A Journey Through Every Stage of Life*, 2 vols.; reviewed *Monthly Review*, March 1754, p. 237. |
| May-1762, Sept. | Scott and Lady Barbara Montagu settle at Batheaston and devise a life of community. |
| 1756 | Scott's brother Robert Robinson, an East India Company captain, dies in China. |
| 1759, 30 April | Geographical, chronological, and historical cards by Scott and Lady Barbara are published. |
| 1760, Nov. | Millar publishes Scott's *The History of Gustavus Erickson King of Sweden, by Henry Augustus Raymond* (imprint 1761); reviewed in *Monthly Review*, Jan. 1761, pp. 54-67; in *Critical Review*, Nov. 1760, pp. 372-85. |
| 1762, 3 March | J. Newbery publishes Scott's *The History of Mecklenburgh*. A second edition is printed that year; reviewed in *Monthly Review*, June 1762, p. 475; in *Critical Review*, April 1762, pp. 312-19. |
| Sept. | Scott and Lady Barbara Montagu give up Batheaston and remove to Bath. |
| 29 Oct. | Newbery publishes Scott's *A Description of Millenium Hall*; reviewed in *Monthly Review*, Nov. 1762, p. 389; in *Critical Review*, Dec. 1762, pp. 463-64. |
| 1764, 26 June | J. Newbery publishes second corrected edition of *A Description of Millenium Hall*. |
| 1765, Aug. | Lady Barbara Montagu dies. |
| 1766, 9 April | Millar publishes Scott's *The History of Sir George Ellison* in 2 vols.; reviewed in *Monthly Review*, July 1766, pp. 43-46; in *Critical Review*, April 1766, pp. 281-88. |
| 1767 | Third edition of *Description of Millenium Hall* is published. Irish edition of *The History of Sir George Ellison*, probably pirated, is published by W. Sleater, J. Potts, & J. Williams. |

| | |
|---|---|
| 1768 | Scott undertakes the Hitcham community experiment. |
| 1770 | F. Noble publishes the "second edition" of *The History of Sir George Ellison* in 2 vols. |
| 1772, 27 Jan. | Thomas Carnan prints for Scott *A Test of Filial Duty*; reviewed in *Monthly Review*, Feb. 1772, p. 165; in *Critical Review*, Feb. 1772, p. 182. |
| 19 May | Edward and Charles Dilly publish Scott's *The Life of Theodore Agrippa d'Aubigné*; reviewed in *Monthly Review*, Oct. 1772, p. 325; in *Critical Review*, June 1772, pp. 477-83. Irish edition published by D. Chamberlayne et al. |
| 1774 | First known publication of *The Man of Real Sensibility* (condensed from *Sir George Ellison*) is published by James Humphreys Jr. in Philadelphia. |
| 1777, c. Aug. | Scott's favorite brother, Morris Robinson, dies in Ireland. |
| 1778, 2 Oct. | Scott's father, Matthew Robinson, dies. Fourth edition of *Description of Millenium Hall* is published by T. Carnan and F. Newbery. |
| 1780, 7 Dec. | George Lewis Scott dies. |
| 1787 | Scott removes to Catton, Norwich. |
| 1795, 3 Nov. | Scott dies at Catton. |

# Note on the Text

~

The text reprinted here is that of the first edition, published by Millar in 1766. Preparation and proofreading of the novel were not executed by the original printer with the greatest of care. I have silently corrected obvious printer's errors and attempted to standardize inconsistent spelling and use of capital letters according to Scott's own common usage; where the author uses both eighteenth-century and modern spellings (e.g., *compleat* and *complete*), I have adopted the modern version. The raised *r*, *rs*, and *t* of the abbreviations *Mr.*, *Mrs.*, *Sr.*, and *St.*, employed by Scott in her letters, and the raised *e* and *r* of *ye* and *yr* employed by Montagu in hers, have been lowered to conform to editorial policy. The modern symbol for pounds sterling (£) has been substituted for the eighteenth-century *l*. The ligatural vowel of *œconomy* has been omitted here and the word spelled *economy*. The quotation marks that sometimes but not always appeared at the beginning of every line of quoted dialogue have been removed, and the erratic use (and non-use) of quotation marks has been silently amended.

# THE HISTORY
## OF
# SIR GEORGE ELLISON

~

VOLUME I

# PREFACE

The usual intention of a preface, I apprehend, is to make the Author's apology; and yet I question whether he might not have a better chance of extenuating his fault (if he has committed one) by abridging his book than by adding to its length.

The doubt I am in as to this particular, will make me, though I comply with the custom, endeavour to do it in as few words as possible; and with all convenient brevity attempt my excuse for offering to the public the following sheets.

The lives of good or eminent persons have been thought an useful study, as they set before us examples which may incite us to virtue, and trace out to us a path wherein emulation may induce us to walk [1]. But the men whose lives are published are generally above our reach, or out of the sphere of common persons. Great generals, or wise statesmen, are rather objects of wonder than imitation to the common rank of men; saints and martyrs we admire and applaud, but are apt to feel the piety of the former above our powers, and hope never to have occasion for the resolution of the latter: Our hearts are warmed by the contemplation of their virtues, but we seldom sufficiently consider, how the motives which led them to such sublime heights, may be applied to the actions of common life; and for want of this application, we lose the benefits we might reap from their examples.

This neglect has often led me to think that the life of a man more ordinarily good, whose station and opportunities of acting are on a level with a great part of mankind, might afford a more useful lesson than the lives of his superiors in rank or piety, as more within the reach of imitation [2]. This opinion induced me to collect all the actions that came to my knowledge of the person to whom I have given the name of Ellison, and to reduce them into the regular form of Biography, in order to lay before the public a life, which in some particulars every man, and in all particulars some men may imitate, his actions being confined within the common sphere of persons of fortune, in several articles within the extent of every gentleman's power.

It may be said by some, that on the same principle I ought to have selected a character more faulty, one wherein the virtues are blended with such imperfections, as bring it nearer the common level, and render it of more easy imitation; whereas a character so free from vice, may discourage the attempt in those who feel a greater mixture of evil in their own dispositions. But I confess myself of a different way of thinking; the chief use I have seen made of mixed characters, has been to gather from them a sanction for the worst parts of our own. We are inclined to say, 'If this good man had such a vice or failing, surely mine may be excused, it is not of a more hurtful kind; or, if it is, some of my virtues are of a more useful nature; therefore taking their superiority into the account, the balance will be rendered equal.' Thus the faults of good people do more harm than the errors of the less virtuous, and when we would exhibit a character proper for imitation, we should rather endeavour to conceal the failings which may have stolen into a good heart, than industriously seek to discover them.

I have already intimated that the name of Ellison is a borrowed one; possibly, if I have any readers in Dorsetshire, some of them may say, they know no such person there; though I rather hope the county contains so many gentlemen who resemble Sir George, that several will be pointed as the originals from whence his character is drawn. But should this hope be disappointed, and the former supposition prove fact, let them consider, that I am at liberty to conceal the place of my friend's real abode, as well as his real name, and may substitute a fictitious one in the place of either [3].

If any one should object, that Sir George Ellison is too good to have existed any where but in imagination, I must intreat my censurer will, before he determines this point, endeavour to equal the virtue of Sir George; a request I may the better make, as by indulging me in it, I may venture to assure him he will reap the chief benefit, and if he attempts it with vigour and sincerity, I am persuaded he will find Sir George's conduct within the reach of human powers, when properly applied, and strenuously exerted; for such exertion will not fail of being rewarded by the necessary assistance.

# BOOK I.

~

## CHAP. I.

Sir George Ellison's father was the younger son of an ancient and opulent family; but receiving only that small proportion of his father's wealth, which, according to the custom of this country, usually falls to the share of a younger child, his posterity had little chance of inheriting any considerable fortune from him; though he had, by the profession in which he was placed,[1] been enabled to live genteelly. Had his diligence been greater on his first entering it, he might have raised to himself such an income as would have enabled him to make a better provision for his family; and when it was no longer time to repair this error, the sense of it gave him great concern; and to make the best reparation in his power, and what indeed was more than an adequate recompense for the neglect he lamented, he dedicated all the leisure his business allowed him to the care of his children's education. Their learning he left to proper masters; the object of his attention was their hearts. He watched the first rise of every passion, and endeavoured to correct it before time had given it strength. The first dawnings of Virtue he perceived with joy, and encouraged with care; cultivating every good disposition, and inculcating the most amiable and solid principles. He instructed them fully in the Christian religion, and shewed them that it was the best foundation, as well as surest support, of moral Virtue.

Before his son George had completed his one and twentieth year, his family, by the death of his wife and two children, was reduced to two sons and one daughter. James his second son was then but twelve, and his daughter fourteen years old. This difference in their ages determined Mr. Ellison to trust in his son George's hands two thirds of the sum of which he was possessed;[2] for this being no more than four thousand pounds, he considered, that when divided, the share of each would be so small as must prove insufficient to place them with tolerable advantage in trade; and the difficulty he had found in providing for his family, had disgusted him with professions; which are better suited to the single, than the married state. By so good a capital, he hoped to secure the success of his eldest son, whose disposition gave him reason to believe he should thereby do the best service to his other children. He knew the young man to be perfectly sober, humane, and generous, and at the same time an exceeding good economist; extremely diligent, and well inclined to that care of, and attention to, his affairs, so necessary for those who undertake merchandize. He had beside a tender affection for his brother and sister, and both loved and revered his father.

Mr. Ellison's conduct may perhaps be censured in this particular. Such entire confidence in so young a man might be injudicious; dangerous it certainly was, and to his son appeared so hazardous, that he opposed, for the first time, his father's inclination, and used every argument prudence could suggest to alter his purpose; but either paternal affection, or real knowledge of George's turn of mind, made him persist in his determination; telling the young man, that, if his success answered his hopes, his protection would greatly repay his brother and sister for any danger they might incurr; but to shew that he was not careless of their interests, he took a bond from his son, which secured to them, in case of their father's death, their share of the £4000 to be paid them in two years after his decease, if by that time of age, and obtained his promise, that during those two years, the money should bear six per cent interest; thus providing for their convenience as much as could be done without hurting their elder brother, whom possibly a more speedy payment might distress.

George Ellison was of a disposition to prosecute warmly and diligently every thing he undertook; therefore, as he entered into merchandize, he wished to pursue it in the most profitable manner, indifferent as to any inconveniences which might attend it. He knew that many, in consideration of their ease, were unwilling to purchase superior advantages in trade, by leaving their native country; a circumstance to which he had perfectly reconciled himself, by considering a man who has his fortune to make as a citizen of the world; and that the country where he has the best means of living, is most properly his own; subsistence being a more rational cause of attachment than birth. He therefore endeavoured to settle correspondences with some of their less adventurous merchants, by whose means he might negociate a quick trade from Jamaica, where he intended to fix; and the character he had established in the city, by his excellent behaviour during his apprenticeship with Mr. Lamont, an eminent merchant,[3] rendered him successful in both these articles; and with warm hopes, though tender concern, he took leave of his father and this kingdom, well provided with correspondents here, and recommendations to the principal people in Jamaica.

As my intention in the following sheets is, not so much to give a minute detail of Mr. Ellison's actions, as to record his virtues, and rather to represent him as an object of imitation than of wonder, I shall pass over a few succeeding years of his life very succinctly; nor do they afford any great variety of incidents, his whole attention being turned to the business he came upon; which he pursued so successfully, that in two years after his arrival he had increased his stock one third; and at the same time, had gained the esteem of all who were concerned with him. He now thought it time to remit half his capital to his father, telling him that he could not be easy till he had restored that sum; for as his sister was become a woman, or nearly so, some advantageous match might offer; and he should think himself very culpable, if by detaining her fortune, he should deprive her of a good establishment. The remainder he would punctually restore before it could be wanted for his brother.

Old Mr. Ellison was surprized and vexed at this action of his son's, who had given him no previous notice, fearing he would forbid it. He represented the injudiciousness of lessening his capital, before there was any necessary call for it; since he might have made so great a profit upon it, as would much have increased his own fortune, before his sister would have any occasion for hers, as it would be soon enough for her to marry many years hence. And as for the remainder, he desired him to consider that, without assuming any advantages from his seniority, the third of the whole was his share; and in taking no more, his brother and sister would have reason to think he treated them very generously; he therefore insisted on his looking upon that sum as his own; for his great industry, and uncommon merits, could never be a reason for his losing a share of his patrimony.

Young Ellison returned only a vague answer to this letter; he had already taken his resolution, and was determined to adhere to it, but saw no occasion to contend with his father's justice and affection, till the time of putting his design in execution. The more generally he became known, the more extensive his trade grew, as every one wished to be connected with him. His fortune daily increased beyond his hopes; and he felt the greater satisfaction in it, from finding that his uncommon success had not excited envy; which possibly might in part be owing to his conduct; for the frugality necessary to a young beginner so far restrained the natural generosity of his temper, that his merit was more conspicuous than his success; his industry, sobriety and temperance, shewed that he had a just title to more than uncommon increase of riches, but his moderation left them so far in doubt whether he had really acquired what he had a right to expect, as prevented their drawing any disagreeable comparisons between his profits, and those of others.

Five years after his first settling at Jamaica, he acquainted his father with his resolution of returning the whole capital he set out with; observing, that he could not think his lawful share was too great a consideration to pay his brother and sister for the hazard they ran in his being intrusted with the whole; a confidence deserving every grateful return to the best of fathers; which at the same time, that it gave him the pleasing and encouraging consciousness of possessing the esteem he most wished for, provided him with the means of making a fortune. That Mr. Ellison might not apprehend he was distressing himself, he informed him, that he had now raised a capital of £6000 to which he should always think his father had as good a title as himself.

## CHAP. II.

If Mr. Ellison's good conduct gained him the esteem of his own sex, we may easily suppose the other was not insensible of his merit; especially as it was accompanied by a very fine person, a face handsome from great symmetry of features, but still more from vivacity, sensibility, and sweetness of countenance; a manner and address polite and engaging, and a turn for conversation peculiarly agreeable. Mr. Ironside observes, that Mrs. Jane Lizard included black eyes and white teeth in her description of a man of merit;[4] perhaps, there are not many women, who on the like occasion would include fewer personal attractions, than found place in Mrs. Jane's. Mr. Ellison, therefore, was sure to please, since in this sort of merit, he excelled as much as in that of a more substantial nature. As the manners of Jamaica are not peculiarly reserved, many intimations were given to Mr. Ellison, of the favourable disposition of the ladies; but his attention was so totally engaged by his business, that the strongest hints were lost upon him. He was deficient in the sensations that render a person most quick-sighted in that particular, he was void of vanity (as much at least as a human creature can be) and perfectly indifferent to the whole sex; Cupid is such a bungler, that he seldom hits a mark that is in motion; against an active mind he usually misses his aim; and he had never been able to find Mr. Ellison's sufficiently at leisure to be wounded;  business is a shield through which Love's arrows cannot easily penetrate. Amidst all the airs that coquetry could play off upon him, he was frequently computing the profits of his last embarked cargo of sugars and spices; and was in little danger of being captivated by the fairest form, except Commerce, as sometimes personified by the poets,[5] had made her appearance before him; the gums of Arabia, the gems of India, and in short the various riches of different climes, with which they deck her, would have greatly heightened her charms in his eyes; while the egrets, pompons, and bracelets of fashionable nymphs appeared to him oftener burdensome than ornamental. The politeness of his behaviour, and the chearfulness of his temper, however, so well concealed the coldness of his heart, that to warm it seemed no impracticable attempt, and prudence as well as inclination might dispose many to endeavour to gain the affections of so worthy and so successful a young man. No woman had the mortification of thinking she had a rival, till a widow lady entered the lists.

This lady was seven years older than Mr. Ellison, having completed her three and thirtieth year. Though the bloom of youth was past, she was still handsome; had behaved very prudently in the different states of life in which she had appeared; was possessed of ten thousand pounds in money, and a plantation of no less value. This last article might have engaged the attention of men insensible to the charms of her person, or the merit of her conduct; but as Mr. Ellison's close attachment to his business proceeded entirely from a desire of succeeding in a thing he had undertaken, and his ardent wishes of being able without imprudence to return into England before the best part of his life was spent, without any of that love of money which renders people eager after every means of gain, he formed no designs on her, or her fortune. The widow was not equally insensible; she saw in him every quality that could recommend him to a woman of prudence; for his youth was a trifling objection she overlooked; and it seldom happens that either sex in the choice of a companion for life are guilty of a less oversight; or if she saw it, she thought it not her business to point it out; that rather was his part. Mr. Ellison's friends perceived the partiality which had passed unnoticed by him; and persuaded him not to let slip so good an opportunity of improving his fortune; since without those advantages, her character and person rendered it an eligible match. Though Mr. Ellison had not till now entertained any thoughts of matrimony, yet it was a state he had always intended to enter, when his affairs should render it convenient, and he should meet with a woman who could engage his affections. He therefore listened without reluctance to the advice of his friends. The lady was agreeable, her fortune desirable; and though his heart was void of those nice sensibilities, which he wished to feel for the woman with whom he entered into so intimate a connection, yet he flattered himself that her merit, joined with her personal charms, must soon excite a strong affection in a heart naturally warm and tender.[6]

There was little reason to suppose his father would object to an alliance so advantageous; but possibly he might have formed some views which this marriage might frustrate, and therefore be disagreeable to him: at least the young man was sensible he should feel double satisfaction if he had his father's sanction, and therefore would not make any direct address to the lady, till he had received that necessary consent. His father took the first opportunity of removing this impediment, sending not only his consent but his approbation, accompanied with the warmest wishes for his happiness.

Mr. Ellison, whose inclination for the lady had increased with acquaintance, received his father's letter with joy; and now making an express declaration of his attachment, in terms of esteem and rational affection, rather than in the inflated phrase of passion, the widow, without coquettish airs, or affected reluctance, accepted his proposal, and the marriage was soon completed.

By the alteration of his fortune Mr. Ellison found his sphere of action extended. But (as is frequently the case) this gave him great uneasiness. The thing which had chiefly hurt him during his abode in Jamaica, was the cruelty exercised on one part of mankind; as if the difference of complexion excluded them from the human race, or indeed as if their not being human could be an excuse for making them wretched. Slavery was so abhorrent to his nature, and in his opinion so unjustly inflicted, that he had hitherto avoided the keeping any negroes; chusing rather to give such advantages to his servants, as rendered it very easy to get the few he wanted from England. But the case was now altered; he had with his wife married a considerable plantation, cultivated by a numerous race of slaves, nor could his affairs go on without them. This much embittered his possession; and perhaps few have more severely lamented their being themselves enslaved by marriage, than he did his being thus become the enslaver of others. According to the present state of the island he was sensible he could not abolish this slavery, even on his own estate, and saw no means of rendering happy the poor wretches, whose labours were to yield him affluence. His uneasiness astonished Mrs. Ellison; she had a reasonable share of compassion for a white man or woman, but had from her infancy been so accustomed to see the most shocking cruelties exercised on the blacks, that she could not conceive how one of that complexion could excite any pity. But they had not been married above a week, before Mr. Ellison gave great offence to her and her steward, by putting a stop to a most severe punishment just beginning to be inflicted on a great number of them, who, intoxicated with the pleasure of a holy-day,[7] had not returned home at the time commanded. The steward, enraged at finding his tyranny restrained, applied to Mrs. Ellison, telling her, 'that all order was now abolished, and if Mr. Ellison proceeded in this manner, their slaves would become their masters, and they must cultivate their lands themselves.' Mrs. Ellison loved her husband too well not to pity his failings, of which she thought this the chief; and attributed it to a total ignorance of his affairs, with which she hoped to make him better acquainted. Accordingly she calmly represented to him the impropriety of what he had done; anticipating all possible consequences. Mr. Ellison allowed that some of them might happen; that he was convinced persons so habituated to slavery, required a different treatment than was shewn to free servants; what difference would suffice, he had not yet been able to determine, but he was convinced cruelty was not necessary, and he was resolved he would find out some medium. 'As for the idleness you suppose will arise from a relaxation of these shocking severities, I protest by all that is sacred,' continued he, 'that were not justice to you in question, for this estate being originally your's, I cannot think that marriage deprives you of your right in it, I would give it all for the extacy I felt at seeing the joy of the poor reprieved wretches. Had you, my dear, been present when they threw themselves at my feet, embraced my knees, and lifting up their streaming eyes to heaven, prayed with inexpressible fervency to their supposed Gods to shower down their choicest blessings on me, you would have wept with me; and have owned a delight which nothing in this world can afford, but the relieving our fellow creatures from misery; a delight even beyond what our weak imperfect senses can well bear, for it rises to an excess that is mixed with pain, since reflexions on their unhappy state mingle themselves with our joy; but the first extacy over, the pleasure becomes more adequate to our sensations.'

'I do not doubt,' answered Mrs. Ellison, 'but they were rejoiced to find their punishment remitted, as they look upon it as a permission to take the same liberty every holy-day; and you may depend upon it they will give you the like opportunity for such another scene.'

'Very probably they may,' replied Mr. Ellison, 'but if my pardon has no other consequence, it will only appear as useless as your steward's punishment; for he confessed to me, that for the same offence he had most cruelly chastised them not above a fortnight ago. Whatever their behaviour may be, let me enjoy the pleasing sensations arising from even abused mercy, rather than the stings of remorse for useless cruelty.'

'But,' interrupted Mrs. Ellison, 'would you have their faults go uncorrected?'

'By no means,' answered Mr. Ellison, 'but I would have the punishment bear some proportion to the offence; and till it does so, it cannot be effectual. These poor creatures would be far our superiors in merit, and indeed in nature, if they could live without committing frequent faults; if the smallest offence, as a too free indulgence of innocent mirth like this I have just pardoned, is punished with the same severity as a malicious or dishonest action, the suffering wretches become desperate; they find, however careful, through the weakness of human nature they must sometimes err, and also that by the barbarity and tyranny of their overseers they shall frequently be punished, even when they are not guilty; and looking upon these sufferings as a misery attending their condition, they do not endeavour to avoid what they cannot always prevent. I am determined henceforward to ease your steward of this part of his business; the produce of the land he may still attend, but those who cultivate it shall be my care; he is not fit to be trusted with any thing but what is inanimate. And that you may not think I pay too high a price for this indulgence of my compassion, or rather this compliance with my conscience, I will endeavour to find a means of rendering our slaves obedient, without violating the laws of justice and humanity.'

Mrs. Ellison was mortified to find her husband incorrigible in so material an article; but recompenced herself for the fears she was under lest their fortune should suffer through his simplicity, by an inward exultation on reflecting, that however it might be in other families, in their's woman was certainly not the weaker vessel, since she was above those soft timorous whims which so much affected him; had always kept her slaves in as good order as any man in the island, and never flinched at any punishment her steward thought proper to inflict upon them. However, with the generosity the strong ought to shew to the weak, she determined to push the matter no farther at that time; but to let the man take his silly way, till experience convinced him of his folly; and denying herself any other triumph over his imbecillity than a smile, which expressed more of contempt than complacency, she was turning the conversation to another subject, when a favourite lapdog, seeing her approach the house, in its eagerness to meet her jumped out of the window where it was standing; the height was too great to permit the poor cur to give this mark of affection with impunity; they soon perceived that it had broken its leg, and was in a good deal of pain; this drew a shower of tears from Mrs. Ellison's eyes, who, turning to her husband, said, 'You will laugh at me for my weakness; but I cannot help it.'

'My dear,' replied Mr. Ellison, 'you will one day know me better than to think I can laugh at any one for a token of sensibility; to see any creature suffer is an affecting sight; and it gives me pleasure to observe you can feel for the poor little animal, whose love for you occasioned his accident; but I confess I am surprised, though agreeably, to see such marks of sensibility in a heart that I feared was hardened against the sufferings even of her fellow creatures.'

This last expression stopped the torrent of Mrs. Ellison's affliction; and indignation taking place of compassion, as she turned her eyes from her lap-dog to her husband, ———— 'Sure, Mr. Ellison, you do not call negroes my fellow creatures?'[8]

'Indeed, my dear,' answered Mr. Ellison, 'I must call them so, till you can prove to me, that the distinguishing marks of humanity lie in the complexion or turn of features. When you and I are laid in the grave, our lowest black slave will be as great as we are; in the next world perhaps much greater; the present difference is merely adventitious, not natural. But we will not at present pursue this subject; the best action we can now do is to relieve the poor little sufferer; let us go into the house, and get its leg tied up; I believe I may venture to take upon myself to be its surgeon.'

This kind offer mitigated Mrs. Ellison's resentment, at having been so disagreeably associated with people whom she esteemed the most despicable part of the creation; and put her in better humour with her husband's compassionate nature; for though she still saw him equally weak in this particular, yet she now looked upon it as an amiable weakness. We will leave them therefore busied in their present care, equally placid, and equally attentive to the poor lap-dog.

## CHAP. III.

Mr. Ellison had determined, while he remained in Jamaica, to take all the advantages it offered him, and not to suffer the increase of his fortune to lead him into a neglect of trade; but his desire of mitigating the sufferings of his slaves was so great, that he resolved to withdraw his whole attention from commerce, till he had devised some means of effecting this first wish of his heart.

Humanity, when sufficiently warm and steady, seldom waits long for the power and opportunity of exertion. He soon formed a plan, and set about the execution of it with the utmost diligence. He erected a great number of cottages, and assigned to each family a comfortable habitation, with a little piece of ground adjoining, well stocked with vegetables, the future cultivation of which he left to themselves; at the same time providing them more plentiful and better subsistence than was usually allowed to any in their station. Two days in the week he permitted them to leave off work at an early hour in the afternoon; and promoted innocent amusements among them at those times; carefully preventing the sale of strong liquors, lest mirth should lead to drunkenness. If the weather were peculiarly sultry, he would make them retire from work in the hottest part of the day, and always took care that they were supplied with wholesome liquor to refresh them. If any were sick, he immediately had all proper relief applied; and by the encouragement he gave to such old women as nursed them well, secured them every comfort their condition could admit.

While he was establishing these regulations, he pretended blindness to many of their faults; but such as could not be overlooked, he permitted to be punished in a manner he thought dreadfully severe, though merciful in comparison with what was usually inflicted; fearing some very bad consequences might otherwise happen through excess of lenity, before he had completed his plan. But when he thought they must be sufficiently convinced of the difference between their condition and that of any other slaves in the island, he told them, he was determined to try whether they deserved good usage: when they compared their situation with that of other slaves they had reason to think themselves happy; but yet their treatment had not been such as was agreeable to him, who did not chuse to consider them slaves, except by ill behaviour they reduced him to the disagreeable necessity of exerting an absolute power over them. 'While you perform your duty,' continued he, 'I shall look upon you as free servants, or rather like my children, for whose well-being I am anxious and watchful. I have provided you with convenient habitations; given you a plentiful portion of all necessaries; assigned to each a small share of peculiar property; taken care of you in sickness; and considered your ease in health; I have increased your liberty; promoted your amusements; and much lightened your punishments. But still these are too heavy; I cannot feel myself so superior to any of my fellow creatures, as to have a right of correcting them severely. I am determined therefore, for the future, to abolish all corporal punishments. I shall require nothing of you that can be properly thought a hardship; but if gratitude and prudence cannot bind you to good behaviour, the first offence shall be punished by excluding you from partaking of the next weekly holy-days; for the second fault you shall not only be deprived of your diversion, but of a day's food; and if these gentle corrections do not reform you, on the third offence you shall be sold to the first purchaser, however low the price offered; and this sentence is irreversible; no prayers, no intreaties shall move me. The man who after so happy a change in his condition can repeatedly offend, is not worthy to be the object of my care; and shall become the property of some master, whose chastisements may keep within the bounds of duty the actions of that man, whose heart cannot be influenced by gratitude, or his own true interest.'

Mr. Ellison's humanity had already gained the affection of his slaves, but on this declaration they almost adored him; and in the strongest terms promised him, and themselves likewise, never to offend so good a master, in such a manner as to bring them under the heavy sentence he had pronounced against those who persevered in disobedience. This was at that time the real sentiments of their hearts, but human frailty, and an acquired indifference to offending, from having been long subject to indiscriminate and unavoidable punishments, left scarcely the resolution of one unbroken. But the fonder they were of diversion, and the more they delighted in their now plentiful board, the more sensibly they were affected by the two first punishments, and few of them were so senseless as to incur the third. The first who was so unfortunate, when he found the sentence was going to be put in execution, and that he was really set up to sale, was almost distracted; he was so enraged at his own folly, that he was with difficulty restrained from doing violence on himself. His importunate intreaties for pardon extremely distressed Mr. Ellison. To deny the poor wretch a farther trial grieved him to the soul; and yet he saw that a strict adherence to his first declaration was absolutely necessary; he therefore resolved to endure the conflict, though not unmoved, yet with unaltered purpose; and to shew them that in despight of his compassion, which was too great to be concealed, yet he was inflexible.

Mrs. Ellison, who met him as he returned from this unhappy wretch, was amazed at his uneasiness; 'Surely,' said she, 'you have less spirit than a sucking babe, if you can pity such an ungrateful creature; you have borne with him too long already. I hope you are sensible it is a great weakness to be so tamely forgiving, as you have already shewn yourself; it is high time he should feel your vengeance; if a slave will indulge his idleness, surely a master has a right to gratify his resentments.'

'Is it possible, my dear,' answered Mr. Ellison, 'that you can imagine I expose this wretch to the cruelty of some implacable master to gratify my resentment! If I could feel the smallest emotion of that nature in my heart, I should detest myself. The poor criminal is more outrageous in his expressions, but I question whether he feels more than I do on this occasion. I am exerting a power merely political, I have neither divine, nor natural right to enslave this man. This shocking subordination may be necessary in this country, but that necessity makes me hate the country. The most atrocious crime only could deserve the punishment I am inflicting; and were it not that all order depends on a superior's inviolable adherence to his own laws, I assure you the poor man should instantly be pardoned. Nor could I go through what I am doing, if I did not hope this example will have so strong an effect on those who are now deploring his fate, that it will prove the last time I shall be reduced to so painful an exertion of power. I see by your smile, that you still despise me for being as you call it so tamely forgiving. You say, Surely, I must be sensible it is a great weakness; how can I think so, when I see such various proofs that the Being, in whom there is no weakness, who is all perfection, is far more forgiving than any of his creatures; He is Love and Mercy itself; can then any portion of the Divine Nature, that part of his image which he stamped on man, be esteemed a failing! How much more disobedient are the best of us to him, than our slaves are to us? yet he does not crush us with his power; he neither sends the lightnings to blast the offender, nor pestilence to consume a sinful country; he bears with us year after year, gives us frequent calls and admonitions to repentance, and leaves us a long season for amendment. He is ever ready to forgive, and lets fall his vengeance only on those who will not ask to be forgiven; who will not even endeavour to amend. He requires only a forbearance of the evils we have before committed, and sorrow for them; he has performed the expiation for us. When we think of the fountain of Mercy, can we call forgiveness or compassion a weakness! To see it in that light, is as contrary to your real nature, as to mine; the difference between us lies only in education; you have been bred in a country, where scarcity of natural inhabitants introduced slavery, which can never be established but at the expence of humanity; the master becomes a tyrant, for human nature always abuses a power which it has no right to exert; and the slave's mind being as heavily fettered as his body, he grows sordid and abject. I, on the contrary, was born in a country, that with all its faults is conspicuously generous, frank, and merciful, because it is free; no subordination exists there, but what is for the benefit of the lower as well as the higher ranks; all live in a state of reciprocal services, the great and the poor are linked in compact; each side has its obligations to perform; and if I make use of another man's labour, it is on condition that I shall pay him such a price for it, as will enable him to purchase all the comforts of life; and whenever he finds it eligible to change his master, he is as free as I am.'

As Mrs. Ellison was not deficient in understanding, she saw there was some truth in what her husband had said; but it was a truth her reason could more easily perceive, than her heart feel, for it was steeled by habit.

Mr. Ellison, soon after his marriage, had desired his father to send him over a proper person to teach reading, writing, and accounts; leaving him at liberty as to the stipend, only desiring the man might be sober and virtuous. As soon as this person arrived, he gave him a neat house, and established him schoolmaster, sending all the children of his negro slaves to be under his tuition.[9] He caused them to be instructed in the principles of the Christian religion, hoping thereby to civilize their manners, and rectify their dispositions. He performed this office himself, to those more advanced in years, believing instruction would come with more authority and persuasion from him, as they respected him as their master, and loved him for the happiness they enjoyed in his service: and certainly such doctrine can scarcely fail of proving persuasive, when the preacher's actions are so eminently conformable to his precepts. In the familiarity of discourse, he rendered all things necessary to be known so intelligible, that the dullest mind comprehended his instructions, and they were all convinced that must be right which produced such a life as his.

By plentiful food, and a comfortable life, Mr. Ellison's negroes became stronger than any in the island; the natural strength of those who belonged to other masters, being consumed by hardships and hunger. His were, therefore, able with ease, to do so much more work, that he might have diminished their number; if compassion had not prevented him. To keep them in sufficient employ, he made such improvements, both as to the beauty and profit of his estate, as were little thought of by others; at the same time, that he was careful to give his slaves as much ease and amusement as they could enjoy, without being corrupted by the indulgence; sensible that the greater their happiness, the more they would fear incurring his punishments. He animated them in their duty by proper commendations and reward, and proportioned his encouragements with exact justness to their deserts. He had the satisfaction of seeing his conduct succeed to his utmost wish. Negroes are naturally faithful and affectionate, though on great provocation, their resentment is unbounded, and they will indulge their revenge though to their own certain destruction. Mr. Ellison gave them no opportunity of feeling this fatal passion, and he had not a slave who would not have joyfully sacrificed his life for him. Their superstition inclined them to think him a deity, rather than a man; and in nothing did he find them less docile, than when he endeavoured to turn their love and adoration of him to his and their Maker. It was difficult to persuade them to look on him as only an instrument in the hands of their merciful Creator, employed by him for their good; and of consequence their gratitude and love ought to be paid to that power, which gave their master the opportunity and inclination to concur with the views of their General Parent, and make them happy. He shewed them plainly that he was but God's steward; that without his blessing, the sower soweth but in vain; that the clouds must drop fatness, or the earth will not be fruitful; and if the sun did not ripen their fruits, all the art of man could not prevent universal famine and destruction:[10] That all the worldly prosperity he enjoyed, all the good dispositions which led him to impart the blessings he received, came from above, and to the Power who had given them, it was their duty to render their thanks. All this he frequently urged, but still their affections could not be weaned from their visible benefactor.

Above a year passed away without his being obliged to sell another slave; which gave him hopes he should never again be exposed to so painful an exertion of his power. And the poor wretch, whose example had had so good an effect on his companions, had all that time suffered the usual severities under a harsh master; which were greatly heightened by comparisons between his present and late condition, and by reflexions on his folly in exposing himself to so dreadful a change. His self-reproaches made him doubly wretched; and as he lived in a plantation adjacent to Mr. Ellison's, he was a constant object of compassion to his former companions, who frequently lamented his fate, and represented his distress with such pathetic simplicity, as touched Mr. Ellison's compassionate heart to so great a degree, that he resolved to re-purchase him at any price. This he effected on more reasonable terms than he hoped, for the poor fellow's dejection of spirits was such, that it undermined his health, and rendered him so weak, that his master was very glad to get the price he had given for him. When he was acquainted with his being again become Mr. Ellison's property, his joy was near proving fatal; the sense of that gentleman's goodness, and his fortunate restoration to happiness, entirely overpowered his spirits, but when he recovered his speech, his thanks were poured forth in such unintelligible extacy, as was far more affecting than the most sublime eloquence. A holy-day was given to all the slaves to welcome his return, and never was the restoration of a monarch celebrated with so much heart-felt, disinterested joy.

But although the gratitude and assiduity of this poor fellow's future behaviour greatly rewarded his master, yet it produced a disagreeable event; another slave was encouraged by it to flatter himself that Mr. Ellison would never again exercise the same severity, since it had proved so painful to him; but above all, not on one who was particularly intelligent and useful, as this slave knew himself to be. On this supposition, he determined to become more the master of his own actions; and, extending his offence to a third time, was dreadfully surprized to find himself, notwithstanding his most earnest intreaties, doomed to be sold. It was with difficulty he prevailed with his fellow slaves to interceed for him; they blamed his ingratitude so much, that they almost thought he deserved his punishment; but when good nature got the better of judgment, and they joined their intreaties to his, Mr. Ellison assured them, all intercession was vain.

The day was appointed for the sale of the offender; but before it arrived, he was seized with a violent fever, and the terrors of his mind, at the thought of the execution of the sentence he had incurred, increased his malady so much as rendered it improbable he should recover, and made him desirous not to do so. Preferring death to slavery under another master, he refused to take the remedies prescribed, and earnestly begged they would suffer him to die. Mr. Ellison thought his condition would sufficiently excuse the reversing of his sentence; and rather than put his life to farther hazard, pronounced a pardon for his past offence; but declared, that if he again was guilty of the like, nothing should procure his forgiveness. The poor man now became as anxious to preserve, as he had been before desirous of losing his life; gave repeated assurances of never being ungrateful for the mercy shewn him, and lavish in professions of future obedience; which the event proved to be the real dictates of a settled purpose, not of a sudden emotion. His mind being at ease, his strength was superior to the violence of his disorder; he recovered from his fever and his perverseness together; carefully avoiding, from that time, all possibility of incurring the punishment from which he had so happily escaped.

Mr. Ellison thought himself not less fortunate in having had so good an excuse to pardon the offender, and was never after put to the same painful trial. The superstitious vulgar look upon the third as a fatal number; but these slaves had great reason to think it so, and carefully avoided it; which was not very difficult; for as Mr. Ellison saw the services of his slaves in the same light as those of free servants, he did not expect them to be exempt from faults; and for such slight offences as in England he would have thought deserved only reproof, he inflicted no other punishment; not using the power received from the custom of the country, but in relation to more material offences.

## Chap. IV.

Having collected in one view such particulars as may serve to give the reader a proper idea of Mr. Ellison's manner of treating his slaves, it is time to say something of affairs still more domestic.

Mrs. Ellison, before the expiration of the first year of their marriage, produced him a very fine boy. Her fortune enabled him to extend his trade; and his success therein always answered his wishes; though his increase of wealth did not bear the same proportion to the capital with which he traded, as it had done before he married. The like frugality was no longer necessary, nor indeed would it have been excusable. He now might safely indulge his benevolent and charitable disposition; therefore, it was his duty to do so; and he thought his wife had a right to partake in the enjoyment of the income she brought him; however, he saw his wealth increase full as much as he desired. Thus far we have looked at the fair side of his affairs; but he was not free from vexations; happily he was reasonable enough to think he had no right to be so, for that the most fortunate man must expect his share of pain and trouble, which we can no way so well alleviate, as by patient submission to this indispensable consequence of humanity.

Mrs. Ellison, as I have already hinted, was a good sort of woman; but many good sort of people, according to the common use of the phrase, make bad companions in intimate society. She was so very fond of her husband, that she was miserable if he was out of her sight. If, when abroad on business, he did not return just at the hour she expected, he found her in agonies, lest some misfortune had befallen him; and with floods of tears, she reproached him with insensibility of the pain she suffered from his want of punctuality; sobbing out that 'poor dear Mr. Tomkins' (her first husband) 'would not have used her so; he would rather have left any business unfinished, than have given her such terrors.' If he expressed an inclination to spend an evening with a friend, she was inconsolable, lamented his indifference, 'he was all the world to her, but she too plainly saw he wished to be any where rather than at home; poor dear Mr. Tomkins never was so happy as in her company; but her lot was now sadly changed.' If he paid the common attentions which politeness required to any other woman, she was fired with jealousy, 'men were ungrateful, inconstant creatures; a good wife was sure to be neglected, for every flippant girl; poor dear Mr. Tomkins, had no eyes but for her; but handsome men, truly, must be admired; the love of one woman would not satisfy their vanity.' When any generous action of his reached her ears, which could not but happen frequently, she would most pathetically lament that, 'notwithstanding the fine fortune she brought, her dear boy would be a beggar'; and most eloquently would she preach against extravagance.

A moderate portion of understanding suffices to discover the weaknesses even of people who are wiser than ourselves; and a little cunning is sufficient to enable us to take advantage of the discovery; for cunning attains its little ends more surely than wisdom; like the despicable mole which works its way through the greatest mountains, while the noble lion cannot penetrate one foot deep into the earth. On some creatures nature has bestowed strength, courage, and wisdom, on others fangs and claws; among these I rank the cunning of our own species, who seldom fail of biting and scratching out their way by means so low and despicable, that the nobler part of mankind, neither see nor suspect their aim. Had Mrs. Ellison openly shewn an intention of enslaving her husband, she would have found him better acquainted with the relative duties of matrimony, than to have submitted to a disgraceful and unnatural yoke. But on their first marriage, she restrained only with silken threads; the fetters were forged by degrees. By the little endearments of excessive fondness, she would bring him to compliance, when he raised objections from convenience, or politeness; and unwilling to appear insensible to so much tenderness, he would sometimes delay business, and break appointments. Every compliance of this sort rendered her applications more frequent, and if he shewed much reluctance, plaintive, affectionate reproaches of want of love, strengthened the request. Every conquest more fully convinced her of his weakness; she perceived that his greatest fear was to give pain; that he could not bear without severe pangs to be the cause of uneasiness to any person; but above all, to one who was rendered susceptible of it, chiefly by her love for him. Against this, therefore, as the most pregnable part of the fortress, she erected her battery of sighs, tears, caresses, and reproaches, which she played off with great art, and equal success. She became however, so lavish in the use of them, that Mr. Ellison at length saw reason to suspect there was more of policy than love in her behaviour; but before he conceived this suspicion, she had brought him to a habit of compliance, which he could not shake off without a stronger effort, than the gentleness of his nature would suffer

him to exert. He was naturally passionate, his emotions were quick and violent, but soon over; a perfect knowledge of this failing in his temper, kept
him so much on his guard, that it seldom broke out; and the fear of not being
able to restrain his anger within proper bounds, if he indulged the smallest
expression of it, made him pretend blindness to many things which he would
otherwise have reproved; lest warmth of temper might lead him to say more
than he thought right. This laudable delicacy assisted Mrs. Ellison's views; he
bore much perverseness from the fear of becoming in the wrong, if he gave
himself liberty to repent; and if at any time she had (what she soon learnt to
esteem) the good fortune to teaze him past his patience, she was sure of carrying every point for some time after; for the concern he felt, at having broken
into angry expressions, against the woman whose affection had led her generously to put herself and so large a fortune into his power, (for in this light he
saw her marrying him) and who therefore had a just title to his gratitude, as
well as his protection, made him seek every means of making reparation for
what he thought injurious treatment; though every other person would have
considered it only as a necessary exertion of spirit, and must have wondered at
his patience in not carrying his resentment farther. Mrs. Ellison was so sensible of the advantages these sudden sallies gave her, that whenever she had a
point to carry, which she knew was extremely contrary to his inclination, she
would contrive to teaze him beyond the power of human patience to support
without resentment, herself preserving such an air of calmness and moderation as well becomes her sex.

By these arts she soon made her husband that slave which he would suffer no one to be to him. Her power indeed was not sufficiently absolute to
force him to the omission of any thing he thought a duty. Not even her tears,
or most tender intreaties, could prevail with him to neglect any office of humanity; he was conscious that he should be very culpable, if he suffered his
weakness to interfere with the good of others, though sacrificing his pleasures
was, at least, an innocent folly. Even any material article of his business she
could not make him omit; but the company of his friends, and amusements
he was fond of, he relinquished; and thus varnished over his weak compliances. 'Affection may operate variously in different minds. A desire to make
happy, to promote every thing that can benefit, or even amuse, the beloved
object appears to me the natural result of Love; but possibly in persons whose
minds are contracted by bad education, and corrupted by the exertion of an
absolute power, which cannot justly belong to any mortal Being, Love may
assume a tyrannic air; and from a long habit of self-gratification, a person

may be brought to seek less the happiness of the beloved, than her own indulgence. The source is amiable, though the spring is contaminated; and it would be cruel to make a woman suffer for her affection, because Education has perverted her understanding, or in some degree suppressed the best sensations of the heart. She gave an evident proof that she preferred me to the charms of money, for she might certainly have married one of the richest men in the island. Can I be to blame then in making some sacrifice in return?'

But if Mr. Ellison stood justified to himself, his friends passed a less favourable sentence. They found themselves deprived of the most agreeable society the place afforded, and were not a little angry with the occasion of it. Some seriously, and sensibly, advised him to free himself from his bondage: others laughed at him for his pusillanimity. A secret consciousness that the advice was good, and the ridicule just, made him receive both with great good humour, but they were equally ineffectual; he eluded them in the best manner he could, telling the first, that 'to throw off the restraint would give him more trouble than he found in submitting to it;' and to the jesters he only said, that 'they must not wonder if his long application to merchandize had taught him to see every thing in the light of traffic; and his wife had bought him at so great a price, that he thought she had a right to make the best of the purchase.' Her power over him could not be a secret, but he had pride enough to wish to conceal the uneasiness it gave him.

None of his acquaintance were so severe upon him as Mr. Reynolds, a near neighbour, who, sensible of Mr. Ellison's superiority of understanding, found no small gratification to his mortified vanity, in seeing him brought nearer a level by this great weakness. If Mr. Ellison had conceived any resentment of the many sarcasms thrown out by this gentleman, he would have had his revenge from Miss Reynolds, a lively, sensible girl, who was one day particularly piqued at her brother's telling Mr. Ellison that he had fallen into strange errors of conduct, for women and negroes were made to be slaves. And Mr. Reynolds being, immediately after making this declaration, called out of the room on business, she cried out, 'How great my brother feels himself! and yet this mighty man, who thinks he is so lordly and so absolute, should be the greatest slave in the world, if my sister Reynolds would let me take my own way.' 'I suspect, Madam,' said Mr. Ellison, 'you rate your abilities too high; by the charms of sweet persuasion, I make no doubt but you might gain entire power over one of gentle nature, but I do not think you have enough of the virago to tame such a temper as Mr. Reynolds's.' 'I allow,' answered she, 'that I am not well qualified to do it by violence, but art would make the conquest easy, as I shall shew you. This absolute Monarch, who is pleased to hold our sex in such contempt, was the most abject slave imaginable to his first wife, though he is a tyrant to the present Mrs. Reynolds. You will say, what occasioned the difference of conduct? Only this, his first wife was a weak, illiterate, low-bred woman; this has an understanding superior to his, education has improved, and good breeding refined it.'

'You account oddly, Madam, for his different treatment of his two wives,' interrupted Mr. Ellison, 'I should suppose the fact would be just the reverse.'

"I find then,' said Miss Reynolds, 'you know your own sex less than I do. My brother's conduct is not unusual. Seeing his first wife inferior to him in understanding, he would not so far affront himself, as to believe she could attempt to govern so wise a Being, one of the Lords of the Creation; he therefore was not on his guard against her. In her, as it commonly is in people of weak minds, the want of sense was amply supplied by cunning, of which she made such full use, that she gained an absolute ascendancy over him, while he, easy in fancied security, never perceived she governed, because he was convinced she had no title to do so. But after her death, he began to suspect, from the ease and freedom he felt, that he had for some time been under no small restraint; and falling in love with his present wife, whose beauty was sufficiently powerful to determine him to marry her in spight of her excellent understanding, which he looked upon as a very alarming circumstance, he immediately resolved to be very watchful in the preservation of his sovereignty; for if so weak a woman as his first wife could endeavour to govern him, what strong attempts might he not expect from one so uncommonly sensible! Thus he reasoned; how justly the event has shewn. In pursuance of this resolution, from the day he married her, he has constantly opposed every inclination she has expressed, although it has frequently been agreeable to his own, fearing lest a seeming compliance should encourage an attempt to enslave him. As a handsome woman he is fond of her, but as a sensible one he envies her; and when he most admires her beauty, he is jealous of her understanding. He is ever caressing, and ever endeavouring to mortify her, by pretending a contempt for her judgment, which he flatters himself will give her a low opinion of it. She perceives his motive, and from a real superiority of sense, neither resents nor despises his weakness; wise enough to feel her own failings, she cannot contemn those of others; and as she is above any great desire for trifling gratifications, she has not the least wish for an influence, which generally makes the wife as ridiculous as the husband; even where she has a choice, she knows the object is not worth a contest; and being free from the obstinacy of fools, she does not wish for a government she is disqualified for obtaining, by being destitute of their cunning. All the means she takes towards her own ease, is to forbear as much as possible expressing her choice, that she may have a chance for seeing the thing she chuses done.'

'I am not quite so passive; for sometimes, more to shew her how she might disappoint his great aim, by the very means he uses to attain it, than for any material purpose, when I know she has any wish, I tell him before her, that she is desirous of the very contrary; which, by his rule of opposition, never fails of producing the end I had in view; and if she would suffer me, I could by this method make every thing go according to her inclination; but her mind is too noble to submit to the use of artifice, and she had rather have every wish opposed than obtain the gratification of it by deceit. I was informed that last winter he designed spending with his family three months at Kingstown;[11] I knew my sister was very unwilling to leave the country; I therefore asked him to gratify us by passing some of the dead months in that town; strengthening my request, by assuring him my sister was very desirous of it. My success answered my expectations, he refused me; and by repeating the petition from time to time, as I judged necessary, I kept him here the whole winter. Nor have I yet been disappointed in this method. Were he more reasonable, I should hope, with the experience he has had of the truth of the fact, to convince him that his wife's good sense is his best security against his being governed, and that he might without endangering his sovereignty treat her with the indulgence due to a rational and virtuous Being; but it is scarcely possible to persuade one of his turn of mind that power is preserved, if it is not exercised in tyranny.'

This account of Mr. Reynolds's absurdity might have afforded some gratification to many men in Mr. Ellison's situation, but as he bore no resentment, he felt only concern on the occasion; from thinking that Mrs. Reynolds, while her husband was so perversely actuated by his groundless apprehension, could not be so happy as she deserved. His humanity never rested in inactive compassion, he always attempted to alleviate the uneasiness he pitied; if success did not crown his endeavours, and bring relief to the suffering persons, he, however, procured to himself for some time the pleasure of hoping to do good, and in the end the happy consciousness of having done all that lay in his power to serve them. Instead therefore of drawing comparisons between his own weakness and Mr. Reynolds's folly, which must have set his own conduct in a favourable light, he immediately conceived a design of conquering, or at least moderating this whim of Mr. Reynolds's; and told his sister his resolution, who rather wished than hoped for his success. It may seem much easier to form this design than to discover the means of executing it. Reason is but an hopeless instrument with which to attack prejudice and obstinacy; and the weakest understandings are least susceptible of conviction, as walls of mud bear the battering by cannon with less damage than those of brick or stone; by making little resistance they suffer the ball to pass easily through, but it leaves a breach no wider than is requisite for its passage; a little mud repairs it instantly; thus by calling a little fresh folly to their aid, simple people efface the small impression reason and argument have made on their understandings. The method that occurred to Mr. Ellison as the most proper for effecting his purpose, as well as the execution of it, must have their place in the ensuing chapter.

## CHAP. V.

Mr. Ellison was sufficiently acquainted with Mrs. Reynolds to know, that far from harbouring a desire of controlling her husband's inclination, with which her own generally coincided, she only wished he would act in pursuance of what was really such, and not relinquish his own pleasure, in order to mortify her, when he perceived her choice was the same with his, as her natural openness of temper rendered it impossible for her to conceal the concurrence of her inclinations; though long experience had taught her that he would forego his strongest desire rather than leave her a possibility of thinking he had shewn any compliance with her's.

As nothing operated so strongly on his mind as the fear of being governed, Mr. Ellison thought the most likely way of succeeding, was to shew him that the effects of that apprehension, lay him open to the very thing he most wished to avoid. Miss Reynolds might have been very useful towards the execution of his plan, but he did not chuse to have her concerned in it, lest it might give her brother offence. Mrs. Ellison therefore was the properest assistant; she was very intimate in the family, and had been sufficiently piqued by some of Mr. Reynolds's jests on the tyranic exertion of her power, to enter very warmly into any scheme that might tend to his mortification, or his wife's happiness. Little contrivance was requisite, as Miss Reynolds had shewn the surest method; the Ellisons had only to consider on the best means of making him, from the spirit of opposition, act for a month or two in direct contradiction to his own inclinations.

In pursuance of this scheme, they united more intimately than ever into society with Mr. Reynolds's family; carefully observed each desire as it arose in his mind, and discovered his greatest dislikes. They then took every opportunity of proposing to him to do the thing they knew he secretly wished, as an action that would oblige Mrs. Reynolds, she being always present; for he would have had no objection to pleasing her, could he have been sure of keeping her ignorant that he knew he should do so. He had now a double motive for refusing every thing they proposed, as he thereby thought he shewed both to his wife, and Mr. Ellison, his manly tenaciousness of the husband's prerogative; and so eager was he to take every opportunity of asserting it, that for about two months, they, by this means, drove him into a regular and constant course of opposition to his own inclinations. Such a series of actions, the most disagreeable to himself, would have tired a man less obstinate out of the principle which occasioned it, but he found consolation in the consciousness of having preserved the dignity of man, and the sovereignty of husband. Mr. Ellison had minuted down every occasion wherein they had thus played on his reigning foible, and at the expiration of two months, gravely remonstrated on the perverseness of his temper, and the absurdity of his conduct; and then urging that he thereby gave a wife more certain means of governing him than she could otherwise obtain, produced as a proof of it the paper, where he had put down every time that, taking advantage of his spirit of contradiction, he and Mrs. Ellison had led him into doing the things most disagreeable to himself, and mortifying every inclination, rather than comply with what he thought agreeable to Mrs. Reynolds. It was easy to shew him, that if his wife would take the same method they had pursued, he must be her tool; and if she did not, it plainly proved that she had no desire to govern him.

Mr. Ellison then proceeded to observe how superior Mrs. Reynolds was to all those little mean views, that lead a woman to wish for a power to which she must be conscious she has no right, and cannot assume without acting out of character, and rendering herself ridiculous: congratulating him on having found a woman whose true and solid good understanding secured him from the object of all his fears; but observing, that he ought to feel some apprehensions, lest his absurd behaviour might excite her contempt; for folly accompanied with ill nature can have little title to excuse even from those who would love, while they compassionate weaknesses that arose from goodness of heart.

Mr. Reynolds could not be insensible to such glaring proofs of his folly; he saw the consequences Mr. Ellison deduced from his principle of action, and saw it with distress; exclaiming, 'Is there then no defence against female encroachments? how are we to preserve the power nature designed us, if in spight of all our endeavours, a way may still be found out to govern us?' 'The case is not so desperate,' answered Mr. Ellison, 'as you imagine: your danger lies only in your fear; I have shewn you that you thereby give your wife arms against yourself. Banish these apprehensions. Where virtue and religion place no bars, let your inclination be your guide; admit no motive but the desire of doing what is best and most essential to your happiness; and learn, that to oblige is as much an exertion of your power, as to mortify, and far more rational, as well as amiable. The conferrer of an obligation stands in a superior light to the receiver of it; let that superiority content you, for it is the greatest we can have. That which you may imagine your sex gives, is lost by shewing a weakness of mind that degrades you; when you appear to act from noble principles, then you shew man in his true dignity, and will be respected and obeyed with pleasure, by a woman who has sense enough to discern your merit. A wife may be obedient to your caprices, but she will all the time feel herself your superior; her submission is such as might be expected from a man enslaved by a race of monkeys, if we can imagine a country ruled by those animals; he would be passive from a sense of their power, but despise them for the capricious manner wherein they exercised it. The man who has the good fortune to be married to a woman of sense and education, has only to make himself beloved and respected by her, and then he is sure of being obeyed with pleasure. The arts of a woman who has more cunning than sense, with whom we comply out of good-nature because we cannot by reason convince her, is what a husband has most cause to fear; for such are the governing wives.'

Mr. Reynolds's prejudices were too deeply rooted to disappear on the first conviction; and after he determined on a change of conduct, old suspicions would recur, and have their usual influence. But Mr. Ellison did not leave his work unfinished; and after a long and close attention to his temper, he had the satisfaction of seeing him live in a state of easy confidence with his wife, and making her happy, at the same time that he rendered himself so. She knew to whom she owed this fortunate change in her situation; but the same delicacy which had prevented her from ever complaining of her husband's former treatment, now made her silent on the obligations which filled her heart with gratitude: but Miss Reynolds was less reserved; acknowledged the benefit received in the warmest terms; and would have thought herself peculiarly fortunate to have had the means of procuring for Mr. Ellison the same degree of happiness that he had given them.

But this was not within the reach of her power. Mr. Ellison's vexations increased with the age of his little boy: he was equally the darling of both his parents, but they differed much in their opinions as to the proofs of that affection. The child was naturally of a passionate and stubborn temper; which his father saw with concern, and thought it his duty to keep him within reasonable control; and if possible to conquer faults, which, when strengthened by time and habit, must prove incorrigible. Mrs. Ellison, on the contrary, called his passion spirit, and his stubbornness constancy and steadiness, and could not bear he should receive the least contradiction. She was continually puffing him up with the notion of his consequence; representing all the people about him as his slaves; and making them seek to please him by the most abject means. She taught him to look on them in the same light as she herself did, as creatures destitute of all natural rights, of sense, and feeling. She was pleased to see him vent his childish passions upon them, and was always ready to gratify his resentments beyond his wish; and so successful were her endeavours, that by the time he arrived at the age of five years, he was a little fury, bursting with pride, passion, insolence, and obstinacy.[12] Not that Mr. Ellison had tamely submitted to her corrupting the mind of a child he doated on: From a gratitude he thought due to her, from an excess of good-nature, that rendered it irksome to him to be the author even of a momentary pain, and from a love of peace, which made him think contention a greater evil than obedience, he had suffered her to gain an influence over him, which, though his reason disapproved, yet his conscience acquiesced in, as it was no moral evil; but when his child's present and future happiness were in question, the case was altered; he considered it as a being intrusted to his care, for whose temporal and eternal welfare he was answerable, as far as education and paternal authority could affect it. He endeavoured to teach her the duty of a parent, and to convince her that her indulgence rendered her the child's most pernicious enemy; but having never reasoned in her life, the faculty was too feeble to enter into the force of his arguments; she was too perverse to attend, and too weak to be convinced.

He then assumed an air to which she had hitherto been a stranger, and told her, 'Though he had sacrificed his own inclinations to her, she must not expect to find the same easiness in him when the welfare of his son was at stake'; and in the most resolute manner declared he would not suffer him to be made a brute. Tears were now called to her aid; she wept for his cruelty; lamented the hatred he bore both to her and her child, and to the latter only because it was her's, for the poor babe was too young to have offended him; called him unnatural father, and cruel husband; and poor dear Mr. Tomkins became again the object of her grief and regret. But all these arts proved now unavailing; Mr. Ellison's heart was too deeply engaged in the importance of the cause of their contention, to be moved by any thing she could say; and he kept so firmly to his point, that she began to think it advisable to calm him by a seeming compliance. In his presence therefore she moderated her indulgence, silently acquiesced in the reproofs the boy frequently received from him, and pretended to approve the sentiments he endeavoured to instill into his infant mind. But this seeming submission was productive of as great evils as her indulgence. In Mr. Ellison's absence, which business rendered very frequent, she tried to make the child amends for his father's cruelty, as she termed his care, by a double portion of indulgence, and treated his advice as a jest; inculcating principles which, as they better suited the child's natural disposition, made a far deeper impression. But lest she, or her dear darling should incur Mr. Ellison's anger, she taught the boy to conceal his thoughts and inclinations, and to assume such a manner in his father's presence, as for a little time gave that affectionate parent great pleasure; but it was not long before he found, that to his other faults, his son had now added a degree of deceit and hypocrisy, beyond what he imagined possible at so early an age; and that while he loved his mother for laying the foundation of his future misery, he beheld him only as an object of terror and hatred. To be superiorly beloved, was so great a gratification to Mrs. Ellison's narrow and ungenerous mind, that she rejoiced in every symptom of his dislike to his father; though beloved by her as much as is consistent with such selfish principles as hers.

When Mr. Ellison found, that all the care he could take towards rectifying his son's temper, was only made the occasion of introducing more evil into his disposition, he determined, as the last resource, to send him into England with a friend who was going thither; and there to have him placed at a school, under the eye of his grandfather, who he knew would watch over him with the most affectionate attention. He was sensible that morals are but very imperfectly taught at schools, and that he could not hope the faults in his disposition would be entirely conquered there; but the violence of his temper must meet with restraint, and his pride with mortification; his faults would no longer be strengthened by encouragement, nor in a manner sanctified by example; and he might find it necessary to his ease, to conquer passions which he durst not indulge. To execute this resolution was a most painful task. Mrs. Ellison, at first, absolutely refused consenting to it; and to force on her the grief of parting with her son, who was then but six years old, gave him more poignant affliction than her heart was capable of feeling for any misfortune whatsoever.

To remove her objections, he therefore proposed their following the child into England, as soon as they could settle their affairs in such a manner, as might enable them to bid a long adieu to Jamaica, without great detriment; but this administered little consolation to Mrs. Ellison, as she had conceived a dislike to England, which even her son's being there could not conquer; but forbearing to declare this, imagining it would make her fondness for the child appear less than she chose it should be thought, Mr. Ellison, after sending away his boy, was very assiduous in hastening the means of their leaving the island; supposing he therein gratified his wife as much as himself.

The most difficult part of his business was to get a steward who would treat his slaves with the same gentleness to which he had accustomed them; and he had nearly settled his commercial affairs, before he saw any probability of finding a person fit for that important office. The first rumour of his intended departure, caused the utmost consternation among these poor creatures; they gathered round him, and falling on their knees, in their imperfect English, cried out, 'Oh! master, no go, no go; if go, steward whip, beat, kill poor slave; no go, no go; you go we die.' Nor could the kindest assurances, of not leaving them, but under the care of one who would treat them with the same lenity, pacify their fears. He assured them, that he looked upon them all as his children, and promised no one should supply his place, that did not consider himself as their father. Instead of being satisfied with this promise, they exclaimed, 'all fathers not good; no father like you,' and such torrents of tears would accompany their words, as frequently staggered his resolution. Notwithstanding the most affectionate assurances he could give them, melancholy constantly sat on their, before happy, countenances; at their holy-day meetings, instead of indulging the jollity of which they used to be so fond, their hours were passed in lamenting their approaching misfortune, and laughter was now exchanged for tears. Mr. Ellison, at length, in some measure prevailed upon them not to anticipate an event which might never happen, and indeed he had reason to fear it would not; for he saw no prospect of finding such a steward, as would enable him to justify to his conscience the leaving a place, where the happiness of so many depended upon him.

## CHAP. VI.

Business having called Mr. Ellison to Port-Royal,[13] he there heard lamented the misfortunes of an English gentleman, who had been established there above two years as a merchant in good credit; his capital not being great, his trade was not very extensive, for he never could be prevailed upon to make that use he might of the good opinion which, from his excellent conduct, every one had conceived of him. To all who would have advanced him money on credit, he replied, that, 'if he could depend on his own prudence, diligence, and frugality, which was rather more than a man moderately humble ought to do, yet he could not answer for success, as the hazards of trade were great, and the losses attending it sometimes inevitable. While he ventured only his own fortune, he could behold those dangers with tranquillity; but if the property of his friends was involved, the thought would be accompanied by intolerable apprehensions.' This gentleman was not more unwilling to receive assistance, than he was desirous of assisting others. A friend and countryman of his, who had a wife and large family, imparted to him his distress at finding his affairs in so desperate a situation, that he had no hopes of avoiding bankruptcy; a confidence he made him without any view of farther relief, than the compassion and advice of an humane and sensible friend. Mr. Hammond (for that was the name of the unfortunate gentleman who was then the subject of conversation in Port-Royal) had just received a thousand pounds in return for some commodities he had exported, and this sum he insisted on his unsuccessful friend's taking for a time, in hopes it might enable him to save his credit, and carry on his trade till affairs took a more favourable turn. By this well-timed loan, the poor man and his family were saved from destruction; but losses by shipwreck, and other accidents, having successively fallen on Mr. Hammond, he saw himself reduced into the situation from which he had relieved his friend; with only this difference, that his was a single distress; whereas a wife and nine children would have been sharers in the misfortunes of the other. All Mr. Hammond's effects were seized, but proved insufficient to discharge his debts. The creditors knew he had lent some money, but were ignorant as to the exact sum: this they pressed him to call in; promising, on the receit of it, to discharge him from prison; even if it did not quite amount to what was due to them.[14]

Mr. Hammond could not support the thought of purchasing his liberty by reducing so large a family to beggary; but as he was sensible his creditors had a just right to all his property, he offered to enter into the most binding engagement to give up the sum to them as soon as his friend could refund it without ruin; and to make him pay them the established interest till that time; but, enraged at this delay, they refused to accept his offer, and declared he should remain their prisoner.

This story very much affected Mr. Ellison's compassionate heart; and in hopes of finding some method of relieving the distress of so worthy a man, he went the next day to the prison to visit him. He found him very composed, and more concerned that his creditors should suffer by him, than at his own confinement; but yet he thought, after their refusal of the offer he had made them, he was justified in not ruining a family, who by a more successful employment of the money he had lent them, seemed in a fair way of getting free from their troubles, and being able in a few years to repay him.

Mr. Ellison undertook to do his utmost, to bring the creditors to agree to what he had offered, and negotiated the affair with great assiduity, but little success. During the course of this transaction, he saw Mr. Hammond frequently, and had so many proofs of his integrity and humanity, that he became tenderly interested for him; and as the only means of delivering him out of his melancholy confinement, acquainted him with the resolution he had taken of advancing the thousand pounds lent to his friend, and becoming himself that gentleman's creditor; assuring Mr. Hammond that he should never ask for the payment, but suffer his friend to suit his own convenience in that respect. He then told Mr. Hammond, that he was sensible, though by this step he might deliver him from prison, yet he should not secure him from distress; he therefore begged leave to assist him in any course of life wherein he thought proper to engage; adding, that he could not but wish he might accept the offer he now made him, of taking upon himself the direction of his plantation and slaves, as he delayed his removal into England only till he could find a fit person for his steward: but insisted on Mr. Hammond's not accepting this office, if it was not agreeable to him, as he should be equally desirous of contributing, as far as lay in his power, to his success in any other plan of life better suited to his inclination.

Mr. Hammond's heart so overflowed with gratitude, that he was warm in expressing his deep sense of Mr. Ellison's generosity, and for a considerable time opposed the transfer of the debt of the thousand pounds; but when he found Mr. Ellison so firmly bent upon it, he told him that it was with great concern he refused the offered stewardship; which, however irksome to him, gratitude would induce him to accept, if he was not deterred by a consciousness of not being qualified to fulfil the duties of the office. The care of the land would give him pleasure, and he believed he might acquit himself tolerably well in it, as a deficiency in knowledge might be made up for by an assiduous desire to learn, and an honest attention to the business; but he knew himself totally unfit for the government of slaves. The severities requisite to keep them in order were such as he was not only incapable of decreeing, but even of beholding; and for that reason had always avoided keeping more than two, and those of the most tractable dispositions of any he could meet with. He then returned his thanks to Mr. Ellison for the assistance he so liberally offered him in any other way of life, but declared he would never consent to accept it, having determined to depend on his industry for support; sensible that no office is beneath a gentleman, if undertaken from honest necessity, and executed with justice; and that as laziness and pride only can deprive a man of a possibility of subsistence, they alone can degrade him.

Mr. Ellison was so pleased with the reasons Mr. Hammond gave for declining his stewardship, that to suffer him to finish his answer was the utmost effort of his complaisance. He then told him how much he was delighted with the sentiments he had expressed, as they confirmed him in that opinion of his disposition, which had first inspired him with the desire of leaving him his deputy when he should depart the island; that the difficulties he had been under in finding a steward, were occasioned by the fears of having his slaves ill treated, who had always been used by him more like children than servants, and had convinced him by their behaviour, that severity was not only unnecessary but hurtful. He desired Mr. Hammond, therefore, if he had no other objection to the stewardship, to go home with him, and after sufficient observation to give him his answer.

Mr. Hammond readily acquiesced. When he saw Mr. Ellison's conduct to his slaves, and how great the difference thereby made between them and all others whom he had seen in that condition; how much less abject their way of thinking; how chearful and assiduous they were in performing their duty; the quickness of their apprehension; and in many, the nobleness of mind, and rectitude of principle, which kind encouragement and fatherly instruction had given them, in comparison of those who are stupified by ill usage and oppression; he no longer beheld the office he was invited to accept in a formidable light.

Mr. Ellison now saw the liberty of departing from Jamaica approach; he had little left him to do, but to instate Mr. Hammond in his office, that by seeing in what manner he executed it, he might be better justified in depending upon him; and likewise so far reconcile his slaves to their new master, that they might patiently see him depart. His mercantile affairs were the more easily settled by his brother's arrival in the island. As soon as he had determined on his return to England, he wrote to his father to send over his brother James, who had been likewise bred to merchandize, as it would be in his power to settle him very advantageously; and to establish him immediately in an extensive trade, by making over his correspondents to him. He found the young man sensible, honest, and diligent; and well deserving the encouragement he designed to give him. Mrs. Ellison was indeed less pleased with her brother-in-law, as she feared her husband might favour him too generously. The young man was shocked to see the arbitrary power she exercised over her husband; and was surprized that a man, who in a late instance or two had behaved with so much steadiness, could bring himself to be so tamely submissive in every other particular; not immediately discerning that there was one thing his brother feared even more than his wife, the reproaches of his own conscience; and though he sacrificed most worldly things to her caprices, yet there was a Being whom he more carefully endeavoured to please than her.

Affairs were in this situation when Mrs. Ellison was seized with a fever, at that time almost epidemical. The attack was so violent, as from the first gave little hopes of recovery, and notwithstanding the best medical assistance, she died in a few days.

Mr. Ellison was sincerely afflicted at her death; her faults he had long pitied and now forgot; while her virtues, or such as he imagined she possessed, were engraven on his memory. But his friends, while they endeavoured to console him, comforted themselves in believing, that tho' habit and gentleness of temper may teach a prisoner to hug his chains, yet when taken off, he will soon grow sensible he is relieved from a burden, and find the removal of constant constraint makes him amends for the loss of many pleasures which accompanied it. But they had not an opportunity of seeing this supposition verified, as Mr. Ellison did not stay long enough in the island after his wife's death, to wear off the grief he felt on the occasion. In a short time, however, he became sufficiently himself to prosecute his plan for settling every thing there to the best advantage. He found Mr. Hammond almost even exceed his hopes; he soon gained the affection of the slaves, an open, humane, and chearful countenance, giving them a prejudice in his favour, which his conduct improved into a rational confidence; and it was a great consolation to them to find, that if they must lose a master they loved, yet they should still be under the protection of one possessed of many of the same virtues, which had rendered him so dear to all his dependents. Mr. Ellison beheld with delight the improvement the children had received in the school he had established; he saw, as their minds opened, the obstinacy so remarkable in negroes abate, and was more than ever convinced that that fault, as well as many others, was in them the consequence of ignorance, and depression of spirits. More than ever desirous of keeping the school-master who had acquitted himself so well, he raised his salary, gave him every advantage that could render his situation comfortable, and left with him a young lad of remarkable good disposition and understanding, as an assistant; but with a secret view of qualifying him to succeed, in case the master should die, or grow weary of the charge. The school-master, at Mr. Ellison's desire, had the second year after his arrival in the island, sent an invitation to a sister he had in England, who, from the affection she bore her brother, readily accepted it, and was by Mr. Ellison made mistress of a school of negro girls, a charge wherein she acquitted herself extremely well. By the instructions these good people gave the children, and those Mr. Ellison imparted to such as were more advanced in years, his negroes were taught to lay aside their superstitions, and became not only sincere, but rational Christians, being much better acquainted with the fundamental principles of that religion, than people of low condition are in most Christian countries. The effect was evident in their conduct; the ferocity of their tempers, that resentful turn of mind seemingly natural to them, were so softened by religion, that it very seldom happened that any symptoms of it appeared.

Mr. Ellison's goodness to this race was not confined to those under his own care. He made it the object of his constant endeavours to prevail with all his acquaintance to treat their negroes with humanity; but his arguments might possibly have proved ineffectual, had not the good conduct of his own slaves, their more than common industry and dispatch of business, shewed the advantages arising from it to their master. This was so obvious, it could not fail of influencing men attached to their own interest; and Mr. Ellison had the satisfaction of seeing the condition of the slaves much mended in the greater part of the island; though a treatment equal to what they received from him was not to be expected from any, as perhaps he had not his equal in benevolence. He gave a liberty to all his neighbours to send as many children as they pleased to his schools, and was happy to find they accepted the permission.

Mr. Ellison was so engrossed by these charitable offices, and the private affliction of a heart which still tenderly regretted the loss of a woman who he was well persuaded loved him, that he did not perceive his brother James had entered into a very tender attachment. The truth was, the youth no sooner became acquainted with Miss Reynolds, than he felt the influence of her charms; she was not insensible to the merits of her lover, and they were so well agreed before Mr. Ellison's departure, that James thought it proper to inform his brother of his inclination, and to ask his advice.

Mr. Ellison was well enough acquainted with the world to know, that in these cases, people seldom ask advice till after the resolution is taken; and the warmth with which his brother expressed himself, convinced him, however he might cloath the question in respectful terms, he in reality asked only for his concurrence, and that if, instead of approbation, he was to give him advice against the match, he should greatly disappoint him. Happily his part was easier to act than is usual on such occasions. A long acquaintance with Miss Reynolds had afforded him good opportunity to discern her merit; his brother could not have chosen a woman he so much esteemed; her fortune, though not considerable, was sufficient to be of some assistance in trade, and her prudence and economy were well suited to his situation. He, therefore, very sincerely gave the approbation desired, and did not clog the pleasure even with a hint that marriage might have better suited his circumstances a few years later. He carried his complaisance still farther, offering to delay his departure, which was fixed for the next week, to assist at their nuptials.

This compliment was too agreeable to the lovers to be declined. Though the younger brother had engaged Miss Reynold's tenderer affections, yet she sincerely loved the elder, and respected him even to veneration. She thought their union would commence under happy auspices, if performed in Mr. Ellison's presence, and under his sanction. If this notion proceeded from some degree of superstition, the event shewed her not mistaken, though in a different manner than had entered her thoughts. The marriage was celebrated at Mr. Ellison's house with great elegance, and general satisfaction. Before the bride went to church, she received from her brother-in-law a present of all the jewels that belonged to his deceased wife. As the necessary attention to business would require them to spend good part of the year at Kingstown, he gave his brother a house he had there, with all his plate and linen, and the free use of all his furniture at both houses; imagining, that when leisure should permit, they would be glad to spend some time at his plantation, where he knew his steward would be attentive to their convenience; and to complete his work, he lent his brother ten thousand pounds, to be employed as long as he found convenient in traffic. To Mr. Hammond, his steward, he allowed £200 per annum, with the liberty of living in his house, and many other privileges; declaring him accountable to no one but himself, not even subject to the control of his brother; only thus far he suffered caution to extend, he desired both his sister-in-law and Mrs. Reynolds, to acquaint him from time to time if Mr. Hammond behaved to the negroes in the manner he recommended to him, and had reason to expect.

Having thus entirely settled his affairs, he set sail for England, leaving his friends and dependents most sensibly afflicted, and sharing in their grief;

though the desire of returning to his country, of seeing his father and his child, and of repairing a constitution much hurt by the heat of the climate, made the change on the whole very desirable to him. His voyage was swift and prosperous; and no dangers called off his thoughts from the pleasure he felt in anticipating, in imagination, the joys he expected from his return to his native land; but disappointment too often follows the hopes which have risen to the highest point, and when we think we are just ready to grasp our pleasures, they elude our touch, and leave us nothing but regret.

## CHAP. VII.

Mr. Ellison had in his imagination formed many delightful scenes, between himself and his father; the evening of whose days he hoped would be greatly brightened by sharing his prosperity, and by his assiduous endeavours to amuse, if he could not relieve, the infirmities of age. He thought with satisfaction that he should now have the power of making a proper return for his father's kind care of his youth, for his many fears and anxieties, by tenderly watching over his declining age; an office which Nature has given, and gratitude requires us to execute well, as a reward for what our infancy has cost our parents; thus rendering human duties reciprocal. But all these flattering hopes were put to flight on his arrival in port; a letter being delivered him there, acquainting him that his father was very dangerously ill; not from sudden sickness, but a gradual decline. Old Mr. Ellison had taken care he should receive this intimation, to prepare him for their first meeting, and render it less shocking. This good man was swelled to so great a degree with a dropsy, the last stage of a worn out constitution, as to be a melancholy object even to those who had none of the tender attachment to him which so powerfully influenced the mind of his son. To render the first interview less affecting, he had sent for his grandson home, in hopes that the joy of the parent would mitigate filial sorrow. Nor was he totally disappointed; Mr. Ellison could not be insensible to the pleasure of seeing his only child in health, and in appearance improved, of which the dying man gave him all the comfortable proofs he could collect. But this, though it in some measure alleviated his grief, scarcely sufficed to render it supportable. The indulgence he had given his imagination made the approaching death of his father more grievous. The good old man, on the contrary, saw it creep towards him with slow but sure pace, without any terrors; life indeed, had acquired a new charm by the arrival of his excellent son; but not suffering his mind to dwell on the pleasures his society would afford him, he was truly thankful to Providence, for giving him, before he left the world, the greatest joy it had to bestow. The happy establishment of all his children, made him think the most desirable period for his life was now come; his mind was free from all cares for them; he was sensible, that were he to remain here much longer, every additional year of life must be accompanied with some new infirmity, or, what was still far more grievous, instead of departing full of joy and gratitude for the prosperity of his children, he might weep over their graves, or participate in some misfortunes which in the course of things might befal them. So happily circumstanced as he was, he must indeed relinquish some very real pleasures, but he firmly hoped to receive far greater in exchange; and could not regret the loss of transitory gratifications, when eternal joys offered themselves to his view.

His son was greatly affected by the calm resignation of his mind; the patience with which he supported his painful distemper; and the chearful and lively hopes of a blessed eternity, which in his eyes disarmed death of all its terrors, and made him look on his last hour with the same placidity, as on any one that preceded it; and so well supported him at the fatal instant, as to render him scarcely sensible of the pains which usually attend the separation of the soul from the body.

Mr. Ellison had less fortitude; the event, though foreseen, gave him the most poignant affliction. He blamed himself for being so immoderately affected, when he considered how happy an exchange his father had made; and while he was overwhelmed with grief for his death, the full persuasion of his father's present happiness, though it could not cure, yet softened his affliction, and together with a just sense of the duty of resignation, made him soon able to submit with patience to a loss which he ever regretted.

Mr. Ellison determined, as soon as he had settled his affairs, to fix in the country. Sir William Ellison his cousin germain[15] invited him to his seat in Dorsetshire, promising to shew him several good houses, any of which were to be hired or purchased; and Mr. Ellison was particularly inclined to fix his abode in that country, as it had been the place of his family's former residence.

He had sent over, before he left Jamaica, £45000 and beside the interest of that sum, he received twelve hundred pounds a year from his plantation, clear of all deductions.[16] His health was impaired by the warmth of the country where he had acquired so good a fortune, but still more by his late afflictions, which induced his physician to prescribe travelling, not into foreign, but in his own kingdom; and during this journey it was, that by the accident which impeded his progress, he was so hospitably received at Millenium

Hall.[17] As he has long ago on this occasion spoken for himself, I shall omit saying any thing of his visit there, as it would only be a tedious repetition; but assume my account on his departure from thence.

Mr. Ellison and his young fellow traveller did not leave Millenium Hall with equal regret; Lamont was extremely pleased with the visit, the novelty had amused him; but though he was not insensible to the pleasure every one not totally depraved must feel in the contemplation of so much virtue, yet it wore an air so aweful to his light mind, as occasioned a restraint which in a good degree lessened his satisfaction. He felt himself more humbled than was agreeable to his natural temper; when he compared the importance those ladies were of in society with his own insignificance, his vanity was severely mortified; he could not conceal from himself, that his highest pretension was to amuse the idle company he frequented, and to assist them to throw away many hours which might be usefully spent; though, how profitable every moment might be made, had never occurred to him till he saw that society. But what rendered this comparison still more irksome to him was, that the persons who so much excelled him in reason as well as virtue, were women, were of that weak sex, which he had hitherto considered only as play-things for men; a race somewhat superior to monkeys; formed to amuse the other sex during the continuance of youth and beauty, and after the bloom was past, to be useful drudges for their convenience. To be disabused of so favourite an error, galled him intolerably; but desirous of throwing a little dust before his own eyes as well as before those of his companion, he observed that, 'he should not have been so much surprized at what they had seen, if the ladies had but just commenced that way of life; for at a certain age, the wisest part women could take, was to retire from all the gaieties of the world, since they could no longer add to them; and he had often wondered at the number who were daily intruding themselves into parties of pleasure, when the power of pleasing was over, as if they emulated the custom at the ancient Egyptian feasts, and personating death's heads, were ambitious to become a Memento Mori to the younger part of the company; but by the time that excellent society had been settled at Millenium Hall, it appeared that some of them had retired while their beauty was in its full lustre, and they still qualified to engage the admiration of the other sex,' continuing to remark that, 'to be sure such a kind of life as they had been witnesses to, was very respectable in women, and was arriving at the highest excellence their sex could reach; but that such retirement would be very unfit for man, who, formed with more extensive capacity, deeper penetration, and more exalted courage, was de-

signed to govern the world, to regulate the affairs of kingdoms, and penetrate
into the most mysterious arts of human policy.'

Mr. Ellison, who, like his friend, had been revolving in his mind all he
had seen, but with far different effect, smiled at Lamont's self-importance,
and asked him if he thought many men capable of the arduous tasks he had
assigned them. 'When in regard to property,' (said he) 'all men were in a state
of equality, a superiority of parts and courage were sufficient to raise a man to
power and command; but since nature's Agrarian law[18] has been abolished by
political institutions, few men have a chance of filling those important offices
you seem to think the property of all. Poverty is an impenetrable cloud,
which will conceal the greatest merit from the rest of mankind; rank and fortune are such steps to honour, that it is difficult for a man to climb to any
height who is not possessed of them: Some degree of one, or both, is absolutely necessary to bring the brightest talents into such a light as can render
them conspicuous; and the whole course of a century will scarcely produce
half a dozen men of such superior abilities, as shall conquer the disadvantages
of a small fortune, or obscure descent, and raise them to that distinguished
rank, for which you seem to think us all qualified; and to which a great estate,
or high birth, will frequently exalt those who are as unfit for it as ourselves.
What visionary ideas, therefore, have you conceived of the dignity of man!
According to you, we are to be all monarchs and law-givers; we are to regulate kingdoms, though we cannot establish a tolerable government in our
own families; we, who busy ourselves in the most trifling occupations, are to
be intrusted with the most important affairs of state. Consider the lives of all
your acquaintance, and see whether man then appears so exalted an animal,
that the offices of benevolence are beneath his notice. Follow them to the
gaming-table, to horse-races, to assemblies, to operas; enquire into their
views, their pursuits; and then judge how well your pride is founded. Believe
me, Lamont, let us leave those high pretensions to the very few to whom nature has given superior talents; and let us allow, that man, as well as woman,
acts in the most honourable character, by pursuing a benevolent course of life.
May those who have talents to benefit mankind, do it by their talents! but let
us, to whom Nature had been less lavish in that particular, benefit them by
our virtues; to which the faculties of our minds, and the goods of fortune
should be subservient. Let the superiority given us appear in the superior
good we do; for while our lives are as trifling and useless as those of the other
sex, we ought to be ashamed to esteem ourselves above them; and should act
more judiciously, in not laying claim to superior talents, without we make a

proper use of them. In my opinion, virtue creates the best superiority; therefore I shall not be ashamed of endeavouring to imitate the ladies who gave rise to this conversation; and do not fear, lest by so doing, I shall degrade my sex, though I confess to fall short of them may disgrace it; and yet I am very apprehensive that will be the case; for, the truth is, benevolence appears with peculiar lustre in a female form, the domestic cares to which the well educated have been trained, qualifies them better for discerning and executing the offices of humanity. With this consideration I may in some degree console myself when I see my own inferiority. Our sex has long aped the most trifling part of the other in its follies; we are grown dissipated, puerile, vain, and effeminate; a sad abuse of talents, which I readily grant were given us for better purposes; so far I agree with you as to the dignity of man; but, however the poets may personify them, the virtues are of no sex; and shall we less esteem any of them, because they are practised by women, when we are not ashamed, as I have said, to adopt their follies! Our dignity does not depend on the situation wherein we are placed, "an honest man's the noblest work of God,"[19] whatever be his rank or station.'

Lamont was so tired of this long lecture, that if he had not felt a secret consciousness it was just, yet he would have forborn starting any objections, to avoid giving his fellow traveller opportunity for adding an appendix. He found his late visit had left some serious impressions on his mind, and did not wish them increased, as they now and then suggested disagreeable scruples, in regard to some parts of his conduct. Acquiescence does not always imply conviction; it is sometimes used to avoid being convinced: Lamont was silent from a mixture of both these motives; and Mr. Ellison, though he wished to improve the new impressions he plainly perceived on Lamont's mind, yet was careful not to surfeit him by an over dose of advice or instruction; and therefore only threw into their discourse occasionally, and seemingly without design, such short reflexions as he thought would have most effect upon him.

Mr. Ellison, finding his health much mended by his journey, was induced to extend his tour beyond his first intention; accordingly they passed through the greatest part of Wales, taking a particular view of every place most worthy notice, glad to lengthen out their progress by amusement; and great was the pleasure they received from the stupendous beauties of that country, and the hospitality and simplicity of manners so remarkable in the inhabitants. Nature there seems to reign alone, unrestrained by art, and uncorrupted by fashion; the face of the country, and the minds of the people, are equally unadorned; and the beauties of the one, and the honest frankness of the other, put all ornament out of countenance, and shew us, what we have now few opportunities of seeing, the charms of artless Nature.

Their progress ended at Sir William Ellison's, where Lamont paid only a visit of three days, and then returned to London. Sir William received his cousin very affectionately; he had not seen him from the time he first left England, but retained a great regard for him, founded on an early acquaintance with his virtues. Though nearly related in blood, there was little resemblance in the dispositions of these two gentlemen. Sir William was a man of sense and integrity, but a humourist.[20] He was now at fifty years old, a batchelor; for having been in his youth jilted by a woman he ardently loved, who, after all preliminaries to their marriage were settled, left him for a man of larger fortune, and more gaudy appearance, he had made a vow never more to address any of the sex; and kept that vow better than is usually done by those who make it in a fit of resentful rage and disappointment. His father died soon after, and left him the possession of £3000 per annum, free from any incumbrances whatsoever; the estate in good order, and the mansion house well furnished, and above a year's income in cash. He had now nothing to desire on the side of fortune; to him who was determined on celibacy, it was extremely ample; his only disturbance was the sight of womankind; his pique was so strong and so general, that the appearance of a pinner[21] or a petticoat was sufficient to put him out of humour. Could he have excluded all females from his family, he would probably never have stirred out of his house, that he might not have been under a necessity of having his sight offended. But the more he tried it, the more he was convinced he could not bring it to bear, without intolerable inconveniencies; for that he tried it is certain. As soon as he took possession of his country seat, he turned away every maid servant, and prevailed on men to undertake their offices; but his bed was so aukwardly made, he could not sleep in it; his linen so ill washed he would not wear it; his china was all broken in a week by the clumsy hands of those who washed it up; his house so dirty, the sight of it made him sick; in short, every thing was so aukwardly performed by these male chamber-maids and landresses,[22] who in all probability being very averse to their master's error, did not acquit themselves to the best of their power, that he found himself reduced to admit the tremendous sex into the house. By degrees the sight of women grew less irksome; but his resolution to avoid much intercourse with them continued. Having no intimacies, he had no exercise for his affections; and according to the nature of us all, the more indifferent he was to others, the more strongly attached he grew to himself. As he loved no one, and was entirely independent, he seldom endeavoured to please any but himself; he indulged every whim, and gave way to every fancy that arose in his mind; by indulgence they grew stronger; and at length he found London, where for some years he had passed good part of his time, become disagreeable, because other people's humours interfered with his, and instead of considering it for his interest to relinquish such peculiarities as were inconsistent with society, he chose to retire from society, in order more freely to indulge them.

When settled in the country he found himself perfectly at liberty to be as odd as he pleased; and judged himself free, in proportion as he differed more widely from others; and while he was an absolute slave to his own caprice, laughed at those who sacrificed insignificant trifles to custom and the world. To philosophic freedom, founded on the government of ourselves, he was as absolute a stranger, as to the pleasures arising from mutual compliances in amiable societies, and was his own tyrant, than which a worse cannot be found; no one can so essentially enslave us, as that which is within us; Nero or Caligula[23] were not worse tyrants than a man's own passions. Fortunately Sir William had no vices; his self-indulgence therefore made him absurdly capricious, but not criminal. He had naturally good sense, was fond of reading, was honest, good natured; and, 'till selfishness grew upon him by giving way to every humour, was generous.

He could not give a stronger proof of regard to Mr. Ellison, than inviting him to his house, as there was some danger that his guest might put him out of his way; but he had been fond of his cousin when a boy, and notwithstanding his thoughts and attention had so long centered in himself, yet he still felt some remains of affection for him. Mr. Ellison, though well pleased with Sir William's reception and conversation, finding he laid him under some restraint, determined not to make his visit very long; and, therefore, soon called upon the baronet to fulfill his promise, of shewing him the houses which were to be purchased in that country. But after seeing them all, he fixed on one almost adjoining to Sir William's, and purchased it with the estate belonging thereto, consisting of two farms of about an hundred and fifty pounds a year each. The house was a large and good old mansion, in tolerable repair; but having stood empty near ten years, during the minority of the owner, was inwardly in very bad order, and the gardens entirely gone to ruin.

This circumstance much lessened the price, but was no disagreeable thing to Mr. Ellison; who rather chose to lay out the place to his own taste, than to pay for what the seller might call improvements, but perhaps to him would appear deserving of no other name than alterations, and possibly those not eligible. Sir William, whose house, gardens, and grounds, were neat to a degree of preciseness, was surprised at his cousin's choice. Not a particle of dust was to be seen in the baronet's house; nor was a dead leaf allowed to litter his garden. The same neatness extended to every article; his table was elegant, though he had few companions at it, not but he was glad to see any who chose to partake of it, but from a notion that to heat the blood by good eating and drinking, while the sun was high enough to have much influence on our bodies, must be extremely pernicious, his hour of dinner approached very near the supper-time of his neighbours.[24] For this reason he never dined abroad, nor was much troubled by company at his own house; though, as he was both liked and esteemed, his neighbours had sometimes the complaisance to pretend to dine with him, having first prepared themselves by a private dinner at home. His chariot was as elegant as his house, and drawn by six very fine bay horses, whose tails and manes took more dressing than the hair of the greatest beauty in London. His liveries were suitable to the equipage; and in every article his neatness and elegance exceeded even female delicacy; though had any thing feminine been brought into a parallel with him, the disgust he would have conceived might have converted him into a sloven. Thus delicate, he might well look with horror on his cousin's purchase; the gardens were overrun with the rankest weeds; and as for the house, spiders had supplied the place of other inhabitants, and like good housewives, had hung every room with webs of their own weaving. Not once in the last ten years had the inimical brush disturbed their peaceful dwelling; the lines once spun to convey them to the ground, or from one side of the room to the other, remained unbroken for the same uses year after year, and by frequent additions, were rendered so strong, that it was difficult to stand in any of the rooms, without being persuaded one was caught in a net. In short, so curious was the workmanship, that had the spinster Goddess beheld it, she might have envied Arachne[25] a second time, and metamorphosed her a-new, into some less artful and less diligent insect. Mr. Ellison felt a little compunction at the thought of destroying so numerous a race, who had the rights of long possession to plead. Incredible was the slaughter; thousands and ten thousands[26] fell by the potent hand of a stout char-woman, and in a few days these usurpers were all destroyed.

As soon as this massacre was completed, Mr. Ellison took possession; having put in the common necessaries for immediate use, and ordered down five negro servants he had left in London; for he brought from Jamaica as many of his domestic slaves as he was sure he could conveniently employ, six in number, three of each sex, and by marriage made them three couple; nor would he give them the pain of leaving their children behind, but suffered those who had any to bring them.

Before Mr. Ellison left Sir William, the baronet advised him very kindly, not to put himself to any great expence on his new house; saying, 'As you are heir to mine, your own will in time become of no use; the gardens indeed may be laid together with advantage.' Mr. Ellison thanked him for his advice, but told him he hoped he would yet provide himself with heirs more nearly related. Sir William walked off in a pet; and was so much offended by the wish, that he could just then have found in his heart to disinherit him.

## CHAP. VIII.

As the ladies at Millenium Hall still retained their place in Mr. Ellison's thoughts, he had no sooner got into his house, than he wrote Mrs. Maynard,[27] begging her to recommend him a house-keeper, one who would manage his affairs with reasonable care and dexterity, treat his family with good nature, and his poor neighbours with humanity.

Had this request been made by a lady, Mrs. Maynard could have gratified it immediately; but as Mr. Ellison was not above four and thirty years old, extremely handsome and agreeable, as well as very rich, she did not think it proper to send him a very young woman, whose character at least, might from her situation have been called in question; nor was Mrs. Maynard sufficiently acquainted with him to judge with any certainty of his principles, though all she had seen of him gave her the most favourable prejudices. She therefore wrote him word, she was not immediately able to comply with his desire, as she yet could find but one person perfectly qualified; and to her she imagined he must object, as she had a daughter of twelve years old, whom she could not persuade herself to part with; but assured him she would make diligent search, and did not doubt but she should soon be able to find one proper for his place.

Those who have a true taste for the pleasures of benevolence, cannot be averse to extending the circle. Mr. Ellison's fortune not obliging him to confine his expences within narrow bounds, he had no objection to his house-keeper's bringing a daughter with her; and thought it a sort of duty, arising from the affluence of his circumstances, to take one who was by that particular excluded from most services. He no sooner communicated his way of thinking on this point, than Mrs. Maynard dispatched her to her new master.

As soon as she was recovered from the fatigue of her journey, Mr. Ellison thought proper to acquaint her with his plan, that she might know the nature of her business. He told her, 'That the desire of imitating, as far as his fortune would reach it, the benevolent system he saw exercised at Millenium Hall, had induced him to apply there for a house-keeper who was well instructed in their method of acting.' He added, 'That a decent and regular economy in his house was what he expected, as far from extravagance and wastefulness as from parsimony. He would have his servants enjoy soberly all the comforts of life, as he thought that to make them happy was his first duty; but this he knew was best done by order, regularity, and decent frugality. He would have such a number of servants, as could perform the business of his house with ease; for he scarcely knew which was more hurtful to them, idleness or too much labour, and he did not like to have them so very full of employment, that the sickness of one servant should make a confusion in the house, as he had seen in many families; for it was apt to prevent the sick servant from being properly relieved and attended to in time, and the rest were overburdened by additional business, when the invalid was no longer able to perform her part. He therefore desired her to consider how many more servants would be requisite. As for the state of the adjacent poor, being yet but little acquainted with it, he could give no particular directions, but wished she would inform him of what she heard on that point, and likewise mention to him the sort of relief she judged most proper.'

Sir William was much diverted at his cousin's female director; he was his own house-keeper, and executed the office indeed with great skill and care, keeping his whole menage in excellent order, without any great trouble to himself; and wondered his cousin would not follow so excellent an example; not considering he was not equally fit for it, having never had occasion to give his attention to domestic affairs, as he got a wife as soon as he got a house. Sir William, like many people who are so attached to their own opinions, as to think no one can differ from them without being absolutely irrational, was full of wonder, equally surprised at what his cousin did, as at what he omitted; another thing which thus affected him was that Mr. Ellison determined to take one of his farms into his own hands. The baronet asked him, 'if he intended to plant sugar-canes, or sow pepper.' Mr. Ellison smiled at a reproof he thought just enough, and replied, 'that he was sensible of his ignorance in farming, but hoped to get so much knowledge from him as might suffice, together with the care of an honest servant, to prevent his being a very great loser; and he had rather suffer a moderate loss, than not have sufficient land to supply his family, since without it the country could not have that patriarchal, hospitable appearance, which constituted its greatest charm.' He had little merit in receiving well the baronet's censures, as they were always made with good humour. Mutual regard, and great taste for each other's society, were the foundation of a very happy correspondence between them, which was rendered more amusing by the different turn of their minds; nor were Sir William's particularities any obstruction to their friendship, as Mr. Ellison avoided intruding at unwelcome hours, and every thing else that could put him out of his way.

It may not be amiss to shew how Mr. Ellison was circumstanced as to a more extensive neighborhood. On the contrary side to Sir William's house, and within an hundred yards of Mr. Ellison's garden, lived Mr. Grantham, lawful heir to the Duke of ———, if that nobleman died without children, which was now highly probable, as he was above threescore years of age, and his duchess but little younger. Mr. Grantham was indeed a very distant relation, yet was heir both to the estate and title; but his branch of that great family having fallen to decay, he inherited from his father only fifty pounds a year. This he farmed himself, and lived in the only house he had, which was little better than a common cottage. His education had been on a level with his fortune, and his manners were those of a plain honest farmer. But though ill qualified for higher company, regard for his birth, and compassion for his narrow circumstances, procured him a due portion of civility from all the neighbouring gentlemen, among whom he took pleasure in being received, and kept up an interchange of visits. This was not so easily performed by his wife, as she could not be equipped for that purpose, suitable to her inclination. Mr. Grantham was a very honest, sober, sensible, and industrious man, and acquitted himself diligently in the most laborious parts of the farmer's business, but was not free from pride of family; and even when following the plow, or stopping up a gap in his hedge, reflected with some inward satisfaction, that he was cousin to a duke, who made as splendid a figure as any man in the kingdom, and if this was a weakness, it might be allowed both natural and pardonable; and produced no bad effects, except the influence it had in his choice of a wife may be called such. He thought he should disgrace his blood by marrying a farmer's daughter, though with such an one he might have got a few hundred pounds, which would have set him much at his ease; and a lieutenant dying in an adjacent town where he was quartered, and leaving a daughter entirely unprovided for, and greatly distressed, he thought her a wife much more suitable to the dignity of his family. Captivated by her gentility rather than by her person, for she was no beauty, he took a pride in addressing the captain's daughter, for the courtesy of a country town kindly bestows the title of captain on every officer, and she was glad to accept of any provision. However, Mr. Grantham was more fortunate than he had reason to expect; his wife proved very notable and industrious, only too prolific, having perpetuated the family of Granthams, of which the duke and he were the last, by bringing him five sons and three daughters; a number attended with great difficulties in their narrow circumstances; but the thought that they might one day be so many lords and ladies,[28] was a sufficient consolation, and made them behold so numerous a progeny with exultation. In this satisfaction Mrs. Grantham had more than her equal share; for though she could not boast any noble blood in her veins, yet she was more proud of being allied to it, than her husband was of possessing it, and felt more severe mortification from their poverty. When in her utmost dignity, mounted on a hard pillion[29] on a trotting cart-horse, behind her husband or his plowman, she would blush to think how unequal her appearance was to that which the wife of the heir of a dukedom might expect; and when milking her cow, or churning butter, she could not forbear venting a few feminine imprecations (for like Piercy's wife, she was not genteel enough to curse or swear like a lady)[30] against their ungenerous relation; and it must be allowed that relation well deserved it, who could suffer his next heir to remain in indigence, though a man perhaps of more real worth than many of the elder branch of the family could boast; and leave the children, who must certainly inherit his title, to be educated in a manner that must ever disqualify them from wearing it with dignity or propriety; a circumstance of which Mr. Grantham was so sensible, that it was the most afflicting part of his poverty.

At the distance of about two miles from Mr. Ellison's lived Mr. Allin, a gentleman who inherited a good estate from his father, but being extravagant in his youth, had reduced it within very narrow bounds, and involved himself in difficulties that had a good deal soured his temper, converting his extravagance into parsimony. His society would not have been very eligible, had it not been for an only daughter who kept his house, whose beauty, accomplishments, and excellent qualities, rendered her the most distinguished young woman in the whole country. A little farther off dwelt Mr. Blackburn, an old gentleman of great merit, who by a due mixture of study and conversation, had greatly embellished an admirable understanding. He had spent many years abroad, at an age when the mind is most capable of improvement from the observation of men and manners; had then entered into the most learned societies in his own country, and enjoyed the friendship of men most distinguished for virtue and abilities; till growing old, and his spirits being much affected by the profligacy and disobedience of an only son, he betook himself to a rural retirement, which he dignified by his extensive knowledge, and uncommon politeness.

On the other side of Mr. Ellison's house, and about five miles from it, lived young Mr. Blackburn, son to the gentleman I have just described; his father having given him an estate with a good house upon it, on his marriage with a young woman of family, but no fortune, whose beauty had captivated the young man; his father being glad to encourage any rational inclination, in hopes the society of a woman he loved might reform him from his vices. But success had not answered his wishes; young Mr. Blackburn soon grew tired of his wife, and returned to his bottle, to hunting, gaming, and women; and behaved with such insolence to his father, when he reproached him for his dissolute course of life, that he banished him his presence, and declared a resolution to disinherit him. This breach had subsisted three years, when Mr. Ellison came into the country; and the father still as much offended, and the son as far from reformation as ever.

These were Mr. Ellison's nearest neighbours, and first visitors, paying him their compliments before he had got a room fit to receive them. But as he aimed at nothing farther than neatness and convenience, it was not long before his house was as well furnished as he desired. As soon as he got into it, he had employed several labourers to clear the weeds and rubbish out of his gardens; but Sir William observed, to his great *surprise*, that before they had half done their business, they all disappeared. He enquired of his cousin the reason, and did not think the fact less odd, when Mr. Ellison told him, that, harvest being begun, he thought it but just to let the farmers have all the assistance they could for a work so important to them, and which could not be delayed without great hazard; and he judged it equally right to the labourer, who at that season was sure of employment; but after it was over, might find in him a very desirable resource.

The Baronet stared at an answer he scarcely comprehended, and asked his cousin, 'what the farmers and labourers were to him? and whether it was for their benefit or his own, that he intended to cultivate his garden?'

'My chief view,' answered Mr. Ellison, 'I acknowledge to be my own gratification, but I would wish that the advantage of the labourers should go hand in hand with it; for both he and the farmer stand in this relation to me, they are of a species which I would endeavour to benefit to the utmost of my power.'

'So you do,' replied the Baronet, 'whenever you employ them; the fellows ought to be very grateful to us improvers, for I know not what they would do without us, and yet they are a set of grumbling rascals.'

'Their advantage from your improvements,' said Mr. Ellison, 'appear to me more certain than their obligations to gratitude. The motive creates the obligation. Your own amusement is the thing you aim at; the good you do is accidental. Now I am so great an epicure, that I love to raise my pleasures as high as I can carry them, and while I amuse myself with improvements, would enjoy the additional satisfaction of intentionally benefiting others; and the best means I know to procure this, is to make the pursuit of my own gratification so far subservient to the good of the labourer, as to hasten, or retard the first, as shall prove most conducive to the latter. I shall therefore let my work stand still when the poor are sure of other employment; and particularly when the success of the harvest depends so much on the quick gathering in of the corn; for if, while I am making an elegant garden, the grain which should bring in a subsistence for my neighbour's family should be spoiled for want of labourers, I could feel little pleasure in walking in it. The good which necessarily follows the indulgence of our inclinations, should excite the labourers gratitude to God, not to us, since it is owing to the wise and gracious order of his Providence, that we cannot gratify ourselves without in some degree benefiting others.'

'Fine talk, fine talk,' interrupted Sir William, 'I find you are very theoretical; when you have lived in the country a little longer, these exalted ideas will be brought down by practice; you will learn the necessity of taking care of yourself, for if you relinquish your interests, you may depend upon it no one else will take care of them. While you are providing for the happiness of others, who is to provide for yours?'

'I myself,' replied Mr. Ellison, 'the private happiness of one man is not only consistent, but in good measure dependent on that of others; self-love and social are the same,[31] and we are guilty of a fatal error when we divide them. As we have observed, we cannot gratify our own inclinations, without necessarily benefiting many; but when with design we do them good, we increase our own pleasures, and feel the strongest conviction that our happiness is closely connected with the good of others.'

'I do not deny but there is something in what you say,' answered Sir William; 'only you carry it too far. I shall like to see these refined notions put to the trial. If by the time the harvest is over, the weather should grow so rainy as to prevent your going on with your garden, should you not be a little vexed at having let slip this fine season?'

'Could I be vexed,' said Mr. Ellison, 'because the fears which induced me to put a stop to its progress were realized? The possibility of bad weather was my motive. Had I been sure the sun would have shone uninterruptedly for six weeks or two months to come, I do not believe I should have dismissed my labourers, as the number was not so great but there remained sufficient hands to get the corn in safely. Therefore, directly contrary to your supposition, if heavy rains come on, I shall feel inexpressible joy in having done my part towards preventing the farmer's losing the reward of his whole year's labour, and the fulfilling of all his hopes.'

Sir William put an end to a conversation which was grown rather disagreeable to him. He was good-natured and humane, but his views were narrow; he had never considered the duties of humanity in so extensive a light. He was careful to hurt nobody, and at times would do kind actions; but it must be when the fancy took him. If any one applied to him, he considered their address as a constraint; and as he persuaded himself that acting from his own pure motion alone was true freedom, they were sure of a refusal; whereas his bounty would liberally relieve those who least expected it. He felt the force of what Mr. Ellison said, and felt it with that uneasiness it will ever give to those who are sensible they stand condemned by it, and yet do not chuse to alter their course. He honoured his cousin, indeed, but was determined to humour himself, and therefore chose to hear no more on the subject.

The case happened as he had supposed. At the latter end of the harvest, the weather grew rainy, and he diverted himself with the expectation of seeing Mr. Ellison's patience exhausted; but to his surprize, in two or three days after, the labourers were at liberty, he saw a tolerable number of them digging in different parts, under the protection of little moveable sheds of easy construction, being composed of only four strait poles, with a bar a-cross to keep them at their proper distances, and over the top was thrown a tarpaulin, which likewise hung down on one side, according to the corner wherein the wind sat. The ends of the poles were sharp enough to penetrate sufficiently deep into the earth to keep them from being blown down; and as the cross bar took off with ease, these sheds were moved from place to place with great facility. I question whether Vitruvius[32] ever received more pleasure from any edifice he erected, than Mr. Ellison did from this invention, as it enabled the labourer to work in such weather as he otherwise could not have done, or at least not without great hazard to his health.

# Book II.

~

## Chap. I.

Mr. Blackburn was much delighted with his new neighbour. His under-standing, and elegance of manners, polished more by humanity than by mixing in the great world, were far superior to any thing he had seen in that country. Mr. Ellison was peculiarly happy in having his virtues uncommonly conspicuous; they shone the brighter for a modest endeavour to conceal them; which was rendered unsuccessful by every line in his countenance, and every sentence he freely uttered. The early part of his education had been a learned one; and if his occupations had denied him leisure to increase his stock, he had however, found time to preserve unimpaired what he had once obtained. He, likewise, being naturally studious, had seldom passed a day without stealing from business some hours for reading, which by his judicious choice of books, and the clearness and acuteness of his understanding, had furnished him with a good degree of knowledge. These qualities, natural and acquired, rendered him a most desirable companion to Mr. Blackburn, whose extensive learning and noble mind made Mr. Ellison find a pleasure and improvement in his society, which he had never yet received from any one.

But there was another house which had still stronger attractions for Mr. Ellison. Mr. Blackburn delighted his understanding, but Miss Allin capti-vated his heart. I have told my readers she was very handsome, but perhaps they will expect a more particular description of the woman that could charm a man who had preserved his reason in defiance of the whole sex till the age of thirty five. Miss Allin, though above the general height, could scarcely be called a tall woman, was elegantly formed, and extremely genteel; her mo-tions, though entirely unstudied, were peculiarly graceful; and her hands so fine, that they had no small share in the admiration she excited; yet, her face alone had sufficient attractions without the assistance of the rest of her per-son. Her features were regular and beautiful; her eyes, of the darkest blue, at every glance beamed forth sweetness and sense; equally penetrating and ten-der, they seemed to tell all they beheld that she could discover their faults, but could likewise forgive them; her nose was after the Grecian model; her mouth beautiful to excess, the shape was perfect, her lips of the finest red, and her teeth could not be equalled. Her complexion extremely fine, clear as alabaster, and heightened with a gentle blooming red in her cheeks, sufficient to animate her countenance, without lessening the delicacy of it; the shape of her face was oval, her hair of the finest brown. But it is not in the power of features or complexion to constitute beauty equal to hers; that could be completed only by the dimples which gave a thousand graces to every smile; and by the sweetness they diffused over her countenance, made an absolute conquest of Mr. Ellison's heart, which felt itself at unison with all the tender benignity her expressive countenance denoted.

Miss Allin's charms were not all confined to her person. She had great sweetness of temper, and exceeding good sense; her father had given her all advantages of education; she played on the harpsichord, not perhaps with the perfection of a person who has made it the business of her life, but with an elegance and facility well calculated to assist one of the finest voices that ever was heard. She understood French and Italian perfectly well, had read a great deal with admirable taste and judgment, having been directed and assisted in her studies by Mr. Blackburn, with whom she was a great favourite; and within the last three years she had learnt the Latin tongue, as her leisure gave full opportunity; but this she endeavoured to conceal, nor was she forward to exhibit any of her accomplishments, being, in despight of all her perfections, modest, humble, and unaffected. Her address was polite, and possibly the more easy, for having been accustomed from the age of seventeen to do the honours of her father's house, her mother dying at that time. Miss Allin was now twenty five years old, an age which might perhaps have a little abated the lovely bloom in her complexion had she lived more in the world; but a very regular life, and country air, had preserved it in full force.

Had not Mr. Ellison's long indifference rendered the point doubtful, one might suppose much fewer charms would have sufficed to make an impression on a heart naturally so tender as his; but it is probable that even all Miss Allin's attractions might have proved ineffectual, had they not found him in a state of leisure. Business first, and then duty, had hitherto defended his heart; these shields were now removed, and it lay open to Cupid's arrows; in such a defenceless state it might have fallen a prey to half her perfections, and could not make the least resistance. Nor indeed did he wish it, he yielded himself a willing captive; for as he had no desire to remain single, he with pleasure encouraged an inclination for a woman he thought so well qualified to make him happy, and whose narrow circumstances gave him reason to hope for a favourable reception.

An inclination we chuse rather to encourage than repress is very quick in its growth. Mr. Ellison had been settled but two months in Dorsetshire, when he came to a resolution of asking Mr. Allin's permission to address his daughter, giving him to understand that his fortune set him above all pecuniary demands. The great advantages his daughter would find in such an union, would have made Mr. Allin sufficiently eager to complete it, had he not been spurred on by the last article, which however was a strong incentive; for the Miser in Moliere was not more sensible of the charms of that part of a lover's address *sans dot*,[1] than Mr. Allin; Mr. Ellison, therefore had not only his consent, but his good wishes, and secretly all the influence of his authority. Unfortunately the father's was not the only will of consequence in this case. The joy Mr. Ellison felt on receiving the permission he asked was soon damped; for on explaining himself to Miss Allin, she burst into tears (having foreseen from the manner in which she was left alone with him, what was to be the subject of his conversation) and the more generously and nobly he expressed his affection, the faster her tears flowed. Alarmed by the tenderest fears, he begged to know the cause of her distress; but before she could assume sufficient power over herself to comply, they heard Mr. Allin coming towards them: dreading his presence, she requested her lover to conceal her uneasiness; and promising to lay her whole heart open to him the next time they met, she made her escape by one door, as her father entered at another.

Mr. Ellison was not much better able than his mistress to support an interview with her father; the most artful hypocrite would find it difficult to dissemble with a heart so painfully oppressed as his was at that instant; but a tender regard for her peace did more than any thing else could have effected; and eluding the old gentleman's questions, in such a manner as gave him no suspicions of what had passed, he pretended business that obliged him to return home directly. Happily it was only a pretence, for he was entirely incapable of transacting any. He shut himself up in his room, in a state of mind which the heart may guess, but words cannot describe. He passed the night in an agitation and anxiety he had before no conception of, the hope which self-flattery would sometimes suggest, only served to prevent his exerting his reason to support what his fears anticipated. He rose before the sun, with a resolution to know his fate ere the day was over; but wished to learn it without Mr. Allin's knowledge.

Unable to contrive any means of effecting this desire, the restlessness of his mind led him abroad; and the impulse of his heart directed him towards

Mr. Allin's house. He wandered in the adjacent fields a long time, uncertain what method to pursue; and fearing to create uneasiness to the woman for whom he suffered so much. At length Miss Allin, who had not rested much better than her lover, going to the window in hopes new objects might divert her thoughts, saw him in a field adjoining to the garden. The delicacy of her mind bore so great a resemblance to his, that she imagined the cause which brought him thither, and desirous to conclude the interview before her father rose from his bed, she hastened to him, with as much speed as a person can use, who feels a very sensible affliction for the pain she is going to give one whom she sincerely esteems.

When he saw her approach, he had scarcely courage to meet her, dreading the explanation he had so impatiently longed for. Maiden bashfulness, with some mixture of concern on one side, and extreme agitation of spirits on the other, rendered them equally unable to speak; but with common, though tacit consent, they sat down together on a green bank at the foot of a tree; a long silence ensued; and it is difficult to say when it would have ended, if Miss Allin had not sooner recovered her spirits than her lover. She tempered the disagreeable intelligence she was going to impart 'with very sincere expressions of concern at the necessity she saw herself under of giving him pain; professed a due sense of his merit, and lamented that when they first met her heart was not so free as his, since then, in all probability, they might have constituted each others happiness, instead of mutually destroying each others peace. She then told him, that she had with her father's consent been engaged above a year to Dr. Tunstall, a young physician in the neighbourhood; and their marriage had been so long deferred, only by the difficulties her father found, or that his parsimonious temper made him imagine, in raising £2000 the sum he had promised to give with her: That she received the Doctor as her intended husband at her father's command, when her heart was so little prejudiced in his favour, that she could without any very severe pang have been equally obedient, had he ordered her never to see him more; but since she had considered it as her duty and happiness to increase the little prepossession she had conceived, the case was much altered, and she was now as strongly engaged to him in affection, as in honour: An engagement she was determined not to violate, though she despaired of seeing it fulfilled; for she had received an express command from her father never to entertain the least acquaintance or correspondence with Dr. Tunstall, but to look on Mr. Ellison as her husband, and she feared he would never revoke this decree; since beside the many reasons which she was sensible there was for preferring him to the

Doctor, his generosity had added one that with her father was insurmount-able, by declining the acceptance of a fortune.' She proceeded to say, 'that she had nothing to expect but her father's anger, which was impetuous and dread-ful; all therefore she had to ask of Mr. Ellison, who she hoped would rather think her unfortunate than ungrateful, was that he would, as far as lay in his power, mitigate her father's rage, and prevail with him to let her live peace-ably in her present condition; for she relinquished all hopes of changing it; and did it with the less concern, as she imagined his partiality for her might render it more vexatious to him to see her married to another, than merely to be disappointed of her himself.'

As I am, like most Biographers, a little partial to my hero, I shall not describe the effect Miss Allin's words had upon him; a writer is apt to see the faults of his favourite through the same medium he does his own; and perhaps cherishes as a virtue, what the unprejudiced censure as a weakness; but I feel also for my hero as one does on those occasions for oneself; how artfully soever self-love may confound the object, and dazzle our judgment till we behold our folly with complacence, a secret consciousness shews a glimmering of sense remains, for it induces us to conceal, what we are too partial absolutely to condemn. Thus it stands with me at present in regard to Mr. Ellison; the tenderness of his sensations, the delicacy of his sentiments, may appear to me more amiable than wisdom and fortitude; but his soft distress may lower him in the eyes of my less partial readers; I shall therefore only say Miss Allin was rather inclined to think with me, and felt so lively a compassion for him, that she forgot her own grief, and said every thing she thought might contribute to his consolation, except what alone could prove effectual; but as she was fully determined to adhere strictly to her engagement, she carefully avoided giving him the least room to hope a change in her sentiments.

As soon as his mind was a little composed, he took his leave; assuring her that he would try every means to secure her peace, though he was not yet sufficiently master of his thoughts to see the manner in which it would be most advisable for him to proceed. Each returned to their respective house, but with different sensations; she found her heart much lightened, since she had acquainted her generous lover with the state of it; but he carried back despair instead of uncertainty. As soon as he got home, he shut himself in his room, and for the whole day would not suffer even a servant to enter. The quiet of the night, and the fatigue his spirits had undergone by the excess of his vexation, brought his mind into some degree of composure; and as soon as he was capable of reflexion, he grew ashamed of himself for having thus indulged a grief, that was not to be justified by reason. He called himself to a severe account for his ingratitude to Providence, in suffering himself to be miserable, because disappointed of one wish, while he remained in possession of so many blessings; and with concern learnt from this instance, how far his heart was from being fixed where it was most due. He considered how incapable we are of knowing what is really best for us; this woman, in the possession of whom he imagined supreme happiness was to be found, might have proved the cause of the greatest distress; her death, or even her being afflicted with a bad state of health; the evils which might have befallen their children, if she had brought him any; by all these ways, and many others, the completion of his wishes might have proved the source of misery; or what was still worse, his fond infatuation might have made him negligent in his duties; and wholly engaged in endeavours to secure her affections, he might have forgot how far more material, and really desirable it was, to obey and please that Being, which ought to have the first place in our thoughts and affections.

In these reflexions he found a strength he had not before exerted, and grew resigned, though not indifferent. He had not yet acquired the power of thinking on any other subject, but he could think on this as he ought; he felt the disappointment of his hopes, but felt it like a religious and reasonable man; he suffered his vexation without repining, and was convinced that this mortification was either designed for his benefit, or might be turned to his advantage, if he received and bore it in a proper manner. As much as I am inclined to do honour to Mr. Ellison's resignation and philosophy, I would not promise, that had the smallest glimmering of hope broke through the cloud of despair in which he was involved, it might not have put to flight all his reason, and baffled his pious reflections; for man is frail, and philosophy still weaker; but as he was put to no such trial, he came off triumphant, though, like many generals, less from the powers of his great courage and wise conduct, than from the enemies not having made the attack on the weakest part, resembling the man in the fable, against the wind of adversity, the blasts of his mistress's scorn, he wrapped his cloak of philosophy close about him, but she might have smiled it away in one gracious hour, had she been so disposed;[2] and possibly all his wise reflexions would have vanished before a soft glance of her eyes; he would have received her as his Creator's last, best gift,[3] without feeling the least apprehension that any pain or evil could spring from such a blessing. We are frequently much obliged to circumstances, for that consistency of conduct which gains us the esteem of mankind, and our own approbation.

## Chap. II.

Though Mr. Ellison grew resigned and patient as to his disappointment, yet he was ardently desirous to restore Miss Allin to the happiness of which he had for a time deprived her; and resolved to perform his promise more effectually than she could expect. Accordingly, three days after he had received his sentence from her, he sent an invitation to Mr. Allin to dine with him; and took that opportunity of acquainting him, 'that since he was last at his house, he had learnt that Miss Allin had long been engaged with his consent to Dr. Tunstall, and therefore had resolved to desist from his pretensions; as he should think himself very criminal, if taking advantage of a superiority of fortune, he should attempt to deprive another of a blessing which must be so dear to him; and indeed he should have so bad an opinion of a woman who could be mercenary or inconstant enough to break her word, though in his favour, as would render it impossible for him to be happy with her.'

Mr. Allin was much disconcerted at this declaration, and answered, 'he might do as he pleased; but that as for Dr. Tunstall, if he intended to marry his daughter, he must wait till business increased, or death put her in possession of his little estate, for he found it impossible to raise a fortune for her, without distressing himself.' From the account Mr. Ellison had heard of his circumstances, he easily believed there was some truth in what he said, and told him, 'he would remove that objection, only desiring him to confirm his former consent with a good grace, and not diminish the satisfaction of his daughter by an apparent reluctance, or even by the coldness of his compliance.'

Mr. Ellison was not slow in executing his purpose. He wrote Miss Allin a letter the next morning, wherein he assured her, 'that as her happiness was more dear to him than his own, he could not support the thought of her being disappointed of the object of her affections; a misfortune which he sensibly felt was most difficult to bear; and therefore hoped she would forgive him, if he endeavoured by the inclosed trifle to obtain her pardon for having thrown impediments in her road to happiness; and he flattered himself she would not refuse him the sole gratification to which at present he was sensible, but suffer him to enjoy the thought of having advanced the completion of her wishes; the only thing that could alleviate the concern he felt at having occasioned the uneasiness she must have suffered.' Adding, 'that he could not expect any other opportunity of asking her pardon, as he must, in consideration of his own ease, avoid her presence, till he could behold her with indifference, an alteration which he did not hope even from time.' In this letter he inclosed a draught on his banker for £2000. Mr. Ellison's generosity went still farther; he feared her father would not acquit himself properly in regard to her cloaths; and considered that as the income of the man she married was very small, to be well equipped might prove hereafter much to her convenience; he therefore sent his housekeeper to the next great town, to buy silks, lace, cambrick, muslins, Hollands,[4] in such abundance, as would not only enable her to make a very genteel appearance on her marriage, but suffice for some years; and he chose to do it in this manner, rather than to make her a present of the money, as the surest means of securing her convenience, to which moderation and generosity might have made her less attentive.

The pleasure he felt in this disinterested conduct, almost extinguished for the time the sense of sorrow; but the heart will have its due; when the gratification began to deaden, vexation returned, and he could gladly have excused the visit Dr. Tunstall made him, in order to return thanks for his generosity; which Mr. Ellison learnt from him was with great pain accepted by Miss Allin; nor could any thing but her father's express and absolute command, have conquered her reluctance in this particular. The sight of a man so much happier than himself, brought so painful a comparison to Mr. Ellison's mind, that the effect was visible to the Doctor, who could not blame the sensation, though Mr. Ellison could scarcely forgive it in himself; and was hurt to find, by this first instance, that he was capable of envy, a passion he had never felt before. His politeness however did not forsake him on so severe a trial; he commanded both his countenance and words so well, as to give his happy rival a kind, though melancholy reception; and, determined to conquer the sensation he so much disapproved, he expressed an inclination to be sometimes favoured with his visits, though he must request him to excuse his returning them.

Miss Allin was extremely touched with Mr. Ellison's generosity; the nobleness of his mind charmed her so much, that had she been left to the disposal of her own fate, she would have preferred a single life, to the gratifying her affection for Dr. Tunstall, at the hazard of giving pain to the best of men, to whom she was more than ever sensible no one deserved to be preferred; but the advice of her father, and the pressing solicitations of her lover, who thought the pain and anxiety he had suffered during Mr. Ellison's courtship deserved some reward, prevailed over her generosity; yet she would not consent to so speedy a marriage as he wished, being determined to leave Mr. Ellison the space of three months to reconcile himself to the event, before it was completed.

Dr. Tunstall and Miss Allin were both too grateful to be silent on the obligations they had received, which from their report soon reached Sir William Ellison's ears, but did not so easily obtain his belief; he looked upon it as a most absurd story, and called on his cousin to tell him what a ridiculous tale he had heard. Mr. Ellison, who had flattered himself that a transaction, wherein some circumstances were of a delicate nature, must remain unknown, was surprised to find it had got air; but making no answer, the baronet continued, 'I told the gentleman who related this curious incident, that to be sure my cousin had acquired some strange high-flown notions, but yet was not absurd enough to reward a girl for her bad taste, nor to facilitate her marriage with another man, except he meant to return the affront put upon him, and give her a proof of his indifference.'

Mr. Ellison was a little nettled at the construction Sir William put on this action. 'It would have been an expensive proof of indifference, Sir William,' (said he) 'and laying a very heavy tax on my own vanity, could I have done it for that reason.' 'It would so,' replied the baronet, 'give it what turn one will, it is too foolish to deserve credit, yet there is nothing too absurd for some people to believe. But you blush, and methinks look a little silly; surely it cannot be true after all; but thou art a queer fellow that is certain.'

'If you see me a little disconcerted,' answered Mr. Ellison, 'it is because your politeness, my friend, is in a scrape that may be rather disagreeable to you, not from my being ashamed of the action, which I cannot with truth deny; for if it is a folly, it is, however, innocent; and so agreeable to me, that I would not have omitted it to have gained the reputation of the profoundest wisdom.'

'How,' interrupted Sir William, 'did it give you pleasure to reward a girl for using you ill? and to reward her too by throwing her into the arms of the man she preferred to you.'

'I have no cause of complaint against Miss Allin,' replied Mr. Ellison, 'all her actions are consonant to the high esteem I had conceived for her. What title have I to any woman's heart, that should make me think it an affront to have another man preferred? but in the present case, however severely my love has been disappointed, my vanity can have suffered no mortification, since her heart and word were engaged to Dr. Tunstall, before we ever saw each other. By inconstancy she might have gratified my passion, but must have considerably shaken my esteem. As for throwing her into the arms of another man, I feel the irksomeness of that step very sensibly; to take it, required a very painful effort, and I fear I shall long feel it a source of great vexation. I confess it would have cost me far less uneasiness to have given her my whole fortune to enjoy in a single state; but such ungenerous sensations ought to be mortified; while I suffer by them, I detest them; and, after all, could I act any other part? Had it not been for me, she would before this time have been united to the object of her affections; every thing was agreed, and all parties happy in the approaching union; when, like her evil genius, I came into this neighbourhood, and cast a thick cloud over the pleasing scene. To her misfortune, she charmed me; my wealth captivated her father's parsimonious soul; and in hopes of saving his money, he broke his word, and required his daughter to sacrifice both her happiness and her conscience to interest. I judged of her distress by my own; but her's must exceed mine, as she was commanded not only to forsake the man she loved, but to marry one to whom she was indifferent, nay, perhaps, one she hated, for the misery he had brought upon her. Her conscience too must have hourly upbraided her for so shameful a compliance. These are aggravations which I am sure my present situation could not support; and I suppose her sensibility is, at least, equal to mine. What then was left for me to do? nothing, certainly, but to repair the injury I had done her, to complete the union I had so nearly broken, and restore her to the happiness I had so cruelly interrupted. My great consolation is, that I have done this; and when I reflect that I have made her happy, I cannot be miserable myself. It is a real satisfaction to me to think, that as far as one can judge on so slight an acquaintance, the Doctor is an amiable man; this, though his rival, I could see through all the prejudice of my passion, and if he makes her happy, I shall consider him as one of my best friends.'

'Very sentimental, and very philosophical, truly,' said Sir William, 'if all men were as refined as you are, Love would not have made such horrid disturbances in society as are laid to its charge; a disappointed lover would no longer be a dangerous animal; as one might content him thoroughly by letting him act the part of father to his mistress, while his rival performed that of bridegroom. I admire this method prodigiously.'

'Some time hence,' answered Mr. Ellison, 'I may be able to laugh with you on this subject; I can see it may afford room for mirth; but the wound is yet green, and bleeds afresh not only in the presence, but on the thought of her who gave it; and therefore with the same seriousness that I began I must continue. Whatever language my heart may yet speak, my reason tells me, that to believe our happiness is entirely dependent on the possession of any one person, is contrary to good sense, to experience, to religion. Lovely as Miss Allin appears to me, I might not perhaps have been happy with her; nor

*Utilitarian*

is it necessary I should be unhappy without her. Our passions are but temporary tyrants, they will torment with whips and scourges for some time, but they wear themselves out by exertion, and at length may be overcome. I see some evils that have already arisen from my too strong attachment to Miss Allin; it has made me remiss in the offices of humanity to others, who had not a due proportion of my thoughts; so much were they engrossed by this passion. Had I been successful in my pursuit, every affection might have centered in her; and from my assiduity to please a beloved wife, all other duties might have been neglected. If this could be the case, as is rendered too probable by the excess of my love, have I not reason to think Providence has been supremely merciful in denying me a temptation I was too weak to resist; and which, from an useful member of society, would have degraded me into a mere fond infatuated husband; and have substituted the ensnaring and intoxicating indulgences of passion, to the calm and solid joys of conscious virtue.'

Sir William, who had listened to the latter part of Mr. Ellison's discourse with gaping mouth and staring eyes, as soon as he found he had done speaking, cried out, 'The strangest fellow breathing! that is certain. You a lover! love and so much philosophy never dwelt in the same bosom; you are made for disappointment.' 'At least disappointment is made for me, Sir William,' replied Mr. Ellison, 'therefore it is my duty to extract benefit from it.'

'I could as soon extract sun-beams out of a cucumber, like the chymists in Laputa,'[5] interrupted the baronet, 'but you are a philosopher, and may do much. When I suffered a disappointment somewhat like your's, I raved and ranted, cursed the whole sex, despised my own, hated my rival, and abused myself. I am provoked to see you so rational; and yet I think I admire you as much as I can a man who is continually putting me in disgrace with myself, by leading me to draw a comparison, wherein I make but a very scurvy figure. To endeavour to be as good as you are, would be an abominable trouble, and ineffectual at last; and yet I do not like to set you off by the contrast; why the devil did you settle just by me? You are like a statuary who should think the beauties of a Venus would not be sufficiently distinguished, if he did not put a Sybil or a Tesiphone[6] by her side.' This compliment led the conversation to different subjects, and the baronet no longer persecuted his cousin on a generosity he scarcely comprehended.

While Mr. Ellison flattered himself with the hopes of marrying Miss Allin, he delayed settling his family in the order he intended, thinking it more advisable to regulate the whole at once; but when that prospect vanished, there no longer subsisted any reason for postponing it. The knowledge he had of his son's impetuous temper, and bad qualities, determined him to educate him at home. Whether he would there acquire an equal share of learning as at school, he much questioned, but the rectifying his heart appeared to him the most essential article towards his happiness; and of all knowledge that he most wished him to acquire, was the knowledge of himself, and the means of governing his passions; in these points he thought he might be better instructed under his own eye than at school; and if thereby he could render him an honest and amiable man, he should have good reason to be contented, though he did not prove a learned one. He had already begun to make proper enquiries after a well qualified tutor; and was likely to succeed, as he had set no bounds to the salary. To save in the stipend of a tutor, appeared to him the worst sort of extravagance and parsimony, most unnaturally mixed together: If a man is not well qualified for the trust, all that is paid him is thrown away; if he is equal to it, there is scarcely any thing he does not deserve; and to refuse to useful and excellent talents, which cannot be acquired but with great expence, and assiduous application, what industrious dulness or lively impudence may acquire, was in his opinion criminally ungenerous. The good education of his son appeared to him of such importance that he did not believe it possible to acquit himself sufficiently of the obligation he should be under to the man that performed it. As this was his way of thinking, he had no reason to confine his demands within very narrow bounds; he required in a tutor an exemplary moral conduct, a good temper, a liberal education, knowledge of the world, and a polite and genteel behaviour. He would have thought he had but half provided for his son's education, if he had not got him a tutor, in whom the gentleman and the scholar were united.

As Mr. Ellison was so great a master in the science of benevolence, that he performed few actions that did not bear more than one good fruit, he had in view the serving Mr. Grantham by the home education he intended his son; and therefore made it a condition that the tutor should teach as many boys as he pleased, with the same care as his own; and desired he might be acquainted that several would immediately be put under his instruction. Mr. Ellison's liberality was soon rewarded. A gentleman of excellent character, great learning, and amiable manners, having met with some disappointments in the profession of physic to which he was bred, was very glad of so eligible a retirement, on a promised salary of £400 a year; the number of scholars was no object to him; he depended on Mr. Ellison's good sense for not giving him more than he could thoroughly instruct; and he did not doubt but each would learn more assiduously and chearfully, for having companions and competitors.

As soon as this great point was settled, Master Ellison was fetched from school; a very good apartment was allowed to Mr. Green his tutor, and the little Granthams were likewise put entirely under his care, spending few beside their sleeping hours at home; for as their father's house almost joined to Mr. Ellison's, they returned thither without inconvenience every night, coming early the next morning; and having at Mr. Ellison's both their corporal and mental food; the first of which was some ease to the narrow circumstances of those good people, and the latter gave their father the most sincere joy, as he now saw them in a way of being educated equal to their birth, and future fortune, of which he had before utterly despaired. Indeed he found his expence much lightened, for Mr. Ellison carefully provided them apparel, in every respect equal to that worn by his own son; and was very watchful that the latter assumed no superiority over them, to whom he shewed him he was in reality greatly inferior; but this was explained to him in the absence of the Granthams; for Mr. Ellison wished for their sakes the thought might not occur to them; and exhorted their father and mother not to destroy one benefit arising from their present low estate, which might greatly add to the happiness of their lives, by instilling into their minds, a pride that must be the source both of private chagrin, and public contempt.

## Chap. III.

Mr. Ellison was not so wholly engaged either by private vexation, or domestic business, as not to extend his attention to all his neighbours. The little estate he had bought lay in three parishes, which gave him a knowledge of the state of each. He found the poor tax ran very high, and yet the poor were but ill taken care of; the farmer was much burdened, the poor but little relieved. When age or sickness rendered them incapable of hard labour, no employment was found for them; the allowances given amounted to a great sum, and yet scarcely afforded a sufficiency for each individual, who really needed the more for having no business; for idleness is a very expensive thing, it gives leisure to imagine wants, that demand their share of an income too small even to provide necessaries, to which they will frequently be preferred. He found it impossible to act in concert with the head people of the parishes, in every method that occurred to him for lessening these evils; and therefore determined, if possible, to get it entirely into his own hands.

He well knew the only way to obtain a general concurrence, was to gain people by their private interest; and therefore offered to take upon himself the care of the poor of each parish, if the principal parishioners would consent to give him half the sum hitherto paid for the poors rate. So favourable an offer was not likely to meet with much opposition; Sir William Ellison was the only person who scrupled it; which he did from an unwillingness to suffer his cousin to undergo the expence he feared he was bringing upon himself, well persuaded the money he required could not by any means suffice, especially for some years. But Mr. Ellison desired, he would not make that an objection, as it was what he himself had foreseen, but chose to incur it rather than suffer the poor to be so improperly provided for; and he believed it possible to put the affair under such regulation, that in a few years the sum contributed might prove sufficient. Sir William, however, generously refused to withdraw his opposition, except Mr. Ellison would suffer him to contribute a large share of the expence; to which the other could have no objection.

These preliminaries being settled, Mr. Ellison hired a row of contiguous cottages, repaired and furnished them comfortably, and then removed the poor into them. His house-keeper undertook to find him a man and woman proper for overseers, who should honestly, and even indulgently, take care to provide them plentifully with all necessaries, and even comforts, carefully watch over their conduct, and see them execute such employments as he should assign them. When we consider where she had been bred, we shall not think this was a difficult task for her to perform; and indeed she with ease found persons well qualified for this office; who were glad, for the good salary Mr. Ellison allowed them, to leave their former abode and friends. There were few of these poor men so old, as to be incapable of cultivating their little gardens, which yielded good part of their subsistence; he required each likewise to keep his own room very clean and neat, and not to expect that service from the women, for whom it was more easy to find out profitable employment; as they could nurse the children thrown upon the parish, attend the sick, do plain work, and spin and knit sufficient cloathing for themselves, and all the rest of the poor, both male and female. Some of the men could assist in the two last employments, and those who could not already do it, were made to learn; rather to take from them the temptation of pretending ignorance in order to be idle, than from any advantage to be expected from them, as they were by age and disuse rendered so awkward, that they could scarcely gain enough to pay for the waste they made, and the wool they spoiled.

Amongst the number of each sex these houses contained, Mr. Ellison found some qualified to teach the children whatever might be useful to persons in their condition, and therefore made it their chief employment, appropriating rooms for that purpose; and he seldom failed a daily inspection of his work-house, examining minutely into every particular. As he killed his own meat, he provided them with food at a less expence than if bought at market, and took care it was of the most wholesome kind. He allowed no punishments, as he thought none could properly be inflicted on the sick or aged, but endeavoured by encouragement and indulgences to make them act as he wished; and promoted social comfort, and friendly intercourse among them; omitting nothing that might conduce to their happiness, and the relief of their infirmities.

By observation Mr. Ellison found that great distress was sometimes suffered by persons, who either by the law had no right to demand assistance of the parish, without giving up some little tenement they had inherited, and wished to leave to their children; or who from an unuseful, and no blamable pride, were unwilling to be ranked among the parish poor; these people were mostly labourers, who in health could gain a subsistence for their families, but by long sickness were sometimes reduced to extreme distress. For the removal of this evil, he set on foot two subscriptions, one among the men, the other among the women; according to which, by paying a trifle weekly, so little as could not be felt in the poorest family, a fund was raised sufficient to afford each subscriber, in times of sickness, an allowance somewhat exceeding what in health they gained by their labour. This he knew was practised in many places; and the only inconvenience that ever attended it arose from the bad choice of a treasurer, the sum proving sometimes a temptation too great for the honesty of the man they trusted; who frequently was as poor as themselves, and embezzled or went off with the money. To secure the people in his neighbourhood from this danger, Mr. Ellison undertook to be their treasurer, keeping a very regular account of the receipts and disbursements; and as a sufficient fund could not be immediately raised to answer any great call, he, out of the money he had assigned for the parish poor, subscribed eight guineas to each fund, which made them equal to all immediate necessities.

Another great evil at that time subsisted in Mr. Ellison's parish; the vicar and his parishioners were at variance. The former was rather too tenacious of his just rights, for it is possible to be too strict even when we have justice on our side; and the latter, however honest in their dealings with each other, thought it no sin to cheat the parson. Even the gentlemen, as well as the farmers, looked on his tythes as an encroachment; the gentlemen forgetting that the establishment of tythes is more ancient than the title most of them have to their estates, and consequently were allowed for in the purchase; and the farmers equally unmindful, that without such deduction a higher rent would be required of them. These sort of quarrels never fail having bad effects; the minister displeased with his parishioners neglects the duty he owes them, and grows careless about their eternal welfare, which is trusted to his care; and they, from hatred to him, become averse to his doctrine, and confounding the man with his office, neglect the duties of Christianity because he recommends them, and from contempt for the preacher think lightly of the precepts; so much does a due reverence for, and consequently observance of the Christian religion, depend on our respect for its ministers.

Mr. Ellison wished this gentleman to have so much indulgence for the ignorance and stupidity of his parishioners, as to overlook some of their encroachments on his rights; till he had gained sufficient influence over their minds, to make their inclination coincide with their duty; when he might have received his dues as much from their good will, as from their honesty. But though he was a man of great worth, yet he was so exasperated by their ill treatment, that he could not bring himself to relinquish his just demands, even for a time; though he plainly perceived Mr. Ellison did not intend it should be any pecuniary loss to him. He wanted the humility which would have taught him that no condescension is mean, that can prove conducive to the spiritual benefit of the ignorant. Could Mr. Ellison have prevailed in this point, it would have rendered his task more easy; however, notwithstanding all the difficulties that lay in the way, he performed his part so judiciously, and had gained so great an influence over all parties, by a conduct which had won both their esteem and affection, that he at length proved successful. The common people were convinced, that a man so benevolent and charitable to them, could have no intention to lead them into any thing that was not for their benefit; and Mr. Shaw the minister, had too much good sense to be blind to the force of his arguments. He persuaded each side to make alternate concessions, and had at last the satisfaction of seeing them perfectly reconciled.

When Mr. Ellison had so far succeeded in his views, as to remove all prejudices against Mr. Shaw, he very strongly represented to him the duties of his office; shewing him that the performance of the church service was the least part of it. His first position, as it was his governing principle, being the duty incumbent on every one to do all the good to others that came within the reach of his power, he observed how much was required from the minister of a parish, who by his instructions and example, might influence all such of his parishioners, as were not incorrigibly abandoned; he therefore was answerable for their souls, and whatever they suffered from his omissions must be imputed to him.

Mr. Shaw agreed in this point, but differed with Mr. Ellison in the opinion he entertained of his influence. He allowed it his duty to do all the good in his power, but asserted that power to be very small, since it depended on the attention and understanding of his hearers, the latter of which was circumscribed within very narrow bounds, and the first less than could be imagined; adding, 'that he did not believe a tenth part of his audience remembered, after they were out of church, one word of what they had heard in it.'

Mr. Ellison replied, 'he was entirely of the same opinion; but that the church was not the only place where a clergyman ought to endeavour to do good, as it was perhaps there that he did the least, except he pursued the same plan in other places; for he was well convinced, that if a clergyman would make frequent visits to his parishioners, familiarly explain the fundamentals of the Christian religion, and affectionately urge obedience to its precepts, he would find his endeavours greatly successful; and his audience, after being thus instructed, would listen with attention to his sermons, because they would understand them, and observe the doctrine, because their minds were previously well prepared to receive it.' Mr. Shaw was conscious Mr. Ellison advised no more than it was his duty to perform; but the disagreeable terms on which he and his parishioners had lived, served as an excuse to his conscience for omitting the practice. He had not, indeed, ever considered it either as quite so important to others, or so incumbent on himself, as Mr. Ellison by a long conversation on the subject convinced him it was; but in spight of his conviction, Mr. Ellison perceived some reluctance in him to begin a duty, the performance of which was a kind of tacit reflexion upon himself for past omissions. To render the matter more easy therefore, Mr. Ellison invited him to make one at his Sunday's party; it being usual with him on this day, to entertain a certain number of the farmers and decent labourers of his parish at dinner, at his own table, to which no other company was then admitted, where he endeavoured in the course of easy and familiar conversation, to instruct them gradually, and seemingly without design, and to instill in the same imperceptible manner such sentiments into their minds, as had never yet found entrance there. This hospitable custom, had greatly facilitated the reconciliation he had effected between Mr. Shaw and his parish; and it offered Mr. Shaw a good opportunity of becoming more familiarly acquainted with his parishioners; and also by his assistance, Mr. Ellison did not doubt but the conversation would be rendered still more useful to them. This invitation Mr. Shaw readily accepted; and to remove totally any remaining reluctance in him to go to their houses, Mr. Ellison engaged him to walk abroad frequently with him, and seldom failed carrying him into the cottages they passed in their way; till his appearing among them became familiar, and he with ease to himself proceeded to visit them even unaccompanied; a condescension received with humble gratitude; for Mr. Ellison had, by the respect with which he treated Mr. Shaw, greatly raised him in their opinions, and created a kind of reverence in them for their minister, which was very essential towards the proper reception of his doctrine; for as Mr. Ellison was sensible that a clergyman's power of doing good is proportionate to the respect his parishioners bear him, he saw it his duty to excite it.

Mr. Ellison perceived that in his own, and the adjacent parishes, a few of the richer sort had usurped the whole government of the parish, excluding all who were not in league with them from any of the public offices; and as it was done merely with a design of advancing their private interests, it occasioned great oppression of the poorer sort, by the illegal rates and assesses they arbitrarily levied; and many other exertions of the power which wealth gave them, over people too poor to contend, in a country where the process of the law is so expensive, that the rich only can purchase its protection, while those who stand most in need of it are excluded from all hopes of redress. These practices he determined to put an end to, not only in his own parish, but as far as the authority of a justice of the peace[7] could extend; for nothing but want of power appeared to him a just boundary to benevolence; for this purpose he obtained admission to that bench,[8] which, if the office were executed with discretion, vigilance, and integrity, would prove one of the most valuable blessings in the British constitution. But few see it in so important a light as Mr. Ellison, who thought it his duty to qualify himself by the study of all the branches of the law, which concern the execution of the office of a justice of peace; wherein he observed many inexcusably ignorant. He took care to be well acquainted with the extent of his power, as well as with the properest means of exercising it; and convinced that he could not do a more charitable action than to plead the cause of the widow and the poor, he undertook to prosecute those who were guilty of any unlawful oppressions. This he performed with success in two cases; and the damages granted the injured were so considerable, as sufficiently to deter others from rendering themselves liable to the same sentence.

Mr. Ellison, by his authority as justice of peace, suppressed all disorderly meetings, lessened the number of public houses,[9] and obliged those that remained, to preserve a very uncommon degree of sobriety and regularity. It was not in his power absolutely to prevent that succession of fairs or wakes,[10] which take the people from their work, during one or two of the busiest months in summer; but he suppressed so many of the entertainments exhibited at them, and so strictly watched over their meetings, that he rendered them too dull and sober to be any great temptation even to the most idle. This care he extended as far as his jurisdiction reached, to the great improvement both of the morals and the circumstances of the poor, for many miles round his house.

He did not oblige any one to go to church, because he thought it should be a matter of choice; but he would not suffer his neighbours to engage in any amusement during divine service, nor to pass that time in ale-houses; this prohibition brought most of them to church, as they had no longer any temptation to absent themselves from it, and they soon began to feel a better inducement for going thither, from having nothing to do in any other place; and what at first was the result of idleness, became their constant practice from inclination.

## CHAP. IV.

Mr. Ellison's benevolent offices were not confined to persons of the lowest rank. His acquaintance with Mr. Blackburn soon ripened into a very strict friendship; which the difference of age rather strengthened, by mixing a degree of reverence with Mr. Ellison's regard, and converting Mr. Blackburn's esteem into a sort of paternal tenderness. They found all the pleasure in each other's conversation, that social intercourse can yield; but the satisfaction each felt in contemplating the other's virtues, afforded still a more refined delight. Mr. Blackburn, especially, was charmed with the excellence of Mr. Ellison's heart, and if additional years gave himself a title to respect, he felt that his friend's more material superiority, his superior merit, excited sensations scarcely short of veneration. The purity of Mr. Ellison's mind, the warmth of his benevolence, his assiduous prosecution of all the duties of humanity, found in Mr. Blackburn a man not only ready to approve and love, but to imitate them. In many cases, indeed, it was necessary Mr. Ellison should strike the note, or it might not have occurred to his venerable friend, but his heart was always sure to be at unison. Age, and ill health, would not permit him to be so actively good, but he was never slow in executing any benevolent action that came within his power; and endeavoured to establish many of the same regulations so successfully contrived by Mr. Ellison; who lent him all the assistance he could in the performance; though the sphere of his own benevolence, required a degree of care and attention, which would have left no leisure to any one, but so excellent an economist of his time.

Mr. Ellison never thought he had done his duty while there remained any good action unperformed. He saw the influence he had acquired over Mr. Blackburn, the effect it had on his conduct giving still more evident proofs than his affectionate behaviour; for though he had been always nobly generous, yet from Mr. Ellison he first learnt the uses of extensive charity. This good man therefore, determined to employ his interest towards reconciling the old gentleman to his son, which he hoped would prove a means of happiness to them both; and that the advantage of being restored to his father's favour, might lead young Blackburn into some degree of reformation.

The young man, though he had little regard for his parent, had, however, so much affection for his patrimony, as to wish ardently for a reconciliation; and therefore so far conformed to what Mr. Ellison represented as the necessary previous steps, as to restrain his irregularities; some vices he discontinued, and others he concealed by a more private gratification; till his conduct appeared enough reformed, to furnish Mr. Ellison with good arguments in his favour, which he took every opportunity of urging. Mr. Blackburn, better acquainted with his son's disposition, was little inclined to flatter himself with the hopes of any considerable amendment; from frequent disappointments, and long experience, he was averse to a reconciliation which he declared he was sure could not be permanent; but at length yielded to continual solicitation; and suffered Mr. Ellison to bring young Blackburn and his family to his house.

The interview was affecting: The son assumed an air of contrition; which Mr. Ellison's honest heart inclined him to think was sincere; and the old gentleman was strongly affected. Paternal love can never be totally extinguished in a virtuous mind; the presence of his son revived an affection, which for his own peace he had long been reduced to suppress; and the sight of six fine grandchildren, touched him in the tenderest part. Yet innocent, they had never offended, and had been instructed to caress him in the most engaging manner, which did not fail of pleasing, though he suspected it sprung rather from the art of the parents, than the inclination of the children. Mrs. Blackburn behaved very properly; her sensations led her to do so, for they were such as she must reasonably wish her father-in-law should perceive. She was rejoiced at being reconciled to him, as she hoped it might be the means of bringing her husband to a more regular conduct, and of securing to her children a good provision, even in despight of her husband's extravagance.

Mrs. Blackburn was a woman of great merit. Though very handsome, and ill treated by her husband, she was entirely free from coquetry, or any degree of levity in her conduct. She had a tolerable share of understanding, and, what perhaps was still more for her happiness, weak passions, and blunt sensations. She saw, rather than felt, her husband's ill treatment; the coldness of her heart preserved her from jealousy, and enabled her to act with more regular propriety and prudence, than the strongest sense could have preserved, if accompanied with proportionate passions. Her convenience suffered much by the poverty to which his extravagance frequently reduced them; her reason told her that the riotous company he brought home, were indecent companions for her, and pernicious examples to her children; and she felt all the uneasiness on these, and other occasions, that the mind can suffer; in short, she was truly concerned, but not wretched, because her heart was not the seat of her pain; for that alone can render us miserable. This disposition, so great a blessing to one in her trying situation, enabled her to perform all the duties of her station; which by more lively sensations, would probably have been prevented; and if she was not with all her charms likely to inspire strong affections, she could not however fail of exciting esteem, being as free from any great degree of love for herself, as for others; which is not always the case with cold tempers, those who have least social affections, being apt to have the strongest self-love.

Old Mr. Blackburn had a great regard for his worthy daughter-in-law, and she had frequently experienced his generosity, even while he was at variance with her husband, whose faults she had endeavoured, as far as she was able, to conceal from his father; but never attempting pertinaciously to defend them, had avoided becoming a sharer in the offence; while her concealments, even when they could no longer avail, were considered by the old gentleman as additional proofs of her merit. She was herself an excellent economist, and was determined if she could not prevent their ruin, though she must partake of the distress, her conduct should preserve her from any share of the infamy.

Mr. Ellison soon saw reason to believe that his good offices would have no lasting effect; for he found that the most watchful attention to young Blackburn's conduct, and the most friendly remonstrances he could make, were scarcely sufficient to keep him from daily giving his father some fresh cause of offence.

Mr. Ellison in his other undertakings was more fortunate. He had the pleasure of observing great improvement in his son, he found his capacity sufficiently good, and that he learnt with ease and willingness. The constant care of the father, and of Mr. Green his tutor, had greatly mended his disposition, and there was reason to hope, that before he was out of tuition, most of his faults might be cured, and amiable virtues implanted in their places. This was a sufficient satisfaction to Mr. Ellison; had his expectations been greater, possibly he might have been mortified to find him excelled by the young Granthams in learning; but his fears for his son had been on points so much more important, that while he conceived hopes of seeing him a good man, he was not very solicitous whether he proved a scholar. He had likewise affection enough for the Granthams to observe the progress of their understandings, and their intense application with pleasure; the two eldest indeed were most remarkable in these particulars; the third was lively and discerning, but not much inclined to study.

Mr. Grantham was extremely happy with the praises given his sons, and would frequently say with exultation, that now he hoped to see Frank[11] (his second son and favourite) something like a lord; while Mrs. Grantham, more delicate in her expression, and more attentive to her eldest son, expressed her expectation of seeing him a fine nobleman, and worthy to keep company with any duke in the land. But she lamented the different fate of her girls, sensible of the disadvantages they laboured under, though she was attentive to the only part of education to which she was equal, the carriage of their persons; and even when they were scouring a pewter platter, or making up butter, would call to them to hold up their heads; observing how disgraceful it would be to lady Betty, or lady Mary Grantham, to poke so vulgarly. Mr. Ellison would frequently intreat her not to mix predictions with her remonstrances, while they could only awaken the pride, which lurks in every heart; her care he approved, for though they were under a necessity of being poor, he did not see it equally necessary to be aukward; and his wishes for their better education corresponding with Mrs. Grantham's, to contribute towards it in the only way that at that time occurred to his thoughts, he prevailed with his house-keeper to teach the girls to read; for which their parents had little capacity, and still less leisure; employing the same master to teach them to write and dance, as attended their brothers and master Ellison. As the house-keeper was willing to give them all the improvement she was able, she engaged a good deal of their time; and Mr. Green, who was master of the French language, undertook to instruct them in it. Thus employed, they, as well as their brothers, became daily residents at Mr. Ellison's; and of eight children, two only remained in their parents hands, and those merely because they were too young to learn, the eldest of the two being but four years old; for Mr. Ellison gave his house-keeper in charge to keep the girls properly dressed, without any expence to their parents, to whom he likewise often made such presents, as he thought conducive to their convenience and reasonable gratifications. Thus he was already, in a manner, father to seven children, and well pleased with his paternity; for the little Granthams, of whom three were boys, and three girls, were all a fond parent could have wished. Another pleasing circumstance to Mr. Ellison was, that Mr. Green proved no less agreeable to him as a friend and companion, than useful in the capacity of a tutor; and was himself perfectly happy in his situation; contented with the application and talents of his pupils, and charmed with Mr. Ellison's frank and polite behavior; for these two qualities were very compatible in a man, whose benevolence and charity were such, that the natural expression of his heart might be termed politeness, being almost always consistent with it.

Mr. Ellison had likewise great satisfaction in all his other undertakings. He saw the poor live in comfort and content; the higher sort in amity; and perceived the good effects of the familiar intercourse he had established between them and Mr. Shaw; though it was frequently interrupted by violent attacks of the rheumatism, with which that gentleman was afflicted, and often rendered thereby incapable of performing divine service. To obviate this evil, and provide more fully for the care of the parish as well as to give Mr. Shaw leisure to attend to his own health, which sometimes suffered for want of it, he offered to pay the salary of a curate, the income of the living not being sufficient to afford it, on condition that he might chuse the person, and that he would daily read morning and evening prayers in his workhouse; a proposal to which Mr. Shaw with joy consented; and a young man of excellent character was made very happy by becoming the object of Mr. Ellison's choice; who allowed him fifty pounds a year as curate, and ten for reading prayers to the poor; beside neatly furnishing a good apartment in a large farm-house for him, which, with free access to Mr. Ellison's table, frequent presents, and little assistances that were no great expence to Mr. Ellison, rendered the young man's circumstances very easy and comfortable.

But of all Mr. Ellison's charities, none gave him such exquisite delight as the release of prisoners confined for debt.[12] This he had enjoyed but once since his settling in Dorsetshire; the month of May being, intentionally, appropriated annually to that employment, setting aside one hundred and fifty pounds every quarter as a fund for this purpose. As the dearness of provisions in winter, together with the expences peculiar to the season, and the disadvantages which attend it to persons in business, rendered that the most probable time for those distresses to happen, he thought Spring the properest season for his visitation of the prisons. In the month of May, therefore, he set out on his progress, beginning with the nearest towns, and extending his course as his money would allow. He visited the prisons wherever he came; enquired into the sums for which the persons were confined; and allowed himself time enough in each place, to examine thoroughly into the characters, former circumstances, and every particular relative to the prisoners; applying to great numbers for information, as the most likely means of learning the truth; for though it occasioned his hearing great contradictions, yet he could by the manner of those who represented them in the worst light, distinguish how far they were influenced by prejudice: He could see malice and pique through the warmth and eagerness with which they censured; and too often discover malignity, and pharisaical pride,[13] lurking under the mask of compassion and wisdom. The good that was told him, he did not scrutinize with equal care; persuaded that more praise than a man has a just title to, is seldom given him, and also because the error would be less important. He made acquaintance with the principal people both in, and near those towns, and always cultivated it with care, not only as their information in these points was material; but as it was no less useful to him to know their dispositions well, whereby he could judge how far he might depend on their representations, and be enabled to draw a just balance between the censure and the praise, so frequently by different persons bestowed on the same man. Though many are confined their whole lives in those loathsome scenes of distress and misery, wretched themselves, and useless to the world, for such small sums as would incline one to believe that six hundred pounds might deliver a great number, yet Mr. Ellison found it by no means equal to his wishes; for considering that he should often do a man but little service in releasing him out of prison, except he could enable him to enter into some method of gaining his subsistence, his bounty extended beyond the debt, and to those for whom he had procured liberty, he gave the means of preserving it, by supplying them with the necessary assistances towards getting a livelihood in such manner as was most suitable to their capacities, or the business to which they had been bred. He likewise had sometimes whole families to cloath, who, by the loss of him on whose industry they depended for a maintenance, were reduced to hunger and nakedness, little habitations to furnish, and the implements of labour to purchase.

In the superior pleasure Mr. Ellison found in this disposition of his money, his taste was natural, for nothing could be more delightful than the scenes it presented to him. The joy a man who has been, for a time that to him appeared extremely long, and which often has been long in reality, confined amidst stench and nastiness, in a loathsome prison; deprived of air, of sunshine, the most general gifts of nature; debarred both of ease of body, and every comfort; with a mind tortured by the sense of his own wretchedness, and sad reflexions on the misery of a family he loves; the distress, perhaps the insults, to which a wife for whom he has the tenderest affection is exposed, the sufferings that afflict the infancy of a beloved offspring, left without the support, the care, the protection of a father; the joy, I say, that such a man must feel, at being taken out of this wretched state, restored to light and liberty, cannot fail of communicating itself to the heart of him whose benevolence bestowed the blessing; nor can words describe his sensations, whenever he beheld one of these, so late unhappy wretches, filled with gratitude and exultation, received with transport by an amiable wife, caressed in the tenderest manner by a family of lovely children, and wept over by a parent, to whose aged arms he was thus restored; all seeming to think every sorrow at an end, and the world become a state of felicity. While divided by the variety of delightful sensations with which they were at once affected, they could not feel that warm and perfect gratitude, which filled the heart of Mr. Ellison, toward the Being from whom he had received the power of dispensing so much happiness.

These scenes were indeed the great feasts of his soul, but all his hours yielded him refined pleasures, because they were all spent in the exercise of benevolence; a desire to do good to others, was so entirely his governing principle, that however engaged in business or pleasure he never lost sight of it, endeavouring to promote it by every action of his life. He would not allow himself to pursue even the gratifications of friendship, without attempting to turn the esteem conceived for him to the benefit of his friend or others. Nor was he contented with doing some good, except it was the best he could do; to serve another did not appear to him sufficient, if he did not serve him to the utmost of his power. As this was the constant fixed principle of his mind, it occasioned none of that eagerness and bustle by which starts of benevolence are generally distinguished, and often excites our admiration by rendering it more conspicuous; on the contrary, all he did was performed with so much calmness and humility, that if the effects had not proclaimed the motive, it would never have been discerned. In short, the stream of benevolence never meeting with any obstruction in his heart, flowed with so gentle and uninterrupted a current, as eluded the observation of the inattentive. The pleasure he felt from this course of life was so great, as to enable him to bear without repining, and even without any very severe pangs, the disappointment of the hopes he had entertained of enjoying Mrs. Tunstall's society; though his affection seemed invincible. He avoided meeting her, banished her as much as possible from his thoughts; and when her image would obtrude itself, duty and reason came to his assistance, and enabled him to suppress the tender ideas which people are too apt to indulge. His conduct evidently shewed, that a passion which makes so much confusion in the world, owes its strength only to our weakness, and that if properly resisted, by the arms wherewith reason and religion can furnish us, it may be restrained within such innocent and moderate bounds, as neither to make us infamous or unhappy, though we may not be able totally to extinguish it. If people would but exert their powers, what various vexations and distresses would they escape! but they too often yield to the impulse of passion, from a persuasion that it is irresistible; a fatal error! believed by indolence and weakness; when it is in every person's power to confute it, if he will but firmly and sincerely endeavour to conquer.

## CHAP. V.

However satisfied Mr. Ellison might be with his way of life, it did not please Sir William; who having long wondered at half his cousin's actions, at last attacked him gravely upon the impropriety he was guilty of in not living up to the dignity of his fortune, which he asserted to be every man's duty, observing that 'without subordination and distinctions society must be destroyed'; with many other the like positions, which in themselves were true; only, as frequently happens, the conclusions proved to be false.

Mr. Ellison allowed the necessity of subordination, &c. but would not agree to the consequences the Baronet deduced from the proposition. 'You may,' said he, 'from my actions perceive that I am no leveller;[14] I enjoy every gratification fortune can yield me; I have a very good house, not only conveniently, but handsomely furnished; I keep a plentiful table, and admit as much variety and elegance in that article, as is consistent with health and temperance; I have an equipage,[15] as many servants as convenience requires, and indulge myself in improving my garden, and the grounds about my house, in the manner that best suits my inclination. What farther distinction can my fortune make? What greater enjoyment can it yield me, while confined to myself? I raise no one to the same affluence that I enjoy, though I endeavour to give them the blessing of plenty; surely then I am far from destroying the subordination you think so necessary; an opinion I am not going to dispute.'

'That you enjoy the comforts of life,' replied Sir William, 'I grant, and all you have said of your manner of living implies nothing more; but where is the figure in which you ought to appear? The dignity your fortune will allow, and therefore requires of you. I make no objection to your house; were it less good, its vicinity to mine would render me so partial to it, that it would escape my censure. I can see no faults in a habitation to which I owe so much of your society; but all prejudice aside, it is spacious and handsome; it is your disposition of it only that I shall criticize; you might have a noble suite of rooms on the two first floors; and I know nothing that bears more the air of grandeur than being led through three or four fine rooms, handsomely furnished, before we are brought into that where the master of the house waits to receive us. This advantage, which so few have houses that will allow, you throw away; you have fitted up but two below, and one above stairs, on account of the prospect, for company, and use no others for that purpose, having appropriated those which should have been included in your grand apartments to other people; as for example, Mr. Green has one for his school-room, your house-keeper another, in a third you have put up a bed where the curate is invited to lye whenever a rainy evening overtakes him at your house. Then Mr. Green and your son have each of them a room that would not disgrace a palace; tutors are not generally treated with so much ceremony; your son is another thing, he is your heir and mine, and will succeed to my title; it is proper therefore he should be used with distinction. I do not object to your furniture, for considering the use to which you have destined your rooms, it would have been ill judged to have put any thing in them that was more than plain and neat. Your equipage'———'Stay, Sir William,' interrupted Mr. Ellison, 'suffer me to answer to the charge against me article by article, or I may make too slight a defence. As for state, my good friend, I am not made for it; on what pretence could I assume it? My fortune is good, and I hope I am grateful to Providence that it is so, but were it ten times greater, what real dignity can be given me by a thing that industrious dulness may acquire, or dishonest arts more certainly, and more speedily, may gain? If wealth was to be procured only by virtue, it would indeed carry great honour with it; but I fear the steps towards riches are seldom virtuous; the way to great wealth lies through quite a different road; how then can fortune give us dignity? Shall prosperous villany be honoured? Shall we respect the man who has been guilty of public rapine or private fraud, because he has accumulated much wealth? Yet this we must do if riches are allowed to give real dignity. For my part, I see them in so different a light, that I am thankful my fortune does not *dis*honour me, and think myself happy that my possessions neither wound my conscience, nor my reputation; so far from expecting honour from them, I am well contented that they are unaccompanied with infamy. Thus, therefore, I disclaim all right to dignity from my circumstances, and to endeavour to assume it would be fruitless. If I have any inherent dignity, I presume it will accompany me in all places; if I have not, the grandeur of my apartments will not bestow it. So much ceremony to bring us into the presence of an insignificant Being, in my opinion, wears an air of ridicule; and if during so long a progress, any ideas of greatness have entered our minds, they only serve to make the master of the house appear still more mean. On such occasions, the custom in some eastern nations of erecting magnificent temples to a monkey,[16] is apt to come into my thoughts. Beside, such state is contrary to my notions of hospitality; a man who receives his guests with pleasure, should be of easier access. A state apartment, as it is unfit for me, could yield me no satisfaction; it is not so with the manner in which I have disposed of the rooms you regret my not giving my friends the trouble of walking through. It is a great gratification to me to see Mr. Green in possession of an agreeable apartment; the office of tutor I think one of real dignity, and I must always have the truest respect for a man who by nature, and the good use he has made of the advantages of education, is capable of forming and instructing a youthful mind, and conscientiously and diligently performs the task. His undertaking is of the most useful sort, and requires the best abilities; I therefore respect the office in proportion to its importance, and love the man both from a sense of his merits, and my obligations to him. Whoever receives a person into their house in that character, who is not equal to it, acts a very weak part; and if he is capable of so noble an undertaking, the man dishonours himself who does not pay him the respect he so well deserves. The office is laborious, it ought to be tempered with all the indulgencies and gratifications we can give. I am happy in having a comfortable room for the worthy curate; I esteem his merits, and I revere his profession. If the smallness of his circumstances may lower him in the eyes of his parish, it is my duty to endeavour to raise him, by treating him with the distinction due to his virtues. Now, my good friend, you are welcome to proceed to my equipage.'

'Give me leave then,' said Sir William, 'to tell you that your equipage is pitiful. Is it decent in a man of your fortune to keep only a pair of horses? Then you never go attended by more than one footman; indeed you keep but two, and they wait less on you than on your friends, at whose command they are always ready. There is not a gentleman in the county, with a fourth part of your income, whose equipage and retinue is not genteeler than yours. I the more wondered at the last article, for as you love maintaining the poor, how can you do this better than by an increase of attendants? and then you would have some figure for your money.'

'I will not,' replied Mr. Ellison, 'say that to your charge I plead guilty; for though I acknowledge the truth of the fact, I do not allow the guilt. As for my equipage, a pair of horses are sufficient for any occasions I have; and serve to supply the demands of Mrs. Grantham, Mrs. Blackburn, or any other of my neighbours, who chuse to borrow them; why therefore should I trouble myself with more? or keep unnecessary horses, at an expence that might afford the requisites of life to a whole family? Neither do I by any means subscribe to the reasons you give me for increasing the number of my footmen; except I were to take the maimed and the blind in that capacity, I look upon it as a very uncharitable action. Every man of moderate age, and tolerable health, is able to gain subsistence, and that by means useful to the community and beneficial to himself; *health to himself, and to his children bread, the labourer bears.*[17]

'But footmen, beyond the number necessary to the business of your house, which never can require many, are maintained in idleness; their health and their morals suffer from want of employment; their education incapacitates them from making any mental use of leisure, and they are freed from corporeal labour by custom; time hangs so heavy on their hands, that vice generally finds them ready to embrace any method it points out to them for getting rid of what they know not how to employ. To give sustenance to those who cannot obtain it, to add some conveniences and comforts to such as can procure themselves only bare necessaries, I think my duty, as far as my power will reach; but to maintain in idleness, men who are able to work, I consider as a double crime, first as I hurt them very essentially, and secondly, as it is spending amiss the money with which it has pleased Providence to entrust me, for better purposes; I may likewise add another very weighty objection, the depriving society of hands whose labour might be very useful to it. My seeing it in this light, is the reason that I never will hire a country lad as a footman; it would deeply wound my conscience to take such an one out of a way of life where he might honestly get his bread, enjoy the blessings of nature with sobriety and industry, to introduce him into a state, where idleness must in all probability corrupt that integrity, which is the only certain foundation of ease in this life, and of happiness in the world to come. The consequences bear great resemblance to those attending a crime I sincerely detest; for next to seducing the virtue of a thoughtless or simple girl, is the corrupting the innocence of an ignorant man; for such must ever be the consequences of idleness. I will always, by giving my servants sufficient employment, endeavour to preserve what virtues they bring to me, and to obstruct many temptations to the vices they have acquired, as well as the opportunity of indulging them; but no man shall ever, by my means, be brought into so dangerous a station.'

'It is dangerous enough, that is the truth of it,' said the baronet, 'but you reflect on these things with strange seriousness. Am I to be the guardian of other men's morals? I know what you are going to answer; you will tell me that I must not introduce them into temptations which may corrupt; there is something in that; but you carry all those matters too far. But to proceed with your way of life. I have no great fault to find with your table; if it is not so splendid, nor so curious as those of some of our neighbours, yet every thing upon it is always excellent, and there is an elegance in the neatness of it, which distinguishes it to advantage; less variety is wanting where every dish is so good, that an Epicure would allow that one sufficient. Plentiful your table must necessarily be, since so many are daily fed at it. But I cannot think without smiling on your improvements in your garden and grounds, and all you have done is beautiful and new, for you have wisely avoided imitation; but to watch the progress, is infinitely entertaining. What tribes of skipping children, and hobbling old men and women are employed! In summer especially, one shall scarcely find an able bodied man in the whole extent. Some of your labourers seem fit to dig nothing but their own graves; first or second childhood always finds favour in your sight. If you employed proper workmen, your whole plan would have been executed before this time, whereas it is not now half done. But this is your business; your garden is finished, and that is the only part I see from my windows; but what vexes me is, that people must think you employ there young and old children out of a spirit of covetousness, having them for a trifle; as indeed you might; though I know you give the poor feeble wretches the wages of the best labourers; and the children double what they deserve. This is a disgrace to you, and therefore, as I said, it vexes me.'

'That you are inclined to laugh at my labourers,' answered Mr. Ellison, 'I do not take at all amiss; I sometimes cannot forbear it myself, when I see two of the poor worn-out fellows, trying with all their might to raise a stone or log of wood from the ground, which I could lift with one hand, till at length, finding their endeavours ineffectual, one of them calls his grandson Jacky or Tommy to add his mite of strength, and thereby perform the wondrous feat, of which they are as proud as Hercules of any of his labours. Sometimes too a little failure of eye-sight leads them into ridiculous errors, wherein I am obliged to let them continue, rather than mortify them with the sense of their infirmities. I do not wonder therefore if you are diverted; but I am sorry you should be vexed. What hurt does it do me, that people mistake my motive; they so frequently charge me with being lavish, that if they sometimes impute a little covetousness to me unjustly, it will only serve to form a kind of balance, which may the better reconcile them to my conduct. By able-bodied men, as you observe, my work might have been done long ago, and with much less expence; but what advantage would that have been to me? my great amusement would be over, for most things give us more pleasure in the prosecution than in the enjoyment; and as for the expence, I should be very glad to be at the same, were I never to have any property in the work. Youth cannot be too early inured to labour. I consider that in the children I employ, I am sowing the seeds of future strength and industry; and in the mean time their parents feel the benefits of a numerous offspring, and learn to see it a gracious gift from Providence, which those cannot easily think it, who find their children a heavy burden for twelve or fourteen years; and as it relieves them from a good deal of this load, it encourages others to marry, who observe that in a very few years, a child may gain sufficient to discharge the additional expence it creates. I look on idleness as so great a curse, that I think I make old age happy in employing it; the decrepid by this means preserve their independency, and while they see they are of some use, they are less sensible of their infirmities; they even admire their own powers, when they behold the beauties which they have had their share in producing; and I verily believe, for that reason, think my garden the finest thing the

world ever contained since the destruction of paradise. I certainly would on
no account give them less wages than their juniors require; their age wants
fuller comforts, and greater indulgencies, and I should be sorry to join with
time in oppressing them. In the summer, as you observe, I have few others: A
labourer is as happy if employed by one of my neighbours, as by myself, he
therefore receives no benefit from my work; and for that reason I chuse he
should become mine only, when no one else has business for him; and in the
interim I content myself with those whom no other person will accept.'

'I am surprised,' said Sir William, 'you ever eat a meal; for you might
always find somebody who had rather eat it, than leave it to you.'

'No, no, my good friend,' answered Mr. Ellison, 'when necessaries are in
question, I first consider myself.'

'I do not understand your way of acting. Is not all you have your own?'
interrupted the knight.

'Not a shilling of it, Sir William,' replied Mr. Ellison, 'I have nothing of
my own. You stare; I will explain myself at once. I consider every thing I
possess, my fortune, my talents, and my time, as given me in trust, to be
expended in the service of the Giver. I am but a steward, and must render an
exact account of all that is delivered into my hands. The best manner in
which I can serve my master, is in benefiting his creatures; I therefore think
myself obliged to spend the greatest part of my fortune in relieving the necessitous, in providing for the good of their souls, and the ease of their bodies.
My understanding is given to direct me in the best way of performing this,
and to have it share in doing good to others, as well as to be exercised in
thankfulness to, and adoration of that Being, who has graciously bestowed on
me so delightful an office; and these ought also to be the chief employments
of my time, and the purposes to which I should apply my health. But as I
believe that my bountiful Master designed I should have a due proportion of
these things for my own enjoyment, you see I allow myself a far greater abundance than I give to any one else; but even that I should not think justifiable,
if I could not make it more conducive to his service, than a contrary course.
Thus, my good friend, I have opened to you my whole heart; these are the
principles which I hope will ever direct me, and prove the rule of my whole
conduct. If I am mistaken, which in this point I think scarcely possible, it is
at least an error which affords me great happiness, and much inward satisfaction; and as my motive is right, I have no doubt but what results from it will
be acceptable; when we act in opposition to pride, vanity, and sensuality, we
are certainly on the safe side. I can claim no merit from mortification; as I

could by no means obtain a happiness equal to what I enjoy from my present way of thinking.'

Mr. Ellison had never made so full a declaration of his principle of action; though he had at different times expressed the same sentiments. He was glad of every opportunity of speaking on the subject, without seeming to seek it, for he wished to bring the baronet over to his opinions, but knew that an appearance of a design to influence him, must frustrate all his hopes. He was therefore well pleased that Sir William blamed his conduct, as by defending himself, he got an opportunity of urging more strongly, arguments which were to him convincing; and had the satisfaction of seeing they made no small impression. They raised such scruples in the baronet's mind, that he frequently resumed the subject, and by degrees was brought to approve Mr. Ellison's conduct, though he could not resolve to imitate it thoroughly. He felt himself more inclined to give his money than his time, for he was indolent but not covetous; and as far as his vanity, and his notions of dignity, which could not be totally eradicated, would permit, he was willing to join with Mr. Ellison in some of his charities, on condition that he should be excused from taking his share of the trouble. As nothing appeared to him so worthy of compassion, as that state which deprived a man of all power over his own actions, and subjected him entirely to the will of another, he desired he might add four hundred a year to Mr. Ellison's fund for the release of prisoners; and gave him liberty to apply to him on any exigence that should offer. The annual four hundred Mr. Ellison readily accepted; but was backward as to the use of the permission he gave him, finding that the peculiarity of his humour made him apt to start objections to any thing proposed; not from an unwillingness to part with his money, but from a reluctance to agree in any other person's opinions.

## Chap. VI.

Though temperance and virtue are the best preservatives of health, yet they cannot secure to any one an uninterrupted state. Mr. Ellison, while employed in assiduous endeavours to alleviate the sufferings of others, became himself the object of compassion. He was seized with a violent fever, which so far baffled the skill and care of Dr. Tunstall, for whom he had sent on being first taken ill, that in three days he was entirely delirious, and his life judged to be in great danger. The grief of his friends and dependents is easier to be imagined than described; but none felt more sincerely on the occasion than Mrs. Tunstall, whose gratitude attached her very strongly to him, tho' she had never been in his company since the morning that determined him to give up all pretensions to her. She always waited the doctor's return with impatient anxiety, and was greatly affected by the account her husband gave her in the beginning of the second week of Mr. Ellison's illness, of the accident which had happened to his house-keeper; who, by a fall down stairs, had put out her ankle, and must be totally confined to her chamber; whereby Mr. Ellison was deprived of a very careful, tender, and sensible nurse, which his situation rendered extremely necessary, and yet the doctor saw no means of procuring him one; any of the servants, or people in the parish, would have attended him with care and affection, but their ignorance disqualified them for the trust. Mrs. Tunstall was shocked to think of the danger he must run in such hands, and asked, 'whether there was any probability that in his insane state of mind he should know her; for if not, she should think herself very happy, if by her care and attendance, she could make any return for the obligations he had conferred on her.' The doctor replied, 'that he did not think there was any chance of his knowing her, his senses were so entirely disordered, but that the fatigues of such an office, together with the anxiety she must feel for so excellent a friend, might prove very dangerous in her present state, she being then in the eighth month of her pregnancy, and therefore he could not easily agree to it.'

'As for my health,' answered Mrs. Tunstall, 'to what dangers ought not gratitude to prompt me to expose myself, for the sake of the man to whom I owe my present happiness; in a word, to whom I owe *You*! I should not deserve you if I did not feel the debt too great to be discharged, but yet endeavour to do all in my power towards acquitting it. The welfare of the child I bear is a tenderer point; but as what I am going to do, appears to me an indispensible duty, I am superstitious or enthusiastic enough, to think it will not be attended with any bad consequences. You will of course be there great part of every day, and will be a judge if there appears to be any danger of its producing very bad effects; I may then, if necessity requires it, relinquish my charge, the worst may by that time be past; and I am really persuaded that my mind will be much more at ease when I am following the impulse of my gratitude, than if I have any room to reproach myself for an omission of duty. Reflexions of that sort, together with my regard for Mr. Ellison, would make his death so affecting, as in my opinion might be more dangerous in my present state than the fatigue you apprehend.'

The Doctor's tenderness for his amiable wife made him very unwilling to consent to her proposal; but she urged it with such persuasive importunity, that he at length, though reluctantly, agreed to carry her to Mr. Ellison's that very day.

She had no sooner given such orders as were necessary for the conduct of her family during her absence, and packed up the linen she should want, than she summoned the doctor to perform his promise. He did not delay the execution of it, but carried her thither; and introducing her to the house-keeper, acquainted her with Mrs. Tunstall's motives. The good woman, whose accident had given her more concern on her master's account than on her own, was overjoyed at finding her place would be so well supplied; and readily granted Mrs. Tunstall's request, of not informing Mr. Ellison, if they had the happiness of seeing him recover, that Mrs. Tunstall had ever been there, which she hoped to conceal from him, by retiring upon the first symptoms of a return of reason. Her motive for this caution was, the fear lest such a token of her regard might awaken any tender sensations in his heart, which she flattered herself had been for some time at ease; though the period he had fixed for avoiding her, that wherein he should be totally indifferent, was perhaps not come, as he had hitherto observed the same care. The house-keeper promised to give the like caution to the rest of the servants.

It is easy to imagine that Mrs. Tunstall must perform with the greatest assiduity an office she undertook out of gratitude. The only rest she allowed herself was on a couch, in Mr. Ellison's chamber; she mixed all his medicines, and gave him every thing he took; but was careful not to approach his bedside on his first waking, lest sleep might calm his delirium, and expose her to his knowledge. She was seldom out of his chamber, except during one or two short visits she daily made his house-keeper, for a whole week that he continued in the same melancholy state; he then began to recover his senses, but was so weak and spent, he took little notice of any thing that passed; she therefore prolonged her attendance for some days, keeping out of his sight, but directing the nurse, and watching that all proper care was taken; and she had the satisfaction, before Mr. Ellison was well enough to discover there was any other person than his nurse in the room, to see the house-keeper able to be brought in, and take the same care she herself had done for some days, though she was not sufficiently recovered to walk, or even stand; she then with great joy resigned her office, and returned home, free from the apprehensions for Mr. Ellison's life which had induced her to leave it.

Every day confirmed her in this easy state of mind; for his recovery, though slow, was uninterrupted; and the many hearts which his extreme danger had oppressed with grief and anxiety were relieved from their heavy burden; more sensible than ever of the value of the man on whom their happiness depended, as all their sensibility had been awakened by his illness. The house-keeper, who was charmed with Mrs. Tunstall's conduct, and had made an impression equally favourable on that lady, was faithful to her promise; being not only silent herself, as to the friendly part Mrs. Tunstall had acted, but taking care that the family should all be equally prudent. The same caution had been given to Sir William, but not with the like success. He had been much concerned for his cousin, though a fear lest his disorder might be contagious, had prevented his entering his chamber. He had called at the house daily, and always asking for Mrs. Tunstall had frequently seen her; but a reluctance to absenting herself from her patient, had made her reduce those interviews into very short compass; only staying long enough to answer his enquiries after the sick man. The appearance of so strong an attachment, the hazard she had run, and the uncommonness of the action, had made such an impression on him, that the utmost his prudence could effect, was to be silent on the subject till his cousin was pretty well recovered; and then, news being brought them as they were sitting together that Mrs. Tunstall was brought to bed, he could not forbear observing, that she had but just had time to recover her fatigue.

Mr. Ellison usually avoided entering into any conversation on a subject wherein he felt himself too tenderly interested, but his sensibility on the present occasion put him off his guard; and he enquired to what fatigue Sir William alluded. The Baronet could no longer resist the desire he felt of acquainting his cousin with Mrs. Tunstall's extraordinary care of him, to which Mr. Ellison listened with equal surprize and pleasure. Her conduct on this occasion had the effect she feared from it, if it came to his knowledge, for it awakened every tender sensation; but these were not accompanied with the pain she thought might attend them. He had brought himself to such a patient acquiescence in the decrees of Providence, that while he cherished the remembrance of her with tenderness, his regret for his disappointment was calm and temperate. He attributed her care to the gratitude of a noble mind, and felt ineffable pleasure in so strong a proof that his esteem was just. The action agreed so well with the generosity of his nature, that to him it appeared natural, and he did not draw from it one argument that could flatter his passion with a probability of her being actuated by any other principle; nor indeed did he wish it; to have believed she harboured a sentiment which must have interrupted her happiness, without increasing his, would have given him pain; with pleasure he saw he had no reason for any such suspicion, and refuted all the arguments Sir William's narrower mind urged, to persuade him that tenderness had as great a share as generosity in Mrs. Tunstall's behaviour. Any virtue in a moderate degree is easily credited, but when it exceeds the common boundary, it is generally misconstrued into some vice, or selfish purpose, by people who cannot comprehend what is so far above their own feelings. I have seldom known an action greatly generous, fail being attributed to some view of private interest, and bring some degree of discredit on the person who would have gained honour by a small bounty. A mind truly firm and noble will disregard this consequence, reaping a pleasure from its own reflexions which far surpasses what the approbation of mankind can bestow; but timid virtue will frequently be discouraged by this injustice, and rather forego, though with pain, the means of conferring a great benefit, than be exposed to imputations which are humiliating.

Mr. Ellison felt himself under great obligations to Mrs. Tunstall for the part she had acted; and acknowledged his sense of it to the Doctor in the warmest terms; and to procure a good opportunity of making a more substantial return, desired he would permit him to be godfather to his new born son, though not present on the occasion; as he intended before that time to leave the country, in compliance with the Doctor's advice to change the air, as the most likely means of perfecting his recovery.

Mr. Ellison designed first to visit his sister, whom he had not seen since he settled in Dorsetshire; and then to perform his promise of revisiting Millenium Hall, which nothing had prevented his doing before, but an unwillingness to leave home, where he thought himself more usefully employed, than he could be in any other place. He set out some days sooner, in order to make his absence at the christening of Dr. Tunstall's child less remarkable. Mr. Ellison had the pleasure of seeing his sister very happily situated; possessing, as well as deserving, the affection and indulgence of a very good husband, and surrounded by a family of very fine children. The cordial reception he met with there, might have tempted him to make a long stay, if his several duties at home, which must suffer in the performance during his absence, had not determined him to observe exactly the time he had allotted for his tour; but to render his departure more easy on all sides, he obtained a promise from his sister, and brother-in-law, to return his visit the first favourable opportunity.

He then proceeded to Millenium Hall, and friendship welcomed him to the house, where hospitality had first received him. He was now treated without ceremony; the politeness of the inhabitants inspiring him with the same ease as if he had been one of the family, a society in which he held it great honour to be included. As he was perfectly acquainted with their charitable institutions, all reserve on that subject was now banished, and they frankly acquainted him with their success and improvements, as well as their plans for new charities. Among these, the most considerable, was one chiefly intended for the benefit of those who appear no objects of charity: but these ladies, far from thinking poverty the only evil which Christian benevolence should lead us to redress, did not even consider it as the most important. The soul, as the noblest, and most durable part of us, was the chief object of their care and solicitude.

The imprudent, and frequently vicious, course of life, into which too many fall, appeared to them evidently to proceed most commonly from a faulty education, whether public or private, the errors therein being numerous, though different. In regard to both sexes the case seemed much the same, but the education of boys was above their sphere; they aimed no farther than to rectify some of the errors in female education.

As the ladies had lived long in retirement, and free from crowds and bustle had led a life of reason and virtue, it is not strange that their way of thinking on various subjects should be a little unfashionable; and perhaps it was not more so on any point than on education; which though the most material, was, in their opinions, greatly erroneous; but in general they thought parents more deserving of compassion than censure. They observed that many were incapable of giving their children much education, having received few improvements themselves, either from early instruction, or later voluntary application; bred in ignorance, they had acquired a narrowness of mind, which conceives no more extensive idea of virtue than what serves to secure us from infamy and the rigours of law; insensible to all those various duties, and social good offices, which, though the safety of our persons and reputations do not depend upon them, yet are so essential to the happiness of all those connected with us; for a woman may be a very disagreeable wife, a tiresome friend, a harsh mistress, and very deficient in the duties of a mother, and yet, according to this narrow way of thinking, be honest, chaste, prudent, and in the common acceptation of the phrase, good natured. To acquit ourselves well in any of these capacities we ought to be thoroughly acquainted with the extent of every virtue, from whence we shall learn, that there is no action so trifling, wherein virtue is not concerned; or, to speak more properly, that scarcely any action is trifling, since in some way it affects the ease and satisfaction of another; and if not immediately hurtful, becomes so, by taking up that time and attention, which might be employed either to our own, or some other person's benefit. Thus, those actions which are called totally indifferent, if we consider them properly, we shall see are so far bad, as we waste on them the hours given for better purposes; for an extensive view of religious or moral duties, will teach us that every action of our lives ought to be useful. Upon these common, and frequent acts, depends in great measure the happiness of those connected with us. Great injuries or great benefits, are seldom in our power; the opportunities for either are few; but by a number of small vexations, we may render a person more miserable than we could by one great injury. There is an elasticity in our spirits, which enables them to rise again after a great and sudden blow, while a frequent repetition of vexations keeps them down, and deprives them of all power of exertion: but a narrow mind sees not the iniquity of such oppression in a right light, because the evils it inflicts are not expressly included either in the prohibitions in the Decalogue or the laws of the land; blind to the spirit of the law, they attend only to the words. Those, therefore, whose ideas are circumscribed within such narrow bounds, are ill qualified to cultivate the minds of their children. But yet it is not from the imbecillity of mothers that children chiefly suffer; there are now few who apply even what talents they have to domestic duties. Amusement is too often the business of their lives; and in the round of diversions they pursue, their children are sometimes forgotten, but always neglected. If they are admitted into their company, the person whose instructions and conduct should lead them to virtue, whose prudence should warn them against vice, and defend their unexperienced youth from all the dangers to which it is unavoidably exposed, sets them an example of nothing but levity and indiscretion; teaches them by the surest means, example, that dress, cards, and dissipation, are the great business of life; and what reason would lead some of the best disposed almost in infancy to condemn, becomes sanctified by the practice of her whom they know it is their duty to respect.

Some mothers have sense enough to see that the company they keep is not proper for their daughters, but instead of changing their acquaintance, and their way of life on that account, and considering that what will corrupt their children, cannot be innocent in themselves, they take another method, and confine their daughters in a nursery, assigning over all maternal care to a governess, who though low in birth, and indigent in circumstances, is supposed equal to a trust, for which few parents, with all the advantages their fortune and station can give them, are sufficiently qualified; and for the poor emolument of a small stipend, she is expected to take that care, which regard for the first and most important duty of life, natural affection, and all the tender ties of maternity, cannot induce the mother to perform. Masters indeed are procured, external accomplishments sometimes are cultivated, and the young ladies may unfortunately excel in a minuet, on the harpsichord, or with a pencil; this I call unfortunate, because it only serves to lay them open to flattery; and vanity destroys what little natural merit remained; for the plant, weak from the barrenness of the soil, and want of cultivation, makes but little resistance. Parents who pique themselves most on the education of their daughters, generally produce them into the world, thus provided with every thing that can render it dangerous, without having attempted to fortify their minds against the temptations that await them, or to give them one qualification fit for domestic life: their attention being wholly fixed on externals, while the hearts and understandings of their children are totally neglected; few good or useful principles inculcated, no true knowledge acquired, no new ideas excited. To improve their public appearance being the great object, no domestic qualifications, no amusements for retired leisure are taught them; their pleasures depend wholly on others, and the hours which are not passed in company, become burdened with all the miseries of ignorance and idleness; in these they must languish if debarred of dissipation, as incapable of amusing themselves as of being useful to others. French, and sometimes Italian perhaps, makes a part of their education; but as they generally learn the one out of Novels, and the other chiefly in Pastorals,[18] their hearts acquire corruption and folly, faster than their heads do the languages; and their understandings, instead of being improved, are perverted by their studies.

## CHAP. VII.

I would not have my reader take for granted, that the sentiments with which the last chapter finished, are my own. I have no title to censure the fashionable world in so material a point; but the ladies who gave occasion to the subject, had by superior merit acquired a right of judging for themselves, and might with justice criticize the manners of a world, that would sufficiently make itself amends by despising them, for leading a life so contrary to its most favourite maxims. However, they were so little addicted to censure others, that they would scarcely have said much on the subject, had they not been determined on an attempt to remedy the errors they blamed. An artist may be thought unreasonable that will not allow any one to criticize his works, who cannot excel him in his art; but these ladies had a title even beyond this: that they could have better performed a mother's part they had evidently proved, without having stood in that relation to any one; but they were desirous of shewing to others how to do the same, and of giving even to such mothers as would not themselves undertake the education of their children, an opportunity of having their places better supplied.

I have related their opinions of home education; and they did not think more favourably of the more public methods. Schools appeared to them in general so ill conducted, that they saw no advantage in sending a child thither, except the removing her from the danger of being contaminated by the example of her mother, and her other relations, which in some cases might be desirable. The ignorance of the persons who keep schools, and the great number of scholars received at them; the little time and attention given by the masters; and indeed the impossibility of so many children being properly instructed by so few persons, were they sufficiently qualified; made them fear that the scholars learnt more evil and folly of each other, than good from the mistress and teachers. Out of the great numbers of young ladies of their acquaintance educated at boarding-schools, very few had they seen improved by it; to any useful or valuable purpose in life they generally returned as little qualified as the day they were sent to it; their acquisitions seldom extending farther, than a little bad French, a smattering of music, a tolerable minuet, a great deal of low pride, much pertness, intolerable vanity, and some falsehood.

To endeavour to teach the ladies the full extent of maternal duty, and to prevail on them to sacrifice the love of gaiety and dissipation to a due care of their children, they were sensible would prove a fruitless attempt. Some, even in high life, set an example in this particular, from which more effect might naturally be expected than from any verbal arguments; and where they fail, no hope remains. But they imagined it possible to mend public education. With this view they determined to establish several schools, and desired Mr. Ellison would take their plan into consideration, and object to any part that he disapproved. Their scheme was as follows.

Having qualified several young women perfectly well for the purpose, they designed to unite four or five in society, who should take boarders at the usual prices, but never above twenty in number, that they might be able to keep a vigilant watch over them, and instruct them fully. The different geniuses of these young women had led them to excel in different talents; one in music, another in drawing, and a third in writing and arithmetic; while another had penetrated more deeply into science; whereby they were enabled, when united, to teach the young ladies committed to their care, every branch of education, except dancing, for which alone they would have occasion to seek for foreign assistance. Their patronesses[19] had rendered them thoroughly sensible, that they were not to undertake this office, merely with a view of procuring themselves a subsistence, or even of reaping honour from any shining qualifications they might give their scholars, but as persons who were to render an account at the last day of the manner in which they had executed it; and who were conscious, that since it had pleased God to place them in that situation, it was their duty to act therein like his faithful servants; breeding up those who should be placed under their care, in the manner most pleasing to him; qualifying them, as far as they were able, to perform well the duties of any station to which they should be called. For this purpose their first and chief endeavours were to be directed towards fixing deeply on their minds the great principles of religion, guarding them equally from superstition and fanaticism, as from levity and carelessness in so material a point. As one means of arriving at this great end, they were to cultivate the children's understandings, and teach them those languages, the acquisition of which are most desirable, and such polite arts as are considered as accomplishments proper for young women of fashion, whereby they would acquire so many laudable and pleasing ways of amusing themselves, as would secure them against the melancholy necessity of being obliged to seek diversions from abroad. These ladies considered that persons of all ages, but particularly the young, must have amusements, otherwise their spirits will languish, and their minds grow too dull even to perform serious duties with vigour; and thought nothing so likely to preserve them from giddy dissipation, and a mad pursuit after public entertainments, as so enlarging their minds by reason and knowledge, that they might see the futility of idle diversions, and feel unsatisfied with every pleasure which their reason disapproved; and likewise giving them a variety of agreeable employments to amuse their leisure hours at home, which every one who aims at any stable happiness, or at performing well the part of a daughter, wife, or mother, should make the principal scene of her pleasures; for we may wildly traverse the whole world in search of happiness,[20] yet shall never attain it but in our own houses, and in the sincere performance of our respective duties.

In consequence of this attention to the improvement of the understandings of these young ladies, care was taken to direct their reading in the most instructive course; to trace out for them a regular series of history; and in every other branch of knowledge, to lead them through the proper gradations with the like regularity; confining them on every subject to the best authors, and not suffering them to fall into that incoherent desultory manner of reading, too usual in the sex, which rather confounds and dissipates, than instructs the mind, and is indeed no better than a serious kind of idleness, productive of little more improvement than more lively sorts of dissipation. With history, geography and chronology were made to go hand in hand; the less abstruse parts of astronomy, natural philosophy, ethics, and the rational parts of metaphysics, were admitted into their studies.

The second rank of schools which came into the plan these ladies had formed, was chiefly designed for such as had no prospect of considerable fortunes; and therefore were not entitled to any higher expectations than marrying men in good trades, country gentlemen of small estates, or men in the church, army, or some other employment, which yielding only a life income, disqualified them from getting wives of fortune, on whom they could make no adequate settlement. The accomplishments to be taught at these schools were of a more humble kind than at the former, and a country situation was preferred, that the expences might be lower. Here the children were to learn all branches of economy; writing and arithmetic was particularly attended to; they were taught to make their own gowns, stays, caps, &c. exercised in cutting out linen, mending it in the best manner, and with the most housewifely contrivance; to make pastry, cakes, jellies, sweet-meats, &c. distilling, cookery, and every other branch of good housewifery. Music was forbidden, as taking up too much time for persons in a middling station, and as a proficiency in it would prove only a dangerous excellence; for it might induce a young woman of small fortune to endeavour at mending her circumstances, by performing in public, or at best introduce her into company of a far superior rank, who would think her sufficiently rewarded for the pleasure she gave them by the honour of their acquaintance, though the expences attending it must ruin her fortune; and as soon as her distresses should be known, her music would lose its charms, and neglect or insult become all her portion. Even drawing was not taught, except where so extraordinary a genius appeared, as gave room to believe it might prove a useful and profitable art. French was cultivated, as the general use of it gave reason to suppose it might be of service; geography was likewise allowed, because it took little time, could never be hurtful, and rendered reading more instructive. Dancing was of necessity permitted, as it was feared no parent would bear the thought of her daughter's not being taught what in all probability she esteemed the most necessary part of education. But though the accomplishments of these scholars were circumscribed, no restraints were laid on any thing that could improve their understandings, as good sense and a liberal mind are equally desirable in every situation. Notwithstanding their housewifery employments, they had a good deal of time for reading, and every possible means were taken to render that instructive and improving.

These two classes of schools may appear sufficient, as many will naturally suppose, that persons of an inferior station would educate their daughters themselves; but this is by no means the case. This worthy society had observed that the lowest shopkeepers in country towns send their daughters to boarding-schools, at so great an expence as renders them as little able to leave their children a subsistence, as those children are to gain one, after having been bred up in idleness and vanity at those seminaries, where little else is taught. These ladies were of opinion that few had so much reason to place their daughters abroad for education as these people, for the business of their shops must frequently deprive them of leisure to look well after their children; but this measure seldom answered any good purpose from the improper conduct of the school-mistresses, who finding their own pride flattered by making their scholars appear considerable, treated them as young ladies; from which the mothers, whose vanity was sure to be at unison with the school-mistresses, felt too much pleasure to disapprove it. This observation occasioned the institution of schools of a third class; entirely designed for people of that rank. At these, the only part of genteel education taught, was writing and accompts, which were carefully cultivated; with every thing that could qualify them for service, or for being wives to men in small trades. All sorts of needle-work, nothing that tended towards economy in their own dress, or that of children, was omitted. In washing, clear-starching, brewing, making of bread, pastry, confectionary, distilling, and cookery, they were instructed. They were made in rotation to do all the business of the house, milk cows, make butter and cheese, and feed poultry. To give them more extensive practice in these things than could otherwise have been afforded them, these schools were placed at the out-skirts of large country towns; needle-work and clear-starching were taken in, at the common prices, because they would not sink the pay for such work as will scarcely produce a maintenance to the performer. But cakes, sweetmeats, and particularly cookery, were there furnished at low rates, in order to bring business enough to keep the girls well exercised in them; and in this eating age, there are few towns that are not furnished with at least one feasting alderman, to purchase joyfully, delicacies which his own kitchen will not afford him. By the profits thus made, the school-mistresses were enabled to take the children at a very moderate price. No dancing-master was allowed to attend, for though the proper carriage of the person is of some importance to every one, yet it was imagined the care of the mistresses might suffice in that respect; whereas the benefit received from the dancing-master would be apt to be over-balanced by the vanity it might inspire. For the same reason, the title of Miss was banished the school, though great civility of behaviour was required; but to preserve this, it is by no means necessary that the children of chandlers and alehouse-keepers should treat each other with the appellations of Misses, and young Ladies; which teaches them to confound the distinction that ought to be kept up between them and their superiors.

In one particular, however, as much care was taken to instruct them as if they were of the highest rank, I mean in the article of religion. They were well taught the fundamentals of Christianity, and the purest and strictest principles of morality were instilled into their minds; but even in this there was some difference made, as the obligation to the duties peculiarly adapted to their stations were particularly inculcated.

When Mr. Ellison had examined the several plans of these various systems of education, he told the ladies that he saw little room to object to any thing therein; but he feared the success of the schools might not prove answerable to what in reason it ought to be; 'for,' said he, 'few people are judges of education; they can see if their daughters dance well, some of them can even discover if they have made any proficiency in music, or talk French fluently; but very small is the number of those who can form any judgment of your more extensive views in education; ignorant themselves, they will neither comprehend the knowledge their children acquire, nor the uses of it. Many perhaps are conscious that some exterior accomplishments, wherein themselves are deficient, would be desirable acquisitions to their daughters, as tending to render them objects of admiration; but I am apt to believe the greater number are well convinced that in every thing of real importance there is no occasion to excel them; many who can scarcely hobble a minuet, and do not know a note of music, may wish to see their daughters dance with grace, and perform well on the harpsichord; but will not allow they can be more prudent, more wise, or more moral than themselves, though they scarcely know how to avoid infamy, or to govern their families; and conceive that morality extends no farther than will just keep them out of the reach of penal laws. Others will be afraid their children's spirits should be depressed, or their understandings worn out by too much study; the health of some will be esteemed too delicate, and because it is not sufficient that the body shall often destroy the soul, after we are arrived at maturity, they are resolved that even in infancy it shall begin to render us fools. To others your plan will appear erroneous as far as it is new, and its greatest merits will be the parts most objected to; for though novelty in trifles seldom fails of pleasing, in affairs of importance it alarms; and the things that are most worth improving upon, and most want it, are alone condemned by the bulk of mankind to remain in their original imperfection. I wish envy does not still prove a greater impediment to your success than even all I have yet mentioned; among those who perceive the excellence of your scheme, I fear the greater part will prove envious of the merit of it, and from that motive oppose, what their own hearts will tell them is superior to their views, or above their power.'

'By our retired way of life' (replied Mrs. Morgan)[21] 'we are grown such Utopians, that what you urge might have appeared very strange to us, if we had not heard the same observations from another friend; and though we are apt to forget the faults and follies of mankind, in part perhaps voluntarily, as too much reflexion upon them is dangerous to one's benevolence; and in part necessarily, from the little connexion we have for many years had with the multitude; yet our memories are not so defective, but when truths of this kind are presented to us, our minds acquiesce in the probability; therefore we are prepared for all the discouragement our schemes can encounter; and have endeavoured to strengthen the young undertakers against it, lest their industry, and application to perform well their parts, may be damped by the smallness of their success; we can preserve them from suffering any thing thereby beyond mental mortification, as a deficiency in profit can with ease be supplied by us, who have set aside a fund for that purpose. I think our views cannot be entirely frustrated, our schools may expect, without any acknowleged superiority of merit, to have some small share, at least, of the great numbers of children destined to a public education, and we would not wish them to have many at a time. These we shall have the satisfaction of knowing are educated in a manner to render themselves, and all connected with them, happy, though their parents may not perceive from whence they have obtained their advantages; a point of no importance either to them or us. Chance will send some scholars; it is our business, as well as the concern of those who are to live thereby, to turn that chance to the benefit of such as are under their care.

'We might have secured to our young women as many scholars as they would have received, by fixing a price for their board considerably lower than other schools, and should with pleasure have appropriated a yearly sum towards their maintenance, as we think that cultivating the minds of the rich is almost as charitable an action as nourishing the bodies of the poor; but we could neither have afforded a sufficient sum, or found a sufficient number of well qualified instructors, to have accommodated all who have recourse to school education, therefore other schools would still have been wanted; and to secure to some young persons the advantages we think may be given them by proper instruction, we should by lowering the price of education, have ruined all who now live by that profession, and whose pay is certainly short of their deserts, if they acquit themselves as they ought; and indeed, all respect to their qualifications out of the case, yields them but just a maintenance, and that very laboriously obtained. You will not think, by what I have said, I shew a disposition to entertain too favourable an opinion of the world, whatever I may before have hinted to that purpose, for it is a severe reflexion on mankind to say, that money is a consideration that can influence people of fortune in so important a point as the education of their children, wherein of all others they should not be parsimonious; but frequently there is nothing in which they so willingly act the economist; and though shame will not suffer them to deny giving the usual accomplishments, yet they are very desirous to do it at as cheap a rate as possible, and little concerned though it is ill performed, if the name of having proper masters does but save their credit, or if they can but find places where they can decently board their children, to remove from themselves the trouble of parental care.'

Mr. Ellison allowed that he feared Mrs. Morgan's reflexions were but too just, and told her, that, though he had declared the discouragements he thought their useful and benevolent plan might at first meet with, yet he was not so positive in his opinion, but that he begged she would promise to admit three young ladies of his acquaintance into one of the schools of the highest class, being unwilling to delay his application, lest, contrary to his apprehensions, they might be immediately filled; and he had determined on the first mention of their plan to send Miss Granthams thither.[22]

His request we may suppose was easily granted; for as these ladies had no greater desire than to find young persons to reap the benefit of their intentions, it was as agreeable to them as to himself; and they even offered to pay for an equal number, if he knew any children of fashion, whose parents could not afford them an education adequate to their birth and future fortunes; observing to him, that to accept this offer would not be putting them to expence, as they did not see much chance for the school's bringing in, for some years, a sufficient income both to defray the charges, and properly reward the school-mistresses; consequently some assistance from them would be necessary.

# BOOK III.

~

## CHAP. I.

While Mr. Ellison remained at Millenium Hall, he made frequent visits to the two societies,[1] composed of the persons those ladies had removed from a state of mortifying dependence; and received great pleasure from seeing their happiness. Observing to them one day how complete their satisfaction appeared, one of the ladies said to him, 'How is it possible it should be otherwise, if our dispositions are not uncommonly prone to discontent and ingratitude! We enjoy not only every circumstance of comfort, but every rational pleasure. All the benefits society can afford are within our reach; all that competence can yield is ours; we have every thing that attends plentiful possessions, but the trouble of taking care of them. We are indeed dependent, but reflexion only can make us sensible of it; here dependence exists without those chains and fetters which render it more galling than the oppressions of the most indigent, but free, poverty. When we see our benefactresses feel such true joy in bestowing, it would be ingratitude even to wish not to receive at their hands; in accepting their bounty, we seem to confer an obligation, and do in reality confer a benefit, by being the cause of so much refined pleasure to them. This is the most exalted part of their bounty; their wealth gives us ease and plenty, but it is their generous noble way of bestowing, that gives us happiness. Nor does this alone constitute our felicity; it is still heightened by comparing our present situation with the past. Light appears with additional brightness when set off by shade. Great as their generosity is, it still rises in our opinions, when we reflect on the painful, I might say loathsome, dependence, from which it rescued many of us.'

Mr. Ellison was not naturally curious, but so baneful is idleness, that having nothing else to do, he felt some inclination that the leisure the afternoon afforded them should be filled up, with an account of the past lives of those who seemed to make the best use of the remembrance of them, by turning former mortifications into an increase of present happiness: He therefore answered what this lady, by name Mrs. Alton,[2] had said, in such a manner as drew her almost insensibly into giving a pretty full detail.

'My father,' said she, 'though he outlived my mother 4 years, died when

I was but eighteen years old. As his fortune was good, I was well educated; for though fashionable accomplishments were not neglected, I was bred to a proper share of good housewifery. I had taken care of my father's family from the time of my mother's death, her infirm state of health having induced her to qualify me for that office, before the usual age for such occupations. I was therefore able to govern a house, but had little chance to have a house to govern; for at my father's decease, I learnt that his whole estate was entailed on my brother; it had not been in his power to charge it with any fortune for me, and, as he had lived to the full of his income, I was left entirely to my brother's generosity. This piece of information shocked me extremely, although I loved my brother well enough, to be contented to accept as an obligation, a provision to which nature seemed to give me a right; and had so good an opinion of him, that I did not doubt of his providing properly for me, were he left to himself; but, unfortunately for me, he had married a young woman of low birth, though tolerable fortune, of whom he was so fond, that I was sensible my dependence must be rather on her than him; and I was not sufficiently acquainted with her disposition, to know what expectations to form in that respect. My brother, however, judged that the concern I was under for the loss of my father, must make any additional anxiety on my own account, too heavy a weight on my spirits, for the strongest constitution to support unhurt, and therefore gave me many kind assurances of his generous intentions towards me, and took me home to his house, where I was well received by my sister-in-law, to whom I endeavoured to render myself useful, as well as agreeable.

'In this view, I shewed a readiness to assist her in the economy of her family, and the care of her children; no unacceptable services, as her mean education had rendered her but ill qualified for either; she knew not how to govern her servants with that composure of temper and steadiness of conduct, which commands respect, and therefore had been troubled with their negligence or insolence; and as for her children, she was capable of giving them but little instruction; working tolerably with her needle being the utmost extent of her knowledge. As almost a continual pregnancy gave her an excuse for indolence, I soon found my desire of serving her would bring a burdensome office upon me, for she constituted me house-keeper, and soon after nurse; and to shew me that my services were necessary, lessened the number of her maid servants, frequently saying, "That as her's was an increasing family, she could not afford any other addition but that of children." On the same principle of economy, finding I understood a good deal of cookery, she changed her cook for a girl, who could not perform the easiest things without direction; and referred her to me for the requisite assistance; thereby introducing me into a third office, and that a very laborious one, as my attendance in the kitchen could seldom be dispensed with for the greatest part of the morning.

'I was in no danger of falling into idleness, my time being well filled up. My first business was to dress the children, and get them their breakfasts; I was then to see the same meal prepared for their parents, and myself. The parts of house-keeper and cook would have sufficiently employed the rest of the morning, but that of nurse was added to it; for the three eldest children were generally with me the whole time, to my great interruption, and their danger, as a kitchen is no safe place at that age; and indeed I was forced to keep a very strict attention to save them from scalding, burning, or some other accident of the like nature; but their mother complained they were too noisy for her, which in some degree might be true, considering her frequent indisposition; but was magnified by her knowing no means of assuming gentility but that of appearing sick, which led her to add much pretence to a little reality.

'As it would not have been decent to have reduced me to the appearance of a servant, I was expected to make one at the dinner I had dressed; and therefore was obliged, when we had company, which was frequent, to huddle on my cloaths in the little intervals the office of cook would allow me; and always to take the same opportunities to new dress the children, who were sure to be soon dirtied by the place they inhabited.

'The afternoon seldom brought me more leisure, for I was then to teach the children to read, to walk out with them, mend theirs and the family linen, till it was time to get them their suppers, and put them to bed. Though I had always been used to business, yet my strength was not equal to the fatigue I underwent, and I felt bad effects from it; but I bore them with tolerable content, while my sister seemed well pleased with my services. I did not long enjoy this gratification. As my brother was a great sportsman, while the season continued favourable to field amusements, he spent a very small part of the day in the house, therefore was ignorant of my various avocations; but when frequent interruptions to these entertainments occasioned his living more at home, he perceived how diligently, I may say laboriously, I was employed in his service, and expressed some unwillingness to give me so much trouble; at the same time complimenting me on the manner in which I acquitted myself; observing how much the children were improved by my care, how well his table was ordered, and how quiet his family; asking me, by what art I managed the servants, to make them do their duty so well and so readily, in a country where they were in general so idle and insolent, that it was scarcely possible to bear with them for a quarter of a year together; (for such he imagined the case, because his wife had seldom kept one two months ) and still more unfortunately made me a present of a few guineas, which by that time were become highly necessary; telling me, that the obligations he and his wife had to me deserved an earlier acknowledgment, but he had really till that moment forgot how much occasion I might have for such a supply.

'From the first period of his conversation, my sister began to redden, but the conclusion completely provoked her. She was glad of my services, but so far from chusing to acknowledge herself obliged to me, she was desirous I should think they were but a very small return for the support I received from her and my brother; and without leaving me time to express the pleasure I felt from his approbation, she said with some sharpness, that he was wonderfully tender of me, in thinking I had so much trouble, strong and healthy as I was, in doing what she, with her unfortunate delicacy of constitution, had done for so many years, without exciting in him any of those apprehensions; any more than that great admiration he expressed, as if there was any such great matter in keeping a family in order, when it was once put in a right way; and she who had had all the trouble of regulating it, to be sure, had no merit; no, it was all to be attributed to me, who had only gone on in the way she had planned out for me, a thing any girl of twelve years old might do: and indeed she thought herself very unlucky in being prevented by ill health from doing the whole herself, as a house could never be well managed but by the mistress of it; but her too delicate constitution obliged her to submit to the inconveniences that naturally arise from the want of a mother's and a mistresses eye.

'My brother, who feared as well as loved her, was hurt at finding he had offended so unintentionally; and in his confusion, by way of excusing himself, replied, that he had no thought of drawing any comparison between us, he never entertained the least doubt of her skill in managing her family; what he had said of the advantages arising from my care, only alluded to those things which had before been in the hands of a house-keeper and nurse, by no means to any particulars wherein I might supply her place.

'If I did not feel myself extremely flattered by being told that I excelled two of his menial servants, his answer was not more pleasing to my sister, who did not much like to have it observed that I performed the office of two of them, beside various other things that would not have been expected from persons of their education, as it did not seem quite agreeable to the treatment due to a sister; she therefore dropt some hints how necessary it was when new expences occurred, to retrench in others; complained of the inconvenience of lessening the number of servants, and how hard it was to be forced to undergo it, and yet to be out of pocket, observing that the board of people who eat in the kitchen cost little, and that servants wages were small in comparison of what people might lavish away in presents.

'I felt myself so nettled at these ungenerous hints, that I feared I might not continue mistress of my temper, and therefore thought it advisable to retire. I was never inclined to draw an exact balance between obligations conferred and repaid; a person must be of a sordid temper who can keep an account of debtor and creditor in generosity; but yet I could not refrain from making some little degree of comparison, which shewed me that my services deserved as payment from my brother, what my relationship to him might alone sufficiently entitle me to. I wished to make all the return in my power for what he should be pleased to do for me; but to be made a slave, and yet reproached as a burden, was more than I could well bear. Since I was doomed to do the office of a servant, I only desired to be thought to deserve my wages; and now felt all the bitterness of my situation, which cost me some tears, and many heart-felt pains, that I endeavoured to conceal.

'From the behaviour of my brother and sister at supper, which assembled us about two hours after I had left them, I perceived the conversation had continued after I withdrew; they were both in but indifferent temper; silence and sullenness appeared in her, vexation and fear in him; she treated me with formality, and he with coldness; being afraid, as I guessed, to exasperate her if he shewed any thing like affection to me. It is scarcely possible for any one to be in a more disagreeable situation; my heart had not lost all its resentment; but my indignation for my sister's treatment of me, was not greater than my concern for the uneasiness my brother visibly suffered, of which I was, though innocently on my part, the cause; and I should have found it impossible to conceal my sensations, had I not been employed in mending one of the children's frocks, which gave me an excuse for paying less seeming attention to the company, though in reality they engaged all my thoughts.

'The consequences of this quarrel did not end with the evening. My sister, who had fancied herself lowered in her importance by the merits my brother attributed to me, thought she might raise her dignity in the house without giving herself the trouble of re-assuming the care of it; and for that purpose determined to be more particular in her directions; accordingly from that time she interrupted me in whatever I was doing; if I was dressing the children, she would order me first to hear them read; if, on the contrary, they were reading to me, I must just then make a pye: she could not indeed find more business for me than I had executed before she had taken up this resolution, but by not suffering me to perform it in the same regular method, I lived in a continual hurry, doing all out of season; and seldom being permitted to finish at once the thing I was about, it required double the time, and at last was not so well done. She likewise took occasion to find fault with every performance, to shew her superior judgment; though it frequently failed of the designed effect, as it was generally so causeless that every one saw her motive; and sometimes she erred so totally, as to blame where most commendation was due. She also was fond of contradicting every order my offices obliged me to give the servants; and did all in her power to prevent them or the children from paying me the least respect, or shewing any obedience to my directions; but in these particulars I fortunately did not suffer: the former had enjoyed so much more ease and peace from the time I was made housekeeper than they had done before, that they were, in spight of her endeavours, sufficiently observant, from a fear lest out of disgust I might relinquish my charge; and the most difficult part of my task was to make them properly respectful to her, who they had before held cheap for her ignorance in family affairs, and now despised for her low jealousy of me, which I would not suffer them to imagine I perceived; and by the respect I shewed her, endeavoured to teach them what was necessary on their part.

'I was not less fortunate as to the children. The nurse whom I succeeded was very ill-tempered, and they had suffered a great deal from her, as their mother had left them totally to her care; the comparison therefore between us had rendered me very welcome to them, and they were fonder of me than of their parents. The best obedience springs from love; this they readily paid me, and I could desire no more. They were indeed fine children, both in person and disposition, and I was truly fond of them; they were my best consolation under the various vexations I suffered; and though they increased my business, yet they repaid me by rendering it agreeable. But this was at length made the subject of severe mortifications; my sister grew envious of the pleasure she saw I took in them, and jealous of their affection for me, which her pride considered as an affront to herself, and every mark of regard or tenderness they shewed me, brought severe chidings, and sometimes punishments on them; though seemingly inflicted for other causes, imaginary offences, which her invention suggested as an excuse; and became much more frequent from perceiving that she thereby most sensibly hurt me.

'My abode at my brother's now became very irksome; he, indeed, privately was more generous to me than I wished; but still it was only in presents, which put me in affluence in the state I was in, but afforded me no means of living independent, as the utmost I could save would not have amounted to a sum sufficient to maintain me, even if I lived there to old age. What comfort could affluence yield me while I was deprived of ease and quiet! I was sensible I did great service to my brother and sister in the economy of their family, but this did not recompence them for the uneasiness I innocently occasioned; as her temper would not suffer him to enjoy peace while she was out of humour. The children, no doubt, received improvement from my care, but this part might certainly be more judiciously performed by some other person, more completely qualified, without exposing them to the treatment they received on my account. Thus I saw that I rather troubled, than increased the happiness of those for whom I sacrificed my own; which, after a trial of between three and four years, I represented to my brother, and intreated him to permit me to leave his family; only begging him to secure to me even less than I then received from his generosity; being determined to live on whatsoever sum he should allow me.

"My brother seemed to think my request not unreasonable, and gave me hopes he might grant it; but I found durst come to no resolution without consulting my sister, and she received it less favourably. Some natures take pleasure in making others unhappy; I would not be so uncharitable as to say this was absolutely the case with her, but if it was no part of her motive for chusing to detain me, she had certainly a very great regard for her pecuniary interest, to which she thought my presence was of use. I was kept in suspence above half a year, my brother finding pretences to delay his denial; till at last, my solicitations for an explicit answer grew so importunate, that he told me in very kind and civil terms, he could not part with me; talked of the use I was of to his children and family; and endeavoured, with no small uneasiness and confusion, to varnish over his unkind refusal. I pitied his weakness, by which he was in many respects a sufferer as well as myself, but severely felt the cruelty of this proceeding. It almost drove me into despair; my present situation appeared the more irksome for the hopes I had entertained of being freed from it; and unable to support the thought of a bondage for life, I determined to spend as little upon myself as possible, laying up as great a share as

I could of what my brother gave me; and as soon as I had accumulated the small sum of two hundred pounds, to leave them, and seek a lodging in a cottage in some cheap place, at the hazard of disobliging my brother, and never receiving any farther tokens of his favour.

'I suppose, in the altercations between my brother and sister, he had expressed some dissatisfaction at her treatment of me; for after this time she was much civiller to me before him, but I suffered the more for it in his absence, for she then made herself full amends for the restraint his presence laid upon her; and by accident I discovered that she endeavoured, by every means her malice could suggest, to injure me in his opinion; and though, I believe, she was not able to make any lasting impression on his mind to my disadvantage, yet she frequently succeeded so far as to put him out of temper for a time, and thereby to subject me to new vexations.

'I had passed near seven years in this situation, and had not completed the sum which I considered as the ransom that was to procure my enfranchisement, when I was told of this establishment, then just instituted. I received the account of it with a joy not to be conceived by any one, who has not been as severe a sufferer from dependence. Hope and distress gave me courage: I wrote a full description of my situation to our patronesses, referring them to all the gentlemen and ladies in the neighbourhood for a confirmation of the truth of my representation, and for my character. Herein I ran no hazard, I had the good fortune to be a favourite with our neighbours, and the transactions in neighbouring families are too well known to each other, for my situation to be any secret.

'When the happy signification of my acceptance reached me, I summoned all my courage, and acquainted my brother and sister with my resolution; who were exceedingly enraged at my disgracing them, by entering a charitable foundation. I frankly told them I thought myself a proper object for it; that while I suffered the worst evils that could attend poverty, I did not feel them at all alleviated, by reflecting that my father had enjoyed a good fortune, and my nearest relations were rich. I set out the next morning for this place, without any damp to my joy, but the pain I felt at parting with my nieces, who took leave of me with many tears. As soon as I got here, I wrote to both my brother and sister, in order to pacify them, as I do not love to be at variance with any one, especially with such near relations; in this I succeeded pretty well, and we now correspond on good terms; and my nieces are likewise permitted to keep up an intercourse with me, from which I receive sincere pleasure.

'I have great cause to rejoice that my brother did not accept my former proposal, as the best I could have hoped from it was quiet, accompanied with the dullest solitude; deprived of the gratifications arising from friendship and conversation, which I here enjoy with the addition of every blessing in life; with all things, in short, that can give pleasure to the mind, or mend the heart. Surely few have had equal reason to be grateful.'

## CHAP. II.

Another of the society replied, 'I do not wonder, Mrs. Alton, you feel so much gratitude to our patronesses; to be rescued from the treatment you received from those whose duty it was to promote your happiness, is sufficient to excite it; but as I do not think I have less reason, therefore I will not allow that my sensations fall short of yours. I have indeed little to complain of beside mental sufferings, and such as I fear few in my late situation are exempt from.

'My father was raised to almost the highest dignity in the church; his alliance to some powerful families having gone as far towards procuring him a bishopric, as his own merit; which, however, was such as did honour to those through whose interest he was promoted. But he was preferred too late in life to enjoy it long, or to provide for the independence of his family. His rank required him to live in some degree of dignity, which frustrated his earnest desire of saving fortunes for his children; who at his death, after all his effects were sold and divided, found their whole inheritance amounted to but four hundred pounds each. I was the only daughter, and being rendered by my sex less capable of getting a livelihood than my brothers, was in the most distressed situation, for my father had been able during his life to advance them so far in the world, as to set them above necessity, though they fell far short of affluence.

'My mother had been dead many years, and I found myself in so melancholy a state, that I was glad to accept the invitation of an old intimate of, and relation to our family, and accordingly went to her as soon as our affairs were settled.

'This good lady, Mrs. Smyth by name, professed great regard for me on my own account, as well as on that of my parents, and assured me I should always be welcome to remain with her, which at that time was no small revival to my spirits. She lived in considerable figure, and kept a great deal of company; a circumstance at first not disagreeable, but I afterwards found great inconveniencies arise from it. Mrs. Smyth did not chuse to maintain an useless person in her house, therefore expected me to do every trifling thing that no one else was ready to perform, which really proved no small business, but by no means irksome to me, for I should have obliged her with joy, had she required nothing more difficult from me; but this was not the case, I soon found I had a more odious task to perform, which was that of flatterer; and as I acquitted myself but ill, she would frequently, by opposite questions, reduce me either to give the lie to my own conscience, or put an absolute affront on her vanity. She would on all occasions ask my opinion, an honour which like many others was very burdensome, since her only view was to have her intentions commended; if I expressed sentiments contrary to her's, it excited her indignation, and she would expatiate on the odiousness of a contradicting spirit; hint that conceit and obstinacy never failed making people disagreeable, as they led them to oppose every opinion but their own, and to think none wise but themselves. It would have been to little purpose to have told her, that I was so unwilling to contradict her, that the greatest favour she could do me, was not to ask my opinion; for though belying my sentiments was very painful to me, yet I was not such a knight errant in the cause of truth, as officiously to endeavour to confute any of her errors; I only desired leave to be silent, sensible that no opposition from me could be of any weight. I found the best method was to acquiesce in my condemnation, suffer myself to be declared a lover of contradiction, opiniative, conceited, and various other things, till her resentment had found sufficient vent, and then, as in case of other storms, a calm would perhaps succeed. But I had still harder trials in the same way; if in company any one differed from her in opinion, or in the relation of a fact, she would apply to me to assist her in defending the one, or to corroborate the other; either of which perhaps I could not do without a manifest breach of veracity; yet to have dissented before company, would never have been forgiven me, and I confess I had not courage to do it. Thus I became in time called upon to confirm every error, and bear witness to every blunder she made; though if she had observed me, she would have perceived it was little to her purpose, as the confusion visible in my countenance, when I could not evade giving a direct answer, convicted me of falsehood; which was so obvious to others, that I have seen the greatest part of the company smile at my distress, while, perhaps, only one or two had humanity enough to pity me; and to endeavour my relief by an interruption of which I gladly took advantage. The mean part I acted on these occasions ought justly have rendered me contemptible, if people had not had good nature enough to excuse it by considering how dangerous it was for me to oppose a woman, who could not support the least contradiction even from her superiors.

'Disagreeable as this blind obsequiousness was to me, yet I believe I should have continued with Mrs. Smyth as my surest resource, if I could possibly have afforded the expence; but that I found was not to be defrayed without gradually wasting my very small fortune. She gave me to understand that she expected me to be always well dressed, that my appearance might not disgrace her. I could not avoid going sometimes abroad; she kept no equipage, yet would not suffer me to walk, because it was not proper a young person who lived with her should appear in so ungenteel a light. If her card party was deficient in number, I was required to play, an expence my pocket could not possibly support. I believe her natural disposition, which was by no means ungenerous, would have inclined her to have made these things more easy to me, if she had not been much streightned in circumstances; but vanity led her to spend so very great a part of her fortune, in the articles that raised her figure in the world, that she could scarcely allow herself the necessaries of life, and was really destitute of the conveniencies, which people possessed of not a sixth part of her fortune enjoy: I could not expect that a person, who sacrificed her own ease to vanity, should make it submit to my convenience, therefore had nothing to complain of; yet after having spent one quarter of my pittance, which with the utmost economy had lasted me little more than three years, I saw myself under a necessity of altering my plan of life; though I was at a loss what course to take. In this dilemma I applied to one Mrs. Mayer for her advice, as she was not only a woman of sense, but had shewn me particular attention, and professed no small regard for me; nor do I mean by the word *professed*, to intimate that it was only profession; I could not doubt but I had a good share in her affection, which excited still more than an equal return in me.

'Mrs. Mayer very nobly desired me to perplex myself no farther with the various schemes I had formed, but to come to her; with whom I should find none of the inconveniences that obliged me to leave Mrs. Smyth, as her large income gave her the power of being useful to her friends, which was her favourite pleasure. I felt some reluctance at accepting so plain an offer of pecuniary favours; it was exposing myself to receive obligations for which it would never be in my power to make a proper return. But my affection for Mrs. Mayer inclined me to think no situation could be so agreeable as living with her; I took my heart to task for its reluctance, and considered it as the result of pride: What else could make me unwilling to receive obligations that I could not repay, when by accepting them I should give the highest pleasure to my benefactress. The best return that can be made, (said I to myself) is grateful affection: a sincere and tender attachment may afford her a gratification, which no pecuniary acknowledgement could give to one as rich in generosity as in fortune; pride alone can make me wish to put myself on an equality with her; and in happiness I must be a loser thereby, for what connection can be so delicate as ours; I must always behold her as one to whom I am indebted for a thousand comforts, as my guardian angel, who protects me from various evils, and showers down blessings upon me; every pleasure I enjoy will lead my thoughts to her with tender gratitude. She will look on me as one made happy by her bounty, and feel an additional complacency from the pleasing reflexions she will always be led thereby to make on her laudable beneficence. With this agreeable prospect before me, I told Mrs. Smyth how entirely the smallness of my fortune put it out of my power to continue with her, expressing at the same time the gratitude due for the goodness she had shewn me.

'Mrs. Smyth easily comprehended the justness of my objection, and not being able to remove it, kindly approved my design of leaving her; wishing she had it in her power to make a continuance in her family convenient to me; and assuring me I should always be welcome to her. So kind a behaviour completed the satisfaction with which I went to Mrs. Mayer, who received me in the most generous and affectionate manner, and for some time, every day brought me fresh motives for tender gratitude. But the bounty which I imagined flowed so freely on my first going thither, from her having observed that I really stood in some need of it, became painful by its continuance. What I absolutely wanted I received with pleasure, knowing that she must enjoy a rational satisfaction by the relief she gave me; but in a little time I found myself oppressed with presents, which would have been proper ornaments to a woman of fortune, but were little suitable to my circumstances, unnecessary in my situation, and made me feel myself a burden on her generosity. I endeavoured as much as possible to restrain her hand, but found it more easy to offend her by the attempt, than to render it effectual. She persisted in her too lavish bounty, and insisted in so peremptory a manner on my acceptance, that a refusal would have been an affront.

'This I believe is no common complaint, and, perhaps, will not appear to you a very heavy grievance; at first I thought it so on no other account than as it rendered me more expensive to her than I wished; but in a short time I had additional reasons to lament it. Strong passions rendered her temper various and uncertain, and when she was out of humour, every action, even such as were done out of the most studied desire to please, offended her; on these occasions she would reproach me with ingratitude, and enumerate the favours I had received from her. She would even cast oblique reflexions on me as being mercenary in accepting obligations, which she did not leave me the liberty of refusing. I now found, what I before had no idea of, that a giving hand, and a generous heart, are distinct things; true generosity of mind must be proof even against the most violent starts of ill temper; for though they can awaken the avarice that before lay dormant, yet they cannot make us repine at, or according to the vulgar expression grudge, those bounties which true generosity inclined us to bestow. A generous person sets so small a value on his noblest actions, that he scarcely sees he confers obligations; for in truth generosity does not consist in gifts, but in the estimation we set upon them, tho' we are apt to mistake the fruit for the tree; and yet vanity, a good natured but transient desire to please, and various other motives, frequently produce the same effects. I was one of those who lived in this error, till Mrs. Mayer taught me to refine on the subject, and to distinguish, that of the many who give, few are really generous.

'This was not the only discovery she led me to make; for if I found her ungenerous, I perceived I was proud; I should but ill have enjoyed the comforts of life when accompanied with such humiliating circumstances; they could not have prevented my feeling true gratitude for the bounty I received, but would have rendered the sensation painful; which on the contrary must have been very delightful, had my benefactress's heart been as generous, as her hand was liberal: but to undergo this humiliation for things which I wished not to receive; to be reminded of the great obligations I was under for presents which I accepted with pain, and only from a fear of offending, was very grievous to me, and I frequently thought gave me more uneasiness than poverty could have inflicted.

'I often resolved to leave Mrs. Mayer, and stand no longer indebted for a subsistence to any thing but my own industry; at other times I only determined not to be prevailed with to accept any presents beyond what was absolutely necessary for my proper appearance in her house; but I as constantly found myself unequal to the execution of either; when a calm returned, the kindness of Mrs. Mayer's behaviour banished my resentment; she seemed desirous of my company, and the gratitude I owed her, would not suffer me to resist her inclinations. When she offered me useless presents, I refused to accept them till I saw her grow angry; my spirit then sunk, and cowardice made me take what my heart rejected.

'I had lived above three years in this disagreeable and fluctuating state of mind; too proud to bear humiliation without severe pangs, and yet so enslaved by gratitude and cowardice, that I had not power to free myself from it. When I first heard of this institution, I felt a strong desire to become one of the sisterhood; and made several attempts to bring Mrs. Mayer to approve my applying for admission; but with so little success, that I suppose I might never have attained to this happiness, if she had not been prevailed with to enter into a party, who were going to make the tour of France and Italy. She kindly designed taking me with her, but sensible of the inconveniencies arising from an increase of numbers, and being in no danger of wanting company, I found her better disposed to listen to my proposal, and I was fortunate enough to gain her consent.

'As the truly generous are more ready to give, than the necessitous to ask, no difficulties lie in the way to admission into this house, if the person who applies has preserved a good character in the world; my desire therefore was soon gratified; and gladly I sought refuge here both from distress and insult; though my joy was not entirely complete, till experience had taught me that here I should find a degree of happiness far beyond my hopes, or even my wishes. I expected ease and tranquillity, but I receive likewise every additional pleasure the world affords, from hands which are the most obedient servants of the noblest hearts: hearts which feel themselves obliged to us for giving them leave to make us happy. How pure, and unmixed with any painful sensation, is the gratitude we feel in this place! except that we pay to the supreme Being, no sensation can be so delightful; they differ only in degree, for they are of the like nature. If we have any cause of complaint, it is the too great delicacy of our benefactresses, which makes them sparing of their advice, lest respect for them should induce us to follow it in opposition to our own judgments; and however great the necessity for reproof or admonition, they would not give it without the greatest reluctance.'

## CHAP. III.

'How various are the uneasinesses,' said another of the company, 'that arise from poverty! Those who are born and bred in indigence, it is true, do not feel the variety; the evils it inflicts on them are generally much the same, because they are chiefly corporeal; but in those who unfortunately have been educated in a superior manner, and in their youth placed in a rank which they have not afterwards the power of supporting, the mind is the seat of greatest sufferance; the pride they acquire during their affluence, and a delicacy of sentiment, which, though amiable, is ill suited to the treatment the indigent too often receive, prove continual sources of mortification and anxiety. This is a truth of which I have good reason to be sensible, having experienced it.

'I had the misfortune to lose my mother when I was about twenty two years old, and with her lost my sole dependence. We had for many years lived on a small annuity, bought for her by my father in the mercers company,[3] and the allowance she received as an officer's widow. Being a good economist, she had maintained herself and me neatly and genteelly on this small income, but had not been able to save any thing for my future support, nor had I wished it; my mother was from her youth accustomed to affluence; and to have retired from the acquaintance of all her friends and relations, would have rendered the latter part of her life, which naturally stands in most need of comfort, very melancholy. I knew I had no fortune to expect, and therefore was prepared for the change her death must make in my circumstances; and so well qualified for it, that I had no doubt of being able to maintain myself, and was determined to receive my support only from my own hands. I had seen enough of the fate of humble dependents to think of it with horror, but felt myself very capable of submitting to the vexations of servitude, or the labours of business; and could not doubt, but with the recommendation of friends, I should easily be supplied with the means.

'As soon, therefore, as my affliction for my mother's death was sufficiently calmed, to suffer me to take any measures for my future support, I consulted with my friends on the subject, and declared my resolution of going to service. Some of my relations offered to take me into their families on a genteel footing, as they expressed it; but my choice arose from such long and mature consideration, that it was not easily changed, and I persisted in my purpose, only desiring their good offices, in getting me placed in a worthy family. Their pride was severely mortified by my insisting on this point; they could not bear that a relation of theirs should appear in so mean a station, and strongly represented the disgrace I should bring on myself and family, by such an action. I frankly told them, that I saw it in a very different light; I could never think myself dishonoured by the exertion of an honest industry; since I had not inherited a provision, I thought it my duty to gain one; as nature had given me the power of supplying, in some measure, the deficiencies of fortune, I was certainly required to make a proper use of its gifts, and procure by my industry, a maintenance which my birth seemed to give me reason to expect from inheritance. To prefer a slavish dependence to honest labour, shewed an abject spirit, but to accommodate oneself with courage and resignation to one's circumstances, ought to be esteemed an honourable part.

'If my arguments were just, they were not availing; my relations persisted in their opposition, and I found I had little chance of getting into any tolerable service, while they were determined to frustrate my views. I then took courage to propose their making a collection for me, telling them how happy and obliged I should think myself, if they would give me ten pounds each, and thereby enable me to enter into trade. I imagined they could not hope to provide for a poor relation at a less expence; but whether the sum appeared too great to part with, or the occupation too mean for one of their family, I shall not pretend to say, but I found them as averse to this design as to the other. At length, desirous to remove from the eye of the world, the shame they thought my poverty brought upon them, twenty of my kindred offered to remit me yearly a guinea each, if I would retire into Wales, where I might live easily on that income.

'I had always been accustomed to social, though not gay life, had kept a sufficient portion of good company, and been agreeably received in it. My disposition was well turned to society, and I found no inclination to inhabit a mountain, and disturb the solitude of goats; but I accepted this offer without hesitation, as it was the only independence permitted me; chusing to retire from all the people I loved and esteemed, from every thing that gave me pleasure, and go into a kind of new world, without connexions, without any agreeable expectations, rather than enter into a servile dependence. I should indeed owe my subsistence to my relations, but yet the sum from each was so very small, that the gratitude it demanded from me seemed no very heavy burden.

'Unable to get any satisfactory intelligence about the country I was to inhabit, I set out, at the solicitation of my relations, who were impatient to get me out of town, with an intention to seek for an abode when I came into Wales. The undertaking was somewhat wild, and rather too much for the spirits of one who had suffered so great a change of fortune, and had just taken her leave of every friend; but the love of independence supported me; and when I considered I was flying from all the insults and indignities, to which dependents are exposed, I seemed new animated, every difficulty vanished, my oppressed heart felt lighter, and my grief received some alleviation.

'Never having been used to the country, I had little taste for it, therefore I fixed in a country town; not from any peculiar charms I found in it, but because it was the first place where I had seen a tolerable lodging for the price I could afford to give; and any town appeared less forlorn to me than a country cottage. But I soon learnt that numbers do not always make society. The people were so different from any company I had kept, for the town was a very mean one, their language so uncouth, their manners so rustic, that I could take no pleasure in their conversation. In this vacancy of mind, the charms of the country drew my attention; and as scarcely any part of the world offers more beauties to the eye, I began to find greater pleasure in rural quiet, than in the company of my neighbours; therefore, after having passed a year in my first abode, I retired to a farm-house, which afforded me a better room than is generally to be found in a Welch cottage. This change of habitation grew seasonable, as it was cheaper; for instead of twenty, I received but eighteen guineas the second year, one of the contributors being dead, and another forgetful.

'I believe our taste for every rational pleasure increases by indulgence. Thus at least I found it with my love for the country, of which I grew so fond, that I seldom regretted the want of society. It is true, I sometimes sighed for the pleasures of conversation, longed to communicate my sentiments to an intelligent being, and to gather new lights from some better instructed person than myself; but when I reflected on the tranquillity and liberty I enjoyed, I acquiesced in the solitude which necessarily accompanied it; and would not suffer the absence of higher pleasures, to render me insensible to the gratifications my state allowed me. The farmer at whose house I lodged, had several fine children, from whom I received amusement, while I hope I was not useless to them. The man and his wife were honest, good-natured, and quiet, and as far as their attention had reached, were sensible and judicious. I could not pretend to make them fit company for me, therefore endeavoured to suit myself to their conversation, which could be done only by acquiring some knowledge of their business. Of the good woman therefore, I learnt the management of a dairy, and became a careful nurse to her poultry; with the man I conversed on agriculture, whereon he had never fallen into refined speculations, but was successful in the practical part. I could seldom get books, nor materials for any of the sorts of work which are thought amusing; the pleasures of the early morning hours made me an early riser; my days therefore were of a length that I should have found it difficult to employ, had I not taken this turn. It proved indeed a great resource to me, for I became as interested for my landlord's success as he himself was, and watched the first springing of the corn, or the safe delivery of his pregnant cattle, with equal care. With more activity I joined in the good woman's occupations; and frequently had no small share in the making of cheese and butter. They indulged me in getting a greater variety of poultry, of which I grew very fond, and became a very successful nurse.

'In this retirement, the world did not exhibit to me its gayest side, but I saw it in an amiable light; the harmony of the family I lived in was highly pleasing; their love was, indeed, void of those various delicacies and refinements, which, under a false shew of yielding us exquisite delight, expose us to a variety of real pains; but was plain, simple, and rational, affording them much solid satisfaction, unmixed with fears and anxieties. Their happiness was perhaps as great as this world can bestow, but so free from the glare which dazzles us, that the most envious might have beheld it without envy, as the possessors enjoyed it without intoxication. I had the pleasure of finding I possessed no small share of their honest love; my conformity to a station wherein they perceived I was not born; my attachment to their interests, my readiness to assist them, my care of their children, for whom I as industriously worked as if they had been my own, not having otherwise much employ for my needle, recommended me to their affection; and the good sale of their corn and bullocks, the hatching of a brood of chickens, or the first bringing forth of a litter of pigs, seemed to give them double pleasure, when they communicated it to me; and they would run to me with the utmost impatience to tell the good news.

'In this tranquil state I could contentedly have passed my life, but every year brought a decrease of income. Death deprived me of some of my benefactors, whose successors gave me no reason to believe they knew that the relationship was inherited; and I died in the remembrance of many, who still lived. Thus by a gradual decrease, the sixth year of my abode in Wales I received but six guineas. Notwithstanding the diminution of my allowance, I had hitherto lived upon it, but the sum now was grown too small, and from what I had already experienced, I saw great reason to fear that even this poor supply would soon fail me. I should have been glad to have remained in my cottage, as long as my money would permit, but the impossibility of getting away when that was spent, put me under a necessity of not delaying the measures requisite for my future subsistence. I therefore determined, while I could defray the expences of travelling, to remove to London, and get into the best service I could obtain; which my relations had no title to impede, since they had shewn me how little they were to be depended on.

'With great regret I forsook my cottage, and the pain with which I took leave of my honest friends, was much increased by the concern they shewed on the occasion; but the measure was necessary, and therefore inclination was forced to give way. When I arrived in town, I found my intention opposed by such of my relations as were there; but I was determined to persist in it; and since my own pride did not obstruct my gaining a maintenance, thought I had good right to refuse permitting theirs to starve me. When they perceived my purpose was fixed unalterably, one of them informed me of this institution, and advised me to apply for admission. Each would gladly have given a guinea a year to have concealed from the world the poverty of so near a relation, but since their number was no longer sufficient to support me, they thought I should be less known, consequently less disgrace them, in this retreat than if placed in the metropolis. I was very ready to follow their advice; well aware of the vexations that attend servitude, I had brought myself to submit to the thought of being subject to the caprice, and perhaps ill temper of a mistress, and the irksome conversation of people who too often unite the lowest mind and manners with pride and affectation, as to a state which I could not avoid, but by things still more disagreeable. I considered it as the lesser evil, but still a very great one; and therefore the hope of escaping it gave me no small joy; and as the benevolent are quick in dispensing comfort, my hope was soon turned into certainty; and here I found an asylum from every evil that seemed to threaten me, and together with equal peace and tranquility to that my cottage afforded, enjoy all the best pleasures of society, agreeable conversation, and sincere friendship. I now find that though corn and cattle, dairy and poultry filled my time, rational intercourse can only fill the heart. Instead of that dull sameness of life, wherein nothing but the hatching of a chicken, or the dropping of a calf distinguished one day from another, I here enjoy variety without hurry or confusion. The liberty allowed to every one of chusing her own amusement, and the full provision of all things that can contribute towards it, occasions such variety of employments amongst so large a number, that as any one may without offence prefer solitude to society, so if one chuses to listen to, or to join in music, to work, to walk, to read, or even play at cards, she may always find a party at each, where she will be agreeably received, as we live in general harmony, though we naturally form more intimate connexions with some, than with others.'

END OF THE FIRST VOLUME.

# The History

## of

# Sir George Ellison

~

VOLUME II

# Book III.

~

## Chap. IV.

The pleasure of seeing others happy is so great, that we cannot wonder if Mr. Ellison passed a good deal of time in a society, where every individual enjoyed the felicity of her situation with sensibility and gratitude. But the pleasure he received at Millenium Hall was a little interrupted by a letter from his brother; who acquainting him with several losses he had suffered in trade, informed him of his intention of paying to him immediately the money he had lent him; fearing, that if his bad fortune continued, he might not long have it in his power.

Mr. Ellison was concerned for his brother's bad success, but not in the least disturbed about his own money; he, therefore, in his answer, insisted on not being payed off, encouraging his brother to hope for a turn in his favour. His brother's letter was not unaccompanied with good news, for he received assurances therein of his steward's excellent conduct, and the happiness of his negroes; which was confirmed by Mrs. Reynolds, and Mrs. Ellison. Nothing could yield him higher satisfaction, as it was a thing next his heart; and in the joy these accounts gave him, the probable loss of ten thousand pounds seemed scarcely to deserve his attention; though for his brother's sake he was anxious for his prosperity, but not to so great a degree, as if he had not been blessed with the power of making his circumstances easy, if fortune should deny him success in traffic.

Mr. Ellison was prevailed upon to prolong his stay beyond the time he at first intended; and received so much pleasure from his visit, that he would probably have made it still longer, if he had not considered his return home as a duty. He was sensible, that a person could not do much good, but by regularly abiding in one place; and feared some of the objects of his care might suffer from his too long absence.

When he came home, he had the mortification to find Mr. Blackburn and his son again as much at variance as ever; which grieved him the more, as he thought it might not have happened, had he continued at his own house; and he could scarcely excuse to his conscience a proper care of his health, if another were to be a sufferer thereby. He saw little hope of a reconciliation;

the old gentleman was so disgusted with his son's incorrigible vices, and repeated indiscretions, that he would not listen to an accommodation, which he knew could be of no continuance; nor did he take well Mr. Ellison's arguing what would certainly expose him to new vexations; and, indeed, even the motive which actuated Mr. Ellison could scarcely excuse his earnestness in promoting a reconciliation, that must, by the young man's imprudence, be soon broken, and the old man's peace again disturbed, in the little time he could expect to remain in this world.

In this exertion of benevolence, Mr. Ellison, therefore, was disappointed; but in other particulars, he was gratified to his wish. He had the pleasure of seeing his son and the young Granthams advance fast in their learning, and improve in every respect; and received Mr. and Mrs. Grantham's joyful acquiescence in his desire of sending their daughters to the first school his good friends of Millenium Hall set up at London, for which he equipped them in a proper manner.

Mr. Ellison had not been long returned home, before the season of the year came for his jail-delivery; which he performed with more than common pleasure, as the sum Sir William Ellison put into his hands for that purpose, enabled him to release many more than usual, and to provide better for them after they were set at liberty. The employ was thus rendered extremely delightful to him, being freed from the pain he sometimes felt before, at the necessity he was under of leaving some poor wretches under confinement, for want of a sufficient fund to discharge them; but he now was not only enabled to relieve all, but even extended his tour to two or three more towns than he had hitherto visited.

On his return homewards, he was met by a messenger from Mr. Blackburn, who desired his immediate presence, and for that reason had dispatched a person to meet him on the road. The old gentleman had been seized with a stroke of the palsy, which for two days had deprived him of his speech and senses; and though he recovered them at the end of that term, yet his case did not appear less desperate. The arrival of Mr. Ellison seemed for a little time to give him a new being. He told him, that 'his utmost wish was now gratified: he had enjoyed a long life, wherein he had possessed a sufficient number of blessings to excite his gratitude to Him who had bestowed, and granted him so long an enjoyment of them; yet had suffered too many vexations in the world, not to be willing to leave it: at his age, every day must diminish his satisfactions here; but he had strong hopes, that in the other world, they would be increasing through all eternity. That from the time he recovered to a sense of his danger, he had only wished his life might be prolonged till he came: as he had never met with a man so deserving of his esteem, he had never felt so warm a friendship for any man as for him, and therefore was desirous to see him once more; but he had still a stronger motive for the impatience with which he waited his arrival, and that was to obtain his promise of punctually performing the will, of which he had made him executor.'

'Of that, my excellent and respectable friend,' answered Mr. Ellison, 'entertain not a doubt; you may afflict me by your will, but no one can make me disobey it. I look upon a due observance of the disposition people make in that manner of their affairs, as one of the great duties of society; and so necessary, that even for good purposes, no examples should be set of violating that trust, lest we thereby contribute to render it disregarded. The power of making a will is a valuable privilege; and as it is a right of which no one in our lives can deprive us, so no one after our deaths ought to render it ineffectual. On my obedience to the commands therein contained, you may therefore firmly depend; but give me leave to say, that I hope there is nothing in it that can bring on my friend the imputation of being deficient in placability, in that forgiving temper, which ought to be the constant state of our minds; but most of all in our last moments, when, as we are near approaching that throne where we must all kneel for pardon, we ought more especially to have our hearts filled with the mercy, which we are told will be the measure of that we shall receive.'

'I understand you perfectly, my dear Ellison,' replied Mr. Blackburn; 'I find nothing can restrain your benevolence and generosity, not even the fear of disturbing my last moments, though you have always shewn an ardent care for my happiness and ease. I know not what construction may be put on my will; but believe me, whatever may be thought to imply resentment against my son, is done out of care for him. My fortune would only increase his vices, and add to the distress of his wife and children, who would feel the want his extravagance must bring upon them but more severely, for knowing how far his fortune should set them above it. The larger his scale of expence, the greater debts he would incur; and the heavier would be their sufferings: His fortune is already sufficient to afford them affluence; but his temper would not suffer them to enjoy it, were he possessed of millions. His children will find I have been just; and in the mean time, the person who will come into the present enjoyment, will make the use of it I could wish, by applying it to the relief of virtuous distress instead of squandering it in vice and folly. But no more, I beg, on this subject; it may suffice for our ease on my account, that

I give you my word, I harbour no resentment in my heart against any person whatsoever, but am in real charity with all; and think, with pleasure that in committing those to whom I wish well to your care and friendship, I leave them the greatest blessing I have to bestow.'

Mr. Ellison was extremely affected by the melancholy condition Mr. Blackburn was in, and not less so by the tenderness of his friendship; but he concealed his sensations as much as possible, from a fear of embittering the last moments of his friend, who beheld his approaching dissolution with much more composure and satisfaction, than Mr. Ellison could with his utmost endeavours assume the appearance of. As the fatal moment was continually expected, he sat up with him that night, and found great reason to admire his courage and resignation, whenever his intervals of ease would suffer him to converse: but the next day closed the scene, and the worthy man expired in Mr. Ellison's arms; whose affliction nothing could repress, but the desire of being useful and assisting to his excellent friend, to the last verge of life.

The day following, young Mr. Blackburn, and some other relations and friends being present, the will of the deceased was opened, by which it appeared, that after specifying some legacies to his servants, and particular friends, he had left his whole estate to Mr. Ellison for his life; and at his death, provided the eldest of Mr. Blackburn's sons had reached the age of twenty-eight, it was to go to him. If Mr. Ellison died before that time, another gentleman was nominated to succeed to the estate, till young Blackburn attained that age.

This disposition of affairs gave less offence to the sufferers than may at first be imagined; for after the treatment Mr. Blackburn had received from his son, no person supposed he would ever inherit any part of his fortune; and many feared that even his children would be excluded: he himself had entertained the same apprehensions, but was little concerned about their interests; nor could one much wonder if a man, destitute of true affection for himself, was not very fond of his children. His thoughtless nature was at this time an advantage to him, as it prevented his behaving with the indecency which might otherwise be expected; and he was sensible Mr. Ellison had so industriously endeavoured to cultivate the necessary harmony between him and his father, that he had no title to shew any resentment against him; who, before he left the house, told Mr. Blackburn, 'as, contrary to his own wishes, he was become heir to the greatest part of the family-estate, he hoped he would give him leave to consider himself as the father of the young gentlemen who were in the succession.' In the language of a true blood, Mr. Blackburn gave his consent, and therefore I shall not repeat the terms: the request appeared to him too trifling to deserve a refusal; he well knew he would not take any care of them himself, but if any one else chose to do it, he had no objection. To his dogs and horses he paid much attention and attendance, but children were insignificant things, below his thought; and the kindest appellation they ever received from him, was that of cursed brats.

Mr. Ellison was so quick in the performance of what he had offered, that he sent all the children mourning, and desired their presence at their grandfather's funeral. He remained at the house, not only till that ceremony was performed, but till he had settled every thing relative to the estate, placed proper persons in the house to take care of it, examined into all the repairs that were wanting, discharged the legacies, and put every thing into order.

He would not expressly contradict his friend's will; but was from the first determined to be no gainer by it, at least in the pecuniary way: for the satisfaction which arises from a generous action, must make him in reality a greater gainer, by the power put into his hands. He considered himself only as steward to the family; and purposed keeping a very regular account of the receipts and disbursements. The will was so expressed, as left him at entire liberty, even in regard to repairs; the old gentleman knowing, that no cautions were requisite: and his confidence was well placed. Mr. Ellison determined to keep the house, gardens, and park, in as exact order as ever they had been; both for the sake of the next heir, and the labouring poor of the parish, to whom it furnished some employ. All the charities Mr. Blackburn had bestowed, he thought it his duty to continue, and in some degree increase, in order to compensate the loss the neighbouring poor must suffer, by the death of a person who spent so large an income amongst them. One of the methods he took for that purpose, was to give leave to any of the labourers that pleased, to keep a cow on part of his ground, which he appropriated to that purpose. He easily obtained permission to send to the best schools, all such of Mr. Blackburn's children, of either sex, as were of an age to be taken from their mother's care, who, though a good woman, was so ignorant, that they could obtain no improvement from her; and the company her husband brought home, were very unfit persons for young people to be accustomed to see. These children he entirely maintained. He wished to provide for Mrs. Blackburn's convenience, but that could not be done, except in secret; he therefore prevailed on her to suffer him to remit privately to her an hundred and fifty pounds every quarter; which, with what her husband might spare her, would enable her to discharge their domestic expences, and keep off all debts on that score; and yet if prudently managed, remain unsuspected by him, so very inattentive was he to his affairs. After the discharge of all these articles, whatever surplus of income remained, he determined to lay by, suffering both principal and interest to accumulate for the benefit of the younger children; fully resolved not to appropriate the least part to his own use.

This intention however he concealed within his own breast, till Sir William Ellison pressed him so much on the uses he designed to make of this increase of income, that he could not avoid communicating the plan he had formed. Sir William, according to his usual custom, *wondered* much at his denying himself a share in the inheritance. The care he took of the children, and of Mrs. Blackburn, he approved; but saw no reason for his not enjoying the overplus. He was still more *surprized* at his keeping this intention secret. 'If I denied myself the money,' said he, 'I would at least have the honour of my self-denial.' 'I much question,' answered Mr. Ellison, 'whether I should get any honour by it, were it known; for possibly more might blame, than approve my conduct; but my own conscience, not the opinion of others, ought to be my guide; and by that I am directed in this point. My worthy deceased friend left me his fortune, because he thought I should make a good use of it, in preference to his heir at law, who he knew would make a bad one: herein, I think, he acted laudably. To give a great fortune to a vicious man is like putting a sword or pistol into the hands of a lunatic; the consequences must be pernicious; and therefore the benevolent regard due to mankind in general, forbids our doing either. I could not have possessed so high a place in Mr. Blackburn's esteem, if he had not been well convinced that I would take good care of his grand-children; and his generosity inclined him to think, that the remainder of the income of his estate, was not too high a recompence for the care of them and their fortunes. But I should fall much short of him in generosity, if I was not of a different opinion. My care and trouble will be overpaid, by the pleasure of acquitting some part of the debt of gratitude I owe him for so sincere a friendship; and in the satisfaction arising from doing service to a family, who have the misfortune of being injured by the person whom nature designed for their protector. Thus I best fulfil my friend's intention; for I could no way so well employ the income with which he has intrusted me, as by dedicating it to those, who I have no reason to doubt will deserve it as well, probably much better than myself, and have likewise a kind of natural and legal right to it. But however prevalent these considerations may be with me, to others they may appear so insufficient, as might prevent my receiving the honour you suppose from my conduct. Yet were that honour certain, it would only dispose me to a more inviolable secrecy. Vanity is so natural to the human heart, that, as far as possible, I wish to avoid every thing that can excite it in mine. Where an action may have various consequences, it is very difficult to be sure of our motives, to perform it. If we know we shall obtain praise, it is too probable that the desire of it will have its share in determining us to undertake whatever may produce it. Not that I entirely condemn ambition to be approved; it is inseparable from benevolence: if we love mankind, we must value their good opinion; but though frequently unblamable, it is always dangerous. Vanity grows imperceptibly; and those who would not have it become one of their chief motives to good actions, should often mortify and repress it; and always, when they can, set it aside. While unknown to others, I act according to the dictates of my conscience, my motive can scarcely be wrong; the singleness of my intention delivers me from all scruples. Here my satisfaction is pure and unmixed; my conscience speaks peace to my heart. In a right action that is public, and applauded, my pleasure is rendered imperfect, by a fear lest a desire of approbation might have some share in producing it; or that this approbation, when gained, may by flattering increase my vanity. In one case I enjoy the pleasure reflexion yields me with peace and security; in the other, I am afraid of giving way to it, and scarcely dare reflect; because the satisfaction arising from being applauded, will insinuate itself into my heart. On this account, I own, my reason rejoices when any right thing I do is censured or ridiculed, as frequently you know happens; the potion is a little bitter, but I am sure it is salutary; and the more disagreeable I feel it, the more sensible I am it is necessary. My sensations on this subject are not very acute; but till I arrive at a total indifference, I hope I shall meet with this exercise of my sincerity.'

'Faith, George,' replied Sir William, 'thou art a very provoking fellow. Is it not enough to have made me relinquish at least half a dozen of my most favourite opinions; but when I begin to think myself almost as good, and as ridiculous as thou art, then comes some high-flown, fine-spun notion, that beats to the ground all my self-satisfaction; and I feel myself crawling on the earth, while you seem soaring almost to an imperceptible height above me. Not that I desire to follow you; every thing may be carried too far. Do not imagine that I approve every sentiment I forbear contesting; I shall let all you have said pass at present, and only ask you, why, as you confess the benevolent must feel a regard for the opinions of others, you will not at least acquaint the

Blackburns with your intention, and receive the satisfaction of seeing them grateful and affectionate for the good you design them?'

'Were I not perfectly satisfied,' said Mr. Ellison, 'with the pleasure I receive from a consciousness of acting rightly by them, I might perhaps endeavour to improve it by the means you mention; but in all probability should find my aim unsuccessful. Much more generosity of mind is required to prevent our feeling great obligations burdensome, than is requisite to enable us to confer them on others. I do not think the Blackburns equal to this effort. Instead of loving me as a benefactor, they might look on me as an oppressor, who loaded them with obligations they could not return. They now make themselves easy, by thinking I only do my duty towards them.'

'I should make them see it in another light,' replied the Baronet: 'if I confer favours, I expect the receiver should feel himself obliged to me.'

'Why so?' said Mr. Ellison, 'is not the pleasure of serving others sufficient of itself? can it want any additions from their gratitude? The mutual intercourse of civilities should be public, they harmonize the mind; such debts we incur with pleasure, because we can easily repay them: as tokens of reciprocal regard, they cultivate friendship; but we should receive much greater pleasure from conferring benefits, if we could do it secretly. The person obliged naturally feels a restraint; he does not use the benefit with the same freedom, as if it came to him by inheritance: if we are silent as to his actions, he fears we blame them; if we advise, he thinks we dictate; in proportion as we serve him, we in other respects abridge his liberty. This I confess arises from the want of generosity, too usual even in men who profusely confer obligations: they expect a subserviency of mind in those they have obliged; if in every point they do not exactly correspond with their wishes, they consider them as ungrateful; and what would not be thought a fault in any other, is an offence in them. When this is so often seen, can we be surprized that people feel obligations burdensome? for they fear this consequence, even where they would not find it; and thus are under such restraint, as takes off all the pleasures of communication, and destroys the freedom of friendship, where we should imagine the affections of it would subsist in their fullest force. When, therefore, we can keep ourselves unknown in the benefits we confer, we enjoy the pleasure of seeing the persons relieved from their uneasinesses, the secret satisfaction of knowing we have been the instruments of their happiness, and yet converse with them without constraint: they impart their designs without fearing our censure, ask our opinions with friendly freedom; and we can give our advice without the danger of being thought to command, in presuming on the influence which we may think our generosity ought to give us over their determinations. Unfortunately this cannot always be done; the hand that relieves must necessarily often appear; but when we have the power of concealment, it would be blindness to our own happiness not to take advantage of it. But I have still another reason in this case; I should fear lest by telling them I would receive no part of this great inheritance, they should imagine I secretly blamed my respectable friend for leaving it me, which would be a most unworthy return for his confidence and affection.'

'I see,' said Sir William, 'with all your generosity, you have not enough to suffer me to think myself in the right in my opinion. You first puzzle, and then convince me; the latter part is yet to come: you have confounded my ideas; time and consideration must clear them. The majority of mankind is against you; that is a plea in your favour; for you know I do not love to follow the prejudices of the multitude. I am called an odd fellow, particular, and an humourist; but I am sure I fall far short of you; who have a head filled with such strange notions, as you will find few adopt; some of them indeed I have agreed to, as much from a conviction that the multitude are always in the wrong, as from the force of your arguments; but you must allow me to model them my own way, for I would not be a servile copy of an angel. I shall not think myself any longer my own master, than while I preserve some originality in my character.'

## Chap. V.

The time for the general election of representatives in Parliament drawing near, the esteem wherein Mr. Ellison was held by all the gentlemen in the county, induced them to invite him to declare himself a candidate, with assurances of being elected by unanimous consent.

Mr. Ellison acknowledged himself much obliged to them for so distinguished a testimony of their good opinion, but declined accepting their offer in the genteelest manner he could. Little expecting this disappointment, they were both surprised and mortified; and some of them went so far as to tell him, that his declining so important and useful a trust did not well suit the benevolence and generosity of his temper, which should naturally lead him to embrace an opportunity of becoming one of the legislature, as he might in that capacity have a power of doing more extensive good than by any other means: that of all men living, he was perhaps best qualified to serve his country, as his excellent talents had been always turned towards benefiting mankind;

for by making it his constant application he must better understand the means, and by his spirit and integrity could more effectually execute them.

Mr. Ellison replied, that they much over-rated his abilities, which were in no degree adequate to the business of legislature; in that situation, though integrity might prevent him from doing harm, yet too narrow a capacity would disable him from doing good. In his present sphere of life he hoped he might be useful to some, and therefore was unwilling to lose that power by aiming at greater. 'Once in a century perhaps,' continued he, 'a man may arise whose single voice will have more weight than that of hundreds, who can convince the most obstinately prejudiced, and warm the coldest heart to virtue; but such an one is a prodigy; nature is sparing of such productions: for in him the purest integrity, the firmest resolution, and most extensive capacity must unite. But what can a man of ordinary abilities perform in that situation? He cannot gain authority enough to bring others over to his opinion, but may vainly struggle through life without obtaining one end he aimed at. Let this man confine himself to a private station, and inclination alone is a sufficient qualification to enable him to do good; but from the desire of rising to a more considerable sphere, we are apt to reject that wherein we might laudably acquit ourselves. That I see the extent of my powers I consider as my greatest happiness, as I am thereby admonished to continue in a situation to which I am equal, and wherein I find very full employment both for my time and thoughts; if many who seek admission into the House of Commons, to the ruin of their fortunes and happiness, would reconcile themselves to the same humble lot, it would be far better for the nation, as well as for themselves.

'However, I confess I have another reason for declining the honour you would confer. The manner in which it is offered would indeed save me from the necessity of absolute bribery, and so far I might avoid perjury and the consciousness of having broken a law of the greatest importance to the constitution, and violated the legislative power in order to procure a share in the legislature; but still my constituents, who are obliged to swear they are uninfluenced by mercenary temptations in their choice of me, must many of them be perjured, since to their fear of disobliging their landlords I should owe the votes of the major part; and I cannot see the taking an immediate sum of money, and the continued possession of a farm on which their livelihood depends, in any very different light: in either case the influence is undue; they would not chuse me as the person most likely to serve their country, but as one by voting for whom they should best promote their private interests. Neither would I act the usual part of candidates, and introduce such a course of drunkenness as is generally done to so pernicious a degree, that the people have scarcely time to be reformed before the next election renews the vice. How many persons who before were sober and industrious are corrupted by those seasons of revelry and intoxication? I should feel myself answerable for all the evil that arose from my election; and as I have always beheld with horror the dreadful consequences attending what ought to be the great bulwark of our liberty, and best part of our constitution, I should be inexcusable if I were myself an aggressor, and took advantage of my friends doing for me what I would do for no one, as will appear; for the utmost use I shall make of my fortune at the ensuing election, is to tell my tenants and tradespeople my opinion of the candidates, as many of them may not be able to form a judgment on their different merits, assuring them at the same time, that they are perfectly at liberty to give their votes where they think they are best deserved, and have no resentment to fear from me though they should reject him whom I prefer, except I find they are induced thereto by interested or vicious motives.'

Mr. Ellison's way of thinking appeared very strange to the gentlemen whom he addressed, and they became better reconciled to his refusal when they perceived him, as they thought, so wrong-headed. They smiled at his scruples, and told him he was fit for Utopia; but that as an Englishman he would find he must relax a little of the strictness of his principles. They, in their hearts, however, highly honoured him for the excess of his integrity; and although they felt that his conduct was a tacit reproach to them, yet, so irresistibly amiable is virtue, they esteemed him still more than ever, and wished the kingdom afforded a sufficient number of such men to effect a reformation, and conquer the universal corruption, which even those must censure who comply with it. There are few so depraved as to love dishonesty, though the consequences allure; were the same advantages to attend probity, it could not fail of being preferred: I say the same, for greater do attend it; but as they are not always so immediate nor so flattering to our passions, they are apt to have less influence.

Mr. Ellison acted conformably to his declaration. When the candidates were declared, he left his tenants and neighbours at liberty to vote according to their own opinions, exhorting them to consider it with the seriousness the importance of the affair deserved, and to make conscience their director, and likewise prevailed with them to forbear appearing at any of the drunken feasts on the occasion. This he did not scruple effecting by bribery, sending to each freeholder a larger quantity of provisions and liquor than he could have partaken of, in order to be socially shared in sobriety with his family and neighbours. By this means he preserved them from present debauchery, and all its train of pernicious consequences, and that with satisfaction to themselves. As his dependents dared not accept a bribe, the greatest part of them, ignorant of the different merits of the candidates, followed his judgment, and voted with him; but a few from prejudice in favour of the one, or some private pique to the other, gave their voices in opposition to his, and found the truth of the assurance he had given them; for he shewed not the least disapprobation of their conduct, but respected even their prejudices, sensible that error was consistent with honesty; and that the man who judged wrong, might yet mean right.

As the care he had taken to prevent the corruption of his tenants had not been followed by others, he saw but too much cause to have his opinion confirmed, as to the evils that arise from election-drunkenness; but was most touched with its ill effects on one of a rank superior to those he apprehended in most danger of being hurt by it. Dr. Tunstall, being violent in politics, had exerted himself much at the election, and during the contest acquired such a habit of drinking, and entered into intimacies with so many people who made it their chief pleasure, that the love of it did not cease with the first inducement. The tender regard Mr. Ellison retained for Mrs. Tunstall, made him sensibly afflicted with this misfortune; and she scarcely suffered more at seeing her husband neglect his business, and spend all his time in hunting, or at the table, from which he never rose sober, than Mr. Ellison did at hearing this was his practice. While he thought her happy, he patiently acquiesced in his disappointment; but he could ill bear the doctor should so little regard and render wretched a woman whom he adored, and whose felicity would have been his most pleasing study. He was sensible that distress of circumstances must increase her mortification, at finding to how unworthy an object she had sacrificed all that fortune and the most generous and ardent love could bestow; and as an additional grief, her children must share in her ruin. Though compassion awakened all his tenderness, yet he was but more confirmed in his resolution of avoiding her; the more lively his affection, the more dangerous would the sight of her become to his peace; and he likewise feared that it would be difficult so to regulate his behaviour as to avoid giving her offence. Any appearance of compassion might be looked on as an insult, a gayer manner might wear the air of exultation, and he would have been sensibly mortified if she had unjustly suspected him of the extreme meanness of being glad that she had cause to repent the preference she had given to another.

So far was he from any such sensations, that had it been in his power to regulate her husband's conduct, her happiness would never have received the least interruption; and he endeavoured to remedy all the evils which could be redressed. He represented to the doctor in the most friendly manner the distress which must fall on himself and family if he continued a vice so brutal and odious, and to him particularly pernicious, as it must be attended with the entire loss of his business. He tried every means of touching him, applied to his conscience, his pride, paternal tenderness, his affection for his wife, his own ease; but all he could urge had no effect beyond the present hour. The doctor felt the force of Mr. Ellison's arguments, and at the time purposed to leave off so destructive a practice; but as soon as his noisy companions appeared, his resolution vanished, and every rational intention was drowned in wine.

Mrs. Tunstall's situation was very melancholy. She daily beheld the man she loved in the most disgustful condition; and, when not absolutely intoxicated, the effects of the former night's debauch so stupified and disordered him, that he was not capable of conversation, nor susceptible of affection. During the season for country sports she saw little of him. He went out by break of day; if he dined at home, he was surrounded by companions very unfit for her society, who remained with him till he was in a condition to be carried to bed; if he dined abroad, as was usually the case after a melancholy day, she had the grief to see him brought home at night in the highest degree of intoxication. She bore this change with patience; and though overwhelmed with silent grief, behaved with such constant good humour to him, as must have touched a generous mind, but had no effect on his. He was naturally good-natured, and therefore treated her with civility and some affection; but if she attempted to hint at the decline of their circumstances, and the consequences that must attend it, she found it gave offence, and feared, as his reason was seldom clear, she might by urging what was disagreeable, bring on the only addition that could be made to her distress, a brutality of behaviour. She therefore confined as much as possible within her own breast the poverty she began to feel, and knew must increase; for she had no hope of relief from her father, who she feared would, on any application she could make of that kind, only reproach her with her injudicious choice, and tell her she deserved the consequences of so ill-judged a preference. Her children, from being the joy of her heart, became additional afflictions, as they must partake of all the difficulties which threatened her; and any distress that could fall upon them was sure to wound her in the tenderest part.

Mr. Ellison's humanity was of so quick and lively a kind, that it did not wait to be informed of a person's particular sufferings; from comparing their income with their necessary expences, he knew when they were under any difficulties in point of circumstances. He did not delay therefore till report told him the poverty of the Tunstalls, but from what his own heart represented their situation must be, determined to alleviate in the best manner he could the distresses of the woman whose uneasinesses were his greatest afflictions. To effect it was attended with some difficulty. In any case, delicacy would have deterred him from appearing in it, but in this he thought it particularly necessary to conceal the hand from whence the relief came; especially as he wished to convey it to Mrs. Tunstall, sensible that what fell into her husband's possession would be spent in the indulgence of his favourite vice.

In this dilemma he applied to her father, and intreated permission to convey money to her through his hands, observing that he might insist on her expending it in domestic necessaries, and keeping it secret from her husband, who thought too little on the subject to discover that some foreign aid must enable them to subsist. With no small difficulty he prevailed on the old gentleman to pretend this was his own gift; it contradicted all his former behaviour, and he was unwilling she should believe him so well reconciled to her choice as to endeavour to remedy the ill consequences that had followed it. But Mr. Ellison urged it with an ardor that was irresistible, and obtained a promise of absolute secresy. Yet this method did not entirely answer Mr. Ellison's wishes. Mr. Allin would not suffer him to indulge his generosity to the utmost, prudently representing that Mrs. Tunstall knew his circumstances too well to believe he could spare her so large an annual supply as Mr. Ellison proposed; and therefore by too lavish a bounty he would frustrate his design, as it must give room for suspicion, and she would certainly refuse being supported at his expence. An hundred a year he would undertake to remit to her, but no more; this he observed would keep her above necessity, without being taken notice of by her husband.

Reason required Mr. Ellison's acquiescence, but as he thought the sum insufficient, he endeavoured to add to it by other means. As his house-keeper had kept up an acquaintance with Mrs. Tunstall, he made her observe what cloaths or linen appeared necessary in the family, or any other deficiency of conveniencies; and would order an ample supply to be sent them from London, without any notification of the giver. They sometimes suspected the hand from whence these presents came, but uncertain of the truth, and not knowing how to return them, they were under the convenient necessity of accepting what they would have been sorry to refuse.

Thus Mr. Ellison saved Mrs. Tunstall from uneasiness as far as his power extended, her fears of extreme poverty were banished, and she felt great satisfaction at the proofs she so unexpectedly received of her father's affection; they were indeed accompanied with reproaches and very bitter reflections on the man who with grief she heard blamed, but this she considered as the failing of her father's temper, and would have thought herself ungrateful had she resented what he said, when his actions made her so kind and generous an amends. The doctor found himself free from duns, and therefore more at his ease, but attributed it to his wife's economy; and was thereby confirmed in an opinion he had (with many other of his sex) always entertained, that a family might be kept at a very trifling expence if a woman was a good manager, which he supposed necessity had taught his wife to become. And he would frequently wonder how some of his neighbours could squander away so much money in their family-expences, which with a little care might be brought within so narrow a compass; on these occasions he would pay some compliments to his wife, observing that women could make money go a great way if they pleased; which carried in it a hint of a former failure, in the article that then made the subject of his praise.

## CHAP. VI.

As business had for some years defended Mr. Ellison's heart from any tender impression, so now it served to lessen the uneasiness he would otherwise have received from it, by forcing his thoughts frequently into another train; being engaged so warmly in benevolent pursuits, that he had not often leisure to give way to melancholy ideas. Thus his beneficence received a double reward: beside the satisfactions arising from reflexion, the sense of his private griefs were suspended by his ardor to do good; and while he assiduously endeavoured to render others happy, he enjoyed intervals of peace in his own breast; and Mrs. Tunstall's unfortunate situation would frequently be banished from his mind, by the joy of those he served.

His charitable cares were not confined within this kingdom; his dependents in Jamaica were frequently in his thoughts. He could not bear to think that the term of their happiness should be as uncertain as that of his or Mr. Hammond's life. Though his son had good qualities, and was such as a father might behold with delight, yet he could plainly perceive that the natural violence and imperiousness of his temper was rather restrained than conquered, which made him think with concern of his succeeding to his plantation in Jamaica, though every means was taken to inspire him with a proper sense of his duty to his dependents. Mr. Ellison therefore appointed by will a continuance of the same steward during his life; and secured to him such privileges, that it would not be in the power of his young master to render him uneasy in his office. He also settled such annuities on the slaves then employed on his estate, as would render them in some degree independent, but yet insufficient to enable them to live comfortably without some labour, designing by this moderate provision to leave a spur to their industry, and yet to give them the power (as he enfranchised them) of chusing their own master, as they would not by immediate necessity be obliged to stay with one that should treat them ill. He was sensible that slaves must be had to cultivate the plantation, and consequently there would always be people there subject to bad treatment if the owner was deficient in humanity; but he justly considered that it would not be so severely felt by those accustomed to it, as by such as had been till then used with gentleness and lenity; and by leaving his son a proper sum of ready money to purchase new slaves, he thought he should compensate sufficiently for any diminution he might make in the number of those who he considered as his own private property, persons for whose happiness he was obliged in duty to provide, because it was in his power to do it.

At some parts of the year his house bore a good deal the appearance of a school, for the young Blackburns usually spent great part of their breaking up[4] with him; Miss Granthams did the same, which, added to their brothers and Master Ellison, made a large number, but to him not troublesome company as he was very fond of them, and beside thought his house a properer place for them than their father's, both as his son's tutor took care that they rather gained than lost knowledge by those recesses, and as the Blackburns could learn nothing but vice, and the Granthams, though their parents were honest, sober people, could acquire only pride and vulgarity at home. He loved these children so much, that he received more pleasure from their holidays than they could do. Their undissembled fondness for him, the good dispositions he observed in them, their innocent vivacity and harmless sports, yielded him great satisfaction; and though he gave them all proper indulgence, he kept a strict watch over their behaviour and tempers, and carefully endeavoured to rectify every thing that was amiss. He likewise assigned them a reasonable portion of employment, that they might not think idleness a pleasure by being allowed it in holidays, nor by a long intermission of application be made to feel it more grievous at their return to school; a practice too common, whereby parents frustrate much of the benefit their children might acquire at those seminaries, and render school very disagreeable to them. The only use he saw in holidays was the opportunity they gave the children's friends of watching the progress of their improvement, encouraging it in the best manner they were able, and rectifying the errors they might have acquired, by the company of so many of their own age. The improvement he observed in the young ladies under his care gave him particular pleasure, being far beyond his expectation; for those who have not made children their peculiar study, do not easily imagine how fast they may improve, when under judicious and assiduous instructors. In the delicacy and nobleness of the principles they had acquired, he saw many traces of his amiable friends; and from the knowledge they had gained, he perceived how well their school-mistresses were qualified for their undertaking; and did not doubt, as the young ladies had good natural talents, but in a few years they would be the most accomplished women in the kingdom, without a mixture of the follies too often learnt in childhood, as he found that the first care of their governesses was to eradicate vanity, self-conceit and pride, and that their virtues were still more diligently cultivated than their understandings. Such was the foundation of Mr. Ellison's satisfaction; what the young people's parents received was of a less rational kind. Mrs. Grantham was rejoiced to see her daughters so genteel, and observed that they looked as if their father were now a duke; she could scarcely forbear already stiling them lady Betty, lady Fanny, &c. and brought every deformed or aukward woman of quality into comparison with them, to shew their superior excellence.

Mr. Ellison's house contained also many children of inferior rank; his servants had intermarried, the blacks with blacks, the white servants with  those of their own colour; for though he promoted their marrying, he did not wish an union between those of different complexions, the connection appearing indelicate and almost unnatural. On marriage a small apartment was assigned to each couple; they were continued in their places; but if the wives proved with child, their work was lightened by assistance from the time they grew unfit to perform it: they were suffered to lie-in in the house, and proper attendants were provided; but they were obliged to put the children out to nurse till they began to walk alone; though he thought it so much a mother's duty to suckle her child, and so beneficial to the health of both, that he suffered the children to lie with their mothers, and to be brought to them two or three times in a day to receive their food.[5] When they could walk they were taken into the house, but on proviso that their parents kept them in good order and quiet, that they might not prove a disturbance. He thought that by promoting marriage amongst his servants he kept them sober, and felt great satisfaction from the several little families thus growing up under his protection; but he carefully avoided shewing particular fondness to any one child, however engaging, lest the infant should be hurt by the notion of being a favourite, and ill-will arise among the parents from the jealousy excited by his partiality. As soon as they came to a proper age, his intention was to remove them to the schools he had established for education. By this indulgence to his domestics his house gave one some idea of those of the ancient patriarchs: he seemed as much the father as the master of his family, and received some reward for his humanity in the assiduity and tender attachment of his servants, who were induced both by interest and affection to serve him well; and performed their duty with double satisfaction, as he received their services with expressions of approbation or benignant smiles, not with the sullen silence and supercilious air of those who think the utmost a servant can do is but just his duty, and therefore only sufficient to preserve them from blame. He was sensible, indeed, that what they did was their duty, but when he considered how difficult it is to perform our duties well, how deficient we are in those we ought to pay to our Maker, he saw great merit in such as acquitted themselves of their duty to him; and would have thought himself wanting in a due return, if he had not shewn that he accepted their services with something more than content.

A man who, like Mr. Ellison, can draw so many pleasures from the inexhaustable source of benevolence in his own heart, can never be unhappy whatever misfortunes may befal him; for a season he may feel the oppressions of melancholy, but the joy that arises from doing good will frequently dispel the gloom, and such rays of sober, heart-felt satisfaction break in upon his mind, as will put all sadness to flight. Hitherto Mr. Ellison had felt no grief but what arose from the disappointment of his wishes to obtain Mrs. Tunstall, and the concern for her melancholy situation, which he could alleviate but not remove. He had found means to prevent her being distressed in circumstances, but the pain she must suffer from the odious change in the man who she so tenderly loved and esteemed so highly, was not capable of alleviation. But now a new affliction befel him; Sir William Ellison, for whom he had a real regard, was taken ill of a fever. The distemper at first threatened to prove fatal, but unfortunately nature withstood the danger, and the fever seized his brain, from whence no art could remove it; for Mr. Ellison applied to all of the faculty, particularly famous for their skill in that most calamitous distemper, but it baffled their endeavours, and they declared it their opinion that he was incurably lunatic.

Sir William's death would have given a far less shock to Mr. Ellison; he had borne severer trials with resignation, and would have known how to submit to this, but a human creature deprived of reason is certainly the most melancholy of all objects. He could not behold his friend without the greatest anguish of mind, and yet thought it so much his duty to see him frequently, that no pain that arose from it could make him forbear fulfilling so indispensible an obligation.

As heir at law, the care of Sir William fell to Mr. Ellison, who determined to acquit himself in a manner that should as much as possible alleviate the misfortune to the unhappy sufferer. Several of his friends pressed him to take out a statute of lunacy, which in case Sir William recovered would secure him from all disputes or vexatious scrutiny; exhorting him to consider, that people once afflicted with that distemper seldom regain so perfect a state of mind as not to be liable to prejudices and passions, which render them unfit for the transaction of business, and therefore dangerous to be involved with in any intricate affair.

Mr. Ellison allowed the justness of what they urged, but would not agree to the consequence; saying, 'he had rather subject himself to any inconveniencies, than that his cousin, if he was so fortunate as to recover his senses, should have the mortification of thinking the loss of them had been made public. He did not pretend to keep his condition a secret, which was utterly impossible, but while any eclat had been avoided, the poor man might flatter himself his calamity had not been generally known; a thing much to be wished, as nothing makes a stronger impression on persons recovered from lunacy, than the notion of the world's being informed of their distemper, from whence they feel a sort of shame and reserve that prevents their full enjoyment of their return to reason.'

## CHAP. VII.

Mr. Ellison had an additional motive for declining to take out a statute of lunacy against Sir William. He had no doubt but his friend's inclination had concurred with the law in making him his heir; he had frequently expressed himself to that effect, and both his honour and affection had put it out of dispute. Mr. Ellison was in no danger therefore of being made to account for the revenue of Sir William's estate, which he was determined to spend in every way wherein he found it possible to make it contribute to the unhappy man's amusement, whereas, had the law been to dispose of it, only a moderate sum would have been allowed for the maintenance of the owner, and the rest have been laid up for his heir; and though Mr. Ellison was that person, and would in time have received the benefit of that accumulation, yet was he wholly averse to it, asserting 'that no one had a right to a man's fortune but himself; that it ought to be applied towards contributing to his happiness; and that it would be more just to deprive a vicious or a vain man of part of his possessions, than to deny the whole to the uses of a lunatic, if he was capable of receiving the least share of entertainment from it: his state required every alleviation; a man of sense could be happy with a little, but one deprived of reason must receive his pleasures from externals; and however puerile his amusements might be, he ought to be indulged in them as far as his income extended, while they did not hurt others; that limitation giving him a better right to his puerilities, than the vicious or vain man could plead to a fortune spent in corrupting mankind.'

Mr. Ellison considered his trust in regard to Sir William in so serious a light, that he paid attention to his favourite opinions during his days of reason; and in compliance with what he knew he would have chosen, determined to maintain him in a degree of figure that Mr. Ellison would not have allowed himself. With great care he established him a household. The minister of a neighbouring parish had been seized some time before with the palsy, which had deprived him of the use of his limbs, and greatly impaired his speech. His wife was a very worthy and sensible woman, of great resolution and spirit, tempered with much sweetness of disposition, humanity, and gentleness of manner. She had supported with great fortitude the misfortune that had befallen them, had carefully endeavoured to keep up her husband's spirits, and concealed all she felt on his account and his children's. Though by birth a gentlewoman, and bred up in all the delicacy usual to persons of that rank, she no longer thought of any thing but conforming to their circumstances, and preventing her husband from feeling any inconveniences from the great change his illness had made in them. The living brought them in but fourscore pounds a year; but this income he had much increased by a school, which his ill-health now obliged him to decline, and divide the profits of his living with a curate. Thus reduced to a very small pittance, with a very amiable, but very sickly daughter, of about fifteen years of age, and a son ten years old, this worthy woman parted with her only female domestic, and became at once the nurse and servant of the family. But as her husband was entirely helpless, and too heavy for her and her children to lift, she continued a man-servant, whose business was to wait on her husband, to wheel him about in a chair[6] for exercise and convenience, and to cultivate their garden. With all her economy it would have been impossible for her to have defrayed the expences of sickness, had not Mr. Ellison's bounty reached her, as well as all other persons whose distress was known to him; and he was much pleased with seeing that the first use she made of the money he sent her was to purchase the chair I have mentioned for her husband; an action that gave offence to many, and was termed by them extravagance: 'for such indulgences,' they said, 'were only fit for the rich; surely he might very well have sat always in one place.' Had the indulgence been for herself, Mr. Ellison might have thought it as well omitted, but he was charmed with the tenderness which induced her to provide for her husband's comfort before her own convenience, and considered it as an action (though of a trifling nature) yet of generous delicacy, rather than extravagance.

This was the person Mr. Ellison judged most proper to take care of Sir William and his family; and with pleasure thought he should at the same time rescue her from her troubles. The nobleness of her mind, which appeared in her endeavours to live within her small income, though she had little reason to doubt but Mr. Ellison's customary generosity would enable her to render that task less laborious, was a security against her frustrating any of his intentions, from mercenary views of her own; and her humanity would make her careful to defend Sir William from any harsh treatment. Every virtue for which she was distinguished seemed particularly adapted to the trust he reposed in her; and he esteemed himself peculiarly fortunate in finding one so admirably qualified for the office, who likewise would be greatly benefited by it. As many painful circumstances, however, attended it, he thought it proper she should be well rewarded; for he always proportioned his salaries, not according to the price at which services might be purchased, but at what they deserved. He therefore proposed to her and her husband to relinquish the whole income of his living to the curate, a man of great merit, and newly married to a woman worthy of him, offering to give them an hundred and fifty pounds per annum if they would remove to Sir William's house, where the best apartment should be assigned them, with every convenience for themselves and children, and where they would be at no expence but for their cloaths, provided they would undertake the care and government of the family (of which she should be sole mistress) and study every means of amusing Sir William, and seeing him made as happy as his unfortunate condition would permit. He told them, that as Sir William had always kept a chariot and six, and would have thought he appeared meanly had his equipage been less genteel, he should continue the same, only changing the chariot into a coach, as it might be advisable to have him attended by more than one companion. Of this he observed Mr. Lyne (that was the name of the clergyman) might take advantage to procure to himself both exercise and amusement.

These good people were much delighted with the offer, which not only afforded them plenty and convenience, but gave them the means of saving a provision for their children; for Mrs. Lyne did not doubt laying by at least two thirds of her salary; and they with pleasure consented to relinquish the whole income of their living, for which they were to be made such ample amends. Small preparation was necessary to their removal; and Mr. Ellison had soon the pleasure of receiving their assistance towards the execution of his plan. Till they came he seldom was absent from Sir William, trying every means of amusing him. His endeavours often failed; but at length he found out so many ways of giving him pleasure, as constituted a good deal of variety, and pretty well filled up his time. He perceived that the poor man grew fond of poultry and other creatures, which in some degree had always been his taste; Mr. Ellison therefore collected a great number both of English and foreign poultry, rabbits, Guiney-pigs, birds and squirrels, appointing an old woman whose sole business it should be to take care of them. He indulged Sir William in the ordering of every thing his fancy suggested as conducive to their convenience, and likewise in making alterations in his garden; only when his conceits were very absurd, and such as might create laughter, he contrived to delay the execution, and then easily found means to turn off his thoughts. He was well pleased that Sir William took delight in these alterations; for though he did not improve the beauty of his gardens, yet he provided work for three or four labourers, who constantly attended his orders.

Sir William had been a lover of music; he tried him therefore in that particular, and found, though his judgment was decayed, the taste continued. To gratify it, as he kept him two men servants, he took care to get one who could play well on the French horn, the other tolerably on that instrument, but excelled on the German-flute,[7] and engaged the organist of the adjacent city, with two musicians who played well on the violin, to come over once or twice in a week, as should prove most agreeable to Sir William. Miss Lyne had a very fine voice, though entirely untaught; as it gave pleasure to Sir William, her mother thought it proper to have her cultivate her genius for music, though it would probably prove very useless in any situation wherein she could expect to be placed: the organist's frequent attendance on Sir William, gave her great opportunity of learning on the harpsichord, and when he was not there, the Baronet was very fond of hearing her sing, accompanied by the German-flute.

As Mr. Ellison wished to vary Sir William's amusements as much as possible, in order to keep up his inclination for them all, he desired Mrs. Lyne to indulge him with playing at cards, to which he shewed an inclination, though before his misfortune he was by no means fond of them; and he contrived by presents to make it agreeable to four or five persons in the neighbourhood to be of his party, which secured a set at a very short notice whenever he chose it. These amusements, joined with airing, kept him constantly diverted; and whoever observed him, would have been apt to think reason of less consequence to our happiness than we generally imagine. Mr. Ellison was ridiculed by many for spending so much money in gratifying the whims of a madman, who, it was urged, had no longer any right to his own fortune, being deprived of the understanding which should direct him in the disposal of it; and was thought to defend himself but ill when he replied, that 'he knew no such necessary connection between sense and money, that should make a failure in the first deprive a man of his property; were any such allowed, he imagined the right of possession would be more difficult to ascertain than at present. He acknowledged that insanity of mind was a sufficient reason to take from a man the power of expending his money, because it might render him incapable of laying it out to his own comfort and convenience, but nothing could deprive him of the right of enjoyment; it must always be his, while he had a capacity of receiving either convenience or pleasure from it; nor was it at all to the purpose whether he was amused with Guiney-pigs and rabbits, or hounds and race-horses: if one was more trifling than the other, the consequences proved, at least, that it was not less rational. Sir William's pleasures were perfectly innocent; they not only made some of the inferior parts of the creation happy, but were beneficial to some human beings, and did not give rise to a single evil, nor cause a moment's pain of heart to any one: he should think that man happy who could say as much in defence of the pleasures which he and his friends most eagerly pursued.' If they disapproved Sir William's alterations in his garden, he would leave his defence in that particular 'to the rich citizen, who, in search of retirement, amuses his leisure hours in building a country house in a high road, and admires the air which comes to him loaded with clouds of dust; who places the figure of stern Neptune in a grove of firs, makes Minerva rise with dignity in the midst of his fish-pond, and hides the door of his hogstye with the statue of a Venus. He did not doubt but such a person would shew, by the most convincing arguments, that every man had a right to indulge his own taste, which Sir William had not done in so extraordinary a manner as several worthy gentlemen in the environs of London; with this difference, that the Baronet aimed only at his amusement, and his works could be seen by few; whereas the desire of exciting admiration seemed to be the principal view of the gentlemen hinted at, by their placing their marvellous structures in the most conspicuous places.'[8] He concluded with observing, 'that though society had a right to require every man to be innoxious, it had not the least title to require any man to be wise.'

Some of Mr. Ellison's acquaintance objected to his conduct on motives they thought more prevalent with him; and expressed their surprize, that a man who was so distinguished for charity and generosity should suffer a fortune to be so trifled away, which if dispensed with the same bounty as he did his own, might relieve great numbers of distressed people. Mr. Ellison, to these charitable-minded gentlemen, replied, that 'he had no right to give away another man's money; the same sum as Sir William had for the last year or two of his life set aside for charitable purposes, he still applied to that end, looking upon it as his real and rational choice that it should be so; and he thought it his duty, as far as possible, to make the expences of Sir William's family administer relief where it was most wanted; were he to do more he should not think himself just, and that can be no virtue which has not justice for its foundation. He considered Sir William as possessed of a double right to the enjoyment of his own fortune, first as it solely belonged to him, a legal and natural right; for if it was not his, it was no body's, no other person could justly lay claim to it: his other title was founded in humanity, no one being so true an object of compassion; for, in his opinion, no poverty was so much to be pitied as the poverty of the understanding; a man who falls from the top of fortune's wheel into the lowest indigence, is less wretched than he who by a total deprivation of his senses, is left at the mercy of his own tormenting passions and caprices, and too often subjected to the cruelty of those who, void of humanity, seem to triumph in an understanding which is our greatest shame if ill applied. A poor man may generally by industry or ingenuity relieve his wants, but the miseries of the lunatic are beyond his own power to redress; and custom has made it usual for no one to attempt to alleviate his sufferings.

For his own part, therefore, he thought Sir William's fortune was spent in the most charitable manner possible; and humanity served only to confirm him in the destination of it.'

These censures gave no uneasiness to Mr. Ellison, nor in the least abated the satisfaction he felt in seeing Sir William really happy. Sir William was not passionate by nature, and though from the time he lost his reason his disposition became warmer than was natural to it, yet it was no difficult matter to keep him from any of the violent flights which must make the most painful part of lunacy. By a succession of such amusements as he best liked, he was not only put in good humour, but preserved from dejection and weariness; and Mrs. Lyne accommodated herself so well to the turn of his mind, that he found great pleasure in her company, though he frequently relinquished her conversation to listen to her daughter's singing, which would have been almost his constant employ, had they not been obliged to draw his attention off to other things on account of her health, which was too delicate to admit of such continual exertion of lungs as would have suited his inclination.

Mr. and Mrs. Lyne thought themselves well rewarded for the attention they paid Sir William, by the enjoyment of affluence, and every convenience of life, and the power of providing for their children; Mr. Lyne found his health improve by the exercise which Sir William's equipage enabled him to take, and Mr. Ellison gave them the liberty of sending it for any of their friends when it was not wanted, on condition that they did not suffer company to interfere with their attendance on Sir William, which could not be done without Mr. Ellison's knowledge, as no confidence in them could make him neglect keeping a constant watch over their behaviour in that point, and in his absence his house-keeper and Mr. Green were equally observing. But the share music, the garden, and his creatures took of Sir William's time, left them sufficient leisure to enjoy their friends, who they might entertain as long in the house as they pleased, the entire command of it being allowed them. Mr. Ellison kept beside a very sober young man, who after having received a gentleman's education, was by his father's extravagance in elections reduced at his death to seek his bread, and not having been brought up either to business or profession, nor inheriting enough to set him out in any way of life, had no means left him but entering into service as some gentleman's valet de chambre. Distress soon becomes known to those who are ever ready to relieve it, and Mr. Ellison was very opportunely informed of this young man's situation, just before the beginning of Sir William's illness, the melancholy conclusion of which afforded him the means of providing well for him, and at the same time attaching to Sir William one in whose care he could confide. He allowed him a very handsome salary, treated him, as his birth deserved, like a gentleman, and required nothing from him but to lie in Sir William's chamber, and accompany him whenever he was out of the house, which Mrs. Lyne could not well do, the fatigue being too great for one of her sex. Thus these good people, by relieving each other, made the labour moderate to all; and if they were sometimes weary of their office, their hours of leisure well rewarded them.

## CHAP. VIII.

Had not Sir William's family been settled so much to Mr. Ellison's satisfaction, he would have found his yearly tour for the release of debtors attended with much disquietude; and more especially, as this year it was prolonged beyond the usual time allotted for it, as well as much increased in expence.

After having performed his wonted visitation, he found two hundred pounds of the sum appropriated to that purpose remained in his purse; and unwilling to leave it unemployed, he determined to extend his circle of benevolence by taking in the chief town of the county next to that which generally had been the boundary of his circuit. According to this usual method he got letters of introduction to some of the principal inhabitants, as one travelling through curiosity, and was recommended to a creditable family where he might have a private lodging, the noise of an inn being disagreeable to him. After having been shewn the cathedral, and whatever else was thought worthy of observation in the town, he expressed a desire to see the prison. His taste was thought rather odd, but was readily complied with. He talked with all the prisoners, enquiring into the causes of their confinement, which all were very ready to communicate, except one young man, who answered him with gentleness and even politeness, but in few words, saying, 'that he suffered contentedly the punishment for debt, as his conscience was free from all reproach of extravagance.' Mr. Ellison would not distress him with any farther questions, but his air of dejection, and something peculiarly amiable in his countenance, touched him extremely; and when he had got out of the prison, his first enquiry was concerning him. His conductor replied, that 'the prisoner had great reason to say his conscience did not reproach him with the cause of his being there, since filial piety was the real occasion of it.' Finding Mr. Ellison was curious to know the particulars, he thus proceeded:

'Mr. Maningham, father to this young man, was heir to a very good estate, and married a young lady with an ample fortune; but through extravagance had spent, before his son was of age, all that was not settled on his wife and son, and was beside overwhelmed with debts. Not contented with having ruined himself, he was desirous of bringing his son into the same state, by getting him to resign the settlement on himself; having so far prevailed with Mrs. Maningham, that she had agreed to relinquish her jointure, if her son would make over his title to the estate on which it was charged. She was sensible of the imprudence of this step; but grieved to the heart to see her husband a prisoner in his own house, and not able to purchase the necessaries of life; and moved by his assurances of a more prudent conduct for the future, if once extricated out of the difficulties that then opppressed him, she not only consented to reduce herself to beggary, but joined her endeavours with her husband's, in order to involve their only son in the same distress. The young man, not able to resist their united intreaties, told them, that when those who gave him being desired to make him a beggar, he could not refuse consenting to his own ruin. With youth and health on his side he did not doubt being able to gain a maintenance, and therefore would willingly relinquish his whole inheritance, did the action affect no one but himself; but when he considered his mother must, by his cancelling the settlement, be left totally destitute of support, if she out-lived her husband, he could not think of so unlimited a compliance, though she herself desired it; therefore the most he could do was to give up all except fifty pounds a year, which in case she was the survivor would just afford her bread, though it could not be deemed placing above want one who was born, and had always lived as she had done.

'Young Maningham's consent, with this small reservation, was readily accepted; the settlements were cancelled, the estate sold, and his father's debts paid: but the relief was short, the small remainder was soon spent, and in little more than a year Mr. Maningham was again distressed. Extravagance, however paradoxical it may at first sound, arises from selfishness. The extravagant, for the gratification of their own private inclinations, injure those who should be the most dear to them, are unjust to the traders with whom they deal; and though they most hurt themselves, yet their views are entirely selfish; voluptuousness, vanity, or some favourite vice, makes them blind to their true interest; if they had any feeling for the good of others they would be less prodigal. As this is in fact the case, you cannot wonder that Mr. Maningham, as if he wanted to make the ruin of his son complete, now pressed him to join in a bond for a thousand pounds, in order to supply the present exigence. The young man resisted till a writ for part of that sum was taken out against his father, and then the fear of seeing him confined in a prison conquered his resolution, and he again complied.

'Mr. Maningham did not out-live this fatal transaction above half a year, and by his death his son became solely responsible for the bond; the money was demanded, but nothing was left to pay; on the contrary, other debts were contracted, but those could not be charged to young Maningham's account; however, the bond creditor was implacable, and two years ago threw him into prison. His mother, miserable at the misfortunes she in part brought upon him, (for though she had no share in her husband's extravagance, yet, as I have mentioned, she strongly joined in persuading her son to give up his patrimony) has endeavoured to prevail with him to sell the little remaining estate, very desirous of relinquishing the present possession, but she cannot persuade him to reduce her to beggary; he says, she has suffered too much by his father already, nothing shall tempt him to complete her distress: he can bear his imprisonment with patience while he knows she has some support, and liberty could have no charms for him if purchased with her indigence. He has offered to make over the reversion, but his creditor, flattering himself that filial piety must at length give way, will accept of nothing but present payment. Were not the debt so great, the esteem all who know this excellent young man have for him, would procure his enlargement, as none would refuse to contribute what is in their power; but the sum puts it past hope, and he is probably doomed to spend in this loathsome prison a life which his virtues, his abilities, and education might render useful to the public. All his friends can do for him is by small presents, and lending him books, to make time hang less heavy on his hands.'

This account touched Mr. Ellison deeply. The debt was great; he could not think of anticipating the fund of the ensuing year, and disappointing the hope of some poor wretch, whose sole consolation might at that time be the expectation of his gaol-delivery; and yet he could less bear to leave this worthy man in his melancholy situation, which seemed already to have impaired both his health and his spirits, and in a little time more might affect them irrecoverably. His strong sensations of compassion had obliged him to bind himself down to a rule of never (if possible) exceeding his income, as he must thereby lessen his future power of doing good; but he did not think it right to keep to this too strictly: he had sometimes before exceeded as far as a few hundreds, believing that if by such means he lessened his capital one or two thousand pounds during his life, his son would have no reason to complain, as so large a part of his fortune was gained by his industry; but the greatness of Mr. Maningham's debt gave him some thought, which however determined on the side of benevolence; and finding the excellent character he at first received of him confirmed by numbers, though not without the imputation of folly for having suffered his father to involve him so deeply, he determined to release him; for in his estimation wisdom was but a secondary merit.

Mr. Ellison had no sooner taken his resolution than he returned to the prison, and enquiring for Mr. Maningham, was conducted to him, where he found his mother weeping over him, and again pressing for his consent to give up the estate to his creditor; which he, with the firmest resolution, though expressed in the tenderest manner, was again refusing.

Mr. Ellison appeared so much moved with this scene, that Mrs. Maningham begged him to join his advice to her intreaties, till her son was convinced that in pity to her, and justice to himself, he ought to comply; insisting, that to become the object of parish-relief, would be far less afflicting to her than to see him in that situation, and know she had reduced him to it. The very mention of her being brought to receive the poor pittance of parish bounty, accompanied with all the usual circumstances which must render it insupportable to a woman intitled to, and accustomed to the elegancies of life, overcame Mr. Maningham's fortitude; and in the utmost agonies of spirit he beseeched her, 'not to raise such shocking ideas in his mind, which were alone sufficient to deprive him of reason, and bring a still greater calamity upon him than that she lamented; desiring her to be assured he could neither blame her or himself for what was passed, as the one had been actuated by duty to her husband, the other by duty to his father; if they had carried it too far, the imprudence was alike on both sides, and the motive equally right.'

The eagerness of both these poor people in the contest, together with the affecting nature of it, for some time put it out of Mr. Ellison's power to interrupt them; but at length addressing Mrs. Maningham, he intreated her to compose herself and be comforted, 'for her son should be released from his confinement without the means which must expose her to the distress she solicited. He should no longer remain in that loathsome prison, nor she be deprived of her scanty maintenance.'

The ravishing sound of liberty suspended the grief of these unhappy people; they gazed at Mr. Ellison with astonishment and incredulity. At length Mr. Maningham cried out, 'Is it possible my creditor should relent!' 'I believe not,' replied Mr. Ellison, 'but his demand shall be satisfied. I should think myself as blameable as him, were I to suffer you to languish out your life in this place, when it has pleased Providence to give me such ample power of releasing you. I should not have thus broken in upon your afflictions, and as it were pryed into your sorrows, but with an intention of assuring you they should speedily have an end, and of learning from you where I should address the hard-hearted man, who I suppose thinks himself justified in making you wretched, because his actions are legal. As soon as I have obtained this information I will discharge your debt, and see you restored to your liberty.'

Before Mr. Ellison had quite finished what he was saying, he found Mrs. Maningham at his feet, embracing his knees, and shedding such showers of tears, that her joy could find no utterance in words. The excess of her rapture alarmed him, and raised such apprehensions in her son, as moderated his joy, which he expressed in the strongest and most grateful terms; but yet in a manner so temperate, as shewed in him a natural dignity of mind, which enabled him to receive blessings with moderation, as he had supported misfortunes with fortitude. No small time was taken up in calming Mrs. Maningham; she alternately embraced Mr. Ellison with the most lively raptures of gratitude, and her son with joyful congratulations: her sensations seemed too strong for her reason, and it was with great difficulty they restored her to any tolerable composure of mind. Nor was Mr. Ellison's in a much better state; the delight he felt at the happiness he had communicated was for a considerable time too much for him, and made him sensible the extremes of contraries almost touch each other, and that immoderate joy excites sensations little different from excess of sorrow.

Notwithstanding the interruption given by the various passions with which these three persons were agitated, Mr. Ellison, before he left the prison, gained a full knowledge of Mr. Maningham's affairs, and an address to his creditor, determining not to leave the town till the debt was paid, and the prisoner discharged. Mr. Maningham begged to be permitted to make over to him his small reversion, that Mr. Ellison might enter into possession after the death of his mother, as it was the only acknowledgment in his power, and he thought it very improper he should ever be master of any property while Mr. Ellison was so great a sufferer by his generosity to him; but his benefactor would not listen to this proposal, declaring, that to deprive him of so small a remains of the inheritance to which he was born would damp the satisfaction he now felt in being able to free him from the most bitter part of his distress, and he should think the work but half done till he could find out some means of enabling him to procure a genteel support. When he had got the intelligence he wanted, he retired to put his design in execution with all possible speed; and left Mr. and Mrs. Maningham to congratulate each other with more freedom on this fortunate event, which still appeared to them almost incredible. They had several relations of rank and fortune, who thought they had acquitted themselves nobly by sending some small supplies to the prisoner to alleviate the miseries of his situation, nor had he ever expected more from them; he could never therefore sufficiently admire the mercy of Providence, who by the hand of a stranger, had sent him a deliverance out of all his sufferings. Mrs. Maningham was inclined to think it really miraculous, and that their benefactor was more than human, supporting this supposition by the very uncommon benignity and sweetness of Mr. Ellison's countenance, which she called truly angelic; and indeed, considering him as a man then upwards of forty years of age, the fineness of his person and his beauty were not to be equalled. Mr. Maningham, being less superstitious, looked on him only as the best of men, and felt similar sensations in his own heart, that persuaded him human nature, properly guided and corrected, was capable of rising to the degree of benevolence visible in his benefactor; but wondered at his own astonishing good fortune in falling under the observation of perhaps the only man of the age, in whom the power and inclination to confer such benefits was so happily united.

## CHAP. IX.

The time Mr. Ellison was obliged to pass in this town, in order to finish his transaction with Mr. Maningham's creditor, proved of great service to another unfortunate person. When he dined at his lodgings, where he boarded as well as lodged, he observed that his landlady, after helping him, cut a plate of victuals, and bid the servant carry it to Miss. As he was never curious, but where he saw distress which he hoped he might be able to relieve, he took no notice of this, till one day his landlord asked his wife, 'why she did not persuade Miss to come to dinner, and not to sit always moping in her own room?' adding, that 'as she used to dine with them she might do it still, for he was sure no one could object to Mr. Ellison.' 'I have told her as much,' replied the good woman, 'but she says she is not fit for company; and though we were so good as to bear with her, she cannot expect the same indulgence from every one. But this, I fancy, is not her only reason: I perceive she is much afraid of being seen; she has no doubt some secret reason to avoid being known; she best knows what that is.' 'No bad one I will be sworn,' replied the man, 'she is a lovely, innocent creature, I am sure; I want no better evidence than her countenance and the gentleness of her behaviour.' 'I imagine,' answered his wife, 'half Miss's beauty would be sufficient to clear her from the least suspicion of blame in the opinion of any man in the world. However, I am of your mind, I am convinced she is as good as she is pretty; but had she ever done a wrong thing, I am sure she must before this time have washed away the offence with tears, for I never go into her room but I find the sweet creature weeping; it grieves my very heart to see her, but as she does not chuse to tell the cause, I do not think it right to press to know it: but I find she is not rich, for she has been asking me to-day if there is no plain work[9] put out in this town, for she should be glad to take some in. I told her then she must dry up her tears, for crying and working together would put out her eyes. She replied, nothing would go so far towards mending her spirits as business, if I could procure her any; which I promised to do.'

The sound of distress immediately drew Mr. Ellison's attention; he now grew curious, and asked many questions; but all he could learn was, that the young person they meant, and in appearance a woman of fashion, came to their house to ask for a lodging about a week before he arrived in that town. They found she came down in the London stage,[10] and not making a custom of letting lodgings to any chance comers, they raised some difficulties, and the more on account of her being very handsome, which raised suspicions as to what kind of woman she might be; but the uneasiness she seemed under at meeting with a refusal, the eagerness with which she intreated them to recommend her to some sober family, and her extreme youth, got the better of their scruples, and they agreed both to lodge and board her; of which they had seen no reason to repent, as her behaviour was extremely amiable; but the continual grief with which she seemed oppressed made them melancholy.

Had Mr. Ellison only heard this young woman was more beautiful than Helen, more captivating than Cleopatra, he would not have pressed to see her; but he no sooner learnt she was unhappy, than he intreated his landlady to find means of introducing him to her acquaintance, which she promised, if possible, to contrive. The best method she could imagine she acquainted him with, telling him she would get her into her room on pretence of delivering her some work, and desired him to come in, seemingly by accident, while they were together. This scheme succeeded to their wish; the young lady could not immediately retire without an appearance of affectation, and they sat about half an hour together engaged in general conversation. After this she had no pretence to refuse her presence at meals, as she now was acquainted with Mr. Ellison; nor had she much inclination, the politeness of his behaviour, and the agreeableness of his conversation gave her pleasure; and the happy turn of his countenance, which I have already mentioned, made every one who saw him feel a prejudice in his favour.

She had joined the society but two days, before Mr. Ellison's generosity to Mr. Maningham reached his landlady's ears; for that gentleman's mother felt too lively a gratitude, to be silent on a topic so delightful. This was immediately communicated to the fair lodger; who now rejoiced that accident had forced her into acquaintance with a man so worthy of esteem, though she had then no thought of reaping any benefit from his benevolence. Soon after she had heard the history of this transaction, he entered the parlour, where she was sitting alone at work; and her thoughts being full of it, she expressed her admiration at the account she had just received of his generosity. He replied, that 'if she had really the good opinion of him she expressed, she had it in her power to give him a strong proof of it, which he hoped might be of service to her; for if she believed him worthy of her confidence, and would acquaint him with what seemed to lie so heavy on her spirits, there was nothing he would not do to procure her ease, if it were in his power to effect it.' She did not expect this consequence from her compliment; it a good deal disconcerted her, and she endeavoured to evade a direct answer; but Mr. Ellison renewed the request, and pressed it with so much sincerity and benevolence, that he staggered her resolution of burying the whole in silence; 'he represented the necessity so young a woman was under of having some protector and adviser; yet how difficult a thing it would be for her to find, since envy in her own sex, and the depravity of the other, would make confidents dangerous; assuring her, that she had nothing to fear from him, whose heart was so deeply engaged to one woman, that the most beautiful of the sex could excite no sensations in him but those of cold admiration, though when under misfortunes, their charms might increase his compassion and esteem.'

This unhappy young woman felt the necessity he urged of a protector and adviser, but had not had courage to seek one; Mr. Ellison's behaviour, and so great an instance of his benevolence, disposed her to feel already a confidence in him; he might at least be able to direct her what course to take in order to provide best for herself, and assist her in the means; at least she could fear no ill from a man so truly generous. These reflections joined with his solicitations, determined her to treat him with the frankness he seemed to deserve; and she told him, she would shew, by a full account of herself, the entire confidence she placed in him.

'My father,' said she, 'whose name is Almon, was a man of good fortune, till the gaming-table deprived him of it. At that time he had the character of a man of probity, and the worst that could be alleged against him was, that he was a dupe; but the poverty which our follies brings upon us is a dangerous state; few perhaps have withstood the trials to which it exposes them, at least my father did not; he determined the gaming-table should repair some of the damage it had done him, and with this view joined a set of sharpers, who after having shared in his spoils, willingly admitted him to partake those of the other dupes that should fall in their way. Thus distress corrupted the man whom folly had ruined. My mother was not more afflicted at the loss of their fortune than at the means my father took to relieve the necessities to which he had reduced her and himself; but all she could urge against it was ineffectual, and served only to exasperate him. The company he had engaged in obtained as complete a conquest over his other virtues, as they had gained over his integrity; and my mother soon found that gaming was not his only vice. As he had lost her esteem, I believe she escaped many of the pains of jealousy; for most of the uneasiness I can recollect having seen her suffer, seemed to arise from the melancholy knowledge she had acquired of the general depravity of his mind, and from her fears for me, whose only chance of fortune must depend on the cast of a dye. Her whole care was dedicated to my education; and while she gave me such an one as might suit her best hopes, she endeavoured to prepare and fit me for the worst that could happen; at least the worst that she foresaw. But I had the misfortune to lose this excellent parent before I was quite fifteen years old. My youth did not render me insensible to the loss I herein sustained; but it was greatly heightened by my father's bringing home a woman, who I since learnt he had long kept as a mistress.

'This addition to my grief was too great for my health; the effect it had upon my mind reduced me into a very declining condition, and every day shewed me fresh reasons to lament the dreadful exchange; for this woman assumed the authority of the most absolute parent, and at the same time treated me with all the appearances of aversion, which the general brutality of her manner made more grievous, as it broke forth in the coarsest and lowest expressions. But whatever cause I and the servants had to complain of her tyranny, my father bore his full share, and was so entirely subdued by the violence of her spirit, that he never attempted to resist her, but was as implicitly obedient as if he had been a child. Her ill usage was not all I had to suffer: the company she kept were like herself, and our house became the rendezvous of the lowest and vilest people; sharpers and prostitutes were now to be my

constant companions; and I have since been very thankful that by being remarkably little of my age, and by my very sickly appearance, I so long seemed
unworthy of their notice. My relations invited me to their houses; but as they
would not visit at ours, my father insisted on my refusing their invitation; in
resentment for their absenting themselves from a place, where no person of
character could with propriety appear.

'In this melancholy situation I continued near three years, still declining in health; but youth resisted sickness. I was reduced to a skeleton, and
looked more like a corpse than a living creature, when my father and his mistress determined on going to Tunbridge, where I was to accompany them,
much against my inclination, feeling very sensibly the disgrace of being seen
with so infamous a woman; but I was obliged to comply, and to undergo the
ignominy of appearing publickly among prostitutes. No young person spoke
to me; the men saw no attractions in a walking corpse; and the young women
were obliged, in regard to their reputations, to avoid me. I met indeed with a
few old ladies, who had no daughters or nieces belonging to them, that
seemed to compassionate my situation, and whose kind notice was a great
relief to my spirits; and taking advantage of the liberty they gave me, I attached myself as much to them as possible, but was obliged to great precautions, to prevent my father's mistress from perceiving that I did it to avoid, as
far as lay in my power, being seen with her.

'Either the satisfaction I received from the civility of these good people,
or the waters, did wonders in regard to my health; my worst complaints left
me; and at the conclusion of the season, my pallidness began to give place to
youthful bloom. The good effects were still more visible after I had left the
place about a month; I grew fat, and acquired that air of health which I still
retain; but soon had reason to wish I had preserved my ghastly appearance.

'A young gentleman just come into the possession of a large fortune,
which he seemed in haste to dissipate in gaming and other vices, made some
acquaintance with us at Tunbridge, where he arrived but a week before we
left it; and upon his coming to town visited us. This civility was frequently
renewed, and in a short time I appeared the object of his attentions. This was
seen with pleasure by my father's mistress; and my father shewed no objection
to it. She often represented to me that I was very fortunate in having acquired
so rich a lover, and would enumerate all the pleasures wealth could bestow;
endeavouring to flatter my vanity in every article, and to render it a snare
to me. In a short time this gentleman was seldom out of the house, and
all opportunities were taken to leave us alone. His addresses were tender and

importunate, but accompanied with a familiarity odious to me, and this even before my father and his mistress, who laughed at my anger, and treated my complaints as the dictates of ignorance and folly.

'At length he spoke his views so plainly, that I fled from him in a rage; and while my resentment was in full force, ran to my father, and told him how vile a wretch he received into his house; one whose sole intention was to render his daughter an infamous prostitute, with many other terms as strong, which my anger suggested. These, together with the disappointment my behaviour gave her, put his mistress, who was present, into a violent passion: she asked my father if he would bear to hear her abused in such a manner? that my resentment was affected, but my insolence to her real; that all I had said was only designed to reflect on her; and for that purpose I had taken advantage of the prejudices of fools; for I could not be so silly as to think marriage was any thing more than a bargain of interest; with much profligate stuff to the same purpose. My father took fire, and treated me as roughly as she had done; nor would he pay any attention to the indignity offered me, which seemed by no means to offend him. This not only shocked, but alarmed me; what had I not to fear in a house where every vice seemed licensed, and where even my father would not protect me! The anguish of my mind was inexpressible. A wretch placed on the brink of a precipice, without any visible means of retiring, could not feel greater terrors than those I lived in. I tried to move my father when alone; but he laughed at my distress, and said, that to have gained the affections of a young man who was master of five thousand a year, was indeed a terrible misfortune. When I urged that it certainly was one to be exposed daily to hear that man declare his dishonourable views, and to bear the continual repetition of his odious, because shameful addresses, anger then took the place of contempt, and he forbad my teazing him with my prudish nonsense.

'I could no longer doubt but my father was totally indifferent, in an article which I imagined would most sensibly affect a parent; but I should never have suspected him of any greater degree of depravity, if one of the servants had not opened my eyes. She was sent by my father to let me know my lover was in the dining room waiting for me, and I must go to him directly. So disagreeable a command drew tears from my eyes; and in the bitterness of vexation I cried out, How can he expose me to the addresses of so unworthy a wretch! why must I again see the man, whom but to listen to is infamy! The woman, looking stedfastly at me, said, Are you in earnest, madam, in the reluctance you express? I imagined so rich a lover must be agreeable, especially as he is certainly a handsome man. How, I replied, can *he* be agreeable whose love only seeks my destruction? I can see no beauty in the man who would dishonour me; nor will I any longer endure his insults; a parent's authority cannot justify my disgracing him or myself. I will not stir out of my room while that man is in the house.'

'I pity you from my heart, madam,' said the servant, 'for I fear all resistance will be in vain. I have yet no right to expect your confidence, but I will deserve it, by telling you more than I suppose you know, or perhaps will believe. You may think ill of me for living in this house, but my pocket being reduced very low by a long sickness, I was so glad to take the first service offered me, that I made no inquiry into the character of my mistress; but I had not passed a day in the house before I learnt into what a scrape my impatience had betrayed me. Had I heard as much before I was hired, I certainly should not have come; because the disgrace of such a service will probably be an impediment to my getting a better; however, when I was once entered, I could not resolve to throw myself again out of place, and therefore determined to stay till I could hear of another, and no longer shall I remain here; this I tell you to shew I may not be absolutely undeserving of your credit; and now must inform you, that as I sat at work in my mistresses closet, I overheard her bargaining with your lover for your person. She required him to give her a thousand pounds when he obtained possession of you; he endeavoured to bring her to a more moderate price, but she insisting he complied, and only desired she would entitle herself to the money as soon as possible, for your behaviour made him fear he should not easily succeed. She bad him not despair, she wished it might be quietly brought about, and therefore desired he would double his assiduity, and omit no means of gaining either your affections or your vanity on his side; the latter, she observed, would be most effectual; though she supposed so passionate a lover would rather owe his success to mutual love; that she and my master would on their part do all they could to drive the foolish girl into his arms; but if gentle means avail not, added she, depend on my word, force or stratagem shall make her yours; but you ought to encourage me by some present token of your generosity. He immediately, I suppose to keep her zeal alive, pulled a fine diamond ring (you have seen him wear) from his finger, and put it on hers. Now, said she, I perceive you are worth serving. This, madam, I wished to tell you a month ago, but knew not how you would receive it. Perhaps I am doing your lover service, by shewing you the strength of his passion. But the thousand pounds is a small part of the price he pays, as my master and he generally engage at piquet or hazard after he has made his visit to you; the little attention he then gives to his play, added to the common gamesters arts, draws great sums from him.'

'I was like one thunderstruck with this narration. At first my heart recoiled, and endeavoured to exculpate my father; but recollection convinced me he could not be entirely ignorant of this transaction; terror almost turned my brain, I rose from my chair, and declared I would fly out of the house that instant, but the servant caught hold of me: That, said she, will be to no purpose, you will be seen and brought back; it will only hasten the execution of the diabolical design. Take my advice, madam, compose yourself, appear ignorant of all I have told you; go to your lover, and lull their suspicions asleep by concealing yours, till you can with a better prospect of success make your escape.

'I saw she was right, but to compose my spirits was impossible; I trembled all over, and looked more frighted than the most guilty criminal; however, I promised to obey my father's summons as soon as I was able; but intreated her to watch my return to my chamber, and to come to me, when we might more calmly consider of the best means to escape the snares laid for me.

'I had no sooner said these words than my lover entered, sent by my father, who apprehended from my delay that I should not attend him. He, perceiving I was in tears, and extremely agitated, enquired into the cause, with all the tenderness he could assume, or perhaps he really felt it; but I was too much disgusted to allow him even the merit of pitying me. He intreated to know the cause of my uneasiness, and professed the highest indignation against any one who could occasion me a moment's pain; but all these affectionate expressions ended in an offer to share his fortune, and under his tender protection to be secured from every vexatious circumstance that might now afflict me; little knowing that he was my principal torment, nor did I think it prudent to acquaint him that it was so; but according to the advice the servant had given me, suppressed my resentment as much as I was able, and seemed less offended by his insolent proposal than before, but with equal obstinacy repelled his addresses; and in a shorter time than usual he was summoned to the card-table.

'When my adviser found I was alone, she returned to me, and agreed to let me out of the house as soon as the family was in bed, and conduct me to a stage waggon,[11] which was to set out at three in the morning, observing that the meanness of the vehicle was the best security against my being discovered; and I might leave it for one better suited to me whenever I thought proper. She added, that were she suspected of having any hand in my flight, she should not care, as she had just heard of a place she might have, and should not be sorry to be turned away directly. The thoughts of getting from a house where I was so dangerously circumstanced, gave me so much satisfaction, that I neither foresaw the difficulties to which I was going to be exposed, nor the precautions necessary to alleviate them; but my guide was more prudent, and having sent me to sit with her mistress, packed up all my things that were of any value.

'After supper, my father and his company sat down again to the card-table; my lover insisted on betting with me; my father encouraged him, and, as I was desirous of keeping them in good humour, I complied; he lost, and again challenged me: thus we went on, till I found myself winner of three and twenty guineas, which proved a fortunate circumstance, as I had not quite five in my pocket, too small a sum for setting out with to seek one's fortune; but the tumult of my spirits had prevented my reflecting on that difficulty.

'At twelve o'clock I retired to my chamber, but the company did not break up till two in the morning. No two hours ever seemed longer to me than these, in which I was agitated by a thousand hopes and fears. All the hazards which attended the step I was going to take, now presented themselves to my view, and excited in me apprehensions adequate to the reason I had for them; but the more certain danger by staying in that house, kept up my resolution. Whatever evils could befal me in my flight, might be relieved by time. Industry can conquer poverty, virtue may put slander to silence, but the misfortune which threatened me in the place that ought to have been my asylum from all such dangers, was of a kind never to be redressed; for shame justly incurred can never be wiped off, nor can the blasted reputation be restored; the vicious may return to virtue, but the infamous can never regain the esteem of the world. The various reflexions which occurred to my mind, therefore, during the tedious two hours, instead of staggering me in my purpose, only rendered me more impatient to execute it; and my joy was great, when my deliverer informed me all the family but ourselves were in bed, and she was ready to attend me. I did not make her wait; she took up my bundle, and having stolen out of the house without making any noise, we arrived at the inn she had mentioned to me, just before the waggon set out. I took an affectionate farewel of my guide, who by this action had much endeared herself to me, and mounted my uncouth equipage.

'We had some hours to travel before break of day, therefore I could not immediately discover my companions, but I found I had some. As they were not of a sort accustomed to ceremony, very slight civilities passed between us, and I perceived that most of them were soon asleep. I admired the power of Morpheus,[12] though I had not the happiness of being under his influence, that could conquer the uneasiness of the vehicle, which for want of use appeared very disagreeable to me; but was no just reason for complaint, as it in some measure interrupted a train of reflexions that were certainly far more painful. The return of day dispelled part of my melancholy, and I was well pleased with my fellow travellers, who seemed sober people, but looked at me with surprize, as on one who they thought rather above that method of travelling; for though I had cloathed myself in the worst things I had, and particularly in an old linen gown, yet all together my dress had too much air and smartness in it; but that was unavoidable, for I had not had time to equip myself more properly. As it excited some curiosity, it exposed me to several questions, but by passing myself off for a lady's chamber-maid, I satisfied them pretty well; they a little wondered at my humility, but commended it; and had so often seen people in that situation, wear the air of their superiors as well as their cloaths, that my appearance no longer seemed extraordinary.

'The better to secure me from being discovered, in case any search was made for me, and likewise out of some regard to expence, as I was sensible I should find sufficient occasion for my little fund, I continued to travel in the waggon till I came within one stage of this town, and then got into the stage coach, thinking I should more easily procure a decent lodging if I arrived in that vehicle than in the other.

'I was so fortunate as to prevail with the people of this house to let me a chamber, and have received very kind treatment from them. The forlornness of my situation, my melancholy prospect for the future part of my life, and a more afflicting retrospection, have made an impression on my spirits, I fear never to be removed. The three last years of my life have been wretched; I am thankful to Providence that those which remain are now not likely to be infamous and guilty; but even the sense of this blessing cannot remove my dejection; time may do much; in that my hopes are placed; and being reduced to gain my subsistence, may be an happy circumstance, as employment is the best cure for the griefs of the mind; and necessity is a spur to industry, without which the melancholy are apt to grow indolent. You will not, I imagine, now, Sir, wonder at my backwardness, in telling the occasion of my coming to this place; a father's shame ought as much as possible to be concealed, and you are the only person here, in whom I feel a confidence that can lead me to reveal what makes the bitterest part of my afflictions; for the pains of poverty are small, in comparison to those I suffer when I reflect on the part my unhappy father has acted towards me. You will likewise perceive why I so carefully avoid being seen; for having appeared a good deal in the world, I am in danger of being known.'

Mr. Ellison told Miss Almon, 'he much approved her reserve; for nothing so well became a child as to conceal the failings of her parents, but few, he trusted, had been so severely tried; for the account she had given him had chilled his blood with horror, and shewed such baseness, as must appear incredible to any person who had not observed how one vice serves only as the first step towards iniquity, always leading to many others; an invincible reason for avoiding the least criminal indulgence. The first sin, he observed, is generally committed with reluctance, and followed by compunction; but by repeated wounds, conscience grows callous; and he who trembled at the first wrong step, rising by degrees to the summit of wickedness, commits at last the greatest crimes almost without remorse.'

Mr. Ellison got time, before they were interrupted, to inquire into Miss Almon's intentions concerning her future way of life, wherein he found her entirely undetermined; and proposed that at some other opportunity they should talk over the most advisable course, he being then equally at a loss.

# BOOK IV.

~

## CHAP. I.

The first opportunity Mr. Ellison had of entertaining Miss Almon alone, he asked her, 'If she had any objection to going to Jamaica, where he had a sister-in-law, under whose protection she would be safe; for between the real danger, and her perhaps too strong apprehensions of being known, she would probably be exposed to great inconveniencies in England.'

Miss Almon replied, 'that no person could have less reason to be attached to her native land, than she who had no friend in it on whom she could depend; and in reality she had rather go into another country, than be as it were an alien in her own; therefore if he could put her into a way of gaining a maintenance there, she should embrace it with pleasure; but begged he would not be offended if she took the liberty of telling him, that if he meant she should presume so far on any personal advantages, as to go over with an intention of seeking a husband, which she had heard was often done successfully, she could not accept his offer, as she might probably disappoint his friendly view; for she had always looked on that proceeding as one kind of prostitution, and she was equally determined to avoid all sorts. Both virtue and pride, she thought, forbad making a traffic of her person; and her chance of marrying must be small, as she should certainly not wed a man for whom she had not a real esteem and regard, and she imagined the probability was rather against her being addressed by one for whom she could feel those sensations.'

Mr. Ellison answered, 'that he had too good an opinion of her delicacy, to entertain any such design. He thought she could not fail of having it in her power to marry advantageously, but he should be sorry to see her go to Jamaica on that scheme. His view was what, perhaps, by many young ladies would be thought more affronting, but he believed would prove more agreeable to her.' He then proceeded to say, 'that his brother had two daughters, his wife was a very worthy woman, with an understanding by nature uncommonly good; but having had no opportunity of receiving any education, she was not capable of giving it to her children. He perceived that Miss Almon had had great advantages of that kind, and he did not doubt but she was able to communicate them; he had particularly in conversation discovered that she was mistress of the French language, and the thing that occurred to his thoughts, was, that if she liked to go over to Jamaica, she would be an agreeable friend to his sister, and a most useful instructor of her children; and might depend on having every thing made as easy to her as possible; for his sister would receive any assistance she gave her in regard to her children, as the highest obligation, and think she by no means acquitted herself of the debt by the best pecuniary returns, or the greatest respect with which she could treat her.'

Miss Almon declared, 'that with the utmost joy she accepted his offer; and could never sufficiently acknowledge how much she was obliged to him. She saw that by plain work she could at best gain but a very scanty provision; so poor an one as must reduce her to go into a much cheaper lodging, and consequently associate with very low people. She could not think of applying to any of her relations, as she could not hope for their protection without she told them how greatly she stood in need of it, and she chose to suffer any degree of poverty, rather than represent her father to them in a light still worse than they already beheld him. Were she to attempt service, it must be very difficult for her, unknown to every one; and without recommendation to get a tolerable place; but were she so fortunate, as he observed, her being discovered, or her apprehensions of being so, would render her unhappy. He therefore had found out the only means of relieving her from her cares, and had reconciled her to the thought of accepting favours from his sister, by making her believe she might be useful, which would be her assiduous endeavour; and in the employment, and the change of country and climate, she hoped to drive from her mind almost the remembrance that she ever had a father, or more lively prospects.'

Nothing can give much higher gratification than to see people readily and joyfully enter into our views to serve them. Mr. Ellison was delighted with the pleasure which appeared in Miss Almon's countenance on this occasion, and he completed her satisfaction by letting her know that a ship, the master of which was his old acquaintance, would sail for Jamaica in a fortnight's time. He immediately wrote to this gentleman to provide her with every thing necessary for her voyage, and desired him to employ some female friend in making proper additions to her apparel, of the kind most fit for the country.

Some people lose the merit of their good actions by the ungraceful manner in which they perform them; but Mr. Ellison was not so bad an economist; he obliged more in the manner of conferring a favour, than in the benefit he bestowed; by the latter indeed he engaged the receiver's gratitude, but by the former he gained their affections. He never left a good office imperfect, and therefore determined to conduct Miss Almon to the ship himself, that under his care she might travel with safety and convenience; but delayed it as long as the time would allow, in hopes of finishing Mr. Maningham's affairs before he set out, that he might not be obliged to return to that town again. This he effected to his wish, and had the pleasure of seeing the young man at liberty; but as he considered that if he stopped there he should but in part relieve his distress, he desired he would meet him at his own house at his return from Miss Almon, and give him the pleasure of his company, till they could find out some employment that would procure him an independence. As Mrs. Maningham was very inconveniently lodged, and the town where, in order to be near her son, she had been induced till then to fix, was too expensive, he offered her a very pretty apartment in a neat farm-house he had built on his estate, and begged she would accompany her son in his visit to him, that she might have an opportunity of judging whether his offer was worth her acceptance.

This affair being so successfully concluded, Mr. Ellison conducted Miss Almon to the ship which was to convey her to Jamaica; and having delivered her a letter of the strongest recommendation to Mrs. Ellison, given every order requisite to her best accommodation, and seen the ship set sail, he returned home, where, among the rest that welcomed him on his arrival, he found Mr. and Mrs. Maningham, who came the day before. As Mr. Ellison felt a kind of paternal affection for all his dependents, a return to his own house was always a season of joy. The object of his tenderest sensations was his son, who first received his fondest caresses; his kind notice then extended through all his family; the little infants of his meanest domestics were brought to welcome him home with smiles, if their tongues were not yet able to lisp their joy, and were all received with tokens of affection. Sir William's family had their share in this intercourse of satisfaction, and all the poorer sort of neighbours, who were below the ceremonies which gentility imposes, flocked to his house with inquiries after his health, and received their answer in the most pleasing manner from himself. The joy that sat on every countenance on these occasions, could not fail imparting correspondent sensations in Mr. Ellison, but this time he received hopes of still higher pleasure, being informed that Dr. Tunstall was dangerously ill of a fever, occasioned by a succession of entertainments, at each of which he had drank to excess.

This news immediately gave rise to some hopes in Mr. Ellison's breast, which he endeavoured to suppress; and took his heart severely to task for its inhumanity in feeling pleasing emotions, from any circumstance that was calamitous to another. He turned his thoughts as much as he could from the flattering side of this event, and with sincerity lamented the fate of a man, who was likely to be so soon sent into eternity, by a vice which rendered him unfit for the judgment to which it hurried him. He considered likewise Mrs. Tunstall as then in a most melancholy situation. It was natural to suppose her affection for the Doctor must be greatly abated; but at such a time the faults of a friend are forgotten, and the vice which has brought with it so heavy a punishment, is diminished by the voice of compassion into a mere unhappy failing; the sufferer is no longer blamed, tender pity takes the place of censure, and remembrance represents nothing to the mind but his virtues: when the first violence of grief is over, the memory becomes more impartial, and recollection then administers consolation. But Mrs. Tunstall's grief, though probably excessive only for a season, touched Mr. Ellison nearly; yet he thought it not proper to enquire in person after her, but sought his information from her father, by whom he conveyed some supply for the necessary expences of sickness, which could not fail to be well received, as she believed it the gift of paternal bounty.

The accounts of Dr. Tunstall's health grew daily worse, and Mr. Ellison found, that notwithstanding his warmest endeavours to suppress sensations he thought ungenerous and inhuman, yet his heart would by no means qualify him for chief mourner; joy and sorrow are generally equally disobedient to our commands, they will neither come nor go at our bidding, though we may conceal, and in some degree restrain their emotions. But we are apt to endeavour assiduously to deceive ourselves. As Mr. Ellison did not approve his sensations on this occasion, he wished to hide them from himself; but nature would exert her power, and frequently make him feel that generosity and reason have their bounds, and whatever pains he might take to extend their sway, nature could not be entirely enslaved; like the generous subjects of a free country, she may be governed by laws, and influenced by wisdom, but she will not submit implicitly to arbitrary rule; and he was reduced to sigh over the weakness of his virtue, which he found was not strong enough to conquer the selfishness that made him hear with secret pleasure that Dr. Tunstall was given over, who in a few days after died.

Had Mr. Ellison obeyed the impulse of his heart, he would have flown to the disconsolate widow, and endeavoured, by all the tender sensibilities that can spring from friendship, to have soothed her grief; but he feared such a conduct might appear scarcely decent in one whose sentiments were so well known; and while he acted only as a friend, her reputation might be wounded by being supposed so soon to receive the assiduities of a lover, and her delicacy offended by any marks of regard which might bear the appearance of so early a renewal of his former addresses. These considerations made him forbear visiting her; and the pleasure that must arise from the revival of his hopes, might well enable him to support patiently the mortification. Not that his hopes were of the most flattering kind. Mrs. Tunstall being left with only the fortune Mr. Ellison had given her, to provide for herself and three young children, he had great reason to suppose, that when decency would permit, she might accept a hand that would make her mistress of large possessions: his conduct too had been such as might have inspired her with an esteem for him, and therefore from inclination, as much as from interest, she might be induced to marry him; but these were neither of them motives that could content a lover of delicacy. Mr. Ellison's passion had suffered no diminution by his former disappointment; he still loved Mrs. Tunstall to excess; and was sensible that if her heart made him no return beyond esteem and gratitude, however satisfied his reason might be, his tenderness would be severely mortified. An ardent lover is apt to be even capriciously delicate, and requiring an equal return of passion, can find nothing but disappointment in the sober, rational affection of one unactuated by the same delirium. These considerations rendered Mr. Ellison's hopes less intoxicating than was necessary for his content; he, who in other cases thought the pleasure of conferring obligations so great, that no gratitude from the receiver was wanting to heighten it, on the present occasion felt, that however delightful it might be to place Mrs. Tunstall in affluence and ease, yet his happiness must be very imperfect if she did not in return yield him the tenderest affections of her heart. In these delicate fears, and lover-like scruples, Mr. Ellison is likely to continue some time, and therefore to him we will leave them for the present, and only observe, that he doomed himself to abstain from her sight for the first half year of her widowhood; an instance of great self-denial, and done more from an apprehension of offending her delicacy (for he knew it was impossible for him to conceal his love under the mask of friendship or still colder civility) than to avoid exciting the tittle-tattle of the neighbourhood, or the censure of the malicious.

About this time Mr. Ellison received a pleasure which he had no pretence to reproach himself for being sensible of: a letter from his brother informed him that fortune was become more propitious, and he now succeeded in his merchandize even beyond his hopes, and was equally fortunate in every other particular; the virtues of his amiable wife, and the delight he took in his lovely children, rendering his domestic life a constant scene of felicity.

## Chap. II.

With Mr. James Ellison's letter Mr. Ellison received one from his steward, in answer to a scheme he had proposed to his consideration, for establishing a school at Port-Royal. Mr. Ellison was concerned to see the disadvantages the West-Indians laboured under in regard to education. There was then no tolerable school in the whole island of Jamaica, except those he had instituted for his slaves, and they were of a sort too low for the heirs to large fortunes, who ought to learn more languages than their own, and not confine their knowledge to the narrow bounds which suit those born to a servile state. The sending their sons into England for education, was subject to some inconveniencies; the unwillingness a parent must naturally feel to part with a child to so great a distance, occasioned its being generally too long delayed: then when in England, being removed from parental care and authority, they were too apt to neglect their studies, or what was still worse, to be seduced into vice and extravagance. Beside, the expence of sending them over for education, was too great for those who had not already made their fortunes; whereby some, who became at length the richest men in the island, were destitute of all literary improvement.

As Mr. Ellison was ever endeavouring to do good, he had formed a plan for a school, and desired Mr. Hammond to sound the inclination of the inhabitants, in order to learn whether, if he could meet with a person properly qualified to execute it, he might hope for encouragement proportioned to his merit. This had been done with success; and his steward informed him that several gentlemen had promised to commit their sons to the care of any one, who brought an assurance from him of being well qualified for the trust. They might indeed safely enter into this engagement, for Mr. Ellison was much more delicate in the choice of a school-master, than they would have judged necessary. A man able to teach the common branches of learning, and whose conduct was not flagrantly immoral, was in little danger of not appearing to them sufficiently qualified; but Mr. Ellison's view would have been but ill answered, if he had not found one as capable of instructing his pupils in virtue as in learning; one whose heart would warmly enter into the importance of the charge, and animate him in the pursuit of the measures his understanding should suggest to him as most effectual; such as were the result of his own reason, and careful observation of the various tempers of his pupils; properly varied and adapted to their several dispositions, and not regulated by custom, and those rules which are indiscriminately applied to all children, though possibly rendered by their different tempers as hurtful to some as useful to others.

Common pedagogues are easily found, but such a man as Mr. Ellison required seemed to promise a long and difficult search; and probably might have proved so, had not Mr. Maningham fallen within his notice. He had invited that gentleman to his house, as much with a design of discovering what way of life was most suitable to his inclination and genius, as to enable him to live with ease and comfort, till he could be provided with some profitable employment. He soon found him a man who had made good use of a liberal education, a master of the Greek and Latin tongues, and well read in polite literature. His judgment excellent, his understanding solid and grave, his temper calm, but firm; and the whole course of his past life joined with all that could be gathered from his conversation, to convince Mr. Ellison that he was uncommonly strict and pure in religion and virtue. He immediately shewed an inclination to employ his leisure in the assistance of Mr. Green, and seemed to find a charm in the business of education, which induced Mr. Ellison to mention his design of establishing a school in Jamaica: but as he always feared to propose any thing of importance to those who were under considerable obligations to him, lest they should acquiesce more out of compliance or grateful submission, than from inclination, he only spoke of it in discourse as if he had no particular view in mentioning it. Mr. Maningham at the time merely approved his design; but enquired into the particulars of his plan, with a degree of curiosity which shewed it a good deal engaged his attention. The next day he led Mr. Ellison into the same subject, and then expressed a wish that he were capable of the office, as it was an employment he should like, and in which he might expect more speedy success than in any other.

Mr. Ellison's desire was now fully gratified; he replied, that 'he could not have hoped to meet with a person so well qualified, and had wished it might be agreeable to him; but had forborn to propose it, fearing to influence him in an affair wherein he was desirous he should act only from inclination; since that so happily coincided with his wishes, he assured him he would joyfully defray all the expences of his voyage and first setting out, and secure to him a very good income, till the number of his scholars made any other assistance unnecessary.'

Mr. Maningham, who had been much at a loss what way of life to embrace, which at his age, and destitute of fortune, was a difficult point to determine, felt his mind much at ease on seeing this dilemma removed. The change of country seemed desireable to one in desperate circumstances; and he depended more on his heart than his understanding, for rendering him fit for the office; to the rectitude of the former he could be no stranger, though of the excellence of the latter he was less convinced than any who conversed with him; but he thought a common share of judgment and good sense, under the direction of a heart that is desirous of acquitting itself to the very best of its power, might enable a man of sufficient learning to do his duty successfully in the education of youth. But when he acquainted his mother with his intention, she was shocked with the apprehension of losing so soon a son, who she seemed to have but just recovered; for while he lay in prison, he was an object of pain, rather than of pleasure to her. After a little reflection, a means of preventing this evil occurred, which was no other than accompanying him; and she trusted, that while she was thus gratifying her fondness for him, she might be of some use, as in a school female care is a necessary addition to the instructions of the master. She acquainted Mr. Ellison with her desire, who much approved it; and Mr. Maningham now prepared for his journey with double pleasure, all his attachment to England being broken by carrying his mother with him, though he was not void of apprehensions lest the climate might disagree with her: but she had no such fears; she thought nothing amiss could happen while she was with her son; to be parted from whom seemed now the only evil that could befal her; and when secured from that misfortune, neither sea nor climate appeared to her accompanied with any horrors.

Mr. Ellison took upon himself the care of providing them with every thing necessary; and as he thought Mr. Maningham might possibly find it difficult to procure proper books there, he bought him all that could be useful in his school; and before he parted with them they were possessed of every convenience. He likewise undertook to remit Mrs. Maningham's jointure regularly. With hearts overflowing with gratitude they took leave of their benefactor; and though they could not bid him adieu without being deeply touched, yet they found great consolation in the warm hopes of being more favoured by fortune in the new world they were going to explore, than they had been in that they left. Their kindred stood in no great need of comfort, for few people grieve at the removal of poor relations, who seem to have a demand upon them, of which they have not generosity to acquit themselves, even to the approbation of their own hearts, though perhaps they are not destitute of regard; but a strong affection is requisite to make the generality of people prefer the ease of others to their own convenience. Mr. and Mrs. Maningham, however, visited such of their relations as had taken any notice of them in their distress, who all approved their undertaking, and were lavish of good wishes for their success; a bounty which neither impoverishes the giver, nor enriches the receiver. Some, indeed, added small presents to their good wishes, while the richer sort could scarcely forgive Mr. Ellison a generosity that bore a kind of reproach to them, and envied him an action which they had not the virtue to perform, though it was so much more incumbent upon them. But if they reproached themselves, Mr. Maningham did not join with their consciences;[1] he had that true generosity of mind, which leads the possessor to do every good to others, but to expect little from them. For we much mistake when we imagine that those who are the readiest to confer benefits, are likewise the most inclined to expect them; the same generosity which disposes them to serve others, suggests excuses for the less liberal, and by making them think lightly of their own rights, and indulgently of other peoples failings, their expectations are small; and when those are disappointed, resentment does not aggravate the injury.

Mr. Ellison had desired Mr. Maningham to take over one or two assistants with him, as he little doubted but he would soon have more pupils than he could properly attend, and engaged to pay them the salaries he should agree upon, till he found himself able to do it; and these were not to be very small, as it could not be expected that persons properly qualified would hazard their health, and sacrifice many satisfactions by changing their climate and country without a valuable consideration. As this article was involving his benefactor in still greater expence, Mr. Maningham would take but one assistant; saying it would be time enough to send for another, when he was himself able to pay his stipend; and he was so fortunate as to meet with a very proper person to share the trust he was preparing to take upon him.

Mr. Ellison endeavoured to alleviate his impatience to visit Mrs. Tunstall by a redoubled attention to all the objects of his benevolence, finding that nothing so well enabled him to abstain from the gratification of his own inclinations as relieving the distresses of others; for while he could dispense happiness, or even ease, no private mortification could afflict him: but though he lessened the sense of this sacrifice to decorum, he could not extinguish it; the terms he had prescribed himself to abstain from seeing the object of his constant affection appeared tedious to him; and he would have been apt to join in the frequent wish of more common lovers for the power of annihilating time,[2] had he considered its uses only in regard to himself; but in the light he saw it, he durst not wish it to pass more swiftly, except he could have more quickly filled it with such actions as would prove he had not squandered it; but with a joy that excluded his usual reflections at the completing any particular period, (reflections on the method he had employed it, and how improved it for the best uses for which it was given) he saw the half year expire; and desired Mr. Allin to accompany him in his first visit to Mrs. Tunstall.

He had judged right in taking a companion; for the agitation of his spirits at seeing the woman he so tenderly loved, and seeing her, if possible, more beautiful than ever, was so strong, that lost in the pleasure of gazing at her, he was for a long time incapable of conversing. The mournful garb of her and her children[3] gave them an appearance of distress, which made him behold them with additional tenderness; and an air of melancholy that her endeavours could not conceal, for as she had been truly afflicted, she had felt no desire of giving any outward signs of it, touched him extremely. A dead rival is no formidable object to the tenderest lover. Mr. Ellison was rather pleased to see that Mrs. Tunstall was not insensible to the loss of a man, whom she had once loved to excess, though his conduct had rendered him unworthy of her. He did not think the affections of a heart he wished to gain could be too tender.

Mrs. Tunstall was less embarrassed; she had reason to believe Mr. Ellison did not see her with indifference; the care with which he had so long avoided her sufficiently proved it; but his sensibility gave her no pain, as she felt for him the most perfect esteem and gratitude, and thereby she thought was acquited towards him; and had no cause to reproach herself for not making a sufficient return to his sentiments. She did not imagine, whatever remaining partiality he might have for her, that he could entertain the least design of renewing his addresses to a woman, who, by a refusal of his hand, had shewn she did not deserve it, and one too who was now encumbered with children; and, she supposed, much altered, by the years of care and vexation which she had passed since he had seen her. Prepossessed with this opinion, her mind was wholly at liberty, and she received him with the regard due to his virtues, and the gratitude she felt for the man, to whom she owed all that she and her children could call their own; but at the same time, with the ease of one who foresaw no consequences from a visit that in civility was her due, and which she hoped would be the first step towards a sincere friendship between them; so far she imagined the share she still possessed of his regard might operate with him; and her heart was entirely ready to perform its part in that kind of attachment.

The easy frankness of her behaviour conquered Mr. Ellison's constraint before the end of his visit; he saw she had no views, nor suspected him of any; and pleased that his sentiments were unknown, he followed her example, and fell into easy and friendly conversation. But as he was reduced to conceal his tenderness for the mother, he made himself what amends he could by caressing the children; whose beauty recommended them to his notice, and could not escape it, as they bore a very strong resemblance to Mrs. Tunstall.

Mr. Ellison frequently repeated his visits, and found all his care was necessary to avoid suffering his thoughts to be too much engaged by this lovely woman. The only bounds he wished to prescribe to his affection were such as would prevent its interfering with his duties; had the joy he received from her company, or the pleasure he felt in thinking of her, and in indulging his imagination in fancied scenes of future happiness, delayed the performance of one benevolent action, he would have thought he no longer deserved her. He did not suffer the critical situation his heart was then in to prevent his yearly benevolent excursion, nor to make him negligent in his enquiry into the merits and wants of the various prisoners who were candidates for his bounty; on the contrary, the delicacy of his virtue, making him fear the desire of returning into her neighbourhood might, imperceptibly to himself, have some influence, he gave rather more than common care to the due execution of his undertaking, and would not suffer himself to make all the dispatch he might easily have done.

## CHAP. III.

The preference Mr. Ellison often gave his duties, to the pleasures arising from Mrs. Tunstall's society, continued her in the opinion of his having no view beyond the enjoyment of her friendship; till the expiration of the first year of her widowhood, during which he had condemned himself to absolute silence concerning the situation of his heart; but having given so much time to worldly forms, he was determined no longer to delay what was due to himself, after having fulfilled all that decorum could possibly exact; he, therefore, declared frankly to her, how little alteration time had made in his affection, and intreated she would give him leave to hope, that she would listen to his addresses with more complacency than when he first made them.

Mrs. Tunstall was somewhat surprized at Mr. Ellison's constancy, and not a little puzzled in what manner to answer him; but as he insisted on a reply, she stammered out some expressions of the honour he did her, the greatness of the advantages he thus offered her, and her high sense of the obligations she lay under, which must incline her to comply with any request of his.

This sort of cold reception was ill-suited to the ardor of Mr. Ellison's passion; he therefore begged that politeness, gratitude, and above all, interest, might be out of the question. He had too good an opinion of her to believe she would marry for sordid views, and therefore trusted he had nothing of that kind to fear, but must likewise beseech her not to suffer gratitude (if she apprehended she owed any to him, which he could by no means allow) to make her sacrifice herself to his wishes; for though it was an amiable virtue, yet his heart was too delicate, or too capricious, to be contented with receiving it in return for his warmest affections; and he should be less unhappy without her, than if she gave him her hand in contradiction to her inclination.

I am persuaded most women must pity Mrs. Tunstall; it is rather cruel for a man to insist on a woman's speaking plain in such a case; allowing nothing to prudery and custom, which have ordained that a little dissimulation is a female duty, and one of the first rules in the science of decorum. Happily men are seldom so humble, as not to attribute to inclination the smallest sign of compliance, from whatever motive it may arise; but Mr. Ellison was deficient in vanity; what can be said of few, he saw the possibility of not being beloved; and he trembled lest he should owe to his fortune, what he so ardently longed to have yielded to his tender affection.

Mrs. Tunstall's situation was rendered the more perplexing, by being really ignorant of the state of her own heart. She had never asked herself whether she felt more for him than esteem and gratitude, because she never expected to have the question put to her; and her heart had not been such a babbler, as to tell her unasked. But as he had given her time to recover the confusion into which surprize had thrown her, she made him an answer, which I am persuaded has been often made to others, but perhaps seldom with equal sincerity; that not having yet laid aside her widow's habit, she had not expected to be addressed; the possibility of it had not even entered her thoughts, too much engrossed by other subjects; therefore she was totally unprepared to give him a direct answer. She had considered him but as a most amiable and worthy friend, and knew not whether she could with pleasure consent to be united to him by a tenderer tie; however, she could safely promise all his delicacy required, not to marry him except he became the free, disinterested choice of her heart.

Mr. Ellison had no sooner received this assurance, than he repented his request; he now began to think that if she married him on no other principle than esteem and gratitude, the tenderness of his passion could scarcely fail of exciting affection in the breast of a virtuous woman, and therefore the danger he had apprehended was not great; whereas, by this excess of delicacy, which rendered him as it were jealous of her virtues, he might lose the possession of the woman on whom his happiness now more than ever depended; and had he not thought he discovered in Mrs. Tunstall's countenance, something that gave him room to hope he should not wait in vain, he had scarcely forborn to intreat her to deny what he had asked, and permit him to endeavour to engraft love on esteem, after marriage had rendered it her duty to assist him in securing her affections.

The poor man's apprehensions were in reality very groundless. Mrs. Tunstall was not quite so indifferent as she imagined. Love seldom rises to a blaze, till it is fanned with hope; she firmly believed Mr. Ellison would never think of renewing his addresses to one who had preferred a man so much less deserving; and would have thought ill of herself if, so soon after the death of her husband, she could conceive a tender prepossession in favour of any other. As her mind was thus circumstanced, it had been for her ease, not to examine into the nature of her sentiments, and she was not ready to suspect herself of what she would have considered as a very blameable weakness. No one could deny esteem to Mr. Ellison; gratitude was due to him from her; these sentiments she approved, and therefore avowed them; any more tender she would have blushed at, and therefore concealed them from herself. But when by the declaration of his passion, all constraint being laid aside, the conversations between them took a more tender turn, his assiduities became doubly engaging, and made impressions on her heart, which she excused, as justly due to so constant and generous an affection; and she perceived that her sentiments exceeded those which are inspired by sober friendship, and rational gratitude: but fear lest he should suppose her actuated by interested motives, of which he had expressed some apprehension, induced her to conceal her sensibility longer than she would otherwise have done, from a man whose long and painful attachment well deserved to be rewarded with all the pleasure he could receive from mutual affection. But the motive must be very powerful indeed, that can enable a woman, naturally sincere, to hide for any great length of time, the true state of her heart, from one who is so tenderly anxious to discover it. Mr. Ellison perceived, with inexpressible joy, that he was really beloved, and was so elated with his happiness, that he now fancied himself greatly rewarded for all he had suffered during the whole course of his passion. Present joy effaces much past pain from our remembrance, as indeed it ought, for present sorrow will sometimes make us forget the pleasures of many prosperous years; immediate sensations are too lively to suffer the past to recur with any great degree of strength. Mr. Ellison at this time found it so, yet he could not think his bliss complete, till the gift of her hand followed that of her heart; but though solicited by him in the tenderest and most passionate terms, and induced by the love which filled her own breast to consent to a perfect union, she could not be persuaded to marry him till a longer term of widowhood was expired. Her delicacy had always led her to dislike second marriages; to love twice, or to marry where a woman does not love, had appeared to her inconsistent with true delicacy; and though she was now obliged either to acknowledge she had refined too much, or to be the object of her own censure, yet she was desirous of fulfilling all that the forms of the world could require of her, and therefore desired permission to complete the second year of her widowhood before she entered into another engagement. This request was distressing to her lover, and by no means agreeable to her father, who thought such nice, unnecessary delays were trifling, compared with the advantages fortune offered her; and being grown cautious with age, and parsimonious by nature, he feared some accident might deprive her of a blessing she was too slow in accepting. Thus disposed, they united their forces; Mr. Ellison urged how long he had loved, and how much he had suffered; and they jointly represented that by having forborne all acquaintance with her from the time she married, and for the first half year of her widowhood, he had made such a sacrifice to decency, as must entirely secure her from any malicious imputations, notwithstanding the continuance of his passion must now be well known to the world. But all their arguments might have proved unavailing, if Mr. Allin had not, contrary to Mr. Ellison's express desire, jestingly told his daughter, that if she did not lay aside her foolish scruples, he would proclaim to the whole neighbourhood that she was guilty of a much greater indecorum than a far earlier marriage, as she was in great measure kept by Mr. Ellison.

Mrs. Tunstall was astonished at the terms her father used, but thought he referred to the fortune Mr. Ellison had given her on her nuptials, which indeed made the whole of what she possessed; till he acquainted her that what since the decline of the Doctor's business she had imagined she received from his bounty, was indeed the gift of her generous lover. Mr. Ellison was distressed at this discovery, which he feared might be humiliating to Mrs. Tunstall; but after she had recovered her surprize, 'I see, Sir,' said she to him, 'that Providence has decreed I should owe every blessing to your generosity; what return can I make to such obligations! accept my thanks; accept me; most amiable of men! such goodness is irresistible; henceforward command my will, for by your's it must ever be regulated; I can no longer resist any inclination of your's; on the contrary, find my affection for you grow so entire, that I must wish to have it made my duty to love you with a warm and undivided heart.'

The frown Mr. Allin had raised on Mr. Ellison's brow, was at once dissipated; the consequences of what he had thought an indiscretion in that gentleman were so pleasing, that his heart could harbour no sensation but joy, which was so strongly expressed by the manner wherein he received this consent, that Mrs. Tunstall reproached herself for having delayed a happiness, it was in her power to have sooner given him. As all the parties were so well agreed, we may believe the day that was to complete their bliss was fixed before they parted, and that at only a fortnight's distance, which was just half a year short of the term she had been desirous of completing, before she entered into a second engagement.[4]

Mr. Ellison felt himself the happiest of mankind; a few days only stood between him and the utmost height of worldly felicity; and those were rendered so delightful by an anticipating imagination, and the tender intercourse between two persons passionately in love, and so near possessing each other, that his impatience to see them expired was scarcely excusable. He now experienced the danger of extreme joy; hitherto benevolence had always possessed the first place in his thoughts, but at this period he was too much intoxicated with his own happiness, to give his usual attention to the happiness of others; he perceived this change, but hoped his mind would recover its former tone when the turbulence of joy was abated by certainty and possession, and his spirits naturally become composed by the removal of all anxiety. Indeed every thing concurred to make him happy; for though at this time every pleasure appeared small in comparison to what he felt in the expectation of his approaching union with Mrs. Tunstall, yet he did not receive with insensibility the thanks of his sister-in-law for the valuable present he had sent her in Miss Almon, whose friendship gave her extreme satisfaction, and whose instructions she doubted not would be of great use both to her and her children; for notwithstanding the difference in their ages, she said, they should equally be Miss Almon's scholars, as her superiority of years did not prevent either her desire, or want of improvement. The accounts from Mr. Maningham were not less agreeable, as he informed him, that before he had been three months in Jamaica, he had a sufficient number of scholars to have contented him, but that his school was still increasing. He likewise told Mr. Ellison that the climate agreed perfectly with him, and also with his mother, since she was become accustomed to it; for on her first arrival she was seized with a fever, but since she recovered that, had been very well, and seemed to take pleasure in the care of her young boarders. He also desired another assistant might be sent him as soon as possible, as he had too many scholars for two persons to instruct sufficiently.

Thus every circumstance seemed to concur to make Mr. Ellison completely happy; when three days before that fixed on for his nuptials he received a letter from Mrs. Blackburn, informing him, 'that her husband was in the hands of the sheriff's officers, and if he did not take compassion upon them, he must be immediately removed to prison, as they were not able to discharge the debt, and the creditor refused to take Mr. Blackburn's bond, knowing his whole fortune was mortgaged. She beseeched Mr. Ellison in very affecting terms to relieve them in this distress, and that with all speed, proposing to make over part of their income to pay him for what he must advance, without which, she said, she could by no means think of applying to him in such a case, after the continual obligations he had conferred on them.'

Fewer intreaties would have sufficed to bring Mr. Ellison to their relief. As for her proposal of reimbursing him, he was determined not to listen to it, though he did not design to pay the debt out of his own pocket, but to charge it in the account he kept for the children; whose loss alone this would be, by lessening the money he yearly laid up for them, according to his first resolution of not appropriating any part of the income of the estate to his own use. He had lent his equipage to Mrs. Tunstall, who wanted to make some purchases at the adjacent town; Sir William Ellison was waiting with impatience while his was getting ready to carry him an airing: Mr. Ellison would not disappoint the poor man of any thing wherein he purposed pleasure, and as his own horse was lame, ordered one he had just bought for his servant, to be saddled for himself, and set out in all haste for Mr. Blackburn's; but he had not gone three miles, when his horse threw him. He was at first entirely stunned by the fall; but pain in a short time brought him to himself, and convinced him that his thigh was broke. His servant sent off a messenger to a surgeon to meet him at his own house, and with great difficulty got him home.

The surgeon happily was there before him, and the bone was set as soon as possible; but the pain, though extreme, could not fix his thoughts entirely on himself; his mistress and his friend were sure of finding the first place in them; and desirous of lessening the uneasiness of both, he sent Mr. Green to Mrs. Blackburn, with full power of engaging to discharge Mr. Blackburn's debt, as soon as he should become acquainted with the sum, which she had omitted mentioning in her letter, desiring him to take care that gentleman was not in the mean time carried to prison. He then dispatched his house-keeper to acquaint Mrs. Tunstall with the misfortune that had befallen him, the most painful consequence of which was the disappointment of his hopes, when felicity seemed so near him; but he flattered himself it would not occa-sion a long delay; and that in the interim she would bless him with her pres-ence.

Mrs. Tunstall was shocked to the greatest degree at this melancholy news; but when a shower of tears had given some relief to her spirits, she declared her desire of attending Mr. Ellison directly, and accordingly went back with the house-keeper.

## CHAP. IV.

Mrs. Tunstall found Mr. Ellison even worse than she expected, his pain and fever having increased after the house-keeper set out; but the sight of his destined bride made him for a time insensible to his sufferings, and he only lamented the mortifying change in his immediate prospects; and that after having so long waited for his happiness, he should be exposed to still farther delays, and that too when he had almost reached the very moment of possession. The postponing of their marriage appeared to Mrs. Tunstall as a small part of the misfortune; the pain he endured, and the danger she feared from the fever she apprehended it had brought upon him, were to her so much more afflicting, that she had no grief to spare for lesser evils; nor could find any reason to lament the delay which sat so heavy on their spirits, except their more speedy marriage might have prevented this unfortunate accident. Her having had the chariot gave her much greater concern, as it seemed in great measure the occasion of what had befallen him; but he would not suffer her to believe he should have made use of it, had it been at home.

Though in some past transactions Mrs. Tunstall may have appeared a slave to the most punctilious decorum, yet she was above all such frivolous niceties where she had any humane and important cause to break through them, and determined that want of the marriage ceremony should not prevent her attendance on him, during his confinement. She had once acted this part from gratitude; and trusted she might now without censure be allowed to perform it through affection. Her tender attentions greatly alleviated Mr. Ellison's pains, but could not effect his cure; the third day after the fracture, a mortification began, which gave the surgeons the most alarming apprehensions.

Mr. Ellison always kept his affairs in exact order, and settled his various accounts, and all his trusts, in as regular a manner as possible, with a view of preventing disputes and difficulties, in case he should not either have time or power to regulate them in his last moments, when, even whatever leisure might be afforded him, he should wish to have his mind disengaged from worldly concerns. But he now found, so complicated as his business was, there was no possibility of being freed from that care, especially in his present situation, which had relieved him from all anxiety on Mrs. Tunstall's account, imagining a few days would secure her an ample fortune. He saw the danger which threatened his life; the surgeons scarcely durst attempt to conceal it from him; and the distress impressed on the countenances of all who approached him sufficiently declared their fears.

Death could certainly never have taken him at a more unwelcome season. He was in full possession of every real good this world affords; no one circumstance was wanting to make life agreeable; he was on the moment of receiving the reward of all the uneasiness he had suffered from his love; and his hopes and expectations raised to their utmost height by the joy which seemed to await him in his approaching nuptials. His affections too were in full strength, for no consuming sickness, no decays incident to age, had weakened his passions, or weaned his affections; far different from those who,

> *Taught half by reason, half by meer decay,*
> *To welcome death and calmly pass away:*[5]

He was taken in the full flow of his joys, the very summit of his happiness; the woman he idolized, the friends he loved, the dependents he valued and protected, all weeping round him, and afflicting with their sorrow a heart which must so sensibly feel the pain of leaving them. But melancholy as his situation will be allowed, no dejection appeared in his countenance. As soon as he apprehended his life was in danger, he considered of the best method of preventing others from suffering by his death. He obliged his executors to follow the plan he had laid down for Sir William's houshold, and put it out of their power to retrench any expence that was conducive to his pleasure. He charged on his fortune the support of all the charities and benevolences he had established, till the objects of his bounty should be removed into a world where all their wants would be better supplied. He discharged Mr. Blackburn's debt, and by his will distributed all he had saved amongst the younger children. He bequeathed ten thousand pounds to Mrs. Tunstall; and as his son's fortune could not fail of being great, since Sir William's estate would come to him, he charged it with annuities for all his dependents; he had not a servant to whom he did not leave some token of his bounty; and not confining his thoughts to England, obliged his son to leave his Jamaica estate in the hands of his steward as long as he should live; providing for all the negroes that should remain on the plantation at the time of his steward's death.

When he had settled his affairs in such a manner that no one could suffer except in the interior of their hearts by his decease, and learnt that though he might linger on for a day or two, there was no hope of his recovery, as all the surgeons had tried failed of the expected success, he dedicated the rest of his time to fervent addresses to his Maker, and to endeavours of being useful to those about him.

As for the first, he found it a pleasing task. Though his services had been imperfect, yet he knew them sincere; his conscience laboured under no load of sin, though it could not proclaim him innocent. He was sensible he had often offended, yet never deliberately continued in any evil. He knew he stood in need of pardon, but Faith told him where to apply for it; and while he lamented that he had not more diligently laboured to fulfill the will of his Creator, Hope assured him that Mercy was at hand, that sincerity would be accepted in the place of perfection, and dispelled every rising fear. He took leave of all his friends and dependents; and believing that what he said at such a time would have double weight, he gave them severally the advice most needed for them, and exhorted them to a constant and fervent performance of the duties of religion, saying every thing that he imagined might raise their love to Him who had purchased a right to it at so great a price.[6] Much of his exhortations must have been lost through the grief of those to whom they were addressed, which frequently interrupted him in his discourse; for in the midst of all this distress, he alone seemed calm in spirits, and blessed with a composure, which neither an unwillingness to relinquish life, nor the pain he suffered, could interrupt.

His hardest trial was yet to come, the taking leave of his son and mistress. For the former he felt a thousand fears, lest his unguided youth might be led into some of the many errors to which that season of life is prone; and he did not more grieve than fear to leave him. He recapitulated the substance of all the instructions he had for so many years been inculcating, and beseeched him with tears, and the tenderest caresses, to imprint them deeply on his heart. The young Granthams were not omitted in this last exertion of his benevolence; he represented to them the duties of the station they would one day fill in this world, and still more strongly what was requisite to their happy state in the next. But his severest task was taking leave of Mrs. Tunstall, who approached his bed more dead than alive. In her presence life appeared to him cloathed in all its charms; these were even heightened beyond reality by the deceitful varnish of passion; and to think that the hand which was so soon to have been united to his, and thereby to have raised him to the summit of earthly happiness, must on the contrary now close his eyes, and perform the last direful office of friendship, was almost too much for his fortitude; but when he was melting into sorrow, and lamenting the approaching separation from the idol of his soul, Religion (long accustomed to recur to his mind on every occasion) came to his aid, he checked the rising passion, acknowledged his own blindness, and the all-perfect wisdom of him in whose hand is life and death; and convinced his dispensations are always both wise and merciful, submitted with true resignation, and exhorted the beloved mourner to patience and fortitude. He bade her 'not grieve for him; since he trusted he was going to the only place where he could find a happiness superior to what he should have enjoyed in her society.' Reminded her 'how soon they should meet again, never more to part,' beseeching her, 'to think of him only as gone a journey, where she in a few years would follow him.'[7] Represented the sin of too much sorrowing, 'since it was our duty to submit patiently to every decree of Providence, and not to repine when our hopes are disappointed by Him who knows best whether they ought to be gratified; and never afflicts his children but for their benefit.' He observed to her 'how many misfortunes might have attended their wished-for union; how happy it might be for him to be taken away at the time most dangerous to his virtue, as it was too possible, had he lived, his extreme fondness for her might have withdrawn his affections from Him who was best entitled to them; and the intoxication of passion have led him to omit the duties of a Christian.' He then told her 'he had left her and Mr. Green executors of his will, in full confidence, that if he had omitted any thing, they would act, not by the letter of the will, but by what they knew of his inclination, and take care that every thing he had established was carried on with the same regularity and propriety as during his life; and that no indigent person should feel one comfort diminished by his death.'

Mrs. Tunstall had no power to answer, but with her tears, which flowed plentifully over the hand she pressed between hers, while kneeling by his bed-side. She had great occasion for all his exhortations to patience, but was not in the best state of mind for receiving them. After the first gust of sorrow is over, resignation may take place, despair sinks us into a sort of calm; but while misery is depending, anxiety will not suffer us to exert our fortitude, nor to listen to the calls of duty. She endeavoured, to the utmost of her power, to conceal the anguish of her mind; but with all the resolution she assumed she could perform it only in part, and so much of her affliction appeared as grew too affecting for Mr. Ellison; his strength both of mind and body began to fail, and fearing lest the grief of parting with the object of his tenderest affections might disturb the tranquillity of his mind in his last moments, he desired her to leave him, while he endeavoured to get a little sleep. She, who wished to give a freer vent to her sorrows, obeyed him without reluctance, and he in reality fell into a sleep, which continued for some hours.

At night, when the surgeons examined his leg, they found the mortification, to their surprize, had not advanced, which gave them room to hope there was still a possibility that the medicines given had at last taken effect; but the chance was so very small, they were afraid of speaking the hope that might be gathered from their countenances. The next day the symptoms appeared still a little more favourable, and Mrs. Tunstall began to flatter herself that she might still be happy; but Mr. Ellison gave little credit to this change, fearing, lest hope might deprive him of the resignation, which, perhaps, he in part owed to despair. However, in a few days, beyond all expectation, he was declared out of danger; and he now found, that the life he could so contentedly have parted with, was still extremely dear to him. But had it indeed lost its charms, it must have obtained new ones from the joy that was diffused over the whole neighbourhood. Mrs. Tunstall's was almost too much for her frame to support; that of his friends and dependents, though less extreme, was equally sincere, and he had reason to believe was perfectly disinterested, as he had, to alleviate their grief on his expected death, informed them, that he had taken care their circumstances should not suffer by his decease. But as this had increased their gratitude and affection, it made their joy on the appearances of his recovery still the greater. The pain Mr. Ellison had endured, seemed now only a refinement on his pleasure, so entire was the gratification he received from such infallible marks of attachment. To obtain love had never been the motive for his bounty; he had, as much as possible, divested himself of all desire or hope of gaining either affection or praise from the benevolence which he shewed indiscriminately to all who came within his observation, because he wished to preserve the motive of his actions more pure, and free from all danger of disappointment; but the real pleasure of being beloved must be greater or less in proportion to the benevolence of the mind; for that which arises from vanity is transient and uncertain; he therefore could not but feel the most refined satisfaction from the tender attachment of so many people; was thankful to the Almighty for having added that pleasure to the many blessings he had bestowed on him; prayed for a sufficient length of life to recompense those poor people for the gratification they had given him, and that he might be enabled to spend the remainder of his life in the service of him who had so unexpectedly prolonged it.

Mr. Ellison's recovery, though slow, was rendered very delightful, by the joy expressed in the countenance of every person that approached him. Mrs. Tunstall was ever rejoicing over his restored life, or on her knees giving thanks for so great a blessing. Mr. Ellison, when he expected almost immediate death, had ordered her children to be sent for, as the best resource her afflicted mind could have, and the most probable means of administering consolation when the fatal hour of separation from him should arrive. Happily this care had proved unnecessary, but their being in the family enabled Mrs. Tunstall to continue in his house with less inconvenience; and she never left it till Mr. Ellison was sufficiently recovered for them to confirm at church the union of their hearts, which love had before completed; an union which every succeeding day rendered more delightful, as a fuller knowledge of each others virtues, by increasing their esteem and rational affection, more than compensated for some abatement of passion which must unavoidably be the consequence of possession, and that certainty of each other's affections which

banishes all the fears and anxieties that fan the fire of love and increase the
passion by vicissitude, mingling pains with its pleasures.

## CHAP. V.

Mr. Ellison had now no wish ungratified. Mrs. Ellison returned his affection in the tenderest manner, and completed his happiness by entering
into all his views, and assisting him in every work of humanity, wherein her
heart was as deeply engaged as his. Mrs. Ellison, during her widowhood, had
dedicated her time and her talents to her children; but by her second marriage she had given to another a just title to share in both: a partnership
which, however, was highly advantageous to her scantily provided for offspring; but both she and Mr. Ellison thought it just to make them the best
amends in their power for the interruption now given to her careful and judicious attentions; he therefore applied to his cousin, Mrs. Maynard, to send a
person qualified to instruct them; being, with his wife, of opinion, that children could never be so properly placed as under the eye of a mother, who was
capable of guiding, and willing to give all possible attention to them.[8] They
were indeed only infants, but their parents thought too early care could not
be taken to prevent the acquiring bad habits, and to give them such as might
best fit them for future improvement. Mrs. Ellison could not, without depriving her husband of too much of her company, be always with them, and
did not think it proper to trust them in her absence with common servants,
whose low education must give rise to various errors, narrow views, and absurd prejudices, which they never fail instilling into the minds of children,
susceptible of every impression.

Mr. Ellison had not been married quite a year when his wife produced
him a fine boy, who made an addition to their happiness, the measure of
which seemed before to be full. In a short time after another family felt perhaps equal joy from a very different event, as death gave rise to it. Mr. Grantham received advice that the Duke of ———— had paid the last debt to
nature, whereby he came into possession of the title and entailed estate. What
was unsettled the duke had spent, beside the income of great appointments.
Mr. Grantham received this news like a rational, honest man. He had always
thought with pleasure of the succession, as he had no acquaintance with the
possessor, had been entirely neglected by him, and could have no esteem for
his character. But he felt himself very unequal to the rank he now bore: the
estate he was sensible would extricate him from all difficulties, and he knew

himself sufficiently qualified to enjoy the comforts of affluence; but he looked upon the title as a burden which would sit ungracefully upon him, and was more grateful than ever to Mr. Ellison for having educated his children in a manner that would make them become their rank.

Mrs. Grantham exceeded him as much in joy as she fell short of him in diffidence. The title gave her at least as much pleasure as the estate, and she had no doubt but she should make an excellent duchess. Her brain was scarcely proof against the delight she took in forming schemes of grandeur. It was with no small difficulty Mr. Ellison prevailed with her to delay making any material alterations in her way of life, till the rents of the estate enabled her to do it with convenience; representing that 'as the entail could not be cut off till her eldest son became of age, if Mr. Grantham died before that period, he could leave nothing to her or her younger children, except what he should have saved; therefore of all people they ought to avoid setting out in debt.' He observed to her, that 'there was far greater dignity in seeming indifferent to grandeur, than in enjoying it; and that by not being in haste to appear in figure, they would assume it with less envy, and be thought to become it better.' But Mrs. Grantham had little taste for the dignity of abstaining from the enjoyment of splendor; and all Mr. Ellison's refined reasonings would have proved unavailing, had he not strengthened them by representing 'how lamentable a condition a dowager-duchess would be in, whose income did not exceed fifty pounds a year.' The notion of being a titled beggar had its effect, and she consented to what prudence had before disposed her husband.

Mr. Ellison undertook to accompany his grace in the necessary inspection of his estate; and to their great mortification they found it in very bad condition: the farm-houses tumbling down, the fences out of repair, the mansion-house in a most ruinous state, and the furniture in tatters; the late possessor having, through extravagance, been always too needy to afford the necessary repairs. The steward's accounts were not in much better order; his late master never took the trouble to inspect them, by which means he had raised a considerable fortune, while his master's had gone to ruin.

To a man who had already passed the meridian of life, this afforded a very disagreeable prospect, as he saw it must be long before he could enjoy the clear produce of his estate; which would not, at the utmost, amount to seven thousand pounds a year; a very moderate income for a man of his rank.[9] The first necessary step was to change his steward, but that could not be done immediately, as he had contrived to render his accounts very intricate; he was, however, ordered to make them up in the best manner he could, and then to bring them to the Duke, who after having minuted down the repairs most immediately requisite, returned home. No rents were likely to come in for near a quarter of a year, but Mr. Ellison prevailed with him to determine to stay in his old habitation till that time, and to fix a resolution to confine his expences within three thousand pounds a year, till his estate and house were thoroughly repaired, and fortunes saved for his younger children.

In this advice Mr. Ellison considered equally the advantage of the whole family. By getting the Duke to fix his expences at £3000 yearly, he hoped it would at least come within four thousand; well knowing that people generally exceed the sum they allow themselves; and that, he thought, was as much as he could spend with a tolerable grace; it would allow a decent portion of figure, hospitality, and benevolence; and any thing beyond must sit awkwardly on people so unaccustomed to high life, as nothing exposes a low education like an aim at splendor, which a person so unqualified neither knows how to order, nor to conduct. So great a change of situation, likewise, is apt to be hurtful to the mind, as it too often gives rise to such a degree of pride and vanity as renders the possessor both unhappy and ridiculous; this is much increased by pomp and shew; and he hoped if he could restrain them in that particular, it might prevent the inordinate growth of those vices. Having so long had the children under his care, he loved them with almost a paternal affection; and was solicitous to save the eldest from that most dangerous situation, high birth with an incumbered fortune. Sensible that the general corruption of this country, arises from the necessitous state of too many of the individuals, who endeavour to supply their private wants by prostitution of conscience and honour, he wished the young Marquis[10] to inherit an unmortgaged estate; for though he knew his heart to be excellent, his principles strictly virtuous, and his understanding both solid and brilliant, yet the pernicious consequences of necessitous circumstances are so evident, that he almost feared no integrity could stand the trial, and therefore was anxious to remove from him so dangerous a temptation. Though he was equally fond of the younger children, yet this was his chief care; he had no doubt of the Marquis's providing properly for them, but as he could not do it but by loading his estate with very heavy incumbrances, the fears I have mentioned, made him desirous to have their fortunes supplied by their father's economy.

Mrs. Ellison had found sufficient employment during the absence of the gentlemen, in endeavouring to fortify the new duchess's mind against the dangers arising from her late acquired dignity. She represented to her, that 'her situation had some disagreeable consequences; that it would expose her to the envy of her inferiors, who would scrutinize her actions with malice, and censure them without mercy: while her equals would be inclined to despise her, and turn every little, unavoidable error, into ridicule. That the only method to save herself from the malice of the one, and the over-bearing pride of the other, was to support this change with moderation and humility: to shew that as she had always reason to expect this exaltation, so she was not puffed up by it; and as she had, in consideration of her husband's birth and expectations, been treated on equal terms by persons far superior to her in fortune, so now she ought to let them see that she was as conscious of what she had been, as they were before of what she might expect to be; for as they had not presumed on their superiority, neither ought she on hers; but behave to them, not with that condescending civility, which is in reality an insult, but with the same ease and freedom she had ever done. She warned her against affecting an air of dignity which could never sit well upon her; and as she could not be a fine lady, to content herself with appearing in a better character, that of a sensible and a good woman; if then any faults were found in her behaviour, they would be charged on the injustice of fortune, which had so long left her in low circumstances.'

Mrs. Ellison had the satisfaction of finding the duchess very docile, after the violence of her first joy was over. As she knew her neighbours would all make her visits of congratulation, she desired her good friend would be present, to assist her in doing the honours to so much company; and after they went away, would ask her how she acquitted herself; and suffer her to find fault with any part of her behaviour she disapproved, as well as to teach her how to rectify it; and Mrs. Ellison with great pleasure heard her conduct applauded, by people who had purposed in their visit to find some gratification for their envy, or some amusement for their ill-nature. She took care to acquaint her grace with their approbation, both as a reward, and an encouragement to persevere in the same behaviour.

Their moderation and prudence in not immediately assuming the figure to which their rank intitled them was much admired; and from the whole of their conduct, people were inclined to believe that the dignity of their minds was even superior to their rank. After the Duke and Mr. Ellison returned from visiting his grace's estate, he and the duchess passed most of their time at Mr. Ellison's, as they could there be better accommodated than at home; and it seemed a middle state between their past and future way of life, and fit a little to prepare them for so great a change in circumstances.

While they were with Mr. Ellison, Sir William was seized with a fever, which carried him off in a few days. Mr. Ellison succeeded to his estate and title, with the satisfactory reflexion of having made his deceased relation happier than ever man was, who had been afflicted with the like dreadful calamity.

Mr. Lyne died about a year before, but his worthy wife still remained, who Mr. or to speak properly Sir George Ellison would not permit to be a sufferer by the cessation of a charge, wherein she had acquitted herself so admirably, as made him esteem himself greatly indebted to her. The young gentleman who had been about Sir William had the same title to his regard. Him he recommended to the Duke of ―――― to supply the place of his predecessor's steward; an office for which this young man was particularly well qualified. He had long entertained a passion for Miss Lyne, who had not listened to him with insensibility; and by the recovery of her health, became a very pretty, as well as very amiable young woman. While Sir William lived, they suppressed all thoughts of uniting; but now those ties of duty were dissolved, they, without fear of meeting with any obstacle either from her mother or Sir George, who was always ready to gratify every virtuous inclination, declared their mutual affection; and met with even more than the success they hoped. Sir George Ellison engaged to give the bride a fortune; and presented them with as much of Sir William's furniture as sufficed to furnish their house. Mrs. Lyne's son he had already placed in a merchant's compting house; where his good behaviour promised he would one day make a fortune. Sir George then settled an hundred a year on Mrs. Lyne during her life; who finding herself made by his bounty so easy in her circumstances, added £500 to her daughter's fortune, out of what she had saved; and settled in a cottage near them, refusing an apartment in their house; for she said, that 'when a woman was married she ought to have no one's temper to study but her husband's; double subjection was too much; and yet, perhaps, it was impossible for a parent to cease from exacting the obedience which she had been accustomed to require, or for a daughter of so gentle a temper as her's, to forbear paying it, even if it was not demanded. She lived at so small a distance from them, that she should be always ready to give any assistance in her power, in case of sickness, or on any other occasion, when she might be useful; could receive the like comfort from them, and enjoy the pleasure of their society; the happiness of which she could not doubt, being perfectly well acquainted with the amiable disposition of both.'

## CHAP. VI.

Sir George Ellison made no great additions to the current expences of his family on this increase of fortune, except in the article of equipage. He removed into Sir William's house, as it was better, and more elegant than his own; and lent his to the Duke of ———, whose seat was too much out of repair to be lived in; and had it been in better order, he could not prudently have inhabited it, as he must have been led into a larger scale of expence, than suited his situation, in a county where he was the superior person, and yet several private gentlemen therein had better fortunes than himself, the condition of their estates considered. By continuing in the neighbourhood where he had always lived, he was more esteemed, and better liked, for the moderate figure in which he appeared, as he did not affect a splendor that excited envy, and yet did not disgrace his rank. His equipage and retinue were as genteel, though the latter, perhaps, not so numerous, as those of any man of his quality in the kingdom. His table was extremely handsome; and every article of domestic expence was agreeable to his rank; but it was all ordered with economy: in the number of their servants they were regulated by the uses they had for them; and not being burdened with unnecessary domestics, corrupted by idleness, and who for want of employment fall into riot and debauchery, their family was conducted with all the regularity and economy of inferior persons. Sir George and Lady Ellison had, at their desire, fixed their household, and settled the whole plan of their expences; for as they had hitherto possessed so little, they were but bad judges how far money would go; and their good friends thought themselves over-paid for their trouble, by the pleasure of seeing them live in so prudent and judicious a manner. They persuaded them not to pass any part of their time in London; sensible, that although their merits rendered them respected in the country, even beyond what their titles might exact; yet, in London, where their worth could not be known, their want of knowledge of the world, and their deficiency in politeness, so little reconcilable to their rank, would frequently make them the objects of ridicule. Those who have specious manners, a good address, an easy assurance, and what we call the savoir vivre, adopting the words of a foreign language, have all the qualifications requisite to render them acceptable in the gay world; but such as are deficient in these particulars, however replete with unadorned good sense, integrity, strict honour, and general benevolence, will make but an indifferent figure there; and are much more judicious, when they fix in a less crouded scene, where people have leisure and opportunity to observe their virtues, sobriety of understanding sufficient to feel their value, and to accept sterling merit as an atonement for deficiency in politeness, and in the small, but pleasing talents for gay society. These, it must be allowed, by accompanying virtue give it a peculiar grace, and render that lovely which unpolished is but estimable; and we cannot wonder, if the want of these advantages depreciate very worthy persons in the eyes of those who have not opportunity to penetrate deeply into their characters; but it is a sufficient reason to deter such from exposing themselves unnecessarily to these superficial observers; and the Duke of ——— saw this propriety in its true light; while his lady acquiesced in his choice, and approved in her judgment, though perhaps her inclination rather prompted her to wish for a little better acquaintance with the amusements of the polite world.

The young marquis, their son, gave them reason to hope that he would be qualified for a greater latitude of election;[11] having the pleasing talents requisite to recommend himself to the world, united with the virtues which grace retirement, and render public life useful. His disposition was truly noble. Generous, sincere, humane, and steady; of an active and lively temper, calm and resolute, yet gentle and docile. He had great parts and a strong understanding; polite and graceful in his manner, with true greatness of soul, but free from pride. Though he was not handsome, his countenance was engaging, and his person fine. Nor did the rest of that young family fall far short of him in perfections. Nature had dealt bountifully with them; and Sir George Ellison, and their tutor, had carefully cultivated and improved their natural endowments, and endeavoured to give their minds such a turn, as might render them most useful to mankind; sensible that their rank must bring them into public life. The change in their father's fortune made none in them, till they were of an age to go to the university, to which they were accompanied by young Ellison, and all committed to the care and guidance of the tutor who had so happily instructed their youth, and was both loved and revered by them.

I have already said, that Sir George had not been married a year before his lady brought him a son; the two succeeding years each inriched him by a daughter. It is not possible to imagine a scene of more perfect felicity on earth, than this family represented. The large addition to Sir George's fortune, greatly extended the sphere of his benevolence; no real distress reached his knowledge that was not relieved; and as his disposition was well known through great part of the kingdom, he received applications from all quarters; but he gave not indiscriminately; he considered all that was bestowed on the undeserving as a robbery of the more meritorious; and therefore enquired narrowly into every case laid before him. If this scrutiny, as was often the case, required much time, and the distress represented was very urgent, he would, it is true, send a little present assistance; rather chusing to hazard the misapplication of a small sum, than that innocent poverty should wait too long for relief. Those who came within the extent of his observation, had seldom occasion to notify their necessities, for his bounty supplied their wants almost as soon as they could feel them. A man whose income was insufficient to the maintenance of his children, and who had it not in his power to increase it, if known to Sir George, never failed, without application, of receiving a half yearly present to enable him to answer unavoidable exigencies. Thus the poorer sort of clergy came in for no small share of his bounty; if he heard of a curate[12] with a large family, (of which he frequently heard, as the number of them is so great) the poor man's difficulties were sure of being greatly lightened; for he felt particular compassion for men, sometimes gentlemen by birth, and generally so by education, who were reduced to live on a less income than a low mechanic,[13] and yet to maintain some gentility of appearance, without which, among ill-judging people, (and what parish is not full of them?) both he and his function would fall into contempt. Where he saw no good purposes likely to arise from gaining an influence over those he relieved, he sent his presents without any notification of the giver; though his character was so well known, that he seldom hereby could preserve the secrecy he intended: but where he hoped to benefit the receiver as much by his advice as by his bounty, he forbore all attempts at privacy; and this especially among the persons I have last mentioned as objects of his beneficence; as he took much pains to persuade them, 'to relinquish all thoughts of laying claim to any gentility for their children, and contentedly to breed them up without any higher expectations or pretensions, than those of the neighbouring and middling farmers; for the richer part of this class,' he observed, 'might look somewhat above them, being able to give a few hundred pounds to their children, which a country curate could not hope.' He exhorted them indeed, 'to give their offspring such advantages as they had more peculiarly the power of bestowing, teaching them to read, write, and cast accounts well; polishing their behaviour; rectifying their language; and above all, instructing them thoroughly in religious and moral duties; and to these,' he said, 'their mothers might, in respect to the female part of their families, add such instructions in feminine business as would prove very useful qualifications; all which,' he urged, 'might be taught them without instilling those notions of gentility that so often render the descendants of the clergy the most distressed of all people, and consequently particularly exposed to temptations from the vicious.' This advice, of which I have succinctly mentioned only the heads, he softened in such a manner that it could not give pain, even though a little pride might lurk in the heart of those he addressed; for he beheld with compassion the pride of people reduced to a situation below their birth, and thought that vice in none so excusable as in them who are naturally led to encourage some opinion of self-consequence, in order to make themselves a little amends for the undeserved indignities they meet with from others. But although he endeavoured to persuade the clergy to relinquish all views for their children above what a common farmer or small trader might entertain, yet he himself always gave them a preference in his assistances towards placing them out in life, if their merits were equal, to those of a lower class, especially when their parents were gentlemen by birth, thinking such distinction then their due; but yet, he esteemed the right of merit so superior to those of birthright, that if he found one of the lowest class excel in virtue and talents, he preferred him to a less deserving man, however well descended; and this not only as he thought such preference just, but because the youth who thus excelled was by his merits enabled to reap much greater benefit from his bounty, than one who had not the same powers of improving the advantages of his situation; for, as I have before said, he was very careful in every action, to order it in such a manner as should produce the most good that was possible; through which care it happened that his charities were far more beneficial than they would have been if performed by those whose liberal hands were not directed by minds equally attentive. If a lad's chief merit lay in industry, he dedicated him to occupations where only sobriety and application were necessary; but placed those of more shining talents in situations where they would be called forth, well knowing it to be as difficult to make a dull mind excel in refined arts, as to sink shining parts to the requisite attention to plodding business, an aim that almost ever ends in the disappointment of him who attempts it, and the ruin of the lads so injudiciously disposed of; and is no less to the detriment of society, as by a wrong application it loses the services which either might have done it, if their different geniuses had been properly attended to in their first destination. Indeed the good of the public had no small share even in those actions of Sir George's which are generally looked upon as merely of a private nature; for when he introduced young people into life, he was in good measure guided by general utility, regulating his choice of their occupations by what was of greatest use to mankind, and wherein additional hands was most wanted; and these are so various, that it did not interfere with his attention to the several geniuses of these fortunate youths.

From all whom he thus took under his care, and were placed at too great a distance for him to see them, he required a letter every two months, to acquaint him with their health, their progress, and their wants; and he never failed returning answers, wherein he gave them every kind encouragement, mingled with such advice and instruction, as he thought their dispositions stood most in need of, or was by their situations rendered most necessary. This method not only served to impress their particular duties strongly on their minds, but kept alive their hopes of his future favour, and their belief of his kind care for their welfare, continuing a dependence on him which could not fail proving of great service to them, both as a restraint on their inclinations to evil, and an encouragement to their virtues. It is true, it occasioned him no small business, the answering so many letters took a good deal of time, but as it was spent in the purposes to which the whole was dedicated, it only made so many steps in his regular walk of life; and he could regret no employment that did not lead him to stray from the chosen path.

I will not deny, but Sir George and Lady Ellison frequently wished they could pass more time in each other's society, separated with regret, and looked forward with impatience to the hour that would restore them to the conversation they had quitted with pain: human frailty will make the best people feel they fall very short of perfection; but these tender sensations, which never were given way to, however uneasy at the time, were far from being a misfortune to this worthy couple; the interruptions of idle pleasures, or turbulent amusements, will sometimes deaden affection, for when the spirits are weary even love will sicken; but it never suffers any diminution from having its indulgences suspended by humanity. If Sir George and his lady parted with regret when benevolence called for their attendance, impatience to renew their conversation gave a double joy to their meeting, the cause of their separation made them behold each other with still additional esteem; and when they mutually related the manner wherein they had employed the hours of absence, the poverty or sickness they had relieved, the timorous doubting minds they had encouraged, the afflicted hearts they had comforted, or the ignorant understandings they had instructed, tenderness was heightened by veneration, and the affection, which in the happiest pair is merely human, seemed in them to be divine; and in reality was so in a good degree, being mingled with that spark of divinity imparted from above, that benevolence and love, which however now defaced, still shews how man might once be properly called the image of his Creator.

Nothing is more conducive towards preserving affection than what prevents a married pair from continuing in each other's company after they are weary of it. Conversation will sometimes flag among the most ingenious and most affectionate; but if it happens frequently, the dulness it occasions is apt to be tacitly charged on each other; and an apprehension that the next day may be deadened by the same weariness goes a great way towards producing it, as the fear damps the spirits of both: thus what would be almost unavoidable in the same connection with any other persons, grows to be considered as some particular deficiency in each other. From this evil Sir George and his lady were secured by the very frequent calls of benevolence, and the various interruptions occasioned by the business in which humanity engaged them: as therefore they were strangers to satiety, they continued to feel the impatience of lovers, and were ingeniously inventive to procure little snatches of each other's conversation, to enliven the long interruptions they could not, consistent with duty (or at least with their notion of it) avoid; for Lady Ellison would have been sorry to have fallen short of Sir George in humanity, a virtue which she possessed in a great degree, and found the source of inexpressible pleasure, not only from the benevolence of her heart, but from perceiving how much it endeared her to him.

Her sphere, indeed, was different and more minute; but if her charities were less considerable in expence and in their various consequences, they were however very important, as they administered to the happiness, or at least comfort of many. Her attention was more particularly directed to her own sex. From her every poor woman was sure, during her lying-in, to receive all the assistance and conveniencies that could administer comfort in her state: she supplied her with cloathing for her child; and pitying the sufferings of such poor babes through the intolerable custom of lacing them up almost as soon as born in stiff stays,[14] a practice, though discontinued among persons of higher rank, still prevalent with the poor, who make the little wretches yet more miserable, out of cruel economy, allowing in the height of their stays for two or three years growth; I say, pitying the little sufferers, she prevailed with the parents to permit her to substitute waistcoats,[15] and continued to supply them with such till they grew near woman's estate, only making them somewhat stiffer as they advanced in size, being as great an enemy to the slatternly appearance of too unconfined a waist, as to the impenetrable boddice worn by the common people in the country. This may seem a trifling circumstance, but was much otherwise in effect, as it proved of great service to their health, and rendered them strong and well-shaped; in this last article the consequence was remarkable, for in fifteen years after she began this practice, there was scarcely a crooked young person to be seen within ten miles of her house: this gift not being confined to the poor; for, though not without difficulty, she prevailed even with the richest farmers to accept it from her, and as an inducement to them to do so, she herself made the waistcoats she gave them, that being her own work might seem to stamp a value upon them. Her attention to children was still more minute; for to prevent their little bodies from being more full of wounds than the anatomical figure in an almanack,[16] through the aukward hands which dress them, and seem to look upon them rather as pincushions than as creatures endued with feeling, she distributed dresses for new born infants that did not require one pin, and even courted people to accept them.

Lady Ellison was as careful of the minds of her young female neighbours as of the bodies of the children; and as assiduously endeavoured to preserve the purity of the one, as the ease of the others. Every girl, who at fifteen was sober, modest, industrious, and cleanly, she formally received under her protection, and gave her on the occasion a scarlet ribbon, which was afterwards worn on Sundays, as a distinguishing mark of Lady Ellison's favour. These young women were called in the neighbourhood Lady Ellison's Maidens; and it was well known, that whoever married them with her approbation, which was easily obtained by an honest, industrious man, was sure of receiving in dower with his wife furniture for a cottage, a cow, a pig, a male and two females of different sorts of poultry, a decent sober wedding-dinner for themselves and their parents, and to the bride more particularly was given a neat linen gown, with every other part of apparel suitable to it, as her bridal garments. This portion seldom failed of getting these maidens good husbands, and the rather as it was known to be the source of still farther advantages if after marriage they continued to deserve it. The scarlet ribbon became esteemed as a badge of great honour among them; if any one presumed to wear the colour to whom Lady Ellison had not given it, the outcry against her assurance and presumption was so great, that she was reduced to lay it aside, and appeared more discountenanced than the jay stripped of his borrowed feathers.[17] If a young man was inclined to marry, he was directed more by the top knot than by the face in his choice of a wife, that being the first object of his attention. If youthful levity at any time led one of these girls to be a little too free in her conduct, if she appeared slatternly in her dress, was remiss in her business, or neglected going to church, if a friend asked her what was become of her ribbon, the recollection never failed producing an amendment; nor was Lady Ellison ever obliged but once to withdraw this mark of favour, and that not till emulation had excited all the young girls in the neighbourhood to aim at the conduct which procured it. By its becoming general it at length grew no distinction, and thereby lost so much of its influence, that one of these young women behaved with great indiscretion, and Lady Ellison thought it necessary, for examples sake, to order her to return the ribbon, that the rest might not be disgraced by a seeming companionship with her. The girl hoped no worse consequences would ensue from the withdrawing of Lady Ellison's favour than the loss of the pecuniary advantages attending it, but she soon experienced effects still more mortifying; for she received such frequent marks of contempt, and was so continually reproached by her friends, that not enduring to live in a neighbourhood where she was despised and neglected, she went into a distant county; a lady, at the secret desire of Lady Ellison, having promised, by means of a friend who lived there, to procure her a service, and give her the means of regaining her character; which she did so effectually, that marrying near the place where she had lived in service, Lady Ellison's bounty reached her, and added comforts to those naturally attending a reformation. This disgrace of this young woman revived the people's sense of the honour of their protectress's favour, and made it as much valued as at first, though by the virtues it had encouraged it was become so general.

Instead of forming schools for girls, Sir George and Lady Ellison prevailed with the ladies of Millenium Hall to establish some of the two lower ranks in their neighbourhood, where they boarded the children they took from over-burdened parents, and those to whose orphan state they chose to supply the want of parental care. The visitation of these schools was one of Lady Ellison's constant duties, and a most pleasing employment, as she saw the school-mistresses endeavours succeed equal to her warmest wishes; and anticipated in hope the great benefit the rising generation in that neighbourhood would reap from so useful an institution.

## CHAP. VII.

It is unnecessary to say, that persons who were so careful of the children of others, paid a regular and extreme attention to the education of their own;

which in every respect answered their desires: both their own children and the little Tunstalls, who by Sir George's behaviour would have been thought to owe their being to the same father, as well as mother, proving remarkably capable of, and inclined to improvement. Their persons, particularly all the girls, except the youngest Miss Tunstall, were as fine as their understandings; the eldest Miss Ellison, especially, was completely beautiful, and though the rest fell somewhat short of her in that respect, yet they were endued with such various attractions that the inferiority was little remarked, except at first sight, or by those who nicely examined and compared their features. Their tempers were equally sweet and gentle, though they differed in their dispositions, the eldest being of the gravest turn, her understanding both solid and delicate, her taste true and refined; and the particular notice which her uncommon beauty very early excited, could not prevent her natural modesty and humility from deviating into bashfulness. Their second daughter was excessively lively, and by no means deficient in judgment, though her most distinguishing talent was wit; but it was so corrected by good nature, that it was a constant amusement to her intimates, and gave offence to no one. In this, however, she was excelled by the youngest Miss Tunstall, whose vivacity was so unbounded as frequently inclined her mother to think that the ravages a very severe small-pox had made in her face was no small blessing. If the flattery of the world, and the intoxicating pleasure of being admired, had been united with her natural disposition, Lady Ellison thought it too probable the good sense, of which she had an uncommmon share, must have been quite borne down by the torrent of her vivacity; but, fortunately, the extreme plainness of her face, amidst so many sisters, among whom even the least distinguishable could not but be allowed pretty, made her much disregarded, and in some measure damped the redundancy of spirits which, if animated by vanity, might have proved dangerous.

Sir George and Lady Ellison were careful by their kind notice to make her so far amends for the neglect shewn her by others, as to prevent her being too sensibly mortified; and as soon as she was of an age to be influenced by reason, endeavoured to turn the disadvantage of her person to the benefit of her mind, not attempting to conceal from her the plainness of her face, but trying to reconcile her to it, and instilling into her a desire of cultivating her understanding. They shewed her that 'public diversions could have no charms for her, as instead of pleasures they would yield her nothing but mortification and disappointment; that it was highly probable she must always remain in her single state, as her fortune would not be sufficient to make the other sex overlook her personal defects:' and then used every argument to convince her, how far she perhaps was from being a sufferer in point of happiness by these circumstances, which in the eyes of many might not appear favourable to it. The turn they wished to give to her mind, by thus teaching her a true knowledge of herself, was towards an ardent desire of improving her understanding, whereby she might be so well provided with amusements as to find no want of the pleasures she could not obtain. Her extreme vivacity naturally disposed her to dissipation; her apprehension was quick, but her attention was small; nothing, therefore, but what would give her somewhat of a graver turn could prove effectual to the end they aimed at; and they qualified the mortification such remonstrances might give her, by shewing even more tenderness for her than for her sisters, and taking every means of encouraging her, which soon compensated in her opinion for the neglect of others.

They had the satisfaction of finding their aim fully answered. Miss Louisa, that was her name, saw there was much reason in what they said; the little notice taken of her proved that she must extract her chief happiness from herself, and that private friendships and home amusements must be the principal sources of her pleasures. Vanity (for she was not without her share of it) corroborated what reason advised. She could not endure the thought of leading a trifling and insignificant existence, while her sisters were rendered considerable by various attractions: she wished to be distinguished too; but this was a laborious task. In general, it would be easy to outshine in accomplishments a whole family of beauties, but this was not the case with the Ellisons; their personal charms proved no impediment to their mental improvement. Their parents were not afraid of obscuring the lustre of their eyes by employing them in reading, nor thought application and serious study would fade the bloom in their cheeks; on the contrary, they imagined their eyes would beam forth more intelligence, and a more animated variety enliven their complexions, by having their minds stored with useful knowledge. If they wished to preserve Miss Louisa from the desire of admiration, they were no less solicitous to arm her sisters against the ill effects of it. The more sensible they were of their daughters' beauty, the more assiduous were their endeavours to leave the young ladies as little leisure as possible to think of it; and as they were convinced of the impossibility of preventing their finding pleasure in admiration and flattery, they thought it very necessary to qualify them for pleasures less exposed to the destroying hand of time, and save them from the trifling, insipid, and dispirited old age which so soon overtakes women whose only perfections are comprized in their faces, whose very life seems to lie in their beauty, and one might almost venture to pronounce extinct when that fades; and on this principle a new kind of bill of mortality[18] might be justly composed: as for example, of late hours, forty-eight; of morphew,[19] five; of pimples, twelve; of their thirtieth year, twenty-six; of their thirty-fifth year, after a tedious decay, sixty-seven; together with many other of maladies mortal to beauty. The Ellisons, not chusing to have their daughters existence circumscribed within such narrow bounds, had rendered them no less conspicuous by their accomplishments than they were by their persons; and though not neglectful of external grace, yet most assiduously cultivating mental acquirements. To excel excellence must be allowed difficult, and yet this was Miss Louisa Tunstall's aim; nor was she unsuccessful. By the hours she stole from sleep, and those she gained by declining the company of persons from whom she could expect no improvement, and who her parents visited only in regard to the necessary civility which vicinity required, she obtained so much time, and so industriously employed it, that she united in herself the various accomplishments wherein her sisters separately shone. Some of them arrived at great perfection in drawing, others in musick; she excelled in both. They were mistresses of the French and Italian languages; she had added to them both Latin and Greek, before she was twenty-five years old. They were well instructed in geography and astronomy, as far as could be learnt of the latter without a knowledge of mathematicks; she added to these geometry. They had gone through an extensive course of history, and all polite reading; she, beside, had made considerable advances in philosophy. The very extraordinary quickness of her apprehension, for her vivacity being all turned to study gave both vigour and quickness to an understanding naturally strong, much facilitated her arduous task; and she found so much pleasure in the pursuit of knowledge, that she frequently considered as an happiness that her form was such as did not deserve any share in her attention. She reaped so much solid satisfaction from her studies, that she stood in no want of the approbation of the multitude, and therefore had not the least desire to exhibit her learning; she felt it sufficiently its own reward, though known only to herself; and was not vain of her excellencies, as she considered that she was prompted to acquire them, by a sense of her deficiency in the article most valued in a person of her sex. In one particular, indeed, she could not excel her sisters, and that was in purity of religion and morals, for all possible care had been taken to instill the principles of the most rational piety into their very hearts, and dispositions good as theirs could not fail being most effectually influenced by the union of such precepts and examples.

Nor was it possible to say which of all these young ladies was most tenderly dutiful to her parents, or most affectionate to her brothers and sisters. They were entire strangers to envy; Miss Louisa would with pleasure assist in adorning their lovely persons, and they with delight observed her extraordinary accomplishments, which they attributed to her superior powers, and candidly admired, though they wished themselves capable of rising to the same excellence. Envy is founded on competition; they were preserved from it by a persuasion of her superiority of understanding; and she had been made so well acquainted with her own person, that she had entirely excluded it from her thoughts, where she was well convinced it did not deserve to hold any place; and would as soon have envied the throat of the nightingale or linnet, as the beauty of her sisters, so foreign did it seem to any thing to which she could form pretensions. And lest she might feel any mortification from thinking that after the death of her parents, she should by living single, as is usually the case, be reduced to a very small income, while her sisters might by marriage raise themselves to a splendid situation, Sir George frequently declared, that although he would give his daughters (for he made no distinction between those Lady Ellison had by Dr. Tunstall, and his own) only seven thousand pounds each in marriage, yet to any that lived single, he would add an annuity of £200 per annum, beside other advantages. He by no means wished his daughters to remain unmarried, but he feared no such consequence from this declaration, as he had too good an opinion of them to believe they would marry only for pecuniary motives.

Sir George considered marriage as a state commanded by God, and very useful to the community; he respected it therefore both on religious and political motives; always endeavoured to promote it with propriety, and heard with pleasure that any of his friends had entered into it with virtuous and rational views. He with great joy received letters from Mr. Maningham and Miss Almon, in the fourth year after they were settled in Jamaica, asking his approbation of their intended marriage; at the same time submitting their inclinations to his direction, to whom, as to one who had been more than a parent to them, they thought not only deference but all obedience due. He joyfully hastened their union, and accompanied his approbation with considerable presents; for though no man's words were more sincere than Sir George's, yet he thought them of so little value, that he always took care to accompany them with something he imagined of more solid worth.

Sir George's life was so uniform, that I shall not undertake to give a detail of his actions year by year. I have said enough (perhaps my readers will say too much) to give an idea of the general nature of them. To enter into more particulars of his beneficence might be tedious. The distresses which seem highly important to those who feel the pains arising from them, or the pleasure of relieving them, would often appear trifling to a reader; and as in the principal articles there is generally great similitude between one case and another, the sameness would tire in narration, though in execution, no variety is wanting to make the joys arising from beneficent actions always delightful; novelty is not requisite here, every relief is given with heightened satisfaction, from a recollection, that it has pleased the Almighty to empower the hand to administer frequent consolation to similar distress.

Year after year passed away in the execution of the plan of benevolence I have already described; the ardour of their humanity never cooled, and the various blessings it produced were ever increasing, by the good success of the means they pursued. Wherever they directed their observation, they beheld happiness, as it were, of their creating, and felt their hearts expanded with rapturous gratitude to the Being which had so graciously bestowed on them the means and the inclination of enjoying such transcendent pleasure; a goodness which humbled them to the greatest degree; for they felt themselves unworthy of the favour shewn them, and were sensible they made a most imperfect return for so much mercy; so far were they from taking pride in actions, the motive to which, as well as the power, was given them from above, and the imperfections in the performance only was their own: imperfections perceived by no one else, for those whose eyes were not opened by the same gratitude to, and love of the giver of all good, could not distinguish the failures which were visible to them, and inseparable from the best human actions.

However pure and warm the piety that glowed in Sir George's and Lady Ellison's breast, it was not of that rigid sort, that inclined them to seclude their children entirely from the world, they only desired to preserve them from its vanities and follies. When, in order to perfect them in external accomplishments, it seemed necessary to carry them to the metropolis, they went there yearly; though it was the most disagreeable duty they had ever performed, not from want of taste for the society, or the rational amusements which it afforded them, but as it broke into their established course of life. They feared that, notwithstanding all their precautions, some person might suffer by their absence; that by the delay of relief a distress might be prolonged, or for want of their watchful eye, and repeated instructions, some irregularities might be indulged, which their presence would have suppressed; or virtue might sicken from the want of daily encouragement.

But after the first year of these London journies, they found a means of rendering them more satisfactory. Sir George Ellison's sister was not unworthy of such a brother; she was a woman of excellent understanding, and admirable conduct, improved by all advantages of education, and long intercourse with the polite world. Her husband had for many years enjoyed a post of great honour and emolument under the government, but by a change of ministry was dispossessed during the first winter Sir George spent in London. This event made so considerable an alteration in their circumstances, that they found it necessary to retire into the country; a change not perfectly eligible to them, who had so long been habituated to a town life, and by drawing much rational and worthy society to their house, had rendered it extremely agreeable. This opened to Sir George, a means of gratifying both himself and them. He offered to his sister his house in town during nine months in the year, without interruption; and requested that during the other quarter she and her husband with their family would be his guests, only asking in return that she would take the care of his daughters during such part of it as he and Lady Ellison should chuse to be absent. He knew they could not be placed under a better guide; and made easy by this well placed confidence, he and Lady Ellison divided their residence during those three months between London and Dorsetshire; never being both absent from their country house above a fortnight at a time; while their daughters continued constantly in town during the three months, except Miss Louisa, who was indulged in her inclination to accompany them in every excursion into the country. Thus Sir George received much gratification from his brother-in-law's loss; and at the same time took from him the most disagreeable of its consequences. This couple, now more at leisure, likewise made them longer visits in the summer, than his necessary residence in town had hitherto permitted.

That season of the year always brought a great increase in their family. The young Blackburns then accompanying Mr. Ellison and Mr. Green, their tutor, to Sir George's during the usual recess at college. The Marquis, and his brothers, who were at the same university, visited their father at the same time; Mrs. Blackburn and her daughters, (Mr. Blackburn being dead) usually met the young gentlemen at Sir George's, and passed good part of the vacation with them. The Duke of ——— and Sir George at these seasons were still more than at others connected, though they always lived on the most intimate terms, but on these occasions they almost constituted one family; much to the satisfaction of all the parents, though indulgence to the young people was the principal motive, all of them respecting and loving Sir George as their father, in gratitude to his having so long acted the part of one towards them all. He received fresh pleasure at every return of this season, by observing the improvement of these worthy youths, whose merit seemed to enforce the benefits of a good education, as one could not expect that by nature so many should prove equally deserving. Their understandings, both in turn and extent, differed a good deal, and consequently their advances in learning; but in their virtues there was great equality; and such entire affection reigned through the whole, that it would have been difficult to discover which were allied by blood.

But pleasing as this society was to Sir George and Lady Ellison, they never suffered it to engross any of the time before allotted to the duties of humanity. Every one knew those were their first engagements, and none could wish to intrude on a destination they could not fail of approving.

## CHAP. VIII.

One summer, when this society was all met together at Sir George Ellison's, Mr Lamont arrived unexpectedly. He had spent several years abroad; and had not been long returned into his native country, before he determined to make a visit to Sir George, who received him with great pleasure. Lamont, on enquiring after his former fellow traveller, heard such an account of his extensive charities, and of that series of benevolent actions, to which he seemed to have wholly dedicated his time and fortune, that he expected to find an amiable recluse; and was not deterred from his design by that expectation; being so wearied with a search after amusement, and the pursuit of variety, that he thought with pleasure of spending a little time in quiet and contemplation, to both which he was yet a stranger; but was greatly surprised at being introduced into a company of between twenty and thirty persons; and still more so, when he learnt that the greatest part of them were lodged in Sir George's house. Instead of the serious, though respectable scene, his imagination had represented to him he found he had entered the seat of rational mirth, and decent festivity; a pleasing chearfulness sat on every countenance, and openness of conversation reigned universally; every individual of the company seemed happy in themselves, and delighted with all around them; but more particularly the master and mistress of the house, whose every feature expressed sublime content. The joy Sir George felt at the sight of Lamont, inspired Lady Ellison with equal pleasure, and she welcomed him to that happy society, with an ease and cordiality, that shewed she esteemed no one a stranger or indifferent to her, who had ever been a friend of her husband's.

Lamont congratulated himself on his good fortune, in having undertaken to renew an acquaintance, which promised to yield him more pleasure than he had before received from it; and when the hour of separation arrived, he declared that in all the countries he had been in, he had met with no society so agreeable. Years had much improved him; the giddiness of youth being past, thoughtless vivacity had given place to reflexion, and solidity of judgment well compensated for the loss of the flashy sallies which he and his companions had called Wit.

After Lamont had spent about a week in this family, he began to think the account he had received of Sir George's extensive charities was somewhat exaggerated; he saw him social and generous, but heard no mention of distresses, no hints at poverty relieved, no intimation of persons supported by his bounty. This induced him to enter into discourse with Mr. Green on the subject, from whom he soon learnt, that what had before been told him, fell considerably short of the truth; but that he could in no place have so little chance of hearing those charities mentioned, as where Sir George Ellison was; for he himself always avoided the topic, and his friends were too observant of his inclinations to speak on that subject if any stranger was present; when only themselves were by, to whom the detail was well known, they often made part of the conversation, as the various incidents relative to the objects of his bounty, afforded much matter for discourse.

Lamont was so well pleased with the company he had fallen into, that he could not resist reiterated invitations to prolong his stay; he found sufficient variety of conversations to amuse him, amidst so large a number; the way of life was entirely new to him; the affectionate harmony which reigned among them, the regularity of the family both in their devotions and employments, was the more agreeable to him, for having never before been in so quiet and tranquil a scene. He began to wish to partake of the sober happiness of domestic life, and to think that to one who was weary of rambling, and had with so little substantial satisfaction passed above twenty years in dissipation, and sometimes guilty, but always trifling amusements, marriage was an eligible state; an opinion perhaps as much owing to the charms of Mrs. Blackburn, as to the real pleasure he found in that society.

Mrs. Blackburn, who had then been a widow above four years, was considerably passed the bloom of life, being thirty-six years old; but she was one of those beauties whom time seems to have only lightly touched with his wings, just brushing off the bloom of youth, without leaving any of those deep traces which by his rougher touches he impresses on many faces. Her appearance would not have disgraced six and twenty; her complexion was still fine, gaining in delicacy almost as much as it had lost in resplendence by the fading of the roses in her cheeks. Her face, naturally small, and inclining to round, was still free from all lines that could betray want of youth; the easiness of her mind seemed to have preserved her from any deep impressions, and her situation had perhaps had its share herein. She had been exposed to so many disagreeable circumstances, that she had never continued long enough in a state of mirth to have any of those laughing traces worn, which, though not unpleasing, as they appear as much the lines of happiness as of age, are yet very destructive to beauty; and the bluntness of her sensations had made her distresses sit so lightly upon her, that the uneasiness she suffered made no lasting impressions on her countenance, which was as free from the lines of anguish, as from those of mirth. She still preserved the same delicacy of person that had in youth distinguished her, and to which probably was owing much of her youthful air. However, Lamont could not be deceived as to her age, how far soever appearances were in her favour, all her children making part of the society he was in, and her eldest son was then avowedly eighteen years old; but with fewer prejudices in her favour than he had conceived, he might reasonably enough have allowed, that the age which is not discoverable in the person, ought not to be considered as a fault, since it can scarcely fail of having good effects on the mind; beside that she was in reality, as well as in appearance, younger than himself.

Lamont's particular attention to Mrs. Blackburn was soon observed, though silently, by the company; but they as little expected it to have any serious consequences as he did, till the young people being on their return to college, Mrs. Blackburn had fixed the day for her departure, which was about two months after Lamont's arrival among them. He then began to grow a little grave; and after having appeared particularly thoughtful for two days, made Sir George acquainted with his inclinations, and desired he would use his interest in his favour with the widow.

Sir George was pleased with the prospect of having his friend fixed in their neighbourhood; and had so good an opinion of him, as to believe he would make Mrs. Blackburn very happy, who would be rendered more sensible of his merits, by the comparison she must unavoidably make between him and her former husband. He thought, indeed, she might live as happily by continuing in her state of widowhood, but that depended on her own opinion; and if she chose to hazard second nuptials, he believed she would not easily make a better choice. He therefore undertook the office with which Lamont had entrusted him, only disclaiming all attempts to influence her.

Mrs. Blackburn had remained longer ignorant of the impression she had made on Lamont, than she could have done had it happened earlier in life. A stranger to coquetry even in youth, she had for some years ceased to imagine a possibility of any man's being in love with her; and could consider herself as nothing but an object of indifference, when she beheld a very pretty daughter on the verge of womanhood, for the eldest Miss Blackburn was near fifteen, blooming and lovely, as amiable in mind as in person, having all her mother's gentleness and sweetness of temper, with more strength of understanding, and tenderer sensibilities. Such a daughter might well exclude all thoughts of conquest from her mother's mind; but Lamont's behaviour had been sufficiently intelligible to excite some suspicions in Mrs. Blackburn of his uncommon attachment, before Sir George explained the commission upon which he was sent; yet she was somewhat surprised to find the prepossession she saw he had conceived in her favour productive of so serious a consequence.

When Sir George had delivered his friend's proposal, Mrs. Blackburn desired him to give her his advice upon it. Sir George immediately considered Lamont's suit as granted, believing that if a woman of thirty-six years old, with children grown up almost to maturity, hesitates on such an occasion, she will not very long resist a lover's importunity. He suspected that she who in such circumstances asked advice, wished for a sanction to her marriage. But Sir George, with all his good nature, was a little perverse on this occasion, and refusing to advise, referred her to her own inclination; only observing, that if she had any thoughts of a second marriage, she might not have an opportunity of entering into it on such advantageous terms, Lamont being a man of sense and merit, of no improper age, and possessed of a considerable fortune, which beside the common recommendations of wealth, had still an additional value, as it was an undeniable proof of his sincere regard for her. Concluding with desiring her to consider what he had said on his friend's behalf, not as intended to influence her in favour of marriage, but only if she was disposed to relinquish a single life, to give his opinion how far Mr. Lamont was an eligible person.

This method of proceeding did not quite answer Mrs. Blackburn's wishes: She was well disposed towards Lamont; she thought him agreeable and deserving; his fortune afforded her some temptation, and his attachment to her was too flattering not to prejudice her a good deal in his favour; but her heart had never been susceptible of that extreme tenderness which excludes prudence, and at the age she then was, would not have excused in herself a prepossession, strong enough to have resisted the advice of a friend. Had Sir George advised her to have refused this offer, she would have complied with a good grace, as she would then have judged propriety required it; but she rather wished to have found him in a contrary opinion, that she might have given way to her choice with dignity. His backwardness in this point left her in a dilemma; and not quite satisfied with seeming to chuse a second marriage, and yet unwilling to refuse it, she could not bring herself to give an explicit answer, but expressed a satisfaction in her present situation, that rendered her little inclined to change it; dropping at the same time some intimations of the advantages she should receive in point of fortune by an alliance with Mr. Lamont, if she could reconcile herself, at her age, to enter again into wedlock's bands, imagining it more decent to be influenced by the love of wealth, than by inclination for the owner of it.

Sir George could not forbear smiling at the difficulties into which his neutrality had reduced her; and did not press for a plainer answer to his message, forseeing that Lamont must be very defective in importunity, if he did not soon obtain a full compliance. He therefore told his friend he had made known his inclination, but left him to discover the effects, as he imagined a lover had a better chance of obtaining a favourable answer, if he solicited it in person, than by the cold intervention of an unfeeling agent.

The event did not contradict Sir George's opinion. Lamont found it no very difficult matter to persuade the widow to relinquish her widowhood; not that she seemed over-ready to make him that sacrifice; conscious worth made her assume a dignity even in compliance; she would 'not unsought be won;'[20] and preserved feminine decorum so well, that she appeared to yield to his reasons and importunity, rather than to her own inclinations. Sir George and Lady Ellison found no small amusement in observing the progress of this affair, and Lamont was not weary of soliciting, as he perceived the event of his suit was not doubtful; for all the objections the lady made, were only intended to heighten his sense of the favour she at last intended to confer, and to keep up her own dignity; views which he was too polite to wish to disappoint. But when all the impediments prudery suggested were removed, there remained another point of some delicacy to be settled, which was no other than a doubt that arose whether Mrs. Blackburn's children ought to be present at the celebration of her nuptials. She felt some pain from an apprehension of their censuring a second engagement, and was conscious she should not better become the character of bride, for being surrounded with sons and daughters who were almost grown up to maturity.

The Ellisons perceived a little aukwardness in this circumstance, but considered it as unavoidable, since in that situation she must in a short time appear, though it were to be avoided on her wedding day; therefore they judged it better to go through it with courage, and not increase any opinion of impropriety, by an appearance of a consciousness which would only serve to confirm it. Accordingly, Sir George took upon himself to acquaint the youthful part of the family with their mother's intentions, and to envite them to her wedding, which was to be celebrated at his house; and she accompanied his letters with others from herself, proper on the occasion.

Mr. Ellison had likewise an invitation to be of the party, that he might do the honours of the house to the young gentlemen, and also from a secret view of his father's, who wished to give him as frequent opportunities as possible of seeing Miss Blackburn; whose uncommon perfections had awakened in him a strong desire to render his son sensible of her charms; believing, that although he might get a wife with a much larger fortune, he could no where find one so likely to make him happy.

The name of a wedding carries with it a notion of festivity, which rendered the invitation agreeable to the young people, and they were not ready to think an action could deserve censure which was to be performed at Sir George Ellison's house, a prejudice in favour of their mother's marriage, which the behaviour of Sir George and Lady Ellison increased; for they endeavoured to win over their approbation, by seeming themselves to approve the alliance. Lamont's conduct had no small share in making his new family perfectly well pleased with acquiring a second father, for he not only shewed them every affectionate attention, but made to each very handsome presents, well knowing that nothing captivates youthful minds more than well judged liberality; and Mrs. Blackburn had the satisfaction of seeing her children take pleasure in an event which in fact promised them some advantages, and could not possibly injure them in any respect, she having nothing in her own power.

Sir George did not mention to Mr. Green his wishes in regard to his son and Miss Blackburn till above a year after this marriage, and then had the mortification of hearing that Mr. Ellison seemed to have conceived an attachment to a young lady who lived near Oxford; Mr. Green telling him, that he purposed giving him this information if he had not thus led him to the subject, and enquiring whether he did not think it advisable on this account to hasten the young gentlemen abroad, as during their travels Mr. Ellison's passion would probably subside. But when Sir George, by his enquiries, found there was no objection to the young lady but her deficiency in fortune, he did not think it proper to alter his plan; saying, that if it might be allowed a reason for sending his son abroad before he was as capable as he wished of improving thereby, it was none for hastening the departure of the rest, who could not fail of suffering by the alteration; and that as the object of his son's affections was amiable, deserving, and a gentlewoman, the continuance of his attachment was no real evil, as he might very well excuse want of fortune in a wife. He had, indeed, ardently wished to make Miss Blackburn his daughter, but as he had no other motive for that desire than a view to his son's happiness, he should readily relinquish a scheme which would no longer answer the purpose he hoped.

Sir George was very averse to the too common method of forming distant views, and anxiously fixing the heart on their accomplishment. He thought great solicitude about any worldly affairs sinful, as it is expressly forbidden us by Him who has the best right to our obedience,[21] and at the same time extremely foolish, as our ignorance of the effect any event will have on our happiness should teach us to submit the disposal of our lot to him who better knows what is really for our benefit, and only calmly and prudently, on our parts, pursue what our reason tells us is most eligible; but contentedly resign our aim when we find we cannot attain it, reflecting that, through the imperfection of our reason, the greatest misfortunes might have arisen from the accomplishment of our wishes.

## CHAP. IX.

However philosophically Sir George might look on the common affairs of life, there were some occasions whereon he found it difficult to exercise the resignation he was sensible was his duty. His patience and fortitude were exposed to a very severe trial, after a long enjoyment of peace and happiness. Lady Ellison, in the midst of a constant course of good health, was seized with a scarlet fever, which brought her life into great danger, and raised the tenderest alarms in her husband's breast, whose thoughts had for some days been entirely engrossed by her illness, when they were called off to another subject; for in passing by the parlour door, he heard his youngest daughter crying most violently, and between her sobs exclaiming, that 'she was sure the man told a cruel lie, for her brother Ellison could not do so wicked, so barbarous a thing.'

Sir George, startled by her expressions, and alarmed at her affliction, went into the room and enquired the cause. The girl, who was about nine years old, endeavoured to evade his question, having been charged to conceal what she had by chance over-heard; but as Sir George urged his enquiry, and she had been bred up in an abhorrence of falshood, she was reduced to tell him, that, as she was passing by the kitchen door, she heard a person saying to the servants, that her brother Ellison had killed a man, and was carried to prison for the murder.

Sir George was thunder-struck at so dreadful a tale; paternal tenderness whispered to his heart that it could not be true; but yet the sound of murder filled him with such inexpressible horror, that it was some time before he had power to enquire into this strange affair of the servants to whom it had been related; nor did he receive any satisfaction from them. The account they gave him was, that the master of a little inn in that parish had been there, to enquire if they had received any bad news of Mr. Ellison; for a gentleman, who changed horses at his house, enquiring who was the owner of the adjacent handsome seat and fine park, and being told Sir George Ellison, a gentleman who rendered all the neighbourhood happy, cried out, 'Poor man! he has not a son at Oxford, I hope.' Being asked why he hoped so? answered, that, 'as he came through that town he saw a young gentleman conducted to prison, and was told his name was Ellison; that he was son to a baronet, the worthiest man that ever lived, and that the young gentleman was committed for a murder; adding, that no sight ever shocked him more, the extremest affliction being impressed on the criminal's countenance, as well as on those of several young gentlemen who attended him.'

Sir George immediately sent to the inn-keeper, but could obtain no farther intelligence; he said, the gentleman who had told him this story was himself ignorant of farther particulars, for being travelling with the utmost speed on account of business, had it not been for the uproar in the streets of Oxford, he should not have stopped long enough to have learnt even so much as he had related. As every one felt himself tenderly interested in all that concerned their general benefactor, the inn-keeper had taken alarm, and came to Sir George's house to know if there was any truth in the dreadful story; and the servants had agreed to conceal it from their master, to avoid giving him possibly causeless sorrow, and at least an earlier grief than was necessary, had not his daughter's affliction made the discovery.

Sir George was in the utmost consternation; he could not forbear giving some faith to the report, and yet it seemed strange that Mr. Green should not acquaint him with so important an event, but leave him to receive the shock from accidental information. He was sensible his son's temper was naturally violent, but for many years had enjoyed the satisfaction of thinking all his passions were totally subdued by reason and humanity; yet he could not but fear that nature had in some fatal instant broken forth, and baffled all the effects of education. Had Lady Ellison been in health, Sir George would have gone instantly to Oxford, rather than continue in his anxious state; but so far from leaving her, he dared not even tell his apprehensions, convinced that the effects in her situation would be fatal; and was obliged to assume such a command over his countenance as would prevent her perceiving the sufferings of a heart oppressed to the greatest degree, for he loved his son with the utmost paternal fondness; but the virtue of his mind was such, that had it been put to his choice, he would rather have seen him carried to his grave, the untimely victim of sickness in the bloom of youth, than that he should have imbrued his hands in blood. Very difficult we may therefore suppose was Sir George's task, to conceal the extremest anguish the heart can suffer, under an air of chearful serenity; and it was rendered still harder by Lady Ellison's being so much better that day as to know him perfectly, and to wish to have him constantly by her, finding the pains of sickness almost dispelled by his assiduous care and tender attentions, which if they did not make her quite insensible of her disease, at least reconciled her to it, by seeing how many delightful opportunities it afforded him of giving her undeniable proofs of an affection which constituted the happiness of her life. Had not Sir George entertained a hope that this dreadful story might prove false, he could not have supported so violent a restraint, and never found the hour of bed-time so great a relief, as he then was at liberty to give way to his affliction.

As soon as he heard this melancholy news he had dispatched a servant to Mr. Green at Oxford, to desire to know what grounds there was for such a report; but that gentleman had left the place before the messenger got there, and arrived the next day at Sir George's before noon.[22]

Sir George was sitting by his lady's bed-side, and endeavouring to dispell the fears she had conceived for his health, from the pallidness of his countenance, which bore strong impressions of the agitation of his mind, and total want of rest, for he had not even been able to persuade himself to go into bed that night, when a servant called him out. He found Mr. Green on the stairs, who to his great vexation had perceived by the melancholy which sat on every face, that he was disappointed in his hope of giving the first information of the melancholy event; but the sight of Sir George, and the distress of mind he plainly saw he suffered, shocked him excessively. Sir George was unable to speak, but with trembling impatience seized him by the hand, led him hastily into his library, and throwing himself into a chair assumed all the fortitude he was master of, and desired Mr. Green to tell him the whole without preface or preparation, for since he had outlived the hearing his son was a murderer, there was no reason to fear any ill effects from relating the most afflicting circumstances.

'Dear Sir,' said Mr. Green, 'do not call your son by so harsh a name; he is indeed very unfortunate, but not guilty.'

A full pardon never gave greater joy to a condemned criminal than Sir George Ellison felt at those words. He rose from his seat in rapture, crying, 'Is my son then innocent?' and with hands and eyes up-lifted, added with a lower voice, 'Heaven be thanked!' A few tears of joy fell from his eyes, and growing more calm, he desired Mr. Green to proceed.

This gentleman told him, that, 'had he imagined the report of this unhappy affair could have been brought him by any other means, he would have hastened his journey, especially as he perceived the relation given him had far exceeded the truth; but hoping fame would not be so great a babbler, he had delayed setting out till he had brought his pupil to a more composed state of mind, and provided every thing possible for his convenience. That he has killed a gentleman,' continued he, 'is certain; and what renders it still more grievous to him, that gentleman was his friend, and the father of the young lady to whom I told you he was so much attached; but the blow was accidental, as they were on a shooting party, in a wood where they had liberty from the owner to pursue their sport; nor would the misfortune have happened, but through the inexcusable carelessness of the deceased. The poor man paid the forfeit of his heedlessness on the spot. The consternation of the whole company was great, but your son's grief was inexpressible. A surgeon was immediately sent for, but to no purpose, the shot had penetrated his brain, and there was no hope. Mr. Ellison immediately delivered himself up to justice, and was attended to prison by all the gentlemen who were of the party, by the Marquis, Lord John and Lord George Grantham, and the young Blackburns; who were all deeply affected by so melancholy an accident, and the extreme affliction it gave their friend.'

'An affliction, indeed,' said Sir George, 'which no time can wholly eradicate; for however innocent of intention, the thought of having deprived a man of life, of having robbed his friends of perhaps their greatest happiness, and possibly sent him into eternity at a time when he was but ill prepared to meet the judgment on which his fate through all ages must depend, will ever hang heavy on the mind.'

'This misfortune,' added Mr. Green, 'is certainly accompanied with very aggravating circumstances. Mr. Blanchard, that was the name of the poor deceased man, was, indeed, a bad husband, and a severe father; but if his temper might reasonably be supposed to render his life less dear to his wife and daughter, his extravagance had however made it necessary. He originally possessed but a moderate younger brother's fortune; his wife married him against the inclination of her friends, and for want of their prudent assistance had no settlements; the whole therefore of their fortunes were in his power, and in a few years he spent it all, and found himself reduced to live entirely on the income of a place, which had hitherto proved so insufficient for his support. This obliged him to retire into the country; and, to Mr. Ellison's misfortune, he fixed near Oxford. He was polite, and agreeable in company; which with the charms of his daughter, could not fail rendering his house very attractive, and making his conversation sought by people of the best fashion in the neighbourhood. With him perished the subsistence of his wife and daughter; and what is still more affecting to your son, by the hand of him whose great ambition was to be united in the tenderest ties to that daughter, if he could obtain your consent; for without it, he would contract no alliance, determined to sacrifice every inclination to your will. All the hope he had so fondly cherished of this happiness is now blasted; he cannot flatter himself that Miss Blanchard will ever behold without horror the murderer of her father; and what still more afflicts him is the fear that they will not accept from so fatal a hand the support of which he has deprived them. He gave, however, into my care an hundred pounds, desiring me to find some means of conveying it to them for the supply of present exigencies, in such a manner as might prevent their suspecting from whence it came; but this I had not leisure to perform, judging that after I had done my first services to my unhappy pupil, the most necessary point was to acquaint you with his misfortune, which I was determined to do in person, as it might prove most satisfactory to you.'

'You well know, my good friend,' replied Sir George, 'that I never designed to controul my son's inclinations, in a particular wherein his choice was so much more material than mine, but had I ever hesitated, this misfortune must have secured my consent, if the young lady's can ever be obtained; as his marriage with her is the best reparation he can make either to her or her mother; but this is a thing not to be thought of now; time, especially if Miss Blanchard has any prepossession in his favour, may bring her to look on him rather as a companion in her misfortune than as the cause of it. I most sensibly feel his distress, but am glad he is so anxious to repair the evil he has innocently brought upon them, without which I should have thought him very deficient in generosity. If these unhappy persons scruple receiving a pecuniary reparation from the hands of the son, they cannot refuse what they have, in honour, a right to require from the father.'

Sir George found his spirits greatly lightened by hearing his son was so entirely innocent; he compassionated his misfortune extremely, but when he considered him as free from guilt, he hoped the violence of his present affliction would soon abate; and he felt some comfort in learning that Mr. Blanchard's faults were such as rendered his loss by no means irreparable to his surviving family.

After having enquired into every particular, Sir George returned to Lady Ellison's apartment, with an happier countenance than when he left her; which was soon discovered by her watchful eye, and removed much of the anxiety she had been under for his health. Her fever was so much abated by the following day, that Sir George sent Mr. Green back to Oxford, with a promise of being soon with his son; and every assurance that he thought could prove consolatory to him. He did not think it advisable to leave home without acquainting Lady Ellison with the cause of his journey, lest she might hear it in a manner, and from a person less proper, and be more shocked thereby, than he hoped she would be if related by him. This delayed his setting out a day or two longer than would otherwise have been necessary, as he feared causing too early an agitation in her spirits; but as soon as he thought it might be done with safety, he acquainted her with the affair in the least alarming manner he was able, and had the satisfaction of seeing her bear it as well as he could expect; but the truth was, she concealed the concern it gave her as much as possible from him, lest she should increase what she well knew he must suffer.

When this necessary step was passed, nothing retarded Sir George's journey; he repaired to Oxford with all speed, and directly visited his son in his prison, where he found him as conveniently accommodated as the place would permit, and attended by his friends, who kindly took all possible care that he should be little alone, till his mind were in a state that would render reflexion less painful. Sir George tried every means of reviving his dejected spirits, and promised to remain with him till his trial was over;[23] which though a mere legal formality, where the innocence of the fact was so evident, yet was a shocking ceremony to him, who most severely lamented the accident.

Sir George found a way of administering still greater comfort to his son: He waited on Mrs. Blanchard, and expressing his concern for what she suffered by the misfortune of one of his family, in a manner the least affecting that he possibly could, he intreated her to compassionate the unhappy situation of the unfortunate cause of their sorrow, and to shew her generous pity by accepting all the reparation the nature of the case would permit, and thereupon produced a settlement of two hundred pounds per annum on Mrs. Blanchard, for her life, and one hundred per annum on Miss Blanchard for her life also; which he took the liberty of insisting on their receiving, as the certain tokens of their pardon.

The ladies were much surprized at this action, and knew not what part to take. They were entirely destitute of fortune, having little more than the hundred pounds which Mr. Green had contrived to remit to them, without their being able certainly to learn from whence it came, though they strongly suspected the generous hand to which they were obliged. Mrs. Blanchard was a woman of sense and merit; but by the long course of ill treatment she had received from her husband, and the frequent pecuniary difficulties they had been under, her spirits and health were both so impaired, that she was not fit to struggle with poverty, yet knew not how to submit to so humiliating a support. Miss Blanchard was in a less helpless state. She had good health, lively spirits, and an excellent understanding; and though since her acquaintance with Mr. Ellison her employments had been of a more learned kind, conducted by his recommendation, and instigated by her desire to please him, yet she was well versed in all feminine business, and very capable of providing for herself; which, so far from looking upon as a degradation, she would have thought more honourable than living on the charity of another; but she was strongly influenced by an apprehension of lowering herself so much by a menial employment, as might ruin all her hopes of Mr. Ellison, to whom she was more attached by affection than even by interest; and whatever judgment might be formed by others, she imagined he would not think meanly of her, from knowing she was one of the objects of his father's bounty. This consideration in some measure conquered her reluctance. Necessity had equal power over her mother; and together with Sir George's pressing intreaties, that they would consent to the only thing that could alleviate the concern he and his son were under, at length determined them to accept of a

218 / The History of Sir George Ellison

provision from him; but they were very desirous of restraining his generosity within narrower bounds; Mrs. Blanchard insisting that an hundred pounds a year would furnish them with all the necessaries of life, and was more than they had any expectations of ever being possessed of after Mr. Blanchard's death, had he lived even many years longer. Sir George was the most obstinate man in the world when an act of generosity was in question; all the ladies could say was ineffectual; he insisted the more pertinaciously for their resistance, and did not leave them till he obtained their full acquiescence in his request.

## Chap. X.

All Mr. Ellison's friends were of opinion that travelling would afford more relief to his spirits than any other means that could be used, and therefore represented to Sir George that it ought to be no longer delayed, to which he readily agreed; and it was determined, that as soon as the trial was over, the young gentlemen should be equipped and sent abroad. Mrs. Blanchard expressed an intention of leaving Oxfordshire, whereupon Sir George prevailed with her to remove to a small house in his neighbourhood, having some desire to be fully acquainted with the conduct and merits of her daughter, who he saw would in all probability become his also; but she thought in decency she ought not to go thither till Mr. Ellison had left the kingdom; for though she could not resent an action so far from his intention, yet she feared the world might censure an appearance of immediate forgiveness; and indeed, notwithstanding her sense of his innocence, the sight of him could not but be extremely painful to her.

The solemn ceremony passed, Sir George left Oxford with Mr. Green, and all that gentleman's pupils; but Mr. Ellison prevailed on Miss Blanchard to grant him an interview at a friend's home before his departure, where we may suppose (without any very good evidence of what passed) that he was not sparing of assurances of the sincerity of his passion, or of vows of constancy; the less credible circumstance is that he kept them, notwithstanding all the dissipation of travelling, the temptations every country offered, and the, so often, chilling effects of absence.

The Duke of ———— had no objection to his sons going abroad directly, and in a very short time after Sir George's return home, Mr. Ellison, the Duke's three sons, and the three Mr. Blackburns, set out on their travels, under the conduct of Mr. Green and Lamont, that gentleman having offered to accompany them, finding his wife well inclined to be of their party. As he was well acquainted with most countries in Europe, and had formed connexions with several persons of fashion in each, Sir George considered his offer as very advantageous to the young gentlemen; but as it was not judged so advisable to carry the young ladies, Lady Ellison desired they would accept of her as a parent till their own returned; an addition to their family which was extremely acceptable to Miss Ellisons and Miss Tunstalls, between whom and Miss Blackburns a tender friendship had been cultivated, as well as with the young Lady Granthams. Miss Blanchard, who with her mother settled in the neighbourhood as soon as the young gentlemen departed, was a pleasing addition to their society, and delighted with it. Greater happiness could not be found on earth, than was enjoyed by this family, who frequently received the most agreeable accounts of the progress their young friends made in their travels, and saw every thing about them go on to their utmost wish; and in this state we shall leave them, having already given so minute an account of Sir George Ellison's actions, that my readers will readily excuse what would be little more than a repetition of his virtues, till the return of the travellers, which was a season of great joy to the whole neighbourhood; but none were more tenderly interested in it than Miss Blanchard, and the eldest Miss Ellison. This young lady had always entertained a strong affection for the Marquis, with whom she had in a manner been brought up, and the attachment was visibly mutual, beginning in childhood, and increasing with their years, though he was ten years older than her.[24] When he went abroad she had not completed her fifteenth year; and themselves, as well as those who observed their fondness, imagined their love was only such as might naturally be expected between persons bred up in all the intimacy of brother and sister; but at his Lordship's return, his friends discovered what he had learnt during his absence, that his attachment was of a tenderer nature; and Miss Ellison's heart soon appeared to correspond with his.

The Duke could not object to an alliance with one to whom he was so much obliged, and Sir George consented with pleasure. He with equal satisfaction completed the marriage of his son with Miss Blanchard, whose conduct and conversation had fixed her strongly in his esteem.

Sir George at the same time delivered up his accounts to Mr. Blackburn; as his father was dead, Sir George thought he might, without shewing inexcusable disregard to his good friend's will, anticipate the time of putting him in possession. By these accounts Mr. Blackburn found himself possessed of his whole estate, not only clear of incumbrance, but in excellent repair, much improved, and some thousand pounds in money; with very good fortunes assigned to each of his brothers and sisters, out of the accumulated produce of the estate; Sir George, according to his first resolution, not having appropriated the least part to his own use.

This was no sooner done, than Mr. Blackburn much surprised Sir George and Lady Ellison by declaring the strongest affection for Miss Louisa Tunstall, whose person had prevented any suspicion of that nature; and, as I before said, she had been taught to relinquish all thoughts of making any favourable impressions on the other sex, and to fix her expectations entirely on 'single blessedness.'[25] The most perfect friendship had visibly subsisted between her and Mr. Blackburn; she had confined her affections within these rational bounds, and he had never declared any views beyond it; determined to conceal his intentions till he was master of his estate, from an excess of delicacy, which made him fear lest he might be thought by that alliance to aim at entering sooner into possession. The uncommon qualifications of Miss Louisa, the excellence of her temper, heart, and understanding, had entirely captivated his affections, and given him such a prejudice in favour of her person, that although he perceived she had no beauty to boast, yet he thought it perfectly agreeable, and indeed the sense and sensibility[26] which her countenance expressed, might to those who knew her intimately, compensate for the irregularity of her features, and the darkness of her complexion. As to her figure it was no way amiss, she was genteel enough, though not finely formed.

It is natural to imagine, that Miss Louisa's affection for Mr. Blackburn soon grew more tender, on finding herself the object of his fondest love; and she must have had little of her sex in her composition, if her vanity had not felt great gratification in so unexpected an event, which from the extraordinary merits of the young gentleman, gave extreme pleasure to all her friends.

The Duke and Duchess of ——— with no small pain removed to the family seat, where they could now afford to live in proper figure, having put their estate in excellent order, and saved fortunes for their younger children. For their second son they bought a commission in the guards, and the youngest chose to take orders. The Marquis and his lady fixed in the house the Duke quitted, desiring to live in Sir George's neighbourhood, where his father and mother made them a yearly visit of no small length, in order to enjoy the society of their old friends.

Mr. and Mrs. Ellison fixed their abode at a very moderate distance; and Mr. and Mrs. Blackburn resided at his family-seat. Of his two younger brothers the one chose the profession of physic, the other of the law; which had been the reason Sir George Ellison thought proper to give them the advantages of travelling, as it was at a time of life when it would not interrupt their studies, but improve their behaviour, and enlarge their understandings. The same motives had induced him to prevail with the Duke of ———— to suffer Lord John and Lord George Granthams to be of the party; an indulgence seldom granted to younger sons.

Some years after, this amiable society, large as it already was, received an increase from the arrival of Mr. James Ellison, his lady and family, and Mrs. Reynolds, who was become a widow. As they had given notice of their intention, Sir George had built them a house, by their desire, in the neighbourhood, there being then none to be hired thereabouts. Mr. Ellison had several years before remitted to Sir George the ten thousand pounds he had lent him, having raised a very considerable fortune. Mr. and Mrs. Godfrey (Sir George's sister and her husband) likewise passed much of their time with one or the other, to their mutual satisfaction; and though the society has been considerably decreased by the marriage of most of the young ladies of each family, yet they are so happily disposed of, that their parents cannot lament their absence: and as they practise the virtues they had learnt both from the instruction and example of Sir George and Lady Ellison, their dispersion serves to extend happiness to a greater number of persons than could reach the knowledge of a man fixed like Sir George chiefly in one place, and indeed beyond what the fortune of one person could supply.

I think I cannot take leave of this worthy family at a better time, than when it enjoys the utmost felicity the world can afford, lest by some of those unavoidable misfortunes, which in the course of time must befal every mortal being, the scene may be overcast, and those who now are the happiest of mortals become objects of compassion; which would deprive us of a fair opportunity of quitting them, for I hope none of my readers would be able to bear the very thought of forsaking a friend in adversity.

F I N I S.

# Notes to the Novel

~

## Preface

1. Here Scott echoes the sentiment of Johnson in *Rambler* 4; see my Introduction, pp. xix-xx.

2. Scott echoes the sentiment of Johnson's *Rambler* 60, which calls for narratives of the common detail of everyday life and of unexalted persons.

3. Scott may actually have had a model in the philanthropist John Howard (1726-90), who from 1756 had interested himself at Cardington, Bedfordshire, in model cottages for the villagers, the encouragement of individual industry among them, and the establishment of schools for children of all sects (*DNB*; *Anecdotes of the Life and Character of J.H. written by a Gentleman* [London: Hookham et al., 1790]; John Aiken, *View of the Character and Public Services of the Late John Howard* [London: F. Johnson, 1792]; and numerous other memorials). Howard is known to have visited Bath in 1766. It is probable that the similar efforts in Yorkshire of Nathaniel Cholmley and his wife (in 1774), Anne Jesse Smelt postdated their marriage and were quite possibly inspired by Scott; when Elizabeth Montagu visited them in 1783 she reported they had built a village near their house and furnished and fitted up the houses for their old or married servants; they also supervised a school for the children (Historical Manuscripts Commission, *Calendar of the Manuscripts of the Marquis of Bath* [London: His Majesty's Stationery Office, 1904], 1:349).

## Book I.

1. Mr. Ellison as a younger son could have entered the church, the army or navy, or the law, and had apparently chosen the last.

2. Perhaps Mr. Ellison was possessed of four thousand pounds. A convenient way to calculate the equivalent today is to multiply by one hundred and state the resultant figure in dollars: $400,000.

3. Ellison had apparently been apprenticed to the father of Lamont, the young traveling companion with whom he had visited Millenium Hall.

4. Nestor Ironside, Sir Richard Steele's persona in *The Guardian* essays, has been named guardian to the Lizard family, a function that allows Steele to explore the

problems and attitudes of the young. In *Guardian* 31 (16 April 1713) the twenty-three-year-old Jane Lizard describes the accomplishments of a man of merit, among which she includes (describing her own lover) white teeth and black eyes.

5. The female figure of Commerce was familiar in both literature and art; see, for instance, Richard Glover's *London: or, The Progress of Commerce* (1739).

6. The character of Jamaican women had already been stereotyped; Charles Leslie in his *New History of Jamaica* (1740) had noted that some read, but all danced a lot, coquetted much, and dressed for their admirers. "Their Education consists entirely in acquiring these little Arts. 'Tis a thousand Pities they do not improve their Minds, as well as their Bodies" (quoted in Frank Crendall, *Historic Jamaica* [London: For the Institute of Jamaica, 1915], p. 34). Wylie Sypher notes that the women were thought to be indolent, gay, vain, proud, some with haughty overbearing spirits which if not checked in infancy, could vent themselves in "turbulent fits of rage and clamour" ("The West-Indian as a 'Character' in the Eighteenth Century," *Studies in Philology* 36: 503-20). A pretty woman with these characteristics might easily attract Ellison but would not subsequently deeply attach him. I am indebted to Keith Williams for the reference to Sypher.

7. Holiday.

8. Sypher notes that Creoles in general were thought to be generous, warm-hearted, and brave, but indolent, reckless, frivolous, passionate, and often cruel to subordinates, a result of the hot climate and of the institution of slavery, which degraded the masters more than the slaves ("West-Indian as a Character," p. 503).

9. Leslie in 1740 noted that learning in Jamaica was at its lowest ebb: there were no public schools in the island, and the office of teacher was looked on with contempt and no gentleman would keep company with one; any man of parts and learning who would employ himself as a teacher would be despised and starve. The children of planters learned no more than reading, writing, and casting accounts. Those planters who could sent their children to school in England (Crendall, p. 33). Sypher adds that there were about three hundred Creole children in English schools in 1750, and by 1770 over three-quarters of the non-slave children of West Indian planters were being educated in England (p. 504). Jamaican slaves were deliberately kept ignorant; by 1760 a colony of Moravians was allowed to instruct them in Christianity but forbidden to provide any additional education (Clinton V. Black, *History of Jamaica* [London: Collins Clear-Type Press, 1958], p. 207). Scott clearly addressed herself to a situation about which she was knowledgeable and had strong opinions.

10. Scott's language is creative, more allusion than direct quotation, but for "God's steward," see Titus 1:7; "the sower sowing his seed in vain," Leviticus 26:16; "the clouds dropping water," Judges 5:4, Job 36:28; "the fatness of the earth," Genesis 27:28, 39; "fruits brought forth by the sun," Deuteronomy 33:14.

11. Kingstown: Kingston, on a splendid landlocked harbor on the southeast coast of Jamaica, was built after the older Port Royal, nearby, was destroyed by earthquake in 1692; in 1703, after fire again leveled Port Royal, Kingston became the commercial capital of Jamaica.

12. The boy shares his mother's Creole nature, with its good and bad qualities,

reinforced by her instruction, and he required early moral education to make him deserving. Scott means to suggest that natural or early faults can be corrected by education.

13. Port Royal, an important commercial town at the mouth of the harbor on which Kingston is situated, was superseded in importance after 1703 by Kingston (see Book I, note 11, above).

14. At this period debtors unable to pay their debts could be imprisoned at the instigation of their creditors, so that their assets would have to be disclosed and, if possible, disbursed. Until the debts were satisfied, they could then be held in common jails, where their penniless families often joined them, at their own expense for food and necessities, until death, good fortune, or a change of heart of the creditor occurred, or until, at least in England, an Act for Insolvent Debtors was passed by Parliament, as irregularly happened every few years in order to clear the overcrowded prisons. Not every debtor, however, was qualified to take advantage of the Act in order to obtain release.

15. "Cousin germain" or "cousin german" meant a first cousin, sharing a set of grandparents, a significant distinction when cousins of remote degree were recognized.

16. If, as a merchant, Ellison could realize 5 percent on his £45,000, his income (including £1200 a year from Jamaica and the income from his farms) would have been about £3,600 a year, or about $360,000; if he had taken a long lease on his estate at a yearly rent he would not have been forced to give up a part of his capital sum.

17. Ellison's visit to Millenium Hall is of course the occasion of his writing the letter describing it which in fact comprises that book.

18. Agrarianism, deriving from Roman laws dealing with the disposal of public lands, is the principle of a uniform division of the lands (*OED*), a concept revived in importance at a time when enclosure of common lands by rich landowners was rapidly proceeding. "An equal agrarian [law] is a perpetual law establishing and preserving the balance of dominion" (*OED*—1656, Harrington, *Oceana*). Note that, to Scott, agrarian law is "natural," i.e., preferable.

19. "An honest man's the noblest work of God": Pope, *Essay on Man*, IV.248.

20. "A humourist" was "a person subject to 'humours' or fancies . . . ; a fantastical or whimsical person; a faddist" (*OED*).

21. According to the *OED*, a pinner is a coif with two long flaps, one on each side, hanging down and sometimes fastened at the breast; such a headdress denoted gentility.

22. "Landresses": obsolete for laundresses (*OED*).

23. Nero Claudius Caesar Augustus Germanicus (A.D. 37-68) ascended to the Roman throne in A.D. 54 through the murderous machinations of his mother Agrippina and thereafter ruled in her own murderous style; Caligula or Gaius Caesar (A.D. 12-41) ruled Rome with even greater cruelties.

24. Throughout the century the dinner hour grew progressively later. In the 1760s three o'clock or even later was the fashionable hour, but dining was probably earlier in the country. The usual hour for tea was six.

25. In the Greek legend told by Ovid, Arachne was so vainglorious about her

weaving ability that she challenged Athena to a contest in which she wove so well that Athena in a rage beat her, tore up her tapestry, and impelled her to hang herself, then revivified and metamorphosed her into a spider, the first arachnid.

26. When Saul and his Israelites had defeated the Philistines, the women came singing and dancing from the cities of Israel, saying "Saul hath slain his thousands, and David his ten thousands" (1 Samuel 18:7).

27. In his first trip to Millenium Hall Ellison encounters one of the presiding women, Mrs. Maynard, who turns out to be his cousin. Scott fails to renew the acquaintance in his next trip to the Hall, when Mrs. Morgan becomes his mentor (see pp. 186ff.). But it is to Mrs. Maynard that he later writes for a governess (p. 98).

28. The sons and daughters of both dukes and earls are entitled to courtesy titles of Lord or Lady before their first names.

29. A pillion is a pad or cushion for an extra rider behind a horse's saddle.

30. Hotspur reproves his wife Kate, who has sworn "In good sooth": "Heart! you swear like a comfit-maker's wife. . . . Swear me, Kate, like a lady as thou art, / A good mouth-filling oath, and leave 'in sooth,' / And such protest of pepper-ginger-bread, / To velvet-guards and Sunday-citizens" (*Henry IV Part I,* iii.i.249-58).

31. In the *Essay on Man* Pope postulates a Golden Age, an original state of nature that was "the reign of God: / Self-love and Social at her birth began, / Union the bond of all things, and of Man" (iii.149-50). Ellison quotes the lines "And bid Self-Love and Social be the same" (lst ed., 1733, iii.138-39) and "And bade Self-Love and Social be the same" (iii.318).

32. Marcus Vitruvius Pollio, a Roman architect of the reign of Augustus, described the theory, history, and practice, including his own projects, of architecture in his *De Architectura Libri Decem.* He was the principal architectural authority throughout the period of the classical revival.

## Book II.

1. *"Sans dot"* is French for "without dowry." In Molière's *L'Avàre*, the miser Harpagon counters every objection to the match between the attractively unacquisitive but too elderly Seigneur Anselme and his daughter with the reminder "Sans dot!" (I.v).

2. Many editions of Roger L'Estrange's *Fables of Aesop* (1692) were printed, including one revised and edited (1740) by Scott's friend Samuel Richardson. Scott refers to the fable of the contest between the wind and the sun to make a traveler remove his cloak.

3. For "Creator's last best gift" see Milton, *Paradise Lost,* V.19, where Adam addresses Eve as "Heaven's last best gift." An echo is Pope's praise of Martha Blount as heaven's "last best work" ("Epistle to a Lady," l. 272).

4. Holland was a linen fabric originally woven in Holland.

5. "Chemists in Laputa" is a reference to Book III, chapter 5, of Swift's *Gulliver's Travels,* where Gulliver encounters the projector who "had been Eight Years upon a Project for extracting Sun-Beams out of Cucumbers, which were to be put into Vials hermetically sealed, and let out to warm the Air in raw inclement Summers."

6. In the ancient Greek world a sibyl (an oracle or prophetess, the most celebrated of whom was the Sibyl of Cumae of the sixth book of the *Aeneid*) might be depicted as wrinkled and aged, while Tisiphone was the avenging principle of the three Furies, who were of frightening aspect, winged, and entwined with snakes.

7. At this period country justice was administered by local squires invested as justices of the peace, too often without any preparation or knowledge of the law. Country justice could be ignorant, inappropriate and arbitrary, and illegal, if not prejudiced, interested, and corrupt. See for instance Henry Fielding, *Joseph Andrews*, Book II, Chapter 11; Book IV, Chapter 5.

8. Bench: the seat of a judge or a justice of the peace.

9. A public house was a tavern; the term was shortened to "pub."

10. Each locality had its stipulated time for license for one or more fairs at which produce of all kinds could be bought, sold, and traded and at which amusements such as shows and various other performances could be seen, and, incidentally, drink taken. A wake was an annual parish festival, often in honor of the patron saint, at which excesses also often occurred.

11. The second Grantham son is here named Frank. On p. 221 the second and third sons are called Lords John and George.

12. See note on debtors' prisons, Book I, note 14. Ellison as a prison-visitor follows the reformer Stephen Hales (1677-1761), appointed in 1751 Clerk of the Closet to the Princess of Wales and chaplain to her son. Hales must have been known to the Scotts. In the early 1740s he invented a ventilation pump for improving the air in prisons but did not interest himself systematically in the relief of debtors. Scott anticipated the efforts of John Howard (see note 3 to her preface, p. 223), who devoted himself to the reform of prison conditions and administration (but not of individual debtors) in the 1770s.

13. The Pharisees were an ancient Jewish sect subscribing to strict interpretation and observation of Mosaic law. They were considered to be hypocritically self-righteous and without regard to the spirit of the law; they are often noted in the New Testament.

14. The Levellers were a political party of the Interregnum (1649-60) led by John Lilburne, who argued that man was born free with certain natural rights, including "manhood suffrage" and what amounted to a leveling of all distinctions of position or rank among males, the abolition of privilege, and the institution of equality before the law. The term "leveller" was in use through the nineteenth century; in the 1760s it was another name for the revolutionary White Boys in Ireland, who attacked landlords and broke down park walls and fences.

15. An "equipage" was a carriage equipped wtih appropriate horses and footmen.

16. In India, particularly in the south, temples to the monkey god Hanuman are numerous, and in Japan there are many temples to him as well. Horace Walpole mentions "some traveller, who viewing some Indian temple, that blazed with gold and jewels, was at last introduced into the *sanctum sanctorum*, where behind the veil sat the object of worship—an old baboon!" (*Walpole Correspondence*, 24:433). A note cites *The Six Voyages of John Baptista Tavernier*, translated by John Phillips (1677), which

contains an account of the temple of Kesava Deva at Mathura that resembles Walpole's (and Scott's) description.

17. See Pope's "Epistle to Burlington," ll. 170-71. This quotation was identified for me by Jack Kolb and Greg Clingham.

18. French novels were particularly popular with young ladies, and although some of the novels of the Abbé Prévost were suitable for girls to read, others were not, and the habit of such reading was viewed with suspicion. The romantic pastorals of the Italian poet Metastasio were also popular reading in England.

19. "Patronesses" refers to their patrons at Millenium Hall.

20. Scott may here refer to Johnson's *Rasselas* (1759), in which Princess Nekayah and her maid Pekuah are in the party traversing the world in search of happiness. It is interesting that Scott (a frequent traveler in Britain herself) admits the possibility of women ranging the world, even in her reference to the young women *not* being included in the party for the Grand Tour (p. 219). Young women, of course, never made the Continental tour, but perhaps Scott toyed with the idea of including them.

21. Mrs. Morgan, whose story corresponds significantly to that of Mary Delany, is described in *The History of Millenium Hall* as, with Miss Mancel and Lady Mary Jones, one of its three principal founders: "upwards of fifty, tall, rather plump, and extremely majestic, an air of dignity distinguishes her person, and every virtue is engraven in indelible characters on her countenance. There is a benignity in every look, which renders the decline of life, if possible, more amiable than the bloom of youth" (p. 8). "The History of Miss Mancel and Mrs. Morgan" is recounted at length by Sir George's cousin Mrs. Maynard in *Millenium Hall*.

22. The (three) "Miss Granthams" is a conventional way of mentioning siblings of the same sex. See also the three Mr. Blackburns, Miss Ellisons, Miss Tunstalls, and Miss Blackburns (p. 219) and Lord John and Lord George Granthams (p. 221).

## Book III.

1. The "two societies" refer to houses provided by the founders of Millenium Hall for "women, who from scantiness of fortune, and pride of family, are reduced to become dependent, and to bear all the insolence of wealth from such as will receive them into their families" (*Millenium Hall*, p. 64). The rules of their society are described (pp. 65-70). Sir George on his first visit found one such society and learned that a still larger mansion had just been leased for the establishment of more such women (p. 71).

2. "Mrs. Alton": As single women grew ostensibly unmarriageable, they were no longer addressed as Miss, but became Mrs. ———, i.e., Mistress.

3. The Mercers' Company was one of the livery companies derived from the medieval guilds; the companies controlled trade and participation in it. The Mercers', which dealt in textiles, was one of the most influential and richest of the companies, contributed heavily to charities, and also functioned as a bank, investing its assets in such things as annuities.

4. "Breaking up" refers to a school vacation, particularly the long summer vacation.

5. A child several months old might make up during the night while sleeping with its mother for less frequent daytime feedings, or various kinds of pap ("soft or semi-liquid food for infants or invalids, made of bread, meal, etc., moistened with water or milk" —*OED*) might be fed it. Barbara Dunlap provided information on this question.

6. The bath or gouty chair, a large hooded chair on wheels for invalids, had been in use for at least several decades: see Richard Quaintance, "Unnamed Celebrities in Eighteenth-Century Gardens: Jacques Rigaud's Topographical Prints," in *Cycnos* 11.1 (1994): 93-106, for a description (102) of two such chairs in a 1733 print of Stowe. These chairs had two wheels in back and one in front, were pushed by a bar, and were steered by a tiller guided by the invalid. Quaintance notes that Louis XIV is depicted in a similar chair in about 1713. Horace Walpole notes the "gouty chairs" still apparently in use at Stowe in 1764 (Walpole, *Correspondence*, 22:247; see also 33:525).

7. Many contemporary songs were scored for the transverse (then called the German) flute. The French horn, of equal use in the hunting field and the orchestra, was also a popular solo instrument, and footmen often doubled as domestic players. See, for instance, Tobias Smollett, *The Expedition of Humphry Clinker*, ed. O M Brack, Jr. (Athens: Univ. of Georgia Press, 1990), pp. 32 and 348, n. 10, which refers for a variety of examples to the Everyman Library *Humphry Clinker*, ed. Charles Lee (London: J.M. Dent. 1943), p. 339.

8. Satire like this on the misguided taste and lack of classical education of the prosperous citizens of London as expressed in their country villas was common: see for instance Sterling's projects in David Garrick and George Colman's *The Clandestine Marriage* (1766).

9. Plain work meant plain sewing as opposed to "fancy work," or embroidery. Such work was often sent home to women by middlemen.

10. The London stage was a coach carrying passengers and parcels at stipulated times between London and another place (*OED*).

11. A stage wagon was "one of the wagons belonging to an organized system of conveyance for heavy goods and passengers by road" (*OED*). The stage wagon would be considerably more comfortless than the stage coach, though both were without springs.

12. Morpheus was the Roman god of sleep.

## BOOK IV.

1. Scott means that Mr. Maningham himself did not reproach them.

2. Scott humorously refers here to an example of bathos—in this case hyperbole or the impossible—in Pope's *Peri Bathous, or The Art of Sinking in Poetry*, "that modest Request of two absent Lovers, Ye Gods! annihilate but Space and Time, / And make

two Lovers happy" (Alexander Pope, *The Art of Sinking in Poetry*, ed. Edna Leake Steeves [New York: Columbia Univ. King's Crown Press, 1952], p. 52).

3. Mourning decorum might vary according to locality and class, but generally a widow wore full mourning—all black with occasional touches of white—for a year, followed by second mourning of lighter colors, often white, with fringed linen. Even very young children or babies in mourning for a parent might be dressed in black, or at least in white with black ribbons and sash. Bombazine was appropriate for the first year, and after that silk. See Phillis Cunnington and Catherine Lucas, *Costumes for Births, Marriages and Deaths* (New York: Barnes & Noble, 1972), pp. 244-48, 273-75.

4. Apparently Scott intends us to imagine that at this point an entire year has passed in Ellison's courtship and Mrs. Tunstall's self-discovering deliberations. "The term she had been desirous of completing" was described on p. 177 as two years. The pair delayed six months more before marrying—till she had outworn her second mourning—just six months short of the two years she had at first intended to wait.

5. Alexander Pope, *Essay on Man*, II.259-60.

6. The reference is to Christ, who had "purchased a right" to love because he died for humankind.

7. Squire Allworthy in *The History of Tom Jones* was a widower who "looked on himself as still married, and considered his Wife as only gone a little before him, a Journey which he should most certainly, sooner or later, take after her; and that he had not the least Doubt of meeting her again, in a Place where he should never part with her more" (Henry Fielding, *The History of Tom Jones*, ed. Martin C. Battestin and Fredson Bowers [Oxford: Wesleyan Univ. Press, 1975), p. 35; see also ibid., n. 1, which gives background to these sentiments, "commonplaces of the Christian *consolatio.*"

8. Locke in his *Thoughts on Education* had emphasized, in much these terms, the danger of leaving children to the influence of the lower servants, a caution again emphasized by Richardson in *Pamela II* and by Sarah Fielding in *The Governess* (see my Introduction, p. xxxiv). Richardson, Fielding, and Scott agreed that conscientious mothers must carefully oversee the moral and intellectual development of their children.

9. On this subject Samuel Johnson quoted Lord Shelburne's opinion that "a man of high rank, who looks into his own affairs, may have all that he ought to have, all that can be of any use, or appear with any advantage, for five thousand pounds [or $500,000] a year" (*Boswell's Life of Johnson*, ed. G.B. Hill and L.F. Powell [Oxford: Clarendon Press, 1934], III.265).

10. A marquis (more properly "marquess") ranks between a duke and an earl. The courtesy title of marquess often goes with a dukedom and is attached to the eldest son.

11. A "greater latitude of election" means he might choose to live in the great fashionable world if he liked.

12. A curate was a clergyman without a church of his own who, as assistant to a rector or vicar, might do the spiritual work of the parish at a fraction of the pay. Dorothy Marshall notes that a curate too poor to afford an episcopal license was in a vulnerable position "not unlike that of the casual labourer" and might receive only thirty or thirty-five pounds a year and certain fees; those who had taken only deacon's orders were "without full professional standing or security," fulfilling "all the qualifi-

cations for a clerical proletariat. They were wage-earners of uncertain tenure" (*English People in the 18th Century* [London: Longmans, Green, 1956], p. 102).

13. A mechanic was a manual laborer, a member of the lower orders. A London laborer earned on the average ten shillings a week, or £26 a year (M. Dorothy George, *London Life in the Eighteenth Century* [New York: Harper & Row, 1965], p. 164). Thus a curate might conceivably earn less than a mechanic.

14. A stay or pair of stays (two halves laced together) was "a laced underbodice, stiffened by the insertion of strips of whalebone (sometimes of metal or wood) worn by women (sometimes by men) to give shape and support to the figure" (*OED*). Much attention was given to ensuring that the body should not grow crooked, so that even infants were encased in stays.

15. A waistcoat was a sleeveless bodice; into hers apparently Mrs. Ellison gradually introduced some stiffening.

16. Many almanacs included a naked male figure with some such caption as "The Anatomy of Man's Body, the parts thereof are Govern'd by the Twelve Signs," showing the figure transfixed with twelve arrowlike pointers designating the parts governed by each astrological sign: Aries, the head and face; Taurus, the neck and throat; Cancer, the breast, stomach, and ribs; and so on.

Pin cushions were an important part of the infant layette; from eight to twelve straight pins were ordinarily used in the dressing of a baby. Dr. William Buchan reported that these had been found "sticking above half an inch into the body of a child, after it had died of convulsion fits, which in all probability proceeded from that cause" (Dr. William Buchan, *Domestic Medicine* [Edinburgh, 1769], quoted in Cunnington and Lucas, *Costumes for Births*, p. 34). Richard Steele in 1709 imagines the recital of a new-born being dressed anew when he cried: his nurse "stuck a pin in every joint about me. I still cried: upon which she lays me on my face in her lap, and, to quiet me, fell a-nailing in all the pins, by clapping me on the back" (*Tatler* 15, quoted in Cunnington and Lucas, p. 34). Straight pins continued in layette use until the invention of the safety pin in 1878.

17. Scott refers to Aesop's fable of the daw (or jay) who struts in borrowed feathers which are detected and reclaimed by their owners, leaving him naked.

18. The annual London Bills of Mortality, based on the records of burials and baptisms kept by the Company of Parish Clerks, provided a rough breakdown of the causes of the total deaths recorded (see George, *London Life*, pp. 21-26). The annual London bills can be reviewed at the end of each volume of the *Gentleman's Magazine*.

19. Morphew is defined as "a leprous or scurfy eruption," but in this case perhaps means "tawny blotches on the skin of the face and arms of elderly people" (*OED*).

20. "Her virtue, and the conscience of her worth, / That would be woo'd, and not unsought be won" (*Paradise Lost*, VIII.501-2).

21. "Expressly forbidden us by Him who has the best right to our obedience" refers to Matthew 6:34: "Take therefore no thought for the morrow: for the morrow shall take thought for the things of itself."

22. The distance from Oxford to the Dorset border would be at least seventy miles, and it would be farther still as one proceeded into Dorset. One could cover fifty

miles a day by coach and considerably more by postchaise or on horseback, but of course one would have to stop for the night at an inn.

23. By law, if a death was in any way suspicious or sudden, a coroner had to empanel a jury and investigate at an inquest; the jury would then decide whether murder or manslaughter had or had not been committed. Young Ellison was exonerated on both these counts.

24. "Ten years older" is an error. When Ellison settled in Dorset, the Granthams already had eight children, of whom the eldest son must have been at least the fourth; he was at least five years old. Mrs. Tunstall had three young children when she was widowed, so another four years at least had passed, and she waited eighteen months to marry Ellison, after which their first child was a boy. At the least there must have been twelve years difference in age between the couple.

25. For "single blessedness" see *Midsummer's Night's Dream*, I.i.76.

26. This is an early use of the phrase "sense and sensibility," and one probably noted by Jane Austen.

# BIBLIOGRAPHY

~

## Editions of *The History of Sir George Ellison*

*The History of Sir George Ellison.* 2 vols. London: A. Millar, 1766. viii, 331, 291 pp. The first edition. 1,500 copies printed for Millar by William Strahan. Microfilmed for the *Eighteenth-Century Short Title Catalogue* collection.

*The History of Sir George Ellison.* 2 vols. in 1. Dublin: W. Sleater, J. Potts, & J. Williams, 1767. vii, 288 pp. A new edition, probably pirated.

*The History of Sir George Ellison*, 2nd ed. 2 vols. London: F. Noble, 1770. Remaining sheets of the first edition reissued with a new title page.

*The Man of Real Sensibility: or, The History of Sir George Ellison.* Philadelphia: James Humphreys, Junr., 1774. [2], 84, [2] pp. The first condensation of the novel found.

*The Man of Real Sensibility: or, The History of Sir George Ellison.* Philadelphia: William Woodhouse, 1787. No copy found; imprint known from an advertisement.

*The Man of Real Sensibility: or The History of Sir George Ellison.* Edinburgh: A. Shirrefs, 1795. 72 pp. A reprint of the Humphreys condensation.

*The Man of Real Sensibility: or the History of Sir George Ellison.* Edinburgh: A. Shirrefs, 1797. 125 pp. A reprint of the Humphreys condensation; text identical to the 1795 Shirrefs publication.

*The Man of Real Sensibility: or, The History of Sir George Ellison.* Philadelphia: H. Kammerer, Jun., 1797. 92 [4] pp. A reprint of the Humphreys condensation.

*The Man of Real Sensibility: or, The History of Sir George Ellison.* Philadelphia: John Johnson, 1797. 92 [4] pp. The same sheets as the preceding publication by Kammerer, with a different title page.

*The Man of Real Sensibility: or, The History of Sir George Ellison.* Wilmington, Del.: Bonsal & Niles, 1800, 72 pp. A reprint of the Humphreys condensation.

*The Man of Real Sensibility: or The History of Sir George Ellison.* Leominster, Mass.: Chapman Whitcomb, c. 1800, 42 [2] pp. A reprint of the Humphreys condensation.

## SOURCES

### *Manuscripts*

Huntington Library, San Marino, California. Montagu Collection. Correspondence between Sarah Scott and Elizabeth Montagu.

Rare Books and Special Collections, Firestone Library, Princeton University. Montagu Correspondence.

Lewis Walpole Library, Farmington, Connecticut. Letters of William Freind, Elizabeth Montagu, Sarah Scott.

### *Published Sources and Suggested Further Reading*

Blunt, Reginald, ed. *Mrs. Montagu, "Queen of the Blues": Her Letters and Friendships from 1762 to 1800.* 2 vols. London: Constable, 1923. A continuation and conclusion to Climenson's work (see below), including copious quotation from the correspondence, including letters of Sarah Scott.

Brophy, Elizabeth Bergen. *Women's Lives and the 18th-Century English Novel.* Tampa: Univ. of South Florida Press, 1991. Analyzes such aspects of women's lives as filial obedience, courtship, marriage, spinsterhood, widowhood, and reputation as portrayed in Scott's novels.

Brydges, Egerton. *Censura Literaria. Containing Titles, Abstracts, and Opinions of Old English Books . . .* , 2d ed. 4 vols. London: Longman, Hurst, Rees, Orme, and Brown, 1805-15, 1: 293-305; 4: 265-70. Brydges, whose second wife, Mary, was the daughter of Scott's brother William, provides what is still the definitive bibliography of Scott's works.

Carretta, Vincent. "Utopia Limited: Sarah Scott's *Millenium Hall* and *The History of Sir George Ellison*." *Age of Johnson* 5 (1992): 303-25. Postulates the importance of Johnson and Richardson in disseminating the idea of an English female convent.

Climenson, Emily J., ed. *Elizabeth Montagu, the Queen of the Blue-Stockings*, 2 vols. London: John Murray, 1906. A life to the year 1761, based on Montagu's correspondence, which is copiously quoted, by Montagu's great-niece. Letters of Scott are quoted. Continued by Blunt (see above).

Crittenden, Walter Marion, ed. Preface to *A Description of Millenium Hall.* New York: Bookman Associates, 1955. An informative introduction to the book.

———. *The Life and Writings of Mrs. Sarah Scott—Novelist (1723-1797).*

Philadelphia: Univ. of Pennsylvania Press, 1932. The only biography published to date, with a discussion of the works, but a dissertation written without a full review of the available manuscript letters.

Doran, John. *A Lady of the Last Century*. London: Richard Bentley & Son, 1873. A biography of Elizabeth Montagu that includes quotations from Scott's letters.

*Gentleman's Magazine*, Dec. 1795, p. 1056; Oct. 1798, p. 827; March 1805, pp. 218-19; Sept. 1805, pp. 811-12. Biographical notices and extracts from Scott's letters.

Gonda, Caroline. "Sarah Scott and 'the Sweet Excess of Paternal Love.' " *Studies in English Literature, 1500-1900*, 32.3 (Summer 1992)· 511 35. An analysis of Scott's treatment of father-daughter relationships.

Grow, L.M. "Sarah Scott: A Reconsideration." *Coranto* 9.1 (1973): 9-15. Samplings from Scott's letters in the Huntington to demonstrate them superior in liveliness and humor to her novels.

Kelly, Gary, ed. Introduction to *A Description of Millenium Hall*. Broadview Press, forthcoming.

*Ladies' Companion*, 10 Aug. 1850, p. 103; 17 Aug. 1850, p. 116; 31 Aug. 1850, pp. 149-50. Three letters of Sarah Scott written to her brother William and his wife, dating from 1761-62, once in the possession of Sir Egerton Brydges.

Montagu, Elizabeth. *The Letters of Mrs. Elizabeth Montagu*. Ed. Matthew Montagu. 4 vols. London: T. Cadell and W. Davies, 1809-13. A valuable collection of selected letters, not always accurately reproduced.

Myers, Sylvia Harcstark. *The Bluestocking Circle: Women, Friendship, and the Life of the Mind in Eighteenth-Century England*. Oxford: Clarendon Press, 1990. A good discussion of the entire circle of which Scott was a part.

Rizzo, Betty. "Reformers: Sarah Scott and Barbara Montagu." Companions without Vows: Relationships among Eighteenth-Century British Women, pp. 295-319. Athens: Univ. of Georgia Press, 1994. An exploration of the backgrounds, relationship, and communal work of the two women.

Spencer, Jane, ed. Introduction to *A Description of Millenium Hall*. New York: Viking-Penguin, London: Virago, 1986. Adds valuable feminist perspectives to a discussion of the book.

Stoddard, Eve W. "A Serious Proposal for Slavery Reform: Sarah Scott's *Sir George Ellison.*" *Eighteenth-Century Studies* 28.4 (Summer 1995): 379-96. Explores the context of anti-slavery texts to establish Scott's novel as an important advocate for both reform and abolition.